THE CURSE OF BILLY THE KID

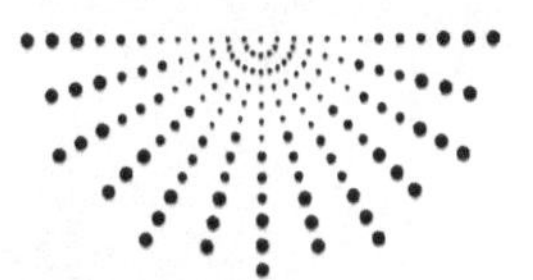

THE CURSE OF BILLY THE KID

UNTOLD LEGENDS VOLUME ONE

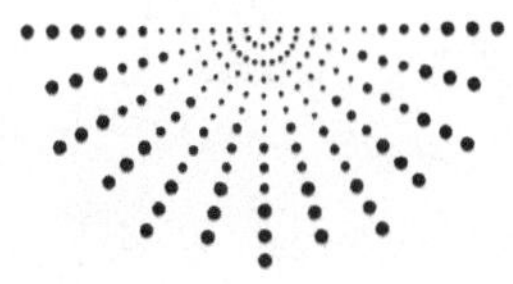

TAMSIN L. SILVER

1

MURDER MOST FOUL

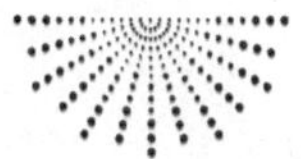

March, 1949

It's weird to be dead.

Or rather, it's a strange feeling when the world thinks you're dead and yet, here you are, walking around, saving the world from evil...

Well, I best not get ahead of things. Let me introduce myself. My name is William Kidwell, or it is for the time being. Back in the day, they called me by another name, but we'll get to that.

I arrived in New Mexico today for a job, and though it's not the first time I've been here since I "died" in 1881, the memories of my life here flooded my brain, making everything I did connect to something back then. Though I'm not the same man I was, what happened to me in the 1870s affected who I've become.

But who am I? Well, I could go back to the beginning and say I was born in 1859 to a poor Irish woman, that she left Ireland for New York City, then took me and my brother out West where she died when I was about fourteen. I could tell you a story about how I was a good kid when it all began...but that shit is boring, and no one, not

1

even me, wants to rehash it. What needs remembering is the year I became a Regulator 'cause that's where my true life began.

I'd just turned eighteen years old, and unfortunately, it was a death that gave me my new life.

* * *

February 18, 1878

The thunderous echo of approaching horsemen behind Middleton and me interrupted the leisurely quiet of the New Mexico canyon, announcing danger. We spun about to see a large posse on horseback coming at us. I knew it had to be the same men we'd been expecting to fight at the ranch until Tunstall had decided he wasn't gonna let anyone die over the cattle in question. So we'd fled early that morning from Dolan's men, yet if I was right, here they were.

Even though it was hard to tell if I was right at this distance with the sun having just begun to set behind the mountains, I had a bad feeling. Because if it was Dolan's boys led by Buck Morton, we were in trouble. I looked over at John Middleton since we were the only two at the back of the traveling party, the other three having gone over the brow of the next hill ahead of us.

"We best not hang about for that to catch up!" I shouted. Without waiting for a reply, I slammed my heels into the sides of my gray stallion's sides, and we picked up speed.

Middleton's bay mare kept pace, and we raced through the newly fallen snow, up over the hill, and past the nine horses we were moving to town. Didn't take long to realize our three friends had split up. Tunstall looked to be asleep in the saddle up to our right while Widenmann and Brewer were off the trail to the left.

Making a quick decision, I shouted, "Get Tunstall outta here! I'll find the others!"

With a nod, Middleton rode hard toward Tunstall, and I veered off the path to the left.

Finding Brewer and Widenmann, I shouted, "We got trouble!"

Widenmann's head whipped around as Dolan's posse came up and over the hill. Seeing them, he shouted, "We can't hold this place! Let's ride to the hill over there and make a stand!"

Middleton shouted at Tunstall, "For God's sake, follow me!"

Without a second thought, I followed Brewer and Widenmann toward an area covered with tall timber and large boulders, assuming Middleton and Tunstall were right behind us. Yet, as Middleton joined us, he was alone.

"Where's Tunstall?" I said, panic clenching my gut.

John Tunstall was the one they would be after. Jimmy Dolan was out for blood ever since John posted a letter in the *Mesilla Valley Independent* exposing Dolan and his pals as the real crooks of Lincoln County.

Middleton spoke up. "I yelled for him to follow. He rode about in a half-circle, and I motioned him in this direction. As soon as he started toward me, I led the way. Maybe he didn't hear me?"

"Or maybe he didn't *want* to hear you," I clarified. "Damn it, John, you can't talk your way out of this one!"

"What?" Middleton asked.

"Not you, the *other* John. We really need to give you a new first name," I said before looking to Richard M. "Dick" Brewer, Tunstall's cattle foreman. "Tunstall thinks he can surrender and fight this in court."

"Damn it! They'll kill him," Dick replied, his voice strained and his eyes filled with worry.

"Let's lay down some cover fire and get him outta there!" Rob Widenmann, Tunstall's best friend, shouted.

Dick's eyes scanned the area, which was no more than vast, unsettled land filled with nothing but brush and trees surrounded by mountains covered in a dusting of snow. We were well hidden, but that caused another problem.

"Billy, you're the smallest. Can you climb?"

I nodded, dismounted, and handed Middleton the reins. I'd have preferred to ride out there and take a shot at them myself, but I understood what Brewer was aiming for. At five-foot-seven and only a hundred and thirty-five pounds, I was the best option for giving us eyes to what was happening on the other side of the hill, especially as it was getting dark.

Spotting a good tree, I started up. Halfway there, an eerie silence filled my ears like water, and a rifle shot echoed off the canyon walls. I came to a halt as dread slammed into my soul.

"Oh, God," Middleton said. "They've killed Tunstall."

I prayed he was wrong and scaled the tree as fast as I could. Once high enough, the scene before me froze the air in my lungs. John Tunstall, a man I admired, lay on the ground next to his horse, his left cheek buried in the snow.

The group of twenty or so men had split into three sections. Most were back a few hundred yards, but four men rounded up our small herd of horses. I recognized two of them right away as Beckwith and Gallegos. That left just three men on horseback looming over John's body. I recognized two of them straight away. It was Billy "Buck" Morton and Tom Hill. The third man looked like the dangerous outlaw I used to ride with, Jessie Evans, but I wasn't a hundred percent sure.

Morton's rifle was still in firing position as Hill dismounted. With swagger, Hill pulled the revolver on Tunstall's belt and fired a bullet into John's head before killing his horse the same way. Laughing, he placed John's hat on the dead horse's head as Morton shouted orders to Beckwith about rounding up our horses.

Eyes wide and jaw clenched, I sat there, unable to move. My innards felt cold to the core while my blood burned as hot as a smithy's furnace. Drenched in a need for revenge, I shook with rage, gripping the tree with all my might to keep from grabbing my gun right then and there. I was on the brink of losing it when Brewer appeared below me. He wanted answers I didn't want to give.

Swallowing the pain, I climbed down and gave the news. Widenmann, a big man with a temper to match, went off his rocker. It took both Brewer and Middleton to stop him from riding out there and getting himself killed.

"There's too many," I told him, keeping my voice down as best I could while the other two held him tight. "You know me. I'm the first to jump into the fray, Rob, but now ain't the time. Not if we want to live to see them bastards pay."

We waited for the safety the dark of night provided and then rode for town. Widenmann had Brewer and Middleton divert to John Newcomb's farm to get help bringing Tunstall's body into town while he and I headed straight to Lincoln.

The whole ride I tried not to think on how I'd left John's dead body lying in the snow out there in the dark. I may not have had much in common with the twenty-four-year-old British businessman, but I respected him, and I didn't think highly of many people.

Since my momma died and my stepfather abandoned me and my brother, I'd not felt part of anything. On the run and alone, I'd been unable to find where I belonged until John had gotten me out of jail and given me a job. He'd believed in me and given me the family I desperately needed. For that alone, I vowed that anyone involved in his murder would die at my hand.

We arrived in town a little after ten o'clock that night and split again. While Widenmann rode to inform Alexander McSween, Tunstall's lawyer and friend who was also under attack by the Murphy/Dolan faction, I headed to where news would travel the fastest: Ike Stockton's Saloon. By midnight, all of Lincoln knew about John, the news traveling like wildfire from town to Fort Stanton and beyond.

By the time I arrived at McSween's and entered his stable, I found the horses belonging to the rest of my gang already settled for the night. Handing my horse off to be taken care of by one of the servants, I walked toward the patio, the outdoor area between the long sides of the U-shaped home. Getting closer, I heard shouting and picked up the pace.

With a hand on my gun, I ran toward the gate of the long west wall of the patio. Stepping through, I saw Henry Brown, and he was as mad as a March hare.

Brown shoved Brewer with all his might, still barely able to move the large man more than a step back. "Where were y'all?" he demanded. When Dick didn't reply, Henry pulled his gun and pointed it at the six-foot-four German man. "Tell me!"

Without flinching, Brewer replied, "I suggest you point that thing somewhere else."

"Or what?" Brown challenged. "You'll leave me to be killed like ya did John?"

Brown had begun the journey with us that morning, but when his horse had thrown a shoe, he'd returned to the Tunstall ranch on the Rio Feliz to get it fixed. As such, he wasn't with us when Dolan's men arrived.

"Henry, it wasn't like that," I said, alerting the group to my presence.

"The hell it wasn't!" he shouted at me without taking his eyes off Brewer.

Widenmann stepped forward. "We didn't leave him!" he yelled, his voice bouncing off the walls of the patio. Quieting down, he continued. "You really think we'd have just thrown him to the wolves to save our own hides? Damn it!"

"Rob," Dick started to say, but Widenmann was on a roll.

"After Waite split off to take the wagon on the road, we all kept drivin' the horses on the trail. Those of us up front ran into some wild turkey. John was half asleep in the saddle but encouraged Dick and me to go catch us a few, sayin' he'd watch the horses with them two," he said, indicating Middleton and me.

"Us two?" I exclaimed. "We were at least five-hundred yards behind y'all, for God's sake. With you and Brewer a few hundred yards to the left of the trail and us that far back, he was a sittin' duck. Why didn't he follow us, Dick?" I asked. "They shot him without a gun in his hand, and I know John, he'd have surrendered, thinkin' he could talk to them about McSween's debt."

"We both know darn well that warrant for McSween is bullshit," Dick said.

"Do we?" I said, keeping my voice down. "He says the bank fees and his own take up a lot of what was owed by that life insurance policy, but for all we know, he's as crooked as a Virginia fence and owes more to Emilie Fritz than he's sayin'.'"

Brewer stared me down, his blue eyes hot with anger. "He might not be the most honest lawyer, but he sure as hell didn't embezzle ten thousand dollars from that woman. It's just a ruse Murphy and Dolan came up with to remove him and Tunstall as their competition."

"More like just Dolan," Widenmann interjected. "Murphy's too sick with the cancer to do anythin'. Hell, bastard's drunk most of the time, leavin' Dolan free to do whatever he wants."

"And an army of men without a moral compass betwixt them to back him up," Henry added.

"Well, I wouldn't say my compass is overly moral bound either," I admitted. "But they killed an unarmed man who's done nothin' but tell the truth. We need to make them pay."

"I'm with Billy," John Middleton finally said. He'd been silent, leaning against the house, smoking a cigarette. He smashed it under his foot and looked to Henry Brown. "I called out to John as we fled. He chose to not follow us, and it was too late by the time we realized it."

Henry settled onto an old chair outside the summer kitchen. "Then this is my fault," he choked out. "Morton followed my tracks in the snow from the ranch back to y'all. If my horse hadn't—"

"Don't start that now," Middleton said. "No one is to blame except Dolan and his men, and if we don't fight back, *The House* will take everything and leave us for dead."

The House was what everyone in Lincoln County called those affiliated with the primary general store/bank/post office recently renamed J.J. Dolan & Company, owned and run by Jimmy Dolan. Anyone who was a part of *The House* fell under the protection of him and the previous owner, Lawrence Murphy. Sheriff Brady himself, a fellow army buddy of both Murphy and Dolan, was obviously loyal to *The House*, as were his deputies. This alone would make getting retribution for John's murder a sticky situation.

With a hum of thought, Dick scratched at his goatee. "McSween isn't one for violence, but Dolan doesn't respond to anythin' else. We have to find a way to compromise."

The idea of not using violence made my trigger finger twitch. "Is that a bluff, or do you mean it for real?"

"I have an idea," Dick said, causing us all to look at him. "We give it a few days. If McSween don't do nothin', I'll go to Mr. Wilson."

"Now you sound like Tunstall," I said. "What is the Justice of the Peace gonna do? You said it yourself, Dolan will only respond to violence, and I'm happy to give it to him."

Dick placed his great paw of a hand on my shoulder. "And you'll get that chance. Just pull in your horns for a few days. Let's see if we can make the killin' of those bastards legal. All right?"

I never had liked waiting. I was a get-it-done-now kinda man, but it made sense, so I agreed, sort of. I might've decided to do something to keep busy in the meantime.

* * *

My momma used to say that idle hands are the devil's playground, and I was living proof of that. That being the case, I did the dumbest thing I could possibly think of that night: I snuck away as a bunch of angry townsfolk debated the situation and headed down the street to poke my nose around the building that housed J.J. Dolan & Company.

I secretly hoped I'd get to shoot one of those sons of bitches, but then big, loyal, honest Dick Brewer discovered me and demanded he come along. As if that wasn't bad enough, it started to snow again. But to tell you the truth, by the time we returned, I couldn't have cared less about either of those things. Because what I saw that night gave me pause...the kind that causes nightmares and makes every bump in the night mean something.

* * *

Except for the activity around the saloons, it was quiet along the one mile long, lazy S of Lincoln's main road. Staying low, we moved silently through the night, hiding behind the houses west of McSween's.

Looking up, the clouds blocked my view of the moon. "What time is it?"

Brewer pulled out his pocket watch and hit it with his other hand. "If this is right, it's just after midnight."

"Then we might have time for a base burner at the saloon after we see what Dolan is up to."

Brewer removed his hat, shook the snow off the wide brim, and placed it back on his head. "You know you're barkin' at a knot with all this, right?"

"We'll see. Come on."

We looped around the back of the Wortley Hotel and Diner, crossed the street, and used the shadows and darkness to work our way to the west side of the Dolan Store. The building itself was the only two-story in the town of Lincoln, and though the main structure was a large, rectangular shape, there'd been a smaller two-level room added on to the west side. Using this to our advantage, we peered around the corner of it and saw a large group of workers.

"Looks like this is where the action is."

"Hell, if action is what you wanted, we can head back to Ike's for that drink," Dick offered.

"You're funny," I said flatly, pointing to the back portion of J.J. Dolan & Company. "Look, all the lanterns are lit up. There's ten to fifteen people goin' in and out as if it's the middle of the afternoon."

"They seem to be loadin' in merchandise from those covered wagons. Nothin' big about that," Dick observed.

"Except it's the middle of the night. The only time John would unload at this hour was—"

"When he didn't want Dolan to see," Dick said, finishing my sentence.

I grinned. "Exactly. Come on, I want a better look."

We moved closer and hid behind the outhouse. Now we could see the back of the building just fine. Men were carrying large boxes into the building, and due to the size and length, it should've taken two men each to move them. Instead, one man would lift a box as if it were full of feathers, so I commented on this.

Brewer brushed it off. "They're probably empty."

I raised an eyebrow at him. "That makes no dag-gum sense. Hell, even if you're right, those boxes are too long. Even our strongest ranch-hands would need help."

"I don't know what to tell ya, Billy."

The full moon escaped the cloud cover for a moment as I peered around the corner, the cold wind blowing in my face, to see a squabble break out between two of the men. A box dropped, causing a ton of ammunition cartridges to roll into the snow. I pointed the heavy contents out to Brewer as heated words between the men turned into punches.

One man was as large and bald as any I'd ever seen, and the other was short and scrawny. I started to bet Brewer some of my poker winnings on the outcome.

"Wait, what's going on?" Dick whispered, looking over my shoulder.

Before I could reply, the little guy hit the other man in the chest with both hands, sending him flying a good twenty feet back. Landing, he skidded another ten, easy.

"Criminy!" I whispered, "Did you see that?"

"If I say no, can we leave?" Dick replied.

The smaller of the two dropped to all fours, his back arching in a horrible and impossible way before running at the big man. He disappeared behind the covered wagons, and I assumed he'd gone into the store, the fight was over. But just then, the night air filled with a howl so strong it vibrated my eardrums. The next second, an enormous wolf bolted into view, heading straight for the bald man.

"We need to go!" Brewer said, grabbing my arm.

"Where'd the wolf come from?" I asked at the same time.

"I sure as hell don't wanna find out! Now let's go before it picks up our scent!"

The wolf collided with the large man, who didn't appear frightened in the least, and they tumbled along the ground, snow and dirt flying about.

"Yeah, we need to go," I said, my eyes now on the back door where people were gathering. "Wait until we…" The rest of my sentence escaped me as I just stared at the door in shock.

"Wait until what?" Dick demanded when I didn't complete my sentence.

I couldn't reply. A woman I recognized from my past had exited the store, tying my tongue. She was slight in stature, with a small waist cinched in, making her skirts seem fuller and her bosom larger.

"That can't be…" I whispered.

"I'm leavin', with or without you," Dick said.

My mind was spinning so loud I barely heard him.

The woman yelled at the fighting pair, who stopped immediately, faced her, and dropped their heads to stare at the ground like scolded children. She continued to bark orders, pointing to the spilled cartridges, while saying something about being finished before sunrise.

I would've sat there longer if Dick hadn't pulled my arm. Losing my balance, I reached out to save my backside from landing in the snow. My hand hit the corner of the shed with a heavy slap, drawing the attention of all outside the store to turn our way. Dick and me stopped moving and breathing until the woman began to start giving orders again.

Once the woman began to start giving orders again, I let out a breath. "We gotta go!"

"That's what I've been sayin'!" Dick complained through his teeth.

Luckily, the moon was hidden again, and we ran through the dark as fast as we ever had, returning to McSween's without so much as a word between us. Entering the house, we found everyone still awake in the parlor, talking about political maneuvers. Brewer and me nonchalantly slipped into the room, and I stood there listening to arguments, even making a few of my own, until my head could take no more. Taking a seat, I dozed in and out until just before sun-up.

Shaking the remnants of bad dreams from my head, I rose and stepped out into the patio area as the sun slipped up and over the horizon, making the unmarked snow on the mountains glisten like the surface of a lake on a windless day. I could hear nature start to wake up and talk, so I lit a cigarette and closed my eyes to listen. Blowing smoke into the cold air, I stretched my neck with a pop and a crack. I was tuckered out, but at least the snow had stopped falling.

Not surprised to hear someone else join me to escape the discussion still going on inside, I turned to see it was Brewer. He stood next to me, looking up at the mountains without saying a word.

Finally, I said, "We speak nothin' of what we saw, ya hear?"

Dick looked dragged out. Rubbing his face to wake up, he caused the blond hair of his mustache to go askew before dragging both hands through his wide, dark-blond curls that perpetually had what my momma called "bedhead." With a heavy sigh, he said, "Who'd believe us anyway?"

"No one," I told him.

Again, we stood in silence. When I finished my smoke and turned to head back in, he said, "I actually came out here to tell you that the new guy, Patrick Garner, wants to speak with us after we go see Wilson and sign affidavits that state who killed John."

"Okay. Why?"

"Don't know." He paused, then said, "What if he asks where we were last night?"

"We say nothing. Anyone who introduces themselves with, 'I was never here, never mention you saw me,' isn't someone I trust right off the bat. Besides, we don't know nothin' about that Alabama boy or why he's even here," I pointed out.

A voice from behind us said, "That Alabama boy is here to help you get justice for Tunstall."

It was Garner himself, all six-foot-three of him, looking like a Barber's Clerk, in my opinion, already dressed in his suit at this early hour. I should've been embarrassed he heard us talking, but I was too tired to care.

"And we appreciate that, Mr. Garner," Dick said.

I huffed and opened the door to the west wing drawing room. "I'm gonna take a nap until we go sign affidavits. I'll catch y'all when the sun's higher in the sky."

I entered the door to the west drawing room and shut the door just as I heard Garner ask Brewer where we'd been while McSween and the rest had been making plans. I was half tempted go back out there to make sure he kept his mouth shut, but I trusted Brewer.

Exhaustion causing my head to feel like I was breathing in and out through my ears, I shook my head to steady my blurry vision and went into the next room. It was a small bedroom appointed for visitors to catch a few hours down. I removed my cartridges and weapons and set them within arm's reach. Still in my clothes, I lay down, shut my eyes, and prayed I wouldn't dream of wolves.

* * *

Just remembering my exhaustion back then seemed to make my eyes burn with it now. I needed sleep if I was going to get moving early tomorrow. The sooner I figured out what happened to Fletcher, a missing Regulator, the faster I'd be out of New Mexico and the memories of this place that haunted me could recede back into the recesses of my brain.

Opening the door to my hotel room, I quickly swept it, gun drawn, to find it empty. Placing my guns in strategic locations around the room, I undressed, laid out my things for the morning, and got a shower before dropping onto the cool sheets of the hotel bed, the smell of laundry detergent puffing up around me. I sneezed, sensitive nose and all.

Getting the pillow the way I liked, I closed my eyes and tried not to think about that night when I'd seen that wolf for the first time. I'd worried I'd dream of them, but I hadn't. Instead, I'd dreamt of the woman I'd seen at Dolan's and the section of my childhood she'd been a part of. Mary had been the first teacher who'd given a damn about me. I once overheard my guardians talking about how I'd transferred my affection from my mother, who'd recently passed away, to Mary.

Looking back, that very likely was true, for I missed my mother dearly back then. Hell, I still did. We were a lot alike, her and me. I even favor her, and not just the light brown hair, but my blue eyes, baby face, delicate hands, and slender build were all her. She had a good head for business, which I, sadly, didn't inherit. But she'd been great with people, had a witty sense of humor, was a wonderful cook, could sing like a songbird, and loved to dance. Those traits I got.

Chuckling to myself at the memory of her dancing with me as a boy, I allowed myself to drift off to sleep. I had a lot to do tomorrow, including introducing myself to the sheriff of Lincoln County. I didn't have high hopes about that...not at all.

2

OFF TO JAIL

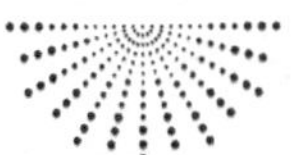

Rob Widenmann was a U.S. Marshal, so he left Lincoln early the next day, the nineteenth, to request military assistance while we tried to move things along in town.

"Then there's Billy here," Middleton said to George Washington, one of McSween's negro servants. "You shoulda heard him! We hand the warrants to Constable Martinez, who has the gall to protest that he might easily get himself killed by servin' 'em, and the kid here says, 'You better take that chance because if you don't, I'll kill ya myself.'"

"Billy, you didn't!" George said, ladling some coffee into a mug for Middleton.

"I sure as hell did, and I'd have done it, too! The law in this city needs—"

"John? Billy?" a steady yet careful voice said from the hall, stopping my train of thought.

I looked over to see my good friend, Charlie Bowdre, who'd arrived earlier that day, along with Fred Waite, who'd been driving Tunstall's wagon. Seeing the look on Charlie's face, I automatically reached for my gun. "What's happened?"

"Newcomb and the others are back with John's body."

No one I'd cared about, save for my mother, had died before. I

15

didn't know what to do. Even still, I found myself saying, "Where is he?"

"The parlor."

I looked to Middleton, who only nodded, and we followed Charlie to the front of the house. I forced air in and out of my lungs as I stepped up to the table he'd been laid out on. I wanted to say so much but didn't know how. After a moment, the only words I could get out were, "I'll get some of them before I die. You have my word."

I turned and walked from the room without looking at a soul. I moved with purpose through the house until I reached the room I'd slept in. I took the door to the outside and exited to the patio with no idea what to do with the burning in my gut.

Without a plan, I headed to the far end, opened the gate, and stepped out to stand by the river. Once I stopped moving, I released the pressure of my pain and anger by yelling up at the sky.

I felt lost again, like when my mom'd left me. Trying to find even ground, I stood out there in the dark of early evening, listening to the silence of the world and marveling at its contrast to the noise inside my head.

I lost track of time standing out back, watching the water. I probably would've stayed out there until I froze to death, but Charlie came and found me. Laying a hand on my shoulder, he said, "Garner is askin' for ya, kid."

"He can piss off."

"He and Brewer are in the west wing drawin' room. You should go. And by the way, it's Dick's birthday."

"What? He didn't say nothin'..."

"When does he ever? Just, keep in mind he's havin' the worst birthday of his life right now, so be nice. Okay, kid?"

With a nod, I headed toward the house and went into the west wing's drawing room, which was nestled between the small summer kitchen and the room where I'd slept. When I stepped in, I noted that Dick sat in an armchair in the corner to my right while Patrick Garner had positioned himself behind a desk-like table directly across from the entrance. He asked me to shut the door, then went back to writing something down. I did as he requested and leaned against it to wait.

Setting his steel nib pen next to the ink well, Patrick stood, his height causing his thick, dark hair to almost graze the ceiling, like Brewer. But where Dick was proportionate, Garner was all leg. "Thank you for comin'. Please, have a seat." He motioned to one of two chairs facing the desk as he walked around to stand in front of it.

"I'll stay on my feet, if ya don't mind," I told him, my thumbs hooked on my belt, my right hand not far from my gun. I wanted him to know I was relaxed but ready.

He seemed to understand that I didn't trust him, so with a simple nod, he rested his backside against the desk and crossed his arms over his chest. "Do you know why I called you in here?"

I turned to Brewer. With just one look, he encouraged me to answer the question as if I knew the answer. Focusing my attention back to the man with the large mustache, I said, "I won a new pony? Hell, I don't know. Maybe ya want me to do a jig. I do like to dance!" I did a few fancy footsteps I'd learned a week back from this beautiful little Mexican woman. Spinning at the end to give my answer some flare, I grinned at him, waiting for his response.

"I want to give you purpose," he said, ignoring my sarcasm. "I want to swear you in as a Regulator for New Mexico."

With no idea what a Regulator was, I waited for there to be a punch line, but none came. I looked to Dick, then back to Patrick, and said, "Purpose? Mister, I got me a purpose. I'm gonna kill every last son of a bitch involved with Tunstall's murder. I think that is a pretty big purpose. Now, are you plannin' to help me with that, or am I on my own?"

"Billy, the Regulators are bigger than that. You need to listen," Brewer said.

Remembering Charlie's words, I sighed, threw my hands in the air, and said, "All right, what is it that will give me purpose?"

"You are a good kid at heart, and talented with a gun, there's no doubt," Patrick said, and I gave him a look that asked how he'd even know that, but he kept going. "However, you're reckless, lackin' in morals, and you speak before you think."

"So?" I retorted. It wasn't my best comeback, but I wasn't used to a man, easily pushing thirty, telling me how to behave. "You're not my daddy, and last time I checked, I was a grown man, so I suggest—"

"Tell me what you saw at the Dolan Store last night."

I slowly turned to Brewer, my narrow eyes drilling into him as if I'd just learned he'd been the one to kill my momma. Birthday or no, now I was mad. I held it in though, only saying, "I thought that trip was between us, Dick."

"He only told me after I explained to him what I'm about to share with you," Garner said, defending Brewer's actions. "What you thought you saw last night, the stuff you're tellin' yourself was your imagination...well, it wasn't. There are things in this world that most know nothin' about."

"Such as?" I prodded.

"Many think of them as just Irish legends, but I'm here to tell you that the Bahvah, the Dahrungah, the Therian Throhophs, and the Lagnick Faylund are real." When I appeared to not have an inklin' to what he'd said, even though I still understood the old Irish language, he clarified. "You may have heard of them under their American terms: witch, vampire, shapeshifter, and lycanthrope...or werewolf, per say."

My chuckle started small but grew to a full-blown belly shaker when Patrick's face remained serious. Slapping my leg, I bent over as I laughed good and hard. Soon I realized Dick wasn't joining me, though, so I cleared my throat, stood up straight, and said, "Really now, did you call me in here to tell me you believe that the members of *The House* are fairytale boogiemen? Come on now, that's absurd. I've known some of these men for years. There is no way they—"

"Could blend in?" Patrick interjected, finishing my sentence. "That's where you're wrong." Coming toward me, eyes intent, he added, "They are master manipulators and out to own the New Mexico Territory. But we, the Regulators, swore that they wouldn't get a foothold in America. They need to be registered and then sent back to England and Ireland. Or killed. You don't want demons like them here, kid."

The man wasn't pulling my leg, and I could see that more laughter wasn't the right course of action, especially with Brewer watching on all serious-like. Poor Dick. He obviously believed this man. The question was, did I play along, or should I walk out the door with a thank you and a goodbye? Unsure which was best, I waited him out. When I said nothing, he continued.

"Tunstall was a Regulator from England, just like his father before him. I've known of his family for years, seein' as my father spent time with his before we came over to this country. We settled in Alabama to chase down a lead that vampires had settled in the south. New Orleans is where they ended up, but that's a whole other story."

"Look, Mr. Garner," I started to say.

"It's Garrett, if you must know, Pat Garrett...and I can prove what I'm sayin' is the truth, and I can do so usin' your own life."

"Oh, do tell," I said. "I love a good story." Deciding to sit for this, I planted my backside into the chair behind the desk and pulled out my loose tobacco and the rolling papers.

"Have you not wondered why your life took such a turn?" Pat asked. "You were a good kid and then...things changed. You were arrested, ran away from home, and by seventeen, you'd killed a man."

"That was self-defense," I said, without looking up from rolling a cigarette.

"Whether it was or it wasn't, that's not my point."

I waved him on. "Then, by the grace of God, get to it, Mr. Garrett."

"In the early fall of 1874, a woman by the name of Mary Richards came into your life."

I halted my tobacco activities to look up at him, for now he had my full attention. "What could you possibly know about Miss Mary?"

"That she was a big influence in your life. Took you under her wing for a year and trained you, so to speak. Not just with writin', but since you're both ambidextrous, she secretly taught you how to shoot with both hands. Told you to call her by a nickname, somethin' that sounded like Scawk...am I right?"

My heart pounded in my chest, reverberating off my bones. I looked up into his eyes, feeling the heat behind my own as I stared him down. "How could you possibly know that? I was fifteen and livin' in Silver City."

"You're not the only 'hero' I've met who she's tainted with her touch. In Ireland, her name would be Scáthach," he said, pronouncing the Gaelic name SKAW-huhck. "She's known as The Shadowy One, and though a great warrior, she is also the creator of monsters. Scáthach finds promisin' heroes and trains 'em. But no matter how pure they are at the start, they are forever tainted by their association with her."

Garrett stepped up to the desk and leaned onto it with both hands, his face lowering to be in mine. "She is evil incarnate, son, and she touched your life. The path you walk down shall forever be filled with death and likely your own at an early age. Unless..."

He let that linger to the point where I fell into the trap. "Unless what?"

"You take that curse and use it to fight back at the monsters she's created. Only then can you save your life and possibly your soul."

That hung in the air, the quiet of the evening wrapping around us like a winter blanket as the weight of what he was saying lay heavy on my heart.

A woman somewhere outside called out to her children. A dog barked. A baby cried. The wind outside picked up enough speed that as it seeped through the window of the room, it whistled. It was a normal night, but everything in my world felt different.

Did I believe Pat? I was tempted to. It would explain a lot. Especially why I thought I saw Mary in the doorway, giving orders at the Dolan Store. But it was a lot to take in. So I stood there, silent.

Unsure of how long it had been, I realized Brewer was saying my name. Ignoring him, I turned to Pat. "Let me get this straight. What you want me to believe is that Mary, the one woman who showed me kindness after my mother passed, rules the dark realm of the Otherworld and she has tainted my life with death."

"Yes," Pat said. "And the only way to break free from the hold she has on your soul is to make the death that follows you count."

"And how is he supposed to do that?" Dick demanded to know.

"Simple. By makin' sure that those monsters she created die by his hand."

Dick laughed without humor behind it. "Are you out of your mind? I've seen the size and strength of those creatures. Hell, Billy and I both have...and you want us to believe *he* can kill those and it'll be 'simple'?"

"Yes," Pat replied with a calm to his voice and demeanor I didn't understand.

"Have you looked at him?" Brewer said.

"Thanks, Dick," I said dryly.

"No offense, it's just...you're not the biggest of men and those things are enormous."

"None taken, I think," I said. "They can be killed with guns, I'm guessin', and I'm the best shot of any of us."

Pat grinned. "Exactly. They can be killed with bullets made with silver. So you see, Mr. Brewer, Billy is not helpless."

"I didn't say he was, it's just...damn it all to hell, he's just a kid!"

"I am not," I said. "I might be ten years younger than you, but that doesn't mean I don't know how to fight for my life."

"For your soul," Dick corrected.

"They are one in the same," I said.

Dick turned to me, his blue eyes darker than usual, and his face grave. "No, Billy. No, they're not."

A chill ran up my spine in a way that unnerved even me. Taking a settling breath, I brushed it off and steadied my gaze back at them. "Then I guess I better not die," I said, and walked out of the room.

I heard Dick call out to me, but I was too busy pretending to ignore him to turn around. Instead, I kept on walking to wherever my legs would take me. Anywhere but there.

* * *

Next morning, having had time away from it all to ponder, I headed back to the McSween home and headed straight to the west kitchen for coffee.

"About time you showed up," Dick said to me as I walked into the kitchen. Filling his mug with coffee, he continued. "Fred's been waitin' on you to go over to Martinez's place so the three of you can go serve them warrants to Brady at the Dolan Store."

"That's why I'm here." I took my hat off, set it on the table, and stepped over to the stove. Ladling some coffee into a mug, I grinned and said, "Well, that and coffee." I blew on the hot beverage and made my way to a small table and leaned against the wall. "I'm surprised you don't see all this as a bit pointless now."

Dick sat at the small table and drank some of his coffee before saying, "Why would you say that?"

"Really? You were awfully sure we was bein' told the truth last night. If what we were told last night is true, why would we care about bringin' Brady or Dolan in for John's murder? If we believe Pat's story, this goes way beyond what we thought we knew."

Dick looked at the other chair and back at me. I took the hint and sat down.

His voice low, he said, "Keep it down, okay? Not everyone can be knowin' about the...the situation."

"The 'situation'?" I said with a laugh. "You mean about the supposed werewolves takin' over our town who are led by my childhood teacher?"

Dick stood up and closed the door that led to the rest of the house. "When you put it like that, it does sound ridiculous."

"Because it is ridiculous! Who says Garner—"

"Garrett," Dick corrected.

"Whatever...who says that boy from Alabama isn't yankin' our chain, or worse, pullin' us into somethin' he *wants* to believe is true."

Dick picked up his mug. "Why would he do that?"

"I don't know. Maybe he's mentally ill...maybe he needs justification for this Regulator thing he's been tryin' to do. Hell if I know. But really, tell me now, do you seriously believe that I'm some cursed being chosen by the leader of the Underworld—"

"Otherworld," Dick corrected again. "Dark realm of the Otherworld."

I stood. "Do you hear yourself?! Jeez-oh-petes, Dick...he's a loony. Simple as that."

Dick motioned for me to keep my voice down, then said, "And if he's not?"

"If he's not...then like I said, don't we have bigger problems than servin' some warrants on Brady and Dolan?"

Dick paused and began to pace the room, scratching at his goatee while he thought. After a moment or two, he said, "Fine. We ask for more proof. I'm sure he can provide it."

"Damn right." I drank down a good portion of my coffee.

"So until he does, we proceed with the plan we had. Deal?"

"Deal. As long as you're the one to tell him we need that proof. I have no interest in talkin' further with Garner on anything." Dick opened his mouth to correct me, and I gave him a look that shut him up. "Garrett, Garner, whatever. Hell, either one of those or both could be lies. Find out more and we'll talk about this later tonight. Right now, I have a dirty sheriff to go arrest."

I downed the rest of my drink, put my hat back on, and walked out into the patio area of the U-shaped home before realizing that Fred was likely inside. By happy accident, he saw me and stepped out from the east wing of the McSween house.

"There you are," Fred said. "We need to get movin'. Martinez is expectin' us anytime now."

"Let me get my Winchester, and we'll head on over."

Fred nodded, we fetched our rifles, and made our way over to Martinez's place.

"I'm gonna swear ya both in as deputies so ya have authority to help me do this today," he said, handing each of us a silver star to attach to our chests. "Just remember, no shootin' at anyone unless they shoot at us first."

I gave Fred a look that said I'd be damned if I let any of them sons of bitches shoot at me first, but I kept my mouth shut, and we headed down to the Dolan Store. There was no sign of all I'd seen there night before last, but there were a bunch of military outside standing at attention.

"What the hell?" Fred started to say.

I recognized the man in charge as Lieutenant C.M. DeLany from Fort Stanton, and approached him. "Lieutenant, what is goin' on here?"

"Sheriff Brady noticed a mob of folks gatherin' at McSween's the past two nights, so he felt he was in danger and called on us to assist in protectin' the office of the law here."

I snorted a laugh. "The law. That's funny."

DeLany appeared confused, but before I could clarify, Martinez stepped up with warrants in hand. "Lieutenant."

"Constable," Delany replied.

"I have warrants here for the men who killed John Tunstall and for Sheriff Brady as well. You'll see the paperwork is in order."

DeLany held eye contact with Martinez for an extra beat before taking the documents. Looking them over, he nodded. "That they are. You can proceed to serve them inside but keep it civil."

"Yes, sir," Martinez said, taking the documents back. "Boys, with me."

Fred and I nodded at him and at DeLany before heading into the bottom level of the Dolan Store. There we found Brady waiting on us, backed by members of the posse that killed John, as well as more military from Fort Stanton.

Without so much as a gun pulled or a word said, all the military inside pulled their rifles and pointed them at us.

"Well, shit," Fred said.

"Hand over your weapons," Brady said.

"The hell I will," I replied.

Martinez stepped forward and handed Brady the warrants. "We are here to deliver these warrants for the arrest of some of your men here, as well as you yourself, Sheriff."

"Excuse me?" Brady said.

"Larceny," Martinez explained, his voice cracking a bit as he did.

"You have got to be kidding me," Brady began to say.

"No sir," I told him. "You fed the horses of these military from the hay in John's store. That's not your property. Nor does it belong to the state. That's larceny...sir."

The static silence that followed weighed heavy on everyone, and tensions rose, soldiers resituated their guns on their shoulder, and my free hand dropped to linger near my revolver.

"He's not wrong," Martinez said. "You had no right to take that hay for the military. McSween has filed a charge of larceny against you for it. With concern to those who hunted down Mr. Tunstall and murdered him, we have multiple accounts on that. We're, at least, placing them under arrest at this time."

"The hell you is!" Frank Baker said from the back of the room. "We didn't kill nobody."

"I was there; I beg to differ," I said, placing my hand on my gun.

"Everyone, stay calm," Martinez said, feeling the anger in the room become palpable.

Brady shoved the warrants into his pants pocket. "No one is bein' arrested today, Constable Martinez...except you three."

"Excuse me?" Fred said. "We are here with legal warrants and badges. You have no valid reason to arrest us."

"Don't need one. I have the gun power."

The rest of the men in the room pulled guns, and I pulled mine from my belt faster than they'd expected and had it cocked and ready to fire.

"Who wants to meet their maker first?" I asked.

"Billy, it's twenty-somethin' to three," Martinez said. "Hand over your guns."

"Over my dead body."

"Do as he says," Fred instructed me as he handed over his rifle to Brady.

My finger rested on the trigger of my gun as I made the decision that I didn't want to get my friend killed. I eased the hammer back, popped the cylinder out, and let the bullets fall. One by one they clattered onto the wooden floor, the sound consuming the room. Holstering my empty revolver, I handed my rifle over to Brady. "My revolver stays with me."

"Fine by me. Boys, shackle 'em," Brady said.

"What?" Martinez exclaimed as multiple men approached us, pinning us against the wall.

Grabbing our hands, the men placed shackles on our wrists and turned to Brady for further instruction.

"We'll march 'em down the street to the jail hold," he said.

Martinez was flabbergasted and furious, rambling on that he was a Constable and Brady had no right to arrest him. I quickly noted there was no mention of Fred or me in that statement and looked to my buddy with a raised eyebrow. He shook his head at me, telling me not to do anything stupid, and I decided, for some reason, to listen to his advice.

"Why you doin' this?" I heard someone ask Brady.

"Because I can. Because I have the power to."

"It'll also send a message to anyone in town what happens if you try to hold the law accountable," Fred said.

Brady grinned but only said, "Take 'em outta here!"

With guns at our backs, the three of us exited the Dolan Store. Lieutenant DeLany was obviously confused at the sight but said nothing, just watched us get paraded by without so much as a word.

"This is downright embarrassin'," I said to Fred as we marched through town in front of everyone.

The farther we went, the more folks came out of their houses to watch us go by.

I felt my face grow red in anger. "Mark my words, Brady will pay for this."

"Yes, he will," Fred said.

We reached the pit *cárcel*, a two-room hole in the ground where prisoners were held, and two men lifted the heavy trap door that covered it. Dropping a ladder into place, they told us to head on down. As Fred and Martinez went down, I noticed that the other room, only separated from ours with a low, dirt wall, held two men in it.

When it was my turn, I stepped to the ladder and hesitated. The barrel of a gun was placed at my temple, and I turned to Brady and smiled. "This ain't over."

Not waiting for a reply, I headed down the ladder into the pit and leaned against the wall, watching the men as they pulled up the ladder and dropped the door to close us in, plunging us all into darkness.

"So...now what?" I asked.

"Now we wait," Fred said.

"I hate waiting."

3

A FURRY CELLMATE

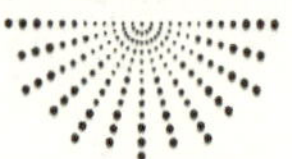

Hours passed in the dark. I slept for a bit but woke up when someone opened the hatch. It was Brady, there to free Martinez but not Fred or me. I cursed him out good, but he still left us there. I fell asleep again. This time though, I woke up to moaning, and not the good kind.

"You all right, Fred?"

"It isn't me."

Raising my voice, I shouted to the two other men in the room next to us. "You two all right?"

"No. My friend is...well, you wouldn't believe me if I told ya," a young, yet strong voice said.

"Oh, I don't know. I've heard some crazy shit in my time, so I might," I replied.

"Full moon was only a few days ago," a different voice said in the dark, one that sounded in pain, and I assumed it was the man who had been moaning a few moments ago.

"And?" Fred prompted.

"And the moon is barely waning and rises soon," the strained voice explained.

"It's pitch black in here with no view of the outside. How the hell can you tell the moon is close to rising?" I asked.

"I can see in here well enough," he grunted. "And I can feel the moon."

"You need to hold it in, Jacob," the other man said. "Please. Think how you'll feel if you wake up and we're all dead."

This got my attention. "Excuse me?"

"Not sure how I'd feel," Jacob said, his voice low and gravely. "The more it happens, the less I seem to care. It gets easier."

I felt my senses become heightened, and I caught the smell of wet dog. Standing up, I shouted, "Is there a way over to you from here?"

"Only up and over," the man not in pain told me.

The wall was low, but I couldn't feel the top of it. "Fred, boost me up."

"Why?"

"Gonna make sure that man is all right, okay? Now give me a hand."

With a sigh, Fred found me in the dark, cupped his hands, and helped me get my foot situated into them.

"One, two, three!"

I pushed off the ground as he lifted, and my hands found the top of the wall. Pulling myself up to my waist, I swung a leg up and lay across the top of the wall.

"What are your names?"

"Timothy," the one man said. "My friend here is Jacob...and he's not in his right mind."

"Okay, Timothy...tell me, ya got a weapon on you?"

"Of course not. They threw us down here just like you, without a damn thing."

I grinned even though I knew he couldn't see it. "What are you two in here for?"

"Disturbin' the peace. Jacob here, however, is also charged with attempted murder."

"That's not good," Fred said somewhere in the darkness.

"It wasn't his fault," Timothy said. "He just—"

Jacob yelled out in agony, and I heard him begin to flail on the ground.

"Oh God...no, please, Jacob..." Timothy said, his voice coming closer toward me. "Timothy? What is going on?"

"He can't stop himself. He can't...it's the moon, you see..."

Suddenly, out of nowhere, I said, "Is he a damn werewolf?"

Timothy gasped in surprise but didn't reply.

My blood heated up. I could feel where Timothy stood and directed my comment toward him. "Answer me, do we have ourselves a furry cellmate?"

Timothy stammered, finally saying, "Yes...it's new. He has no control. We could all die!"

Jacob made a sound that was not human in any way, shape, or form.

I reached out. "Take my hand, Timothy, and get over here on our side."

"What is going on?" Fred shouted.

A roar filled the air, and I felt my senses become acutely aware as adrenaline surged into my system. "Now, Tim!"

He reached for me, and with my senses on full tilt, I could see his movement in the blackness. After one failed attempt, I got a good hold on his arm and pulled up as I let my body start to fall over to Fred's and my side of the pit cárcel.

"Fred, help me pull him the rest of the way over."

"What?"

"Now!" I shouted.

With no idea what was going on, Fred helped me and Timothy over, both of us landing with a thud on the dirt floor just as something large and strong slammed into the wall between the two rooms.

"What in the hell was that!?" Fred yelled at me over the wolf's roar.

"Umm...it's a werewolf, Fred, and if he breaks through that wall, we're all dead. Any ideas?" I said.

"I gathered that much...what I mean is, why do you know about this, and when did you learn?"

"Wait, you believe me?" I asked.

The wolf hit the wall again and dirt flew all around us.

Coughing, Fred said, "My people have known of the lycanthrope for centuries. My question is why do you know and why are they in Lincoln County?"

"I'll explain in a minute," I said. "But first, do either of you have any matches?"

"Better," Timothy said, "I've got a converted flintlock pistol."

I had no idea what that meant until I saw a flash and a flame sprout up, lighting the room.

"It's a lighter. Traded my old mule to some German guy for it."

A roar shook the air, and looking up, we watched as paws came over the wall, followed by a head. Thankfully, he got stuck at his midsection.

"Keep that light on a minute," I said, pulling my gun. "Handle has some silver in it. Up, Fred!"

Without questioning me this time, Fred helped me leap up. With a well-placed swing, I hit the beast in the head, causing him to shake his head, likely due to seeing stars. We sent me up one more time, and with the extra energy I felt, I hit him harder and knocked him out. Slowly, he slid backward and dropped to the floor on his side of the pit.

Timothy closed his lighter. "Will he be okay?"

I turned toward his voice. "Will he be okay? Seriously?"

"He's my friend."

"Right now he's not," I said. "And the sooner you accept that, the longer you'll live."

I sat down and felt Fred sit beside me. Tim chose another part of the room, and before I knew it, he was snoring.

"Good, he's asleep. Tell me what's goin' on, Billy."

"Not sure I'm supposed to say...hell, I'm not even sure I believe it."

"You're gonna tell me anyways," Fred said.

I sighed. "Yeah, I'm gonna tell you anyway."

* * *

The topic of Garrett and his beliefs helped Fred and I make it through the night, thankfully only having to knock Jacob out one more time before the moon set. No longer a threat to us or himself, Jacob boasted of other "great" qualities. Namely, a hot temper brought on from the screaming headache my beatings gave him or possibly werewolf anger issues. Either way, we got lucky that next afternoon, the twenty-first, when two Brady lackeys lowered some food to us. However, that was the only time we were fed before we went through another round of dealing with Jacob.

By the crack of dawn on the twenty-third, I was close to losing my mind. I'd just knocked Jacob out again when the door above opened, and a figure holding a torch in the darkness of early sunrise stared down at me.

"Billy? Fred? You boys still alive down there?"

I'd never been so happy to hear the booming voice of Rob Widenmann in my life.

"We sure as hell are!" Fred answered.

"Any chance you got a ladder?" I said.

"Funny you should ask," Rob said with a deep laugh as a ladder got lowered into our side of the pit hole.

"God bless you," Fred said.

"You go first," I told him.

As he ascended to the land above, I looked to Timothy and quietly said, "You want to follow us? I can't leave you my gun, and he'll kill you if he wakes up while the moon is still up. He'll find a way over or through that wall."

"What kind of friend am I if I leave him?" Timothy asked.

I raised an eyebrow. "A breathing one."

Timothy looked torn, but when Jacob moaned lightly next door, he headed straight to the ladder and went up without a lick of hesitation.

I followed him up but looked down on Jacob in the other room once I was high enough. He definitely wasn't staying unconscious this time around. Seeing him begin to shift, I said, "That's my cue," and I rushed up the ladder.

"What about him?" Rob asked.

"Nope!" I said, blocking his view of Jacob as I pulled the ladder up. Handing it to Fred, I slammed the trap door shut. Looking about, I saw no sign of Timothy and couldn't blame him for getting the hell out of here. "We got anythin' heavy to put on the door?"

"Why?" Rob asked.

"Oh, just don't want to make it easy for them to toss us back in," I lied.

Rob pointed out a large boulder or two nearby. "We might be able to roll one of those over here."

"Sounds like a good idea."

Once we'd completed that task, the three of us hurried to the McSween home where we found a detachment of soldiers waiting. I hesitated and looked at Rob.

Putting a hand on my shoulder, Rob said, "They're here with me to look for the men who killed Tunstall."

"We already tried that. We ended up in that hole," Fred said.

A man rode over on his horse. I could tell by his uniform that he was a lieutenant. "Brady's been arrested for that larceny charge and is not going to be an issue. His small band of boys is no match for my men."

"Thank you, Lieutenant Goodwin," Rob said. "Besides, that was a few days ago, and I doubt those military from Fort Stanton are still at the Dolan Store, but if they are, we'll take care of that. You still sworn in as a deputy, kid?"

"I sure am. So is Fred."

"Good, then let's go see if we can find us them bastards that killed John."

"We need rifles and ammunition," I told him.

"I got you covered," a voice behind me said.

I turned to see Dick coming toward us with two rifles.

He handed one to me and one to Fred. "You two are a mess."

"Gee, can't see why," I said, checking the rifle to find her loaded.

Fred did the same. "When we're done with this, I want a bath, food, and some sleep, in that order."

Dick grinned. "And you'll get it. But we need to do this first."

Everyone agreed, and we were off. Most of us Tunstall/McSween men were on foot while the soldiers went in on horseback. Once we reached the Dolan Store, Rob and Lieutenant Goodwin threw a cordon around the store, a ring of soldiers letting none in or out except those of us with warrants to re-serve. However, when we entered the building, we found nothing but a few of Dolan's men who were not on the list of those being served for John's murder.

Being a physically large and aggressive man, Rob moved through the store like a bull in a china shop, telling us to look for anything that could help us find the bastards that killed John.

We tore the place apart, trying to find any bit of evidence that would lead us to Morton, Baker, Evans, or Dolan but found nothing but a letter and a book of notes. Seeing as it seemed important, we confiscated it and decided to take it to McSween.

When we could do no more at *The House*, Rob led us down to the Tunstall Store, still guarded by Brady and Dolan's men.

"He's gotta know they're not there," Fred said to me as we moved east.

"Of course he knows," I said. "He's mad as all hell. And as loyal a friend as he is, he's just as mean. They killed his best friend, and he intends to make them pay. That includes taking back possession of John's store, and he means to do so today...now."

"It's rash and imprudent for him to do this," Fred said.

"Imprudent? Using that college education, I see," I said with a wink.

Fred laughed. "I just am not sure this is the best move."

Overhearing him, Rob said, "Fred, I want to entrust you with this book and letter we found at the Dolan Store. Can you take these to McSween?"

I knew what he was doing. This way, Fred could sidestep being involved in the Tunstall Store raid if he wanted.

"I can do that," Fred answered.

"Thank you. Wash up and get some rest. I'm sure there's breakfast on the stove by now, too."

Taking the items, Fred thanked him and gave me a look that offered up the chance for me to come with. I shook my head, and with a shrug, he headed off to the back door of the McSween home.

"Rob, who's all going in?" I asked.

He rattled off names of those I knew, like Brewer, Scurlock, Middleton, Corbett, and the Coes, along with those I didn't. We were easily twenty men strong without the military. The joy of knowing we were likely going to take back some of this town energized me in a way that put spring in the step of my exhausted body.

Using the military to get us in the door with the pretense of looking for the wanted men, we rushed in, and as we looked for the men we knew weren't there, we forcibly took the keys to the store back and rousted Brady's men out and onto the street. As they began to argue, we pulled our guns and stood between them and the store.

"Take these to McSween," I heard Doc Scurlock say to Sam Corbet as he palmed him the keys to the store.

Corbet was gone faster than a bull running into a pasture of cows while the rest of us created a barrier between John's store and Brady's men, which consisted of Jack Long, Charles Martin, John Clark, and a few others. A few minutes later, as things were becoming more heated, Sheriff Brady showed up as well.

Seeing both sides with guns raised, Lieutenant Goodwin stepped up. "Everyone needs to calm down."

"If you want, Lieutenant, you and your men can withdraw, and we can shoot this out once and for all," Rob shouted. "This is John's store. They took it without a valid, legal reason, then killed him. That's why we're taking it back."

"If a fight breaks out, I'll put my troops between the two sides, forcin' all of ya to stop shootin' or pay the penalty for woundin' or killin' soldiers. So, what's it gonna be?"

I refused to lower my weapon, as did any of the others protecting the Tunstall Store.

Brady stepped forward and ordered his men to lower their weapons and didn't even try to take the store back, claiming he didn't want any more bloodshed. I think it was because he knew we'd slaughter them all. We outnumbered them five to one.

Once all their weapons were lowered, we did the same. Then Rob, with the insistence of Lieutenant Goodwin, worked to get everything calmed down.

As the rush of taking John's store back began to leave my body, the exhaustion from the past few days seeped in and I excused myself from the party staying to deal with all the warrants and legal situations. I was going to get some of that breakfast Rob mentioned, strip out of these disgusting clothes, bathe, and get some rest. Once I had done all that, I'd talk to Brewer and go give my answer to Garrett.

* * *

I woke up as the sun was about to set, got dressed, and headed to the McSween home. Once there, I went looking for the man from Alabama, and he was right where I'd left him days ago. I thought about joking that he'd never left, but I held my tongue and just smiled.

"I take it by the look on your face we gained some ground today?" Pat said, motioning for me to take a seat like he had the first time.

This time I nodded and sat facing him. "We took Tunstall's store back, and Sheriff Brady had to post a two-hundred-dollar bond for stealing hay from it. Widenmann also found a ledger book of some kind and a letter at Dolan's. Fred brought it to McSween."

"Good to hear. Does that mean you've come to give me an answer?"

"God knows I've had some free time on my hands to think about it."

Garrett fought a smile, then said, "Look, Dolan's crew and all those seen as part of *The House* aren't just citizens who want special treatment and protection. They are demons, and back in England, it's a Regulator's job to, well, regulate and track 'em, keep 'em under control. Here in America, we hunt them down and kill 'em if they won't leave. So, this is the last time I ask, are you in or are you out?"

Still unsure if I believed him regarding my part in this supernatural situation, I did know two things; that werewolves were real and that Dolan's men were involved, giving me a second reason to gun them bastards down. Because of that, I said, "I'm in."

"Good."

"I got one question. Do ya plan on telling the rest of the men how you believe I'm cursed?"

Pat shook his head. "No. In fact, I don't recommend you do either. Brewer needed to know because of what he saw and because he's your friend."

"What's that have to do with any of it?"

Pat pulled a small tin from his breast pocket. "Forgive me, but I suppose I thought you'd want someone to talk to about all this, other than me."

"Assumin' I believe you," I countered, not mentioning that Fred knew now, too.

Opening the tin, a tiny grin crawled up one side of Pat's face. He pulled out a toothpick, opened his mouth, and bit down on it. Holding it between his teeth, he said, "You do. The sooner you admit that, the more effective you'll be."

I reached for my container of rolled tobacco. "Oh, I'll be effective."

Pat handed me a toothpick. "Here, these are cheaper and better for ya." Once I reluctantly took the little stick of wood and put it between my teeth, he said, "Now, I head for Fort Sumner soon, so we leave for trainin' tomorrow. Go pack your gear. We'll will meet up at the Ellis Store for breakfast and ride once the moon sets."

"Which is?"

"Eleven in the mornin'," he said.

I stood, wiggling the toothpick at him, and though I thought he was loco, I nodded in agreement before leaving the room and heading off to find Brewer. I needed to let him know I had all the proof I needed of werewolves and we were going to need to tell the rest of the Regulators. As far as Pat's thoughts about me, we would keep all that quiet. The last thing I needed was a bunch of cowboys looking at me like I was the devil himself.

* * *

You expect us to believe there's supernatural mumbo jumbo going on in this town and that's why John was murdered?" Sam Smith said.

Fred stepped forward. "I spent three nights with one in a hole in the ground. So yeah, believe it."

"Not like you could see it though," Henry Brown said.

"Not true," he said, and told the men about Timothy and his lighter.

The room was silent for a moment and then everyone began speaking at once.

"It's gonna be a long night," I muttered.

"Yeah, it is," Dick replied.

Lucky for us, the boys had asked enough questions and headed home around ten o'clock that night, giving me just enough time to pack, catch four hours of sleep, and be at the Ellis Store in the morning. There we met, ate, and headed up into the mountains where we were given silver bullets, wooden and silver stakes, and other unusual weapons.

"Now what?" I asked.

Garrett grinned. "Now you learn to fight with 'em."

4

THE CURSE

In the late 1800s, Lincoln County was almost the size of South Carolina. With its thirty-thousand square miles, it took up most of the southeastern part of New Mexico and was plagued with corruption and violence, with murder being almost a daily occurrence. Thus, our activities weren't as noticeable as one might think. You could go days without seeing another human being in New Mexico. It made it a perfect breeding ground for Scáthach's demons.

We trained for a few days, our last exercise being after sundown on the twenty-sixth and went all night with no moon to help us so we would learn how to work in utter darkness. We finished just before the moon rose, a waning crescent in the winter sky, around five in the morning of the twenty-seventh.

Hungry, cold to the bone, and no real light since the sun wouldn't be up for another hour and a half, Dick and I built a fire. The other Regulators either headed to the chuck wagon for some breakfast or went to grab some shut-eye, many choosing to snooze sitting up in their tombstone chairs. Garrett, on the other hand, took this opportunity to explain the political side of it all to Dick and me. That's when we learned that like any rotten business today, the canker sore that fueled our troubles started at the top.

I poured scoops of ground coffee into the pot of water on the fire. "You're tellin' me it's not just District Attorney Rynerson who's a friend of Dolan's, but U.S. Attorney Catron, Governor Axtell, and Judge Bristol as well?"

"I am," Pat said, rolling out his *sudan*, a waterproof bedroll. Pausing to take a drink from his canteen, he handed it to Brewer before laying down. "That group of high rankin' officials is a part of what's called the Santa Fe Ring, and you can bet *The House* answers to them."

"Damn it, Pat," Brewer said. "How we gonna fight all of 'em? There are only nine of us."

"So far," Pat said, long legs stretched toward the fire. "You'll get more."

"Besides, we got the tools," I said, touching my belt, which now held more weapons than just guns.

"That's still not enough to put a dent in a mob this size," Brewer pointed out before taking a drink from the canteen.

"Brick by brick, boys," Pat said, leaning back, his elbows resting on his rolled blanket. "We just have to take them out one by one. We do that, steadily and with care, and we'll send 'em packin'.'"

The sound of a howling wolf pierced the night air, and we all went still. The days of fearing a simple wolf were long past. Now we all feared it could be something larger and more dangerous: a werewolf.

I pulled my gun with its silver bullets and spit the toothpick I'd been chewing into the fire. "Let's do a sweep of the area, Brewer."

Dick handed Garrett back the canteen and took off his hat, setting it by his bedding. "Sounds far off. Let's not assume—"

"He's right," Pat said, standing up, his eyes looking from me to the burning toothpick. "Gentlemen don't spit things out, Billy."

"Piss off, Pat," I said with a smirk on my face. "Now let's go take a look, shall we?"

Dick grabbed his weapons. "I do not have a good feelin' about this."

"So noted. Take your lamps, and I'll go alert the others," Pat said, and headed over to the chuck wagon as Dick and me spread out.

I grabbed my Regulator-issued bahvah-lamp from my belt. Each one was a different shape and size, made from a stone called honeycomb calcite and roughly the size of the fist of the man it was given to. Holding up the yellow stone with white lines running through it, I said, "Luminaire." Touched by witch magic, the rock brightened up the dark, glowing from within itself.

We'd not been looking long when Dick yelled out, "I think I found somethin'."

I walked on over to him adding my light to his to stare down at an enormous paw print.

"What'd I tell ya?" I said with a grin.

Dick grunted. "Why are you always right?"

"It's a curse," I said and winked. "Get it?"

Dick's face went flat. "That's not funny."

"Oh, come on, it's a little funny."

"Can you take nothin' seriously? Not even the fate of your soul?"

Standing up, I smiled and said, "Awe, come on now, Dick, you know—"

A bullet hit me in the chest, causing words to fail me as I fell to my knees.

"Billy!" Brewer yelled, but before he could check on me, something enormous and hairy tackled him, knocking his bahvah-lamp to the ground.

My chest burned like Hell itself had taken up residence inside as I rolled over to face Brewer, now farther away. Lifting my gun, I took aim on the enormous beast, whose teeth snapped mere inches from my friend's neck.

"Stop movin' and I'll shoot the thing!" I shouted.

Two other men from our group jumped into the fight, giving Brewer the chance to clock the beast in the jaw with a set of silver-plated iron knuckles he'd been wearing.

"Stop movin'? I don't think so! Shoot the bastard!" Dick said, dodging the creature.

I focused on the four of them, worried the wolf's speed would cause me to hit a friend, but I fired, and the training paid off. The beast wailed and fell. As he did, I felt a surge of energy and could stand. Doing so, I drew my second gun as the thing attacked Brewer again.

Walking toward the hairy monster, everything went into slow motion. I could see teeth, silver, blood, and sweat flying this way and that, but aiming now wasn't difficult. I emptied both of my weapons with precise accuracy into the werewolf, taking his life.

A rush of energy like I'd never known flowed into me, numbing the pain in my chest completely as we watched the creature's horrific change. The wolf's bones began to shift under the skin as the fur vanished, leaving behind a naked, dead, human man. Everyone stood in shock, staring at him, as another bullet whizzed by, causing us to remember there could be more out there that wanted us dead and didn't walk on four legs.

"I'm empty! Brewer, your rifle!" I yelled out.

Without hesitation, Dick threw his Winchester to me. I grabbed it mid-air with ease and turned to fire into the night, which didn't appear so dark anymore. Bullets flew toward us, and everyone else took cover, but I was too wired to even consider it.

Heading toward the gunman—I could see him now as clear as day—I fired two more times. The first was so close that it burned by his hand, causing him to drop the gun, while the second hit him in the head. Again, energy flooded my being, and this time, I had to rest a hand on my knee to catch my breath from it.

Cheers went up all around, and Pat came running toward me, Dick close on his heels.

"He was shot!" Dick told him. "We need to make sure he's not bleedin' out, seeing as he's acting like a loon. What were you thinking, walking out in the open toward a man with a gun?"

I stood, feeling a bit drunk, and handed the rifle to someone. "I had a gun, too." When Dick just glared at me, I said, "I don't know. I just saw him so clearly that I thought I'd take him out."

"See him? This far from the fire, almost no moon, and without bahvah-lamp? It's pitch black out here," Dick pointed out.

I looked around and the night was anything but dark. The stars and the sliver of moon seemed to light up the sky like the sun was already on the horizon. I would've said so, but just then I noticed that Pat had his hands all over my chest, hunting for something. "What in tarnation are ya doin', Pat?"

"I can't find the wound the bullet made," Pat explained.

"Let's take him near the fire," Dick ordered. "Besides, there could be more comin'."

Pat got an arm around me. "Not tonight there won't be. A one man, one wolf team is a typical scouting party. We should be good for the rest of the night but stay alert."

He and Dick helped me back, forcing me to sit on a wooden supply box close to the fire so they could look at my chest. As Dick pulled off my coat, Pat sent all the other men to take care of the bodies, except Fred and Charlie, being that Fred had gotten a bit tipsy one night and told him about my curse.

"There! He's got blood on his right side," Dick pointed out.

"He sure does," Fred confirmed.

Pat unbuttoned my shirt and pulled it open whilst I protested like a drunkard, swatting at his hands but without enough conviction to do anything.

"I don't get it," Charlie said. "There's blood but no wound."

Dick sat on Pat's *sudan*, obviously babying his left arm, his face the epitome of confusion.

"Are you okay, Dick?" I asked.

He ignored my question. "Pat, how is that possible? There's blood. He was obviously hit."

Fred untucked my shirt and something plopped onto my boots. Hearing it, Pat leaned over and picked up the item. Lifting it into the firelight, I saw that he held a forty-five-caliber bullet.

"It seems the curse has fully set in," Pat said quietly. "If you didn't believe me before, you should now."

"What are you babblin' about?" I looked down where I'd felt the fiery pain earlier to find my shirt soaked with blood but not a mark on my flesh at all. "Uh, Pat?"

Garrett eased down to sit next to Brewer but addressed me. "How soon after you were shot did you wound the werewolf?"

"Pretty quick," Dick answered first.

"I suppose," I agreed. "What's that got to do with anything?"

"I only know one other like you," Pat explained. "I thought the affliction was just for him. But it seems not. Must be all her heroes."

"Affliction?" I asked.

"The minute you mortally wounded your first werewolf, it must've set in," Pat said.

"I'm not injured. Isn't that a good thing?"

"You feel light headed?" When I nodded, Pat said, "You take on the human life force of each demon you eliminate: a small amount upon injury, the whole enchilada upon death. It'll always heal you, rejuvenate your body. Once used, that soul will cross over, released from Scáthach's grasp."

"I don't understand," I said, my mind beginning to clear up and stop spinning.

"The other man I know like you, his name is Tom," Garrett said. "He hasn't aged a day since he started killin' demons. He told me that until he rids the Earth of Scáthach or kills all the monsters she personally made the year she cursed him, he cannot let himself die."

"What if he stops killin' 'em? The demons, that is," Dick asked.

"If he's used up all the souls in him, he can age and die...but there's no promise that he'll have killed enough demons to save his soul, for he sacrificed it for this gift," Pat explained.

Horrified, I said, "I did no such thing!"

"Are you sure, Billy?" Fred asked, staring at my freshly healed skin.

"The absorption of their energy is why you were able to see in the dark as well as they do. You take on some of their supernatural powers when you take their soul."

"Such as?" Dick asked as I sat there numb.

"Other than better sight? Strength, hearin', longevity, flexibility, and stamina."

"That would explain why he could see better in the jail hole," Fred said. "He'd injured that wolf."

"And his extra strength and instincts came because he was near one as it changed," Pat added.

What they were saying made sense, in its way, but one thing stuck in my craw. "But I've been aging just fine since I met Mary."

Pat frowned. "You'd not killed a demon yet."

"Why didn't you tell him any of this before?" Dick demanded to know, and I could hear the indignation in his tone.

"I wasn't a hundred percent sure he was a warrior of Scáthach. Tunstall was the one who believed. He had the natural instinct to spot your kind, Billy. Just like his dad. It's a shame John was lost to the cause so early on."

Heated anger lit my brain for multiple reasons, one of which I wasn't willing to confront. The other I let loose on Pat with abandon. "Lost to the cause? Is that what you think?"

I stood and paced to the other side of the fire. "How about murdered in cold blood on the orders of a little man who drinks like a fish and has a temper the size of Texas just because he was mad about an article in the paper? Dolan, and Murphy too for that matter, see themselves as demagogues who have to have the last word and always get their way. You knew that, yet you sent John here unprotected?"

"He had you all," Garrett said.

Those four words stung my heart to a level that they took my words away as I swallowed down the bile rising in my throat.

"That was out of line," Fred told Pat, his eyes on Brewer, who sat with his head in his hands.

Seeing this, anger flamed in my chest the size of a forest fire, and I ran at Garrett. Grabbing his shirt in one hand, I yanked him to me as I jumped to stand on the box I'd been sitting on before. "How dare you! Like McSween hasn't already made Dick feel like it was his fault, you have to go and throw accusations around like that? Fuck you, Garrett. You and your club of Regulators in England. You damn well knew John should've had protection! Someone who knew the truth of what was going on, but instead you left us in the dark, and now he's dead. You get to own that, not me, and definitely not Brewer."

Unable to get much air due to my hold on him, Garrett wheezed in what he could. "His assigned Regulator Network Liaison never returned from La Mesilla."

"His what?" Dick asked.

I let up on my hold a bit and Garrett continued. "There's a team trained to assist Regulators with communication and protection. They're called Regulator Network Liaisons, and each Regulator, or group of them, gets one, but John's never got here. We assumed he was killed in the line of duty, and another was dispatched as soon as John let us know. However, that replacement is still on his way here, and he's the top of his class. I know because I picked him out myself for you all."

"Well, their best candidate can't do anythin' if he ain't here!" I shouted, feeling the extra strength of the soul energy still inside me and knew if I wanted to, I could crush Pat's windpipe with one hand, and I wanted to. I desperately needed to make someone hurt like I did.

"Billy, let him go," Dick said, his voice low and soft in a way that told me he understood my fury and pain. "You can't kill him; we need him."

"The hell we do," I said, but even I could hear the waver of my conviction in that statement.

"Billy," Charlie said. "Take a breath."

"If he'd only been *truthful* with us from the start!" I said, pangs of guilt thumping hard in my chest for Tunstall, but I did what Charlie said, and the red at the edges of my vision faded. I let go of Garrett with a shove that sent him sprawling onto the damp ground a good ten feet from us as the sun slid up over the horizon.

Fred Waite placed his hand on my arm. "Billy, maybe you should..."

I looked around and saw all the other Regulators standing there. My eyes landed first on Henry Brown, then slid down the line to Josiah "Doc" Scurlock, "Big Jim" French, José Chavez y Chavez, "Tiger Sam" Smith, and John Middleton. I had no idea how long they had been watching, but it'd been long enough to hear the argument and see me throw a man a foot taller than me farther than I should've been able to.

Without a word, I jumped down and ran off. I needed time to think without Pat in my face or any of my friends staring at me like I was a leper. I headed into the trees, and as soon as I found one good for climbing, I scaled up her with ease and sat on a branch over-looking the land as the New Mexico sky turned colors only she could . With pinks, purples, blues, and oranges, the sun painted the sky as it began to rise, throwing light onto the world again.

I sat in such a way that I couldn't see the others. I didn't want to be able to watch them when what I needed was to focus on what I saw inside myself. My mind whirled, trying to not only comprehend what had just happened, but how. When had I willingly handed the owner-ship of my soul to Mary? I couldn't remember. It must've been a trick on her part. I couldn't imagine I'd have ever wanted to not grow up. At the age of fourteen, that's all you want: to be an adult. Now I never would.

The truth of this sank into me. I was gonna outlive all my friends and have to watch them die just like I had my mom and Tunstall. It was either that or I would be forfeiting my soul and never see either of them again. The pain of this twisted my gut as I watched the sun take to the sky with the moon.

Usually the moon was alone in the sky, just like I had been since I ran away from Silver City. But then I, too, had been joined by the sun. An educated man with ambition saw promise in me, and just like that, a group of men, as well as many in the town of Lincoln, embraced me. They made me feel for the first time since my momma died that I had family.

Now I would lose them all. People would learn the truth and run, or even if they didn't, time would take them from me. Whether by choice or not, everyone I loved would leave me, again, just like everyone else in my life had so far: my father, mother, stepfather, brother, John...and Mary. What had she done and how?

I groaned, my thoughts coming full circle. Leaning back, I closed my eyes just as my stomach growled. Did I take the chance of rejec-tion by heading back now, or did I wait, giving those who were scared of what I was a chance to slink off?

"Screw that!" I said, jumping down from the tree and landing on my feet without so much as a twinge of pain. "If they want to run from me like scared bitches, they can be forced to explain that to my face. I'm not gonna make it easy on 'em. Not one bit!"

I stormed down the mountain and into our camp to find everyone calmly eating breakfast, which brought me up short. Conversations halted as they saw me. I stood there, my emotions a hodgepodge mixture of surprise and anger at the events that'd happened as well as things yet to come. With no idea what to say, I counted heads. Nine. We were missing one. Garret wasn't here. I spun to look for his horse, and it was gone, too.

"He felt you would calm down more if he let you be," Fred said, standing up. Setting his tin plate down, he walked over to me. "He left something for you on your bedroll. Oh, and he explained the truth to everyone before he left."

"And yet, you're all still here?" I asked, confused.

"We all took a magically sealed oath with some spell Garrett had from a witch," Fred said.

"About me?"

Fred grinned. "Yes, you. Well, you, John, his family...England...the whole thing."

Josiah Scurlock, nicknamed "Doc" because he'd been a dentist at some point, making the fact that he was missing his two front teeth hilariously ironic, stepped forward. "Why would you think we would leave, Billy?"

I looked at Doc, with his big ears that stuck out from a head that held the brain of a professor, and said, "Because I'm a cursed being who doesn't even own his own soul."

"Or maybe you have a soul but someone else holds the deed and you've got to get it back."

I nodded at Doc. I liked that better. It wasn't great, but it wasn't as horrible sounding either. "And everyone knows and is okay with it?"

"Yes, and they are still here," Dick said as he stood. "We've got your back no matter what. Now get some food in you so we can go home. Moon sets about an hour before noon, and I wanna be on the road by then."

My eyes locked on his, and I saw the truth there. Though they all wore their acceptance of me on their faces, it was Dick Brewer who held my gaze. With personal understanding of loss oozing from every pore and an empathy for me that seemed to sit at his very core, I knew I wasn't alone in all this. Then, like the day Tunstall hired me, I swelled with pride and happiness.

I nodded at him, then turned to the group. "Thank you."

After an awkward silence, Charlie stood up. "For God's sake, eat already, or we're never gettin' outta here and I wanna see my lady."

"He wants to be *in* his lady," I heard someone mutter, which caused everyone to laugh.

It broke the tension, and though I could feel they were all still a bit unsure, they were solid in their resolve to be Regulators with me. We were a unified front with a cause driving us forward. We would get revenge on Buck Morton, Jimmy Dolan, and anyone else who had a hand in taking Tunstall's life. They were going to pay, and we were going to serve them the bill.

5

FRANK MACNAB

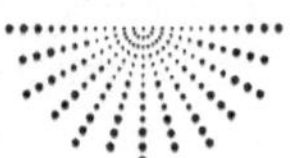

It was time to put my head back into the present. Looking out my hotel window at the New Mexico of 1949, I wondered if the territory I'd loved as a young man had ever really escaped the wound that Scáthach etched into her. Today I was gonna drive back to where she'd done the most damage, Lincoln, and speak to the current sheriff, Sally Ortiz, who'd been voted in the previous year. If she was the culprit of the new demon outbreak, she'd be the sheriff with the shortest career ever.

I pulled on a clean white t-shirt and my new pair of Levi's. Putting a crisp, white dress shirt over the former, I buttoned it, tucked it into the latter, and fastened the jeans up.

I stood in front of the mirror comparing. "Tie, no tie, tie, no tie...no tie wins."

On the bed lay my new black leather belt. She was a dandy, and I was in love with her. In fact, I'd named her Lilith, Lilly for short. I wove Lilly through half of the loops on my jeans then slid the two-gun holster piece on to rest at my back, one on either side of my spine, before looping Lilly the rest of the way and buckling her.

Both of Lilly's sides had a bunch of silver half-circles along her bottom where I could attach different accessories. Today I connected

50

a matching leather rectangular bag to the left side and fastened the bottom of it around my thigh. Inside held extra ammunition and other weapons I might need like stakes and knives. It also had a few protective pockets for potions and such.

After packing my duffle bag, I fetched all three of my guns: one from the bathroom, one from the desk, and one from the bedside table. I checked all three to verify they were fully loaded, yanked up my pant leg, and clipped my Remington 51 on the inner side of my left calf in my boot holster. Easing my pant leg down to cover it, I slid my two Walther PPK/S pistols, one holding silver rounds and one lead, into Lilly's spinal holsters, grips outward.

To hide the PPKs, which is what I called them for short, I pulled on my fitted black leather jacket. Built for me special by a man I met on the job in Poland in the 1920s, the coat hung to mid-thigh and was lined with a special silk and the leather spelled by witches to stop bullets. Not that one could kill me, unless I was out of soul-energy, but they sting like hell, and to be honest, I'd gotten tired of replacing bloodstained shirts.

I shoved my wallet into my back pocket, shouldered my leather duffel, placed my modified sugar loaf sombrero on my head, and headed to check out earlier than needed for my appointment with Sheriff Sally Ortiz. I wanted to stop somewhere before I paid my possible target a visit.

It didn't take long to find my detoured spot since my hotel was on Highway 60 right by Fort Sumner. Once I parked my car, I made my way to the tombstone, took to one knee, and crossed myself. The top of the marker said, "PALS," and it listed three names, claiming that Tom and Charlie had been buried here with me. Truth was, only Charlie was here. As Pat said, Tom has my affliction, so he sure as hell wasn't dead and buried at this spot. Last I knew, like me, he was still on the job working in New York City for the Regulators, who were now called MI-4, as we now fell under the supernatural division of SIS.

The name used for me on the stone always made me laugh. The first name and middle initial were right, but they'd put my mother's maiden name seeing as I was using it at the time I supposedly died. I felt that fitting as my real father's last name brought shame to me.

I reached through the fence to touch the stone and was deep in thought when a boy around the age of ten tapped my shoulder.

"Mister, could you take a picture of me and my friends by the gravestone?"

I smiled when I saw he was accompanied by two other boys, one about his age and one older, not unlike how Charlie, Tom, and I had been. "I'd be happy to. You got a camera?" I asked.

"Well duh, Mister, of course we do," the youngest said as he handed it to me, his attitude reminding me of myself back in the day.

I stared at the contraption for a moment, marveling at how it had changed over the years while I appeared...well, almost exactly the same. Sure, I'd aged a bit from the two years I stopped hunting, but that was subtle. Mainly, I'd had my teeth fixed, but I was still young looking, bare faced, and short by today's standard. I wasn't as scrawny now though, come to think of it. I'd filled out a little, and though still slender, I wasn't weak anymore. I suppose I was lucky that the curse wasn't rigid.

"We're ready, Mister."

The boy's voice pulled me from thoughts, and I looked up at his friends, posing as if they were tough cowboys, hats and all. I spit the toothpick from my mouth with a grin and said, "Y'all ready?" When all three cheered, I raised the camera and took three pictures before handing it back. "Hope one turns out all right."

"Thanks so much, Mister."

"William Henry, at your service," I told him, and tipped my hat to them all.

"Holy cow! Just like Billy the Kid!"

I smiled wide and winked. "Just like."

With a wave, the young boys ran off to a mother who was calling him.

I saluted Charlie Bowdre one last time, then turned and headed off to do the job I'd come here to do. But now I had a smile on my face and thought about how I should call Tom Folliard and tell him about the kid at our gravesite. He'd get a good laugh, that's for sure.

Approaching my car, I wondered what the boy would think if he knew that Billy the Kid still walked the Earth. That he was cursed to do so until either his soul was his again or he vanquished the evil that made him this way. He'd probably wet himself, truth be told.

With a loud laugh, I lit a hand-rolled cigarette and began to hum the chorus of "Turkey in the Straw" as I meandered toward the parking lot of the Fort Sumner museum I was "buried" by. Sliding into my special order black 1950 Aston Martin DB2, I removed my hat and slid on sunglasses. Shutting the door, I revved the engine and headed to the one place I never thought I'd go again: Lincoln, New Mexico.

The two-hour drive from Fort Sumner is scenic, but other than that, it's rather dull. However, I used to do this stretch on horseback, so I wasn't about to complain about the driving time. I just cranked the radio and floored it, like usual.

We won't talk about my many speeding tickets.

As I drove, my mind traveled back in time to the day the curse of Scáthach set in and what awaited me and the other Regulators when we, too, returned to Lincoln.

* * *

Just as Dick wanted, we were on our way after the moon was fully set. It was Wednesday, February twenty-seventh, and on the road back to Lincoln, we ran into McSween.

"Widenmann finally convinced you that you'd be safer if you weren't in town, I take it?" Dick asked.

"Yes. As much as I hated to admit it, he was right," McSween said.

"Susan still in Missouri with her family?" I asked.

"Yes, better she's not here for this anyway. I did send her a telegram tellin' her about John and left her a letter at home to find when she returns. Her sister, husband, and family are goin' to take the east wing of the house though."

53

"What about the Ealys?" Fred asked.

"Movin' them to Tunstall's old quarters in those two rooms on the east side of the store, now that we've taken it back. Rob Widenmann and Sam Corbett are watchin' over our side of the house until Susan gets back."

"Anythin' we should know before you go?" Dick asked.

"I've mostly just been writin' letters about Tunstall's murder to those who can help with makin' Dolan and his men pay for what they've done."

He listed off Sir Edward Thornton, the British Ambassador in Washington, and John Lowrie at the Presbyterian Missionary Board in New York. I had no idea why, so I asked.

"I'm workin' at displantin' Fred Godfroy from his position as the Indian Agent as well as gettin' the British government involved in John's murder since John was still a British citizen."

I secretly thought he was wasting his damn time, but I knew nothing of what they were doing or why. To me, it would all be worked out by using my guns. No letters could bring justice for Tunstall like my six-shooter could. But I sat on my horse and nodded like the rest of them. Hell, maybe they understood, who knows? Either way, I was itching to get back to town and put our plan into action.

Just before we parted ways, McSween said, "Just so you know, Isaac Ellis has been appointed administrator of the Tunstall's estate, and Widenmann went and got himself poisoned by someone of the Murphy/Dolan faction, or so he claims, but he seems fine now. I'll write more letters to the British Ambassador of England and to Tunstall's uncle in British Columbia while I'm gone. Be careful, boys. I'll be back when I can."

I was thankful to have him on his way, seeing as compared to that conversation, the boredom of the road seemed like a *bailé*. And I said so to Brewer, but his mind appeared to be elsewhere.

"Are you even listenin' to me, Dick?"

"Huh?"

"That's what I thought," I said.

"What were you sayin'?"

"Just how this borin' road is more interestin' than listenin' to McSween talk about letters…or did you miss all that, too?"

Dick rotated his shoulder. "No, I heard him. He's goin' about the right channels to get justice for John his way. We're goin' to go about it our way."

"You gonna let Dr. Ealy look at that shoulder when we get back?"

"It'll be fine. I told you, just a dislocated shoulder that I popped back into place. Nothing to worry yourself about."

"Uh-huh. Sure thing." I knew he was lying, but I left it alone. If he wanted to tell me, he would.

Lucky for me, we rode back into town on Thursday in time to help the Ealys move their belongings to Tunstall's old living quarters on the east side of the store. This gave me an excuse to chat with Dr. Ealy, who I usually called Reverend.

"I don't care how you make it happen, just find a way to get a look at Dick's left shoulder. The big man is avoidin' medical attention and he needs it."

This got the reverend to spouting about leaving an injury unattended and what that could cause. I tuned out, nodding at the appropriate times as I carried things down the road, secure now that he'd corner Dick and force medical attention on the giant.

The next morning, March first, Dick and I headed over to see Justice of the Peace J.B. Wilson, again. This time, he appointed Dick a special constable and me his deputy.

Leaving there, it was evident Brewer was on a mission. His usual walk of casual strength had morphed into heated purpose. Normally a man careful of folks as he maneuvered past them, saying hello or excuse me, he just barreled through space like he owned it, long-legged strides eating ground at an exponential pace and no pleasantries on his lips. If ya asked me, he didn't even see those who dove out of his way.

Trying to keep up with the man, I asked, "So now what?"

"We form a posse to go get these bastards," he finally said as we went through the gate of the little white fence that surrounded the McSween home.

"I thought we—"

"Hold that thought," he said, double-knocking on the front door before opening it and walking in, where we found all the sworn-in Regulators.

There was John Middleton, Fred Waite, Doc Scurlock, Charlie Bowdre, Jim French, Henry Brown, Sam Smith, José Chavez y Chavez, and a bare-faced man I didn't know but recognized from the day we'd raided Dolan's store. Obviously, the newly appointed constable didn't know him either.

"And who are you?" Dick asked, reaching over my head and shutting the door behind me.

Stepping forward, a man of average height, light green eyes, and sun-touched brown hair offered his hand to Dick. Speaking in a Scottish brogue, he said, "Frank MacNab is the name. John Chisum and your Alabama friend, Pat, sent me."

Dick took Frank's hand. "A Scotsman?"

"Born and raised, came to this country with me family early on though." He cleared his throat and began to speak like he'd lived in New Mexico his whole life. "But I can sound like one of y'all in a heartbeat."

"Then why keep the accent?" Fred asked.

"The ladies, obviously," MacNab said, going back to his Scottish brogue.

Dick laughed. "I'm Richard Brewer, constable for this party. What did you do for Uncle John?"

MacNab let go of Dick's hand and rubbed his chin like it was a nervous tic . "Um...well, as you know, he's part of the cattle firm, Hunter and Evans. I've been workin' as a detective with them for a year or more. Before that, I was Chisum's ranch foreman."

"Mmm-hmm," Dick said, listening and hoping there was more.

Charlie stepped over. "Frank here is a good man and an excellent shot. Middleton and I have known him since we lived in Kansas, and I vouch for him."

"I can, too. None better from where we used to be, Dick," Middleton said from where he stood in the corner of the room.

"That would put us at ten men, Dick. That's a good startin' number. Besides, if Charlie trusts him, I'm not against him."

Doc piped up, "And we all know how picky Charlie can be, too."

This caused the men in the group to laugh.

One corner of Dick's mouth ticked upward. "All right. Pat swore you in, I take it? Told you all the pertinent information?"

"Yes, sir."

"Good, saves me time. Everyone listen up," Dick said, and then told them about what had transpired at Wilson's house.

"Someone made you a deputy twice in a week's time, Billy?" Charlie said, giving me a hard time. "Are we sure Wilson has got his wits about him?"

Dick fought off a grin and said, "Billy is the one with the curse and the power to help us win this, so I'm good with him bein' my second in command. But I'm goin' to deputize each of you as well. After that, we need to pitch in and help build what will be a twelve-foot-high stone and adobe wall around this place that started construction earlier this morning."

"When do we leave to catch these bastards?" Henry asked. "I'm itchin' to get movin'."

"As am I," Dick told him. "Tomorrow mornin' we'll head out just before the sun rises. I've heard rumor that these men who killed John are hidin' out from us at the Dolan cow camp. If they don't have the balls to come here, we go to them."

The men cheered.

Dick quieted them down. "I don't know when we'll be back this way or when you'll be home next. Because of that, if you didn't already head home to pack a war bag, do so. Select a good horse, too. Today is your day to prepare for our time on the road. But at least help with the wall as long as you can. The sooner we can fortify this location, the sooner McSween can come home."

"Hear hear!" said a few while others grunted agreement.

Dick swore them all in as deputies before we headed outside to help out with the wall.

We'd been at work only an hour or two when I saw a group of men coming our way, led by Sheriff Brady and his mustache. I'd not seen anyone with a larger one this side of the Rio Grande. I often laughed when he spoke, for ya could barely see his lips for the darn thing.

Brady knocked on the front door of the McSween house and Robert Widenmann opened it. To know what was going on, I used the one extra soul in me to enhance my hearing.

"How can I help you, Sheriff Brady?" Rob asked, obviously swallowing the more hateful words he wished to say.

Speaking in as heavy an Irish brogue as my mama used to have, Brady said, "You can come on out here."

"And why would I come outside, sir?"

"You're under arrest."

"What for?" Widenmann demanded to know.

I walked over to Dick. "In case you're interested, Brady's arrestin' Widenmann right now."

"What? The hell he is!" Dick set down the adobe brick he was holding and it broke. He didn't notice and marched off toward the front of the house, yelling out, "Can we help you, Sheriff?"

Everyone else took their cue from Brewer. Regulators with blood in their eyes and hands on their guns came around the corner of the east wing of the house, filling the front yard. Brady turned toward Dick, the Army veteran not flinching an inch at the sight of us all.

"I have a warrant here for the arrest of all those who participated in riotin' at the Dolan Store on February twenty-third," Brady said.

"Riotin'?" Robert blurted in disbelief. "I'm a U.S. Marshal, and I had a warrant to search the premises for the men that shot and killed John Tunstall, since they'd been seen there earlier."

"Were they there?" Brady asked.

"You know damn well they'd already left, but we—"

"Well maybe you should check your sources more carefully."

Rob leaned his large frame toward the sheriff. "Maybe you should check who you consort with, Sheriff, for I have on good authority that they were there with you on the twentieth and you did nothin' to arrest them."

"On what charges? I have no warrants for them."

Dick grinned. "I do, would you like me to get you a copy?"

Brady's face went cold. "No. I don't need your warrants. I have my own." He handed them to Dick.

Leafing through them, Dick said, "Seems like there's one here for each of us except you, MacNab."

"You know, since you wasn't in town at the time," I lied, giving the Scotsman a stern look before MacNab could correct Brady.

"Exactly," Dick said. "The rest of us will just head on over to see Justice of the Peace Wilson with the sheriff and get this straightened out."

"But Dick," I started to say.

He cut me off with a look, then said, "If we want them to consider our warrants valid, then we need to treat theirs the same. Come on, Rob. Let's get it over with."

"Dick, you can't be serious."

"Let's go," Dick said, and though he and the rest grumbled, we all obeyed. "MacNab'll stay here and keep an eye on things, won't ya?"

"Yes, sir," Frank MacNab replied.

We followed the sheriff at a distance, and I used this opportunity to state my concern. "Leavin' just one man to protect all our interests? Sure, why not, what could go wrong?"

Noting the bite to my sarcasm, Dick said, "All the bad guys are with us. He'll be fine."

"All the bad guys we know are in town at the moment, that is," I said.

"I stand corrected," Dick responded, looking over his shoulder at MacNab. "He looks capable, and really, we're just going across the street, Billy."

"And we were in the same canyon with John," I pointed out.

Dick's face went flat and cold. "Don't remind me."

"I'm not tryin' to be a pecker; I'm just pointin' out that there could be a bigger plan in them yankin' us away from the house all at once."

"Damn it..." Dick said, and turned around and ran back.

"Where does he think he's goin'?" Deputy George Peppin demanded to know.

"He heard your sister is workin' at the brothel in town," I said with a grin.

Peppin got into my face, but I didn't budge. "You think you're funny, don't ya, Billy? But I got six pieces of lead that I bet could wipe that smile off your face."

I stared into his eyes, such a light blue that they seemed unreal, and I wiggled the toothpick between my teeth at him. "And I got twelve. Who you think will cry for their momma first? I got ten dollars says it's you."

I knew exactly what Dick was doing. He was giving his pistol loaded with silver ammunition to MacNab. Thus, I held Peppin's attention until Dick returned, then walked off. Out of the corner of my eye, I watched as MacNab pretended to just be wandering, but he was definitely heading to the back of the house.

Coming out onto his front porch, Wilson said, "Well, y'all ain't gonna fit in here. So let's just have the sheriff, one deputy, and then Rob and Dick. You four can talk it out in here. The rest of ya, stay right where ya are."

We all grumbled in agreement and took different sides of the porch. I stared at the McSweens' home, waiting to see what happened, wondering if MacNab was gonna get to prove his worth today or not. Two minutes later, a shot rang out, echoing around us, but I could tell it came from behind the house.

The Regulators all started to move in that direction when the deputies pulled their guns on us.

"Where do you think y'all are goin'?" Jack Long asked.

"Seems to be gunfire behind the McSween house, sir," Fred Waite said, politely as he could. "Don't you think we should make sure everythin' is all right?"

"For all you know, someone is just cleanin' their gun. Stay where you are or we'll open fire."

"Billy?" Fred Waite asked me.

"He's not the law here!" a deputy sheriff snapped at Fred.

I wasn't, but as Dick's number two, I did happen to be the top-ranking Regulator outside the house. In fact, I was about to tell them to stand down while I checked it out, when Wilson's door opened.

"Thank you, Mr. Wilson," Dick said as he stepped out. Turning to us, he added, "Where'd that shot come from?"

"Behind the house," Fred told him.

"Billy, go see what it was."

"You got it, Constable!" I said to Dick. Then, with a wink at Peppin, just to tick him off, I ran off across the street and around the house, into the open area of the U-shaped home. There I found MacNab standing over a dying wolf, his boot firmly planted on that wolf's throat, and Dick's gun pointed at the furry bastard's face as blood poured from the wound in its side.

"Well, shit," was all I could think to say.

6

REGULATORS RIDE

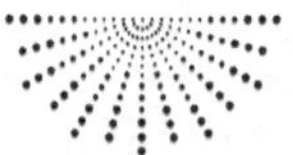

Keeping his eye on the wolf, MacNab stretched his arm toward me. In his hand was the ledger book Widenmann had confiscated during the raid of the Dolan Store. "This was in his mouth as he exited the house. I'm guessin' this is important in some way?"

I took it. "Sure is. Well done, MacNab. I knew this whole trumped up riotin' charge seemed like an excuse to get us all away from the house."

"You want I should finish him off?"

I was about to say no when Dick and the rest of the men came through the gate and into the patio area. "That's up to the constable."

"What's goin' on?" Dick asked.

We filled him in, and before we'd finished, Rob Widenmann stepped up and took the little book from me.

"Is this what he was takin'?" Rob asked.

"Yes, sir," MacNab said.

"See, Dick, I told you it was bullshit," Rob said. "I was actin' on a warrant as a U.S. Marshal, there's nothin' they can do about that. It was all to try and get this back. Sons of bitches! And they sent a trained dog to do it? Just so odd."

With that, Widenmann thundered back into the house, slamming the door shut behind him.

"What did Wilson say?" I asked.

"He could only take so much of Rob's yellin', so he bound it over to April term of court and told us we could go. No bail or anything, no fine."

"I hate court," I muttered. "Hope they don't expect me to show up for this."

"Kill him," Dick said.

"What? Kill Wilson? Why? Is he a demon, too? Damn, I thought he was a good—"

"No, you idiot, the wolf, kill that before it gets too late because they come lookin' for him."

"Why me? MacNab can—"

"You know why. Garrett said if you built up the life energy in you, you'd have more power. Be able to do things. So, take him out."

"Garrett just likes to hear himself talk—"

"Billy?"

"Fine." I pulled out my silver loaded gun with the ivory handle wedged into the waistband of my pants at my back and without looking at the poor beast, shot him in the head.

The wolf demon part of him slid away, leaving only the exorcized human man lying there as naked as the day he was born. I didn't recognize him, nor did anyone else, and I was about to ask where we should put him when the wave of his life force slammed into me, and I had to sit down on the ground.

"Billy, you all right?" Dick asked.

Giggling at my light-headedness, I fell back to lay in the grass. Running my hands through it like I was making a snow angel, I looked up at the blue of the sky and watched a bird fly by, counting the feathers on its wings, for that's how clear he was to me.

"Billy?"

"Shhh...I'm counting feathers."

Dick took my gun. "Get him inside. He's useless like this."

"What's wrong with him?" MacNab asked, squatting down to grab an arm while Fred took my other.

"The energy of the life force makes him loopy for a few minutes, like he's drunk as a skunk. Take him to lie down on one of the beds inside. He'll be okay in a few minutes."

Fred and MacNab hoisted me up, and I looked at MacNab. "You're a pretty boy, ya know that? We could put you in a dress and pass you off as a girl."

"Says the man who has done that before," Fred muttered.

"Shush, you, he's new, he don't need to know all the dirty laundry just yet! So, MacNab, have you ever dressed like a woman?"

Dick laughed, and it was contagious. Everyone began to as well, and I was taken into a west wing room to wait it out. Tired as I was, I nodded off, the effect wearing off in my sleep.

"Sleepin' beauty, you gonna get up and be worth a damn around here or are you goin' to just be a useless cur?" someone said, tapping my noggin with the butt of a pistol.

"A useless cur sounds about right," I muttered, opening my eyes to see Dick looming over me. "Criminy, Dick, do you ya need to hover, ya big galoot? Jeez!"

Dick stood, his head almost hitting the ceiling. "I got a big boot, too, and that's going to be on your ass if you don't get movin' in about thirty seconds." He handed me my silver-bullet-filled revolver. "You got your war bag packed?"

"No. I need to go do that."

"Best get it done now, with the lull in activity around here."

I sat up with a groan. "Did I really tell MacNab he was pretty?"

Dick covered a laugh with a cough. "You did."

"Shoot me."

"You'd just heal. Come on."

I stood and followed Dick out to the parlor where I found all the Regulators wearing skirts and bonnets over their attire. They all started to wave hankies at me and bat their eyes, cooing my name.

"I hate all of you," I said, then started to laugh as I got a good look at John Middleton. He might've only been twenty-four years of age, but he was a tall, heavyset, swarthy man with black hair and eyes, plus a large handlebar mustache. To see him in a skirt and a lady's bonnet was unbelievably funny. Wiping tears, I said, "John, that is not a good look for you...but MacNab, it's good to see I was right."

Everyone laughed, and Charlie came up to me. "I told you he could take a joke!"

I smiled. "The mustache really makes the outfit, Charlie..."

"Ya think?"

I knew he was the one that put them up to it. I didn't even need to ask. Because of that, I grabbed him and kissed him on the lips with a real loud *smack*. "Stunning, just stunning!" To see the startled face of my best pal made me laugh so hard there were tears running down my face as the men around us applauded.

With a bow, I left the room out the front door and headed to the small place I shared with Fred Waite so I could pack. War bags tended to hold an extra set of clothing or two, extra ammunition, playing cards, bill of sale for your horse, a musical instrument if portable like my harmonica, precious letters or things from your sweetheart if you had one, and maybe a few spare parts for your saddle or anything horse related you might need. I was in the process of packing it as Fred walked in, this time without the skirt and bonnet.

"That's a better look for you, but I think that's just due to the mustache you got goin' on."

Fred grinned and smoothed his long 'stache out to the sides with pride. "I'm considerin' growin' a goatee to go with it, but just this line under my bottom lip. What do ya think?"

I looked at Fred, who was half Anglo and half Indian, his features a perfect mix of both, giving him the high cheekbones you saw on a lot of the Chickasaw. "You know you're askin' the man who can barely grow chin hairs, right?"

Fred started to pack. "Are you bitter right now, my brother?"

"Ha! Hell, no. You all have to shave every day. I just wake up this pretty."

"Even with those teeth of yours?"

"Especially with them," I said with a grin, showing off my two front teeth that stuck out due to the ones next to them that'd grown in mostly behind the fronts.

With a snort of laughter, Fred leaned forward and pulled something out of his bag. "You are not pretty; this is though." He tossed the item at me. "Smell that."

I caught it and made the mistake of leaning too close, forgetting my sense of smell would be more acute, and sneezed.

"What did you do, snort the thing up your nose?"

"Still gettin' use to these enhanced senses." I took a lighter whiff of the scarf, and it did smell nice. "Your lady friend, I take it?" I tossed it back to him.

"Yes. But she is promised to some man her daddy wants her to marry. I'm hopin' to change his mind."

It was good that the rest of the Regulators could think about the other aspects of their life during all of this. I was having a hard time doing that. But if the last hour had helped remind me of anything, it was that I needed to not only focus on revenge. Problem was, it was my mission to kill these demons, and anything else was secondary, which was sad because I did like the ladies...a few in particular.

"Billy! Where'd you go?"

I snapped out of it. "Nowhere, sorry."

Fred tucked the keepsake into his war bag and tied it closed. "Come on, let's head on back and get our horses ready."

"Yeah, good idea. Who knows when we'll be back home."

* * *

We left town on March second around five in the morning, working our way down the Pecos Valley, and for the first few days, there wasn't much to do but ride, talk, and play friendly games of monte. We also took turns arm wrestling, competing in acts of brute strength, and then of course we'd shoot at stuff to pass the time. The first two I normally bow out of, but considering I had two souls in me, we wanted to see how much I could do.

Interestingly enough, I was now strong enough to beat Brewer in arm wrestling and lift more than John Middleton. That said, while my strength wasn't supernatural yet, my hearing, sense of smell, and vision were a bit off the charts. I could see better in the dark, smell things I often wish I couldn't, and I was needing cotton in my ears at night to drown out the snoring of some of my compadrés.

One night when Middleton was exceptionally sawing logs, I awoke with a grumble, turned over, and in the distance noticed Brewer pacing about. He was rotating his left shoulder again and appeared to be in pain, which was bothersome. He shouldn't still be sore unless he'd torn something. I considered getting up and confronting him, but I let it be, drifting back off to sleep.

Waking up on March sixth, I was beginning to think we were chasing our tails when our luck changed. Riding just below the crossing on the Peñasco, we noticed some men sitting on the bank of the river. When we got closer, I recognized one of them.

"Dick, that's Buck Morton, the man who shot John."

"Let's go have a chat with them then, shall we?"

We urged our horses into a cantor toward the five men at the river, causing them to notice us, mount their horses, and get moving.

"Word travels fast if they're runnin'," Charlie yelled out to me.

This didn't surprise me at all. We'd been on the road for four days, and people have nothing better to do than talk.

Dick shouted words of encouragement so his horse would pick up speed, and we all followed suit. Gaining on them, the five men split, three going one way and two another. With one hand motion, Dick indicated for us all to stay on the group of three that held Morton.

Dirt flew, filling the air around our party with choking dust as we rode at breakneck speed toward them. Each of us pulled the scarf we wore around our neck up over our nose and mouth so we could breathe easier. The loud thundering of horse hooves pounded like a steady heartbeat as we crossed over the plains, excitement of the chase coursing through our veins.

This was it! We were finally close to getting justice for Tunstall! I rode like the devil was on my back, passing others until I caught up with Brewer. We rode side by side, gaining on them.

By now I could tell who was with Morton: Frank Baker and Dick Lloyd. I shouted this out to Brewer just as they fired on us. Eagerly returning it, I watched a few lead bullets hit them without much reaction on their part. That's when I knew.

"We need silver!" I yelled out.

"What?" Dick shouted back at me.

I pulled my ivory-handled revolver and showed it to him. Everyone knew I kept silver in that gun, so as I pulled it and showed it to Brewer, all those who saw me firing with it understood.

The headlong pursuit became a running firefight and Lloyd's horse, too tired to keep up, gave out and came to halt. Without even a look to one another to verify our next move, the Regulators ignored him and stayed focused on Morton and Baker.

We were beginning to really gain when their horses gave out like Lloyd's had. Jumping off their exhausted mounts, the two men ran for a large patch of tule reeds to make their stand.

"Can't see 'em in there, Captain," Fred said.

"And it's not safe to follow in after 'em," I pointed out so none of the boys would get a stupid idea.

Dick nodded, and we followed him as he rode up to where Morton and Baker had gone in, all ten of us gathering up just out of range of their six-shooters.

"So, what now?" MacNab asked.

"We kill 'em," I said.

"We force them out into the open," Dick said, giving me a look.

"Okay, then we kill 'em," I said.

"No, we arrest them."

I looked at Dick in confusion for a moment. "Pardon me for sayin' this, but that's pointless. The minute we turn them over to Brady, they'll be let go. Hell, those sons of bitches will probably never even have to stand trial if the Santa Fe Ring is involved."

"He's right," Charlie chimed in. "This would all be for nothin'. That warrant you hold is just paper; it can't make them pay for what they did."

"And a quick death is enough punishment?" Dick asked.

"You want them to rot in jail, I take it?" I said. "They'll get out just like the Boys did before. So what ya gonna choose?"

Dick was up against a wall, being squeezed by his moral code and the truth as it stood before him. He placed both of his large hands on his rifle that lay across his lap. Then, without warning, he lifted it and fired into the reeds. Raising his deep voice, he said, "William Scott 'Buck' Morton and Frank Baker, I hold warrants for your arrest regarding the murder of John Henry Tunstall. Surrender or we'll burn you out!"

"There's a choice," I muttered.

There wasn't any reply, so Dick fired another shot into the reeds. "You have thirty seconds to decide!" He looked to me. "Billy, you got matches?"

I felt a giddy bubbling in my chest. "Ya know I do!"

"Get 'em out. If they won't surrender, we'll set fire to this patch of reeds on all sides and that'll be that."

With a nod, I turned to the bag tied up behind me and reached into a side pocket to get my matches.

"Last chance!" Dick yelled. "We're gonna set all sides ablaze."

That seemed to put some get up and go into their step and both raised their hands high, not a gun to be seen.

"We surrender," one of them shouted.

Keeping his rifle pointed at them, Dick replied, "Come on out, and keep your hands up high where we can see 'em. You reach down once for a gun, and I'll put a bullet in your chest without a second thought, just like you did John."

The two men walked out of the reeds, hands up high, guns in their holsters, not making a move toward them in the slightest.

"Doc? MacNab? Get their guns and bring 'em here," Dick ordered. "Middleton? Waite? Get their horses."

Those with a task began to move while the rest of us sat there, wondering what Dick was going to do with them now that he had them. He knew where Charlie and I stood on this, which is likely why we weren't asked to go get them. Dick wasn't stupid. He knew if we had the chance, we'd kill them without a second thought.

They were marched up to us, and I got a good look at them for the first time. That night out in the valley when they shot John, I could see them, but it wasn't as clear as now.

"They them?" Dick asked me, as if reading my mind.

"Yeah, I recognize 'em," I said. With a nod toward Baker, I added, "That one was in the party, but not the three who, you know."

"The three who what?" Baker demanded to know.

"The three who murdered John Tunstall in cold blood," I said, enough heat in my voice to cause Baker to flinch.

Dick must've noticed it, too, for as he held his rifle trained on them, he said, "You thought no one witnessed your little show in the valley that night, didn't ya? Hate to break it to you, but someone did, and you're goin' to jail."

"Now wait a minute," Baker said. "I had no idea that—"

"Shut up, Frank," Morton said.

Baker did as he was told, and seconds, slow as sap in February, ticked by.

Coming to a conclusion, Dick said, "You can lower your hands, gentleman."

"You're not going to shoot us?" Morton asked.

Dick lowered his gun. "Truth be told, I would've preferred not to have taken you alive, but now that we have, you have my word that you'll not be harmed."

It was like a match lit the fire in my chest. "What? Your word? Dick, are you out of your damn mind? These two will not serve a day if we turn them in! No, no way in hell are they gettin' to go scot-free." I pulled my gun with the silver in it and took aim.

"Stop!" Dick yelled.

For no reason I know, I did, even though rage had my arm shaking. I could feel this compelling need in me crying out to kill them. I'd never felt this before and could only assume it was the curse working to undermine my personal choices.

"We're not killing any man who surrenders, Billy, and that's that," Dick said.

"But they—" I ground out between clenched teeth.

"It would make us no better than them," Dick explained, his voice quieter than before.

Charlie was fit to be tied as well. "So you want to what? Hand them over to Brady for a few minutes and then throw them a goodbye party as they head to Mexico and disappear?"

I jumped off my horse and walked toward the two men, placing the barrel of my gun against Morton's forehead. "I'm not hearin' a good enough argument to not kill these sons of bitches here and now."

I stared into Morton's face, one called handsome by many who'd described him. His eyes were intent and showed no fear of dying at my hand. That was likely because he didn't realize I had silver in this gun or he just was one brave S.O.B. I leaned in toward him. "I know what you are, and I'd happily mount your head on a stick and parade it around town. You get me?"

"That's enough!" Dick yelled as Middleton and Doc grabbed me and pulled me back.

I could've fired then, and I almost did. I could feel my strength rise and knew I could overpower Doc, maybe Middleton, too, but not without hurting them, and that gave me pause.

"Don't you dare," Dick said. The power behind the words and the underlying tone was enough that I, as they say, fell into line. As did Charlie, who also had his gun out and aimed at Frank Baker. "Put the gun away and let's come up with another plan."

I lowered my weapon and headed straight to one of my saddlebags to grab two silver cuffs disguised to look like steel. Stepping over to Brewer, I offered a silver cuff to him. "Care to do the honors with me?" When he looked at the bracket like a Brussel sprout, I tossed it to Scurlock. "Help me out, Doc."

He caught it. "Sure thing."

I pointed to Charlie. "Keep that gun on 'em."

Charlie nodded at me, and I clamped the cuff to Morton's ankle.

"This is ridiculous," Baker said. "What is this one little cuff supposed to do?"

Doc grinned at Baker, revealing his two missing front teeth before bending down to put the cuff on him. He then pulled out an actual set of wrist irons. "That will make these effective on the likes of you, that's what."

"What are ya doin', Billy?" Dick asked.

Middleton placed another set of irons on Morton's wrists while I explained.

"Ya see, these silver cuffs will keep 'em from changin' and reduce their strength so the irons do their job."

"Sun is up," Dick pointed out.

"The moon could be, too, and we'd not see it," I said. "If we learned anythin' during that charade of an arrest Brady did yesterday, it's that they can change when the moon is out, doesn't have to be night." I paused and patted Morton on the shoulder when I saw the surprise on their faces. "Oh, by the way, we know all about you."

With a Regulator holding the reins, we let Morton and Baker mount their tired horses. This left both men to ride the horn for balance, a degrading thing for any cowboy worth his salt as a rider.

"Where to?" Fred asked Dick.

"It's gettin' late, so we'll head up river to Bob Gilbert's ranch for the night."

With a nod, I mounted my horse. "Sounds good. We only have light till around six o'clock, so we best get a move on."

"Agreed," Dick said, then he turned to our captives. "If you try to escape, my word no longer holds, and Billy here will put a silver bullet in your brain. Got it?"

Both men nodded, and we headed back out onto the road, keeping a steady pace. Halfway to the Gilbert ranch, Charlie rode up next to me and I could tell he had something on his mind.

"Spit it out, pal," I said.

"How do you know about the moon and sun so much? You never used to."

"Garrett gave me this book that talks about the stages of the moon and gives times of sunset, sunrise, moonrise, and moonset through the year. Figure if I'm supposed to fight these demons, I should know their schedule, right? I've been readin' it a bit here and there. I check it each mornin' for that day's schedule. For example, after the sun rose this mornin', the moon rose about an hour afterwards. It's only a sliver. With the sun out, it's hard to see."

"Sliver?" Charlie asked.

"What do they call it again? Oh, yeah, a crescent. A waxing crescent. And it'll set about two and a half hours after the sun does tonight. That means we'll only see it for a short time. If the research by other Regulators is right, they can only change when the moon is up at a crescent or more. The new moon makes them unable to change, and a full moon means they have to change."

"You're sayin' they could change right now?"

"Yep, but we put a solid silver bracelet on each of their ankles, so that'll keep that from happenin'. If it was a full moon, that wouldn't help at all, but it's not, so we should be safe."

"If we're not?"

"I'll put a bullet in each of their heads. No hesitation."

"Even if they're not runnin' away?"

I hated to go against Dick, but I knew my answer. "Even if."

7

MORTON AND BAKER

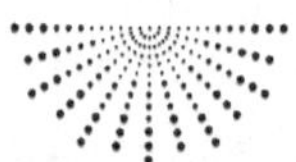

Once we reached Gilbert's ranch, the sun was setting, and I pointed out the moon to Charlie as we dismounted and got settled. Thankfully, we only had two and a half hours to watch our captives extra close. Once the moon set, they would be stuck in human form, and then anyone could guard them, not just me.

By eight-thirty, Fred and Doc came to watch 'em for a few hours, and I got excited about heading to the kitchen to fetch a bite to eat and maybe playing a good game of cards. But what they told me as we swapped places changed my plans for the night.

"William McCloskey is here."

I spun to look Fred in the face. "You're not jokin'?"

"Nope. Seems he was here helpin' translate for Bob. Heard him say to Dick that he'd ride with us tomorrow."

"The hell he is! He was in the party that—"

"I know, but...well...you should go talk to him and Dick. They're outside the kitchen. Food was held for you."

"All right. Thanks."

This was an interesting turn of events. Last we'd spoken to the "other William," as I tended to call him, was three in the morning the day John died. Knowing McCloskey had a few friends in the posse coming for the cattle, Tunstall dispatched him to Turkey Springs, where the posse was meeting up. McCloskey's job there was to inform whoever was in charge that although the seizing of his stock was being done against his consent, there would be no resistance.

But that wasn't what made all this awkward. It was the fact that the last time we'd seen McCloskey, he was riding with the posse Morton led to kill Tunstall. That did not bode well for him, and if we found out he'd had a hand in helping Morton find us that day, warrant or no, I was gonna arrest him.

Trying to keep my anger in check, I walked slowly, going over all the facts as we knew them and chose a plan of action. Arriving at the kitchen door, I found Dick sitting outside by a fire with McCloskey. They were just talking casual-like, but my gaze met Dick's, and I took the cue I saw there, saying, "Well, if it isn't the other William; I heard rumor you were here!"

"Hey, Billy, how are you?" he asked, standing up and coming toward me, hand outstretched.

I wanted to grab his hand, yank him in, pull my blade, and demand the truth. Then ram it into his gut if he'd betrayed us. Instead, I shook his hand and smiled. "I'm good, you?"

"Never been better."

"That's good to hear," I lied. "I'm gonna go get me my dinner before it's too cold. I'll be back. Don't you go nowhere."

"I'm just sittin' here, talkin' with Dick."

"I see that," I said, a tiny bit of bitterness lighting into my tone.

Dick gave me a cautionary look. "Go eat, grumpy."

"On it, Captain!" I said, saluting him and heading into the kitchen where I had to collect myself. I might've been able to calm down, but Middleton came in as I was eating.

He sat with me and stared me down. "What are we goin' to do about this?"

I tried to play it off. "About what?"

Middleton pointed a finger in my face. "You know damn well what I'm talkin' about. How are we not supposed to talk to him about that day?"

"Isn't Dick doing that?"

"I've not heard him say anythin' about it yet, and I've been sittin' around the corner listenin'. Just been pleasantries and ranch talk."

"Dick will ask. He can't *not* ask—it's who he is. He'll have to know. Give him time."

"I think he's been waitin' on you, so it's two against one."

"Dick *is* two people," I joked, picking on the gentle giant's size.

Middleton laughed. "Ain't that the truth. But he knows you're the only one who really saw him, so he'll need you to back him up."

I finished my food and went over to the basin filled with soapy water. Washing my dishes, I said, "Well, I'm about to go out there, and we'll see what happens."

"All right. I'll be 'round the corner if you need me."

"Good to know," I said, and I meant it. It was well known that John was not only an excellent marksman, but a fist-fighter as well. He'd be the first man I'd pick to be on my team, after Brewer, that is.

I set my dishes on a rack to dry and, with a nod at Middleton, went back outside. I crossed to the opposite side of the fire to keep the house and McCloskey in my sights. Plus, between the house, Brewer, Middleton, and me, the other William had no way to run.

Squatting down by the fire, I put my hands toward the flames to warm them. Firelight on my face, I looked at McCloskey, then Dick, and raised an eyebrow. I got a slight nod from the big man, which I took as the go-ahead and decided if it wasn't, he'd stop me.

"She's still the best horse I've ever owned," McCloskey was saying. "Wouldn't sell her for two hundred dollars."

Seeing my opening with that, I said, "Was she the horse you rode to Paul's ranch that night?"

There was a hiccup in the chatter as he took a moment before answering with, "It is. What a horrible turn of events. I couldn't believe my ears when they told me."

Dick grimaced, as did I, but while I hid mine by looking down from the fire, he didn't even try to. "Ears?" he asked. "Don't you mean eyes, Will?"

McCloskey looked to Brewer. "I'm sorry?"

"You were *there*. We saw you ride into that canyon with Morton, Baker, Evans, and the rest of them. Tell me, were you a member of the posse?" Dick asked.

McCloskey suddenly understood the tone in which the discussion had turned, and his voice went up in pitch slightly. "What is that supposed to mean?"

"Were you privy to their plans in killin' Tunstall?" I stated flatly.

"What? Why would you think that?"

"Why else would you be with them?" Dick asked. "Did they force you to ride with 'em?"

"Force me? No! I have friends in the group, so I tagged along."

"That makes no sense," I said, standing up. "Why would you want to ride all the way out there? Do they have somethin' on you? Do you owe *The House* money?"

"No, I do not owe them money or anythin' else!"

"Then?" I prompted.

"I went with them over to Tunstall's ranch as planned. As they were leavin', Buck asked if I was heading into town. I was, so I figured a ride with pals was better than ridin' alone."

"Or maybe you just hold your alliances closer to that side than ours," Dick said, sitting up, hands on his knees.

I took the cue and stood, hooking my right thumb on my cartridge belt not far from my gun. "Are those friends closer than the ones you helped fortify John's place with the night before?"

"Whoa, wait a minute, both of you. I did not sell John out. I swear! I tagged along for the reasons stated and to help with translation if anything got heated."

"Translation? Morton speaks English just fine." I looked to Brewer. "That was English he was speakin' earlier when we arrested him right? Or was I imaginin' that?"

McCloskey looked astonished. "You arrested him? Is that why you're here?"

"Yes," Dick replied. "We've got a warrant for his and Baker's arrest, and we'll be turnin' them both in to the law in Lincoln. They'll go to trial for killin' John."

"Should you be joinin' 'em?" I asked.

"No! No, I should not!" McCloskey protested. "I had nothin' to do with that. I simply was ridin' with them to Lincoln. You have my word."

I could tell Dick wasn't sure he believed him, but we had no proof otherwise, so the big man decided to play it cool. He leaned back in his chair again, feigning a relaxed state, saying, "Okay, we believe you."

McCloskey stood and looked between me and Brewer. Without a word, he walked away.

Tilting his hat over his eyes, Brewer added, "Oh, and Will?"

He stopped and turned back to us. "Yeah?"

"If we find out you're lyin', you'll be lucky if I have time to get a warrant and arrest you."

"How's that lucky?"

I smiled wide. "He means, you'll be lucky if I don't kill you first. Have a good night."

Eyes wide, the other William quickly turned and headed off.

"You believe him?" I asked, sitting next to Brewer.

Hat still down, he said, "For now." Then, out of nowhere, I heard him make a noise that almost sounded like a low growl. With teeth clenched, he added, "But God help him if I find out he lied to me."

Right then and there, I knew that if we learned that McCloskey was indeed a turncoat, I'd have to beat Brewer to the man if I wanted to be the one to kill him. It seemed Dick did have a breaking point after all. Thing was, I may have been the one who threatened to kill him outright, but if Dick's reaction was any indication, he'd do worse to the man than I would...and that scared even me to consider.

* * *

Two nights later, we made our last stop before heading into Lincoln to turn Morton and Baker in to the authorities. We'd even sent a rider ahead to alert those at the Chisum Ranch in South Springs of our plans.

The sun had set behind the mountains, so it was hard to see all

Chisum's place, referred to as South Spring Ranch. However, I knew from previous trips here that it was a long, one story, Spanish style ranch. It was surrounded by a white picket fence that stood no farther than ten feet from the thick adobe walls that protected all who were inside from attack.

Unlike the common flat rooftops in the region, the majority of the one on the Chisum home angled to a point at center, sloping down to the sides. The overhang doubled as a cover for the narrow porch that ran along the entire front of the building, save for the center section where a narrow adobe wall hid the front entrance.

Dick knocked on the door politely.

For a change, a woman answered the door, and for a moment, I thought Uncle John had gotten himself a lady-friend, until I noted her age. She was closer to mine than Dick's, let alone Uncle John's. Fair in complexion, she had long blond hair that fell loose about her shoulders.

I grinned and took off my hat.

"Hello, is Uncle John at home?" Dick asked, using the name the Cattle King of New Mexico had asked us to call him.

"He is. May I ask who's callin'?" she said, her voice holding a Texas twang to it.

"Richard M. Brewer, William Bonney, and the Regulators, ma'am."

"We sent word ahead with Charlie Bowdre. Did he make it here all right?" I asked.

"He did," she said with a nervous smile as she opened the door farther. "I'm Uncle John's niece, Sallie. A pleasure to meet you Richard and William. My uncle is expectin' y'all. He's had nothin' but nice things to say about you since we heard you was comin' by this way."

Dick took off his hat and entered the house. "Thank you, ma'am. Billy, keep a n eye on things out here. I'll be right back with word from Uncle John."

"You got it, Captain."

Sallie held her lantern toward me as Dick disappeared into the house. "Billy? As in Billy Bonney, the outlaw?"

"That'd be me, ma'am," I said, bowing to her with a big ol' grin on my face.

"Why, you're nothin' but a boy."

I laughed. "Well, I guess I am. What did you think me to be, Miss Chisum? Old and gnarly like the cook, Gotfried Gauss?"

"I have yet to meet Mr. Gauss, but rumors make you sound like a hardened man, Mr. Bonney."

I slid a hand into my pocket. "Please, call me Billy, Miss Chisum."

"Sallie," she said, a smile as bright as the sun spreading across her face.

Seeing as I felt a nickel still in my pocket, I pulled my hand out so she could see it was empty. "What's that in your ear, Miss Sallie?"

"My ear?"

Carefully reaching out, I said, "May I?"

She looked skeptical but nodded.

I reached out and flipped the coin the way I'd been taught and pretended to pull the nickel from her ear. "Why this, 'tis a funny place to be saving your money."

"What?"

I produced the nickel for her to see, and with lips pressed together, she fought a smile. "Billy Bonney, you are not what I expected at all."

"If you thought he was a pain in the rear, you'd be right," Dick said, walking up behind her. "John said we're good to stay. Some will have to bunk with the other ranch hands in the cow camp, but for now, horses to the stable for the night, and we get Morton and Baker situated."

"Where they staying?" I asked.

"Here in the house. We'll figure it out. Miss Chisum," he said, bowing his head slightly before stepping past Sallie and out onto the porch, where he put his hat back on.

I tipped my hat to her as well before placing it on my head, then followed Dick back to the men, where he told everyone the plan for the night.

After getting our mounts settled at the stable, we cleaned up and headed inside the house, which contained eight rooms, all surrounding a patio at its center. A beautiful home she was, complete with carpet in many of the rooms, except the dining area. It had a wooden floor and often after large meals at a table that sat twenty-four, Uncle John would have it pulled to the side to make room for dancing. Tonight was no different.

Without the Coes there to play violin, Sallie took to the piano, and all but our two fugitives enjoyed some music and dancing after a good meal.

During a pause where Sallie hunted for music, Dick approached me, a curious look on his face. "Billy, did you take the silver off Morton and Baker?"

"Hell, no. Moon comes up at quarter to nine in the morning. Best we not take any chances if we oversleep."

"Agreed, but they're goin' to be mighty uncomfortable all night then."

"Yes sir, and that there gives me pleasure." I smiled at him wide and flicked a glance toward Miss Sallie as she searched through sheet music for another tune.

Dick missed nothing. "Seein' as you seem to fancy the girl, go find out what she took 'em after dinner."

"I do not fancy her," I demanded, quietly. "She's nice, smart, and pretty. And all I've had to look at lately is your mug and the rest of the Regulators."

Dick grinned. "So...you're sayin' I'm not pretty?"

I laughed a good belly laugh since Dick rarely made jokes these days. "Sure ya are, Dick, but the rest of them ugly sons of bitches is weighin' on my soul. I'm in desperate need of enjoyin' the company of a young woman for a change."

"Well, she seems taken with you—"

"Like all smart women are," I said in jest.

He rolled his eyes. "Well then, why d on't you find out what she took our prisoners while you're flirtin' with her, okay?"

"On it now," I said, smacking his left shoulder without thinking.

Dick winced, his eyes almost crossing with the pain my slap caused, and I immediately felt like an ass.

"I'm so sorry! Are you all right? I thought you had that looked at!"

Dick grimaced, and through clenched teeth, he said, "I did. Still healin'."

His ruddy complexion appeared redder than usual, and I took that as my cue.

"I'll go ask Sallie about that stuff..."

"Yeah, you do that," he said and walked away, grumbling.

I sauntered over as she began to play and sat next to her, singing the song with her as the rest danced behind us. As the song finished, she turned to me.

"Why, Billy Bonney, for a dangerous outlaw, you sing like a bird."

I winked. "Don't believe all the rumors ya hear, Miss Sallie. I'm not that dangerous."

"Not like those two men you brought here, I take it?"

She opened that door of conversation, so I stepped on through. "It was mighty nice of you to offer your room to our fugitives. No windows make it a perfect spot for them, so thank you for that. I just hope you'll have a place to sleep though."

"You're welcome, and don't you worry about me. My uncle has moved me to his room for the night seein' that he plans to bunk out here with y'all."

"I see. Well, thank you all the same, for that and for allowin' me to share your piano bench." I started to stand up but leaned back over and said, "By the way, what was it our two fugitives asked you for?"

"Oh, just some paper, a candle or two, and somethin' to write with. Said they wanted to write their sweethearts before they got locked away. Isn't that, well, sweet?"

"It could even be true," I said. "But you are sweet, that's for certain." I took her hand and kissed the top of it before askin' her, "Do you know 'Turkey in the Straw'?"

"Sadly, I do not," she said.

"I do," Uncle John said, walking over to us with his fiddle.

I put my hand out to her. "Well then, Miss Sallie, might I have this dance?"

She looked to her uncle, who nodded. "He's the best dancer here."

Sallie tentatively took my hand. "I'll believe it when I see it."

"Oh! A dare, my boys!" I said. "Y'all better stay back. I'm about to show Miss Sallie how it's done here in Lincoln!"

They boys hooted and hollered at this as Uncle John began to play. They stomped and clapped as I took Sallie's hands in mine, twirled her about, and danced her feet off.

It was a grand night, and for once, I slept well. However, by morning, when Doc and I went to fetch Morton and Baker for breakfast, they were as pale as death, and Miss Sallie made sure to say so at the breakfast table, giving us all the evil eye.

We all knew it was because of the silver they wore, but it wasn't like we could tell her, so we all just kept to eating and said not a word, letting her believe it was due to their windowless room and fear for their lives.

As we were getting ready to leave, both our prisoners approached Miss Sallie with things in hand, and I used my enhanced senses to hear what they were saying.

"I want to make my last request on Earth to you, Miss Chisum," Baker said. "I will never live to get to Lincoln. When you hear of my death, I wish you would send this watch and bridle, which I plaited myself, to my sweetheart, and mail this letter to her."

"I will, but there's no reason to think you'll not make it to Lincoln. Mr. Brewer seems to be a man of irreproachable character. I would think he'll keep his word to you."

"If it were up to him alone, ma'am, I would agree. But it is not just him in that party." He paused. "Thank you for this."

With no idea what else to say to him, she told him he was welcome, and Morton stepped up to her next, handing her one of two letters he held in his shackled hands. Feeling eyes on him, he turned to see me watching him closely and appeared to swallow what he was about to say. Instead, he just said goodbye and shook her hand with a mighty grip, his eyes sad as they looked at her with words he wanted to say but didn't dare with me so close.

"Come on, you two. Quit taking up all of Miss Sallie's time. You have an appointment today with the Justice of the Peace," I said.

They nodded and walked away, leaving her standing there a bit dumbfounded, unable to find the words to comfort them as she held a bridle, a gold watch, and two letters.

Uncle John approached Dick and me as we reached the stable. "Brewer, before ya go..." He stopped close to us and dropped his voice. "I just spoke with one of my ranch hands who returned late last night from a trip to town for supplies. Word has it that Dolan's got twenty or so men on the road between here and Lincoln. He plans to ambush you and rescue his two men from your custody."

"We have legal warrants for them," Brewer said in our defense.

"I'm not sayin' ya don't. I'm sayin' to be careful. *The House* is always one step ahead, which means the deck is stacked against you."

"Normally I'd say we can take Dolan and his goons," I said. "But it's our ten to his twenty. I don't like those odds."

"Neither do I," Dick agreed. "Hell, they're more likely to kill Morton and Baker than allow us to get them to court."

"Well, that's just fine with—" Dick hit me in the stomach, knocking the wind outta me, making the last word of my sentence sound like, "Oof!" as I doubled over.

"I made them a promise," Dick said, glaring down at me. "We'll go the way of Agua Negra and take that trail that swings around the base of Capitan Mountain."

"Military use that route," Uncle John offered up.

"I know, but not that often, and it's a much less traveled road than the one that follows the Hondo. It'll bring us into Lincoln from a different direction and under cover of night. That way if Dolan is layin' in wait for us, we might get lucky and bypass him all together."

"Smart idea," Uncle John said, handing Dick a letter. "Give this to McSween when you see him."

"Will do. Thanks again, Uncle John."

I stood and wheezed out my thank you to Chisum as well, and with a hand on my gut, I followed Brewer. "I deserved that. We even now?"

Dick looked at me with narrowed eyes over his good shoulder. "Not yet."

"Just dandy," I muttered and mounted my horse with a groan that made him chuckle until we noticed McCloskey approaching us on his horse, holding the reins of Morton's, who sat quietly.

"Dick," McCloskey said. "We need to stop at the postmaster in Roswell on the way to Lincoln."

"Why's that?" Brewer asked as he carefully hoisted himself up into the saddle of his favorite horse, a b ay mare he'd named Mattie.

"Buck needs to register and mail out a letter," McCloskey explained as Morton nodded in confirmation.

"No way," I said, spinning my pony about to face McCloskey. "Ash Upson is the postmaster there, and we all know he's pals with good ol' Jimmy Dolan."

"What is that supposed to mean?" McCloskey countered.

I ignored him and looked to Morton. "Sallie was good enough to mail one of your letters. Why not this one, too?"

"It's all right, Billy," Dick said before Morton could answer me. "We can stop. Besides, it wouldn't hurt to pick up a few things while we're there."

I didn't like the feeling I was getting in my gut. "Let me see that letter."

McCloskey handed it to me. It was addressed to H.H. Marshall in Richmond, Virginia, and I began to wonder if we should've let them write anything at all. But before I could rip it in half, Dick told me to give it back, and McCloskey snatched the letter out of my hand.

With a curse on my tongue, we left South Spring and headed toward Roswell.

8

MEET THEIR MAKER

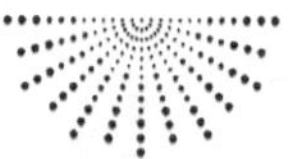

We reached the Roswell post office around ten o'clock in the morning. Sure enough, Ash Upson was on duty. With Dick's shoulder hurting, I volunteered to go in with McCloskey and Morton.

"Are you in any danger, Buck?" Ash asked, noticing the man's wrists were shackled and our posse.

"No. But if anythin' happens to me, I need my people notified," he said, handing Ash the H.H. Marshall letter.

"Buck," McCloskey said, laying a hand on Morton's shoulder. "If they want to harm you two, they will have to kill me first."

I raised an eyebrow at that, and once outside, I told Charlie and MacNab what McCloskey said. They thought it odd as well, but by half past the hour, we were on the road to Lincoln with a long day ride ahead of us.

Twenty miles in, we were strung out for about two-hundred yards along the trail as we slowly moved toward Agua Negra, now only five or six miles away. Charlie and I were in the lead with McCloskey, Morton, and Baker. The three were almost riding abreast and talking amongst themselves right in front of us. MacNab and Middleton weren't far behind us, and the rest were

86

strung out, with Dick riding last so as to keep an eye on the whole party.

With Agua Negra so close, I began to daydream of resting my horse and getting food for him and me. But that's when everything went straight into the shitter.

Being as Morton and Baker had no knowledge of my abilities, as soon as they felt they were far enough ahead of us, they began to speak freely to McCloskey, and what I heard wasn't good.

"What you gonna do, William, when they realize you helped lead us right to Tunstall that day?" Baker said.

"Shh! Keep your mouth shut," McCloskey said.

"You'll be in the same boat we are, if not worse," Morton pointed out. Let's make a break for it. The silver cuffs are off. We can shift and be gone before they can even think about tryin' to catch us."

"And it's not like they can explain what we did to anyone, or they'd sound like they were off their rocker," Baker added in.

"Oh no," I said real quiet-like to Charlie. "We got ourselves a problem."

"What?" Charlie asked.

I moved my horse closer to him but pulled my gun with the silver bullets. "McCloskey is a turncoat. They got him to remove their silver cuffs somehow when we were at the post office. They're about to make a run for it," was all I got out before I saw McCloskey reach for his gun.

Seeing McCloskey's gun working round to me, I fired at him from my hip, and it hit him under the jaw, knocking him off his horse. Without hesitation, Morton and Baker took off on horseback. But as soon as they realized their tired horses weren't going as fast as they needed, they began to shift and soon leapt from their horses and began to run on all fours.

Suddenly my vision became crystal clear and my focus zeroed in on the two wolves running off trail. I shouted, urging my horse to follow them, and Charlie wasn't far behind, both of us firing our weapons.

I hit Morton in the spine just as Charlie hit Baker in the chest.

Both went down into the dirt but kept crawling as best they could with silver beginning to poison their system. Jumping off my horse, I ran the rest of the way to them, holding a revolver on each while the rest of the party caught up. But by then Morton had died, his life force flowing into me, leaving only Baker.

"Do it, Billy, before Dick gets up here," Charlie said.

MacNab agreed. "He's gonna die anyway. You might as well store up and just put him out of his misery."

Feeling light headed, I stared at Baker, and though he was dying, his eyes stared into mine, and I didn't see a demon there. I saw the man, and it gave me pause.

"Billy, it's now or never. Brewer's comin', and he's gonna be hoppin' mad."

That was an understatement.

"I'm sorry," I mouthed to the wolf, and he shut his eyes just before I pulled the trigger and shot him in the head. The weight of his life force, paired with Morton's, knocked me on my ass, literally, making me giggle like a schoolgirl.

"Billy! Taking lives is not funny!" Sam scolded.

This only made me chuckle more, prompting Charlie to come to my defense as I sat on the ground rocking back and forth with laughter singing, "Morton and Baker meet their maker."

"He's drunk on soul-sucking-mumbo-jumbo," Charlie said. "Byproduct of soakin' up the life force of the soul he takes. He's never had two hit him so fast without needin' one to heal somethin', so as John would've said, he's bloody drunk as a skunk!"

The eight men around me couldn't help but chuckle at Bowdre's attempt to imitate Tunstall's English accent.

"Here comes Dick," MacNab said. "What do we want to do?"

"Uh-oh, Daddy's gonna be mad," I said, rolling on the ground in laughter.

"Tell it like it is," Charlie said. "Or rather, Billy can once he sobers up."

"And that'll take how long?" Henry Brown asked.

"Give or take five minutes," Fred Waite told him. "Ten, maybe?"

"Why they naked?" Sam asked, referring to Morton and Baker.

"Lost their clothes in the change," Fred explained.

"What in hell have you done, Billy?" boomed Dick's voice as he jumped off his horse and stormed over.

I sat up and snorted a laugh before looking to Charlie. "He was like two hundred yards behind us. How does he know it was me?"

"Because you are trouble," Charlie replied with a grin.

I fell back onto the ground to stare up at the sky. "You speak the truth, Charles. You speak the truth!"

"Damn it all to hell," Dick said, breaking through the group like Moses parting the Red Sea. Eyes landing on the two dead men, he took off his hat and squatted next to them. "Damn," he said under his breath, and all of us were quiet as the call of a raven filled the air.

Dick looked up at Charlie. "What the hell happened? I want to know this instant!"

"Well..." I began to say.

"Not from you, Barbara May, you're worthless right now, I can tell. Charles?"

"They shifted and made a run for it. Billy and I pursued, and they died from silver wounds, simple as that."

"It is not as simple as that! Why is McCloskey dead back there? What happened?!"

"Well, it seems that—" I started to say again.

Dick spun to face me, his ruddy cheeks now bold red with anger. "Did I ask you?" he yelled. "I made those men a promise. Where do you get the right to make me a liar? You alone do not get to decide who lives and dies, William H. Bonney, not on my watch." He looked away from me to Morton and Baker. Emotion filling his voice, he said again, "I made them a promise."

Getting up on my knees, I said, "I'm sorry for that, Dick. I am. But you should know—"

"Did I say I wanted to hear your lousy excuse?" he yelled, hovering over me. "Just shut up and ride out your high." He turned and began to walk off.

Now I was mad. Standing with a wobble, steadied by Fred, I yelled out, "The hell I will, you overgrown ogre!"

Dick stopped in his tracks. Slowly, he turned around, and his eyes landed on me with the need for vengeance all over his face. "I suggest you choose your next words carefully, William."

"Okay, Richard," I said, using his full name as well, just to be a pain in his ass. "You want the damn truth, here you go."

I explained what had happened exactly, my head becoming less twirly as time passed.

Dick looked to the sky. "So Billy killed Morton with one shot, and Charlie wounded Baker, but Billy killed him for the soul. Yes?"

Everyone mumbled their agreement.

Dick looked down at the ground and began to pace as we all stood waiting. Finally, he said, "We need to dress them."

Charlie grimaced. "Uh, why?"

"You two shot 'em, so you can dress 'em. Who has clothes that'll fit either of 'em?"

A shirt was offered, then pants, and so on until we had enough. Now fully sober, I hunted for the silver bullets so they'd not be found. When they were nowhere to be seen, I called Doc over and asked if he had an idea as to where they'd gone.

"Why do you think I know why? I was a dentist, Billy, not a super-natural surgeon."

I sighed. "I figured you'd know more than anyone else here."

Dick wandered back over to us. "What's taking so long?"

I explained and watched Dick as he processed the info, scratching at the blond stubble on the side of his face. "Garrett never addressed this, but is it possible that the silver kills them because it liquefies into their body?"

"It would have to stop their heart to kill them since they didn't bleed out," Doc added.

"Says the dentist," I teased.

Doc rolled his eyes at me, and I couldn't help but snicker.

"I think Doc's right," Fred said, and seeing that he'd had the most education of us, being as he'd gone to college and all, we were all inclined to listen.

"If that's the case," I said, "then let's get these bastards dressed and then shoot them with lead so we can get outta here."

"We're takin' them with us," Dick said.

Charlie began to put a shirt on Baker. "Are you out of your mind?"

"No, I just happen to not believe in leavin' two men out on the land to rot like they did to John. Dress them and we'll take them into Agua Negra and have them buried."

"After we shoot 'em with lead here," Charlie stated for clarification.

"Yes. Doc, come with me," Dick said, waving the ex-dentist to follow him to McCloskey and his horse.

"Is it me, or is Brewer actin' peculiar?" Charlie asked as he fastened Baker's shirt.

I began to dress Morton. "It's not just you."

"Somethin' is going on with him," Fred said. "The question is what."

Once we got to Agua Negra, we found a place to eat while Dick looked for men who'd bury our three outlaws. By the time he rejoined us, we'd already eaten, but told him we'd wait on him to do so before getting back on the road.

He waved us off. "I'm not hungry anyway. Let's saddle up and move out."

We'd followed him to the horses when John Middleton, who'd been mostly quiet until now, said, "Where to now, Captain?"

"We get our story straight first of all."

"What story is that?" Charlie asked.

Dick thought for a moment, then said, "I hate lyin', but we have no choice."

"Not like we can go into town yelling about werewolves," MacNab said.

Dick pointed at him in agreement. "We keep it simple. We'll say that we were about five or six miles shy of reaching Agua Negra when Morton, who'd been ridin' side by side with McCloskey, snatched his gun and shot him dead." He paused, taking Mattie's reins in hand.

"Then he and Baker took off on horseback, Morton firin' shots at us with McCloskey's gun. We returned fire, overtook 'em, and they died from wounds received during the attempted escape. That's it."

"What about the silver cuffs McCloskey removed from them bastards?" I asked. "Those were our only two."

Dick hoisted himself up into the saddle. "MacNab, you willin' to go find 'em? Spread our story of what happened? You can meet back up with us in San Patricio later."

MacNab mounted his horse. "Consider it done. I should reach Roswell by Sunday. I'll head to San Pat after."

"Godspeed," Dick said.

MacNab headed back the way we came while we moved on to Lincoln. Reaching town by nightfall, Dick sent us on to San Pat, saying he'd take care of this on his own.

As the rest started to head east, I turned to Brewer. "Ya sure you don't want help with this?"

"I'm sure. Remember, we can't tell McSween about your curse. Him or Widenmann. Garrett's orders. I'll take care of this. Go do whatever you want, like usual."

I cringed inside and headed east, catching up with the rest of the Regulators, for I knew damn well that Brewer was still mad at me, and there was nothing I could do about it.

* * *

That seemed to be my lot in life. Pissing Brewer off, waiting for the big lug to forgive me, and then waiting until we repeated that. It became a pattern for us, you could say. Sitting in my car, I chuffed at the memory, then went right at the fork where Highway 70 and Route 380 split. If I stayed on 70, I'd head to San Pat like we had that day, but I had other business I needed to take care of.

As I passed the sign alerting me that I'd entered Lincoln, my heart began to beat a little faster in anticipation of what the town I used to love so much would look like. Back in the late 1870s, Lincoln was the liveliest of towns; its dusty road was filled with people of all walks of life. Mexicans, Anglos, Apache, and buffalo soldiers could be seen coming and going as they purchased or traded for goods before stopping in at one of the saloons for a spell to have a drink and catch up on the latest news.

Children and dogs had played in yards while chickens ran around town like they owned the place. Farmers with burros carrying panniers loaded with fruits and vegetables would wander the street shouting what they had for sale while the poor old man who owned the water cart dragged that thing from one end of town to the other each day.

Open doorways spilled the sounds of life out onto the street. From the banging of metal as the smithy made horseshoes to the sound of music coming from homes, to the laughter and the voices of drunken men from the saloons...the air was filled with life. It was never dull in Lincoln. Until now.

I slowed my car to a crawl and stared in horror at what seemed to be a ghost town. I saw not a soul outside, not even children at play or animals in yards. There was no one selling food or chatting outside on a porch as I drove past what had been the Tunstall Store. It looked much like it had back in the day, if not a little larger. Slowing down, I inched along past where the McSween home used to be, and my chest tightened at the memories of those who lost their lives there.

I continued westward past buildings I didn't recognize and pulled over at my planned stop, the Wortley Hotel. However, as I put the car in park, I stared in horror at what remained of the old diner and hotel. Turning the car off, I stepped out and stared in disbelief at the charred remnants of what had been the Wortley Hotel.

Shutting the car door, I walked up what must've been the side driveway, the only sound the gravel under my boots. Standing there, I examined the destruction and quickly realized my home had changed, and not for the better. Looking to my left, I saw that The House still stood, but it now had double staircases outside. During the war, when Murphy and Dolan lived on that top level, they didn't exist. But one of the two were built when Garrett had been sheriff years later.

The silence was deafening, yet the ghosts of my past were loud inside my mind. That's when I remembered the river. Where was it? I couldn't see or hear it from here. Turning, I headed north to the water and saw it was way farther down the hill than it'd been when I'd lived here. It wasn't nearly as wide either. I understood the concept of erosion, but even this seemed a large drop for such a short period of time.

"I can't stay here," I said aloud to no one, and turned to head back to the road.

By the time I reached my car, another had appeared on the street across from me, and a man with a jangling set of keys made his way to the double doors of The House. Before really making a decision to do so, I was moving toward the man at an accelerated speed. I had to know what had happened here. What killed the town I'd loved with all my heart?

I prayed it wasn't my fault.

* * *

San Patricio was a small town not far from Lincoln. If Dolan could say most of Lincoln were his friends, most of San Pat's were ours. Because of that, we tended to throw a *bailé* there on Saturdays every now and again, and tonight would be no different. Secretly though, I wanted to stay in Lincoln with Brewer. Not that I needed to go play law-boy, but I was wanting to corner Brewer about his shoulder once and for all without the others around.

However, seeing as he made it evident he didn't want any company, there was no way to stay without it getting weird. Besides, there was a *bailé* to attend, and not only did I love to dance, but the *señoritas* in San Pat were beautiful, and I was in the mood to have some time with the ladies.

Figuring we'd not see Brewer again for a while, meaning no work, we all had zero reservations with leaving our guns outside and going in to have some fun. Unfortunately, that didn't last long.

Spinning a voluptuous *señorita* about the dance floor, I caught sight of a very tall man arriving about halfway through the evening, his hat hiding his face as he ducked his head to enter through the doorway. I knew better, but I ignored his arrival, my focus totally captivated by the low-cut dress and beautiful brown eyes of the *señorita* in my arms.

As the song ended, we clapped, and my dance partner leaned in and whispered tantalizing words into my ear.

"*Soy todo tuyo*," I said to her, with a wink.

"Actually, he's mine first," came a voice from behind me.

I turned. "Brewer, what the hell are you doing here?"

"I have news. Get the rest of the Regulators and come with me."

Without waiting for my reply, he moved deftly through the dancers on his way to the door.

"This is not going to be good news," I said to no one in particular.

The pretty *señorita* I'd been dancing with heard me and said, "*¿Qué dijiste?*"

"*Nada*," I replied, then politely excused myself from her company with a promise to return shortly. Catching up with Dick just before he exited the room, I placed a hand on his good shoulder. "Whoa there, cowboy, what's on fire?"

"We are," he said. "Axtel has made us outlaws. Now get the boys and come outside." He jerked his shoulder out from under my hand and ducked back out into the night.

"Damn it," I muttered, and did as he asked.

Once we were all outside and away from anyone who'd be trying to listen in, Dick said it again. "Governor Axtel has made us outlaws."

"How?" Charlie demanded to know.

"Seems while we were riding back with Morton and Baker, the governor arrived in Lincoln, escorted by Colonel Purington, and spent the day investigating the trouble going on."

"The *trouble*?" I parroted. "That's what they're callin' John's murder? You have got to be—"

"Oh, there's more," Dick said. "Seems after an *extensive* interview process, and when I say extensive, I mean three hours spent primarily with Murphy and Dolan, he removed Justice of the Peace Wilson from office and voided all processes issued by him."

"Wait a sec," Doc Scurlock said. "He can't do that. It would bring into question every single action, includin' arrests, weddin's, and warrants for the past two years. That's a lot of retrials, annulled marriages creatin' illegitimate children, and—"

"It would negate Widenmann's U.S. Marshal status," Middleton added.

"As well as our warrants for Morton and Baker," I pointed out, "which is why we're outlaws, since they died by our hand while not truly under arrest."

Dick nodded. "You're all correct. He also declared that startin' today, the only valid legal processes for Lincoln County are by those issued by Judge Bristol in La Mesilla and Sheriff Brady in Lincoln. Brady's deputies are the only officers empowered to enforce both."

Fred Waite, a good law-abiding man, stepped forward. "All legal power in Lincoln County, hell, in all of New Mexico, is now in the Santa Fe Ring's hands. Is that what you're tellin' us?"

"Yes, that's what I'm sayin'. Good news is our Regulator Network Liaison is in town. The one meant for John. I told McSween to send him to find you here, Billy. Have you met him yet?"

"Not yet."

"I'm sure he'll show up tomorrow then," Dick said.

"Is the governor still in town?" Big Jim French asked.

"Nope. Hell, he wasn't even there when I arrived. He'd already headed back to the capital. McSween said that Axtel briefly spoke to him, Isaac Ellis, and Widenmann, but he declined to listen to their views on John's death."

"McSween needs to get out of that town again or he's a dead man," Charlie said, his hand resting where his gun should've been. "We need to fetch our weapons and get him outta there."

"I told him as such, but seein' as he just got back, he's not wantin' to leave again so soon. Good news is he's still protected by, and in the custody of, Deputy Sheriff Barrier."

"That's not real protection," Henry interjected, "but at least it's some."

"Like Barrier is any match for the lot of them if Brady and his boys decide to shove their way into the McSweens' house," I pointed out. "Damn it all to hell!"

I had to walk off the mad, take a moment to calm down, so I did. It wasn't the idea of being labeled an outlaw that upset me. God knows that wasn't new. It was just that each time we seemed to gain a bit of ground, the Santa Fe Ring pulled the rug out from under us.

Hearing someone approach behind me, I spun about, hand reaching for my hidden gun.

"Just me," Charlie said.

I nodded my apology for almost drawing on him. "What do we do now? My gut instinct is to always go for action, but that might not be the best for everyone."

"We probably just need a few days to figure it out. Lay low, see how the chips fall."

I looked over at Dick and the rest of the men and felt a heavy weight on me. I refused to show it though, and said, "You know what? Axtel can try all he wants to hold us back, but we still made headway today. I'm gonna go back inside, dance with that pretty little *señorita* again, and maybe..." I winked at Charlie, "maybe I'll steal me a kiss or two."

I didn't give him a chance to reply. Instead, I headed back to the *bailé* and did exactly as I said I would, and more.

9

THE DANGEROUS ONE-MILE RIDE

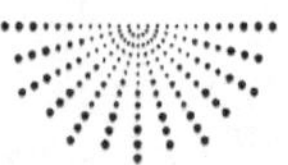

The next day we attended Sunday morning services at the church with the rest of the town. Considering my curse, plus where I'd spent the night, I was mildly surprised I didn't burst into flames upon entering. Once we'd sung hymns and been warned about how our souls could end up spending eternity in Hell, which gave me the jitters, we all assisted the other menfolk with setting up chairs and tables for the Sunday shared meal. I even pitched in with moving food from individual kitchens to the building they used for the town hall.

At some point, after everyone ate their fill and people were beginning to head home to nap or do chores, us Regulators found a way to excuse ourselves to talk privately behind the building.

"Are they sure he's dead?" I heard Henry ask Doc.

"Are they sure *who's* dead?" I said as Charlie and I joined them. "Make my day. Tell me it's Brady...or better yet, Dolan."

"No," Doc said. "Heard rumor while we was eating that Tom Hill was killed yesterday durin' an attempted robbery at a sheepherder's camp near Tularosa."

"Well there's some good news, boys!" I said, leaning my back against the building until a stink beetle came crawling over. With a shudder, I stood back up.

Dick walked over looking pale and ill. He barely was able to nod at us as he shoved his hands into his pockets and leaned against the nearby tree.

"That's not all either," Doc said, now that he had everyone's attention. "In the process of the botched robbery, Jessie Evans got shot in the arm, shatterin' his wrist, then fled to Shedd's Ranch. Once there, he got arrested by some railroad constable and taken to Fort Stanton."

"Well, that'll be nothin' more than a slap on the wrist at Stanton," I said.

"If it's the correct wrist, it'll hurt a lot," Fred pointed out.

This made me laugh. "Too true. Serves that bastard right. Both of 'em. So, what's our next move, Dick?"

We all looked over at Brewer, who'd not said a word, just stood there quietly as usual. Thing was, his eyes looked unfocused, and he seemed exhausted. Remembering it wasn't that long ago that he'd had smallpox, I wondered if he was having a relapse.

"Dick?" I prodded, when he didn't reply at first.

"I say we lay low for now," he finally said. "Of the three men who cornered John, two are now dead and the third is in jail. We take that win, and we wait for the rest to get sloppy. Besides, there are crops and chores at my ranch that need my attention. I'm heading home for a bit. If anythin' big happens, Billy, you come on out to let me know."

With that, he turned and walked off, which wasn't his usual way of doing things at all. Nor was it like him to state for me specifically to do anything.

"That's it?" I said, following him. "You're gonna go tend to your farm while we what, just hang about waitin' on you to be done?" When he didn't respond, I naturally reached out to grab his shoulder and turn him around. Without thinking, I grabbed the left one.

Dick yelped in pain and turned around angrier than my question should've made him. "Yes, that's it! Now go play poker or steal something, that's what you do, isn't it? I have honest work to tend to."

"Hold on there!" I said. "You know damn well I'm good at a lot more than stealin' horses or playing Monte. What is going on with you? You look like shit. Are the smallpox comin' back?" I asked, keeping my voice down on my last sentence.

His long face filled with sadness. "No, it's not that...and I thought that was bad. Just...just let it go, okay? It's the tenth. I'll come into town on the twenty-fourth, and we'll figure things out. Our silver ammunition should already be at the Ellis Store by now. We'll pick that up and get back to work. That gives me two weeks to tend to the farm and you all two weeks of freedom. Enjoy it. Because when I come back, we're going to go after the rest of them."

"Now that's what I wanted to hear!" I said. "Go do your work, farmer boy, and we'll meet up at Ellis's in ten days." I carefully tapped his right arm this time and turned around to go back.

"Billy?"

It wasn't my name that brought me to a halt, but the slight desperation behind the word that stopped my feet from moving. Turning about, I said, "Yeah?"

"If I don't show up on that day, come make sure I'm okay, would ya? Don't bring the whole team, maybe just Middleton or French. All right?"

"Uh...okay...we can do that."

"And keep that between us for now," he asked, wiping sweat from his brow with the back of his right arm.

"Is everything okay, Dick?"

He tried to smile, but it barely showed. "I hope so." Turning, he walked off, and I stood there with no idea what to say.

* * *

By Monday morning, I was still stuck on the strange plan Brewer had asked me to follow. Because of that, when I ran into Charlie and Fred while tending to my horse, I lied to them, saying Dick wanted me to ride into town and get our silver ammunition. I sweetened the pot by saying while I was there I'd pick up anything they wanted and ask for news on Hill and Evans.

"You're not going now, during the day, are you?" Charlie asked, as he worked knots out of his mare's tail. "Someone will see you and turn you in."

"Good point. I'll leave just before sunset, that way I get to Lincoln around dark."

"Okay. Well, maybe you should send word through the Regulator Network and let Isaac know you're coming. That way he can make sure no Murphes are around tonight."

"First off, did you just call the Murphy/Dolan faction, Murphes? And second, I'm not so sure about that network Garrett told us about. Think we can really trust that Regulator Network Liaison that couldn't get here in time to save John?"

Fred spoke up. "No better time than the present to find out."

He was right. "Fine, I'll try to find the spot here in town when I'm done and not leave until it's safe from being seen."

This was a lie, too. I wasn't safer for leaving later. The moon was already up and wouldn't set until around one in the morning. Thus, there were worse things than being seen and turned in for being an outlaw...there was dying by the jaws of a werewolf.

* * *

I went into a saddlebag and pulled out the small box of toothpicks Garrett had given me. On the inside of the tin was the symbol of the Regulator Network: a circle inside a circle with the skeleton of a wolf's head in the center. Unsure where to go, I just began to wander town, stopping to chat with friends here and there.

Garrett said that Tunstall had found places for dropping off information in both Lincoln and San Pat, but so far, I'd found nothing resembling the odd circle anywhere. That was until I wandered through the graveyard near the church.

Staring down at the rectangular stones outlining one of the bodies in the cemetery, I saw the symbol engraved into one of them. Squatting down, I laid my hand on it, surprised to find it wasn't cool to the touch like the rest of the rocks. Pressing on the circular symbol with my thumb, it depreciated. With a click, a drawer under it opened. Pulling it out farther, I found a space lined with white muslin, containing a pencil and a small rolled book with a leather cover.

Pulling it out, I unwound the leather strand that held it closed and found it to be a notebook of sorts. Taking the pencil, I wrote my note, ripped it out of the scroll, folded it up, and addressed it to Isaac Ellis. Putting all three items back in the hidey-hole, I left the paper on top, and slid the stone back in until it clicked into place.

Making sure no one saw me, I leisurely moseyed past the church, where a young man with blond hair sat on the steps.

"Afternoon," he said as I walked past.

"Afternoon," I replied, hoping he didn't ask me what I was doing in the graveyard.

"Lightnin', lazy, or leave it?" he asked.

I raised an eyebrow at him. "I'm sorry?"

He pulled out a tin case like mine, opened it, and pulled out a toothpick, which he stuck in his mouth. "Fast delivery, take my time, or someone else is comin' for it?"

Now I understood. This was our Regulator Network Liaison. "Lightnin'."

"You got it."

Without another word, he fetched my note and was gone.

I walked back to find a lot of the Regulators talking about doing some training while Dick was off working on his ranch. Doc was game to lead the group, and I thought it was likely wiser than sitting around here waiting for the law to come grab us up.

"Wait to leave until MacNab gets back," I said. "My guess is he'll get here tomorrow. If I'm not back by then, I'll join y'all when I return. Just leave me a message on where you go."

"With who?" Doc asked.

"Not who, where." I told them about the network box in the graveyard.

Around half past five, I packed up and left for Lincoln, arriving just after the sun set. I tied my horse in the corral behind the L-shaped building and knocked on the back door. A tall, slender young man in his mid-to late-twenties opened it.

"Hey, Ben," I said.

Isaac's son grinned, hazel eyes shining. "Heard you was comin' by. Get on in here; my dad's waitin' for ya."

"Thanks." I took off my hat as I entered the store section of the building and followed Ben back to the family's living quarters. There I found Isaac kicked back in a chair reading by candlelight. "I hear you got my message."

He set his book down. "Hey there, kid. Yes, I did. Nice fellow, that Roy. Got a message or two from him that McSween sent earlier this week. I didn't know you knew him, too."

"New acquaintance."

"Good one to have. He's a ghost. Appears outta nowhere and is gone before you can say goodbye. Hell, I don't even know his real name. I just call him Roy, and he answers to it." Isaac laughed and stood up. "Back this way. Your stuff arrived yesterday." He struck a match and lit the wick of an oil lantern. "They're in the back. I'd have brought 'em up front, but they're downright heavy."

"They? I thought it was one."

"Two arrived."

I nodded and followed him into the back of the store. He tapped the top crate of two stacked. Inside it would be the order of silver bullets that Garrett was sending us. I'd planned on taking half and leaving half.

"Did you open it?" I asked, offhandedly.

"Son, do I look like an idiot to you?"

I laughed. "No, sir."

"Well then, my only question is how are you gonna take it all with you? It's heavier than you can carry on your own, that's for sure. Did you bring a wagon with you?"

"Like I own a wagon."

Isaac smiled. "Well then, what do you wanna do with all of whatever it is?"

"It's a special type of ammunition. I'd like to take some and leave some, if that'd be okay. We just can't let the Murphy/Dolan guys find it. How often do they go through your store?"

Isaac set the lantern down. "Not often, but it'd be wise to take them down to the McSweens' house. It bein' just a residence and all. Not sure if Susan is back or not, and Alex left town again today after comin' in to get a few things. But the Shield family should be there in the east wing. I can have it taken down there tomorrow afternoon."

I considered that, but delivering a bunch of ammunition while the town watched was not a good idea. Taking it after dark was preferred for sure, but the moon was up, and that was something I didn't want to deal with. More importantly, I couldn't deal with it alone. Isaac was too old for me to put in harm's way like that, and George Coe would never forgive me if I did.

That left only one valid idea, and he wasn't gonna like it. Hell, I didn't like it, but I asked anyway. "How's your son Ben with a gun, sir?"

"He's a downright good shot, he always hits his mark, and...wait a sec, why do you wanna know?"

I explained the dilemma, except I used the word "men" instead of "wolves."

"Well, that'd have to be Ben's decision."

"I'll go," Ben said, stepping into the room, holding a lit lantern of his own.

"Were you eavesdroppin', boy?" Isaac asked, his tone both irritated and amused.

Ben gave his dad a guilty, lopsided grin as he nervously ran his hand through his short, straight, brown hair. "Just a bit. Sorry, Dad." He turned to me. "Billy, I got a horse who ain't scared of nothin'. We'll take her and the smaller wagon. She's fast, too. We should be able to get down there and back safe enough."

Silence hung heavy, and I took the opportunity to grab the crowbar and crack open one of the crates to find it filled with small to medium boxes. Smaller boxes would hold the bullets for our revolvers while the medium boxes would hold the needed ammunition for our rifles.

"I'll leave you boys to organize it as you see fit," Isaac said. "I'll bring the horse and wagon around to the back door."

"Thanks, Isaac," I said as he left.

I noticed Ben was wearing a cartridge belt and his six-shooter. "You'll need new ammo for this trip. Trust me."

"If you say so."

"Take off your belt. I'll have you load it up, just in case. Same with your rifle."

"Any chance you're gonna explain why, or should I just smile and nod?"

"The latter is a wiser option. In short, it's goin' to be a dangerous one-mile ride. Just, know that." I paused, trying to think of how to change the subject and got an idea. "Have you heard any information about Jessie Evans and Tom Hill?"

Ben began to load his cartridge belt with silver ammunition. "I have. Tom is dead, just like Morton and Baker. Did y'all really kill those two men?"

I sat and began to fill up my belt as well. "We did. Killed them while they were tryin' to escape."

"Serves 'em right, then," he said, and filled me in on the word he'd heard from customers and the like. It all matched up to what we'd heard, except that he'd been told Jessie's elbow had been hit, shattering his arm.

"We heard it was his wrist, but either way, son of a bitch is in a hospital in pain and botherin' no one since he's under arrest," I said, finished with my reload.

"Jimmy Dolan broke his leg yesterday."

"And I thought there couldn't possibly be more good news!" I joked, standing up and brushing the dust from my knees. "How the hell did he do that?"

"Stupid S.O.B. was on horseback, chasin' some man who was on foot. He jumped off his horse while she was still at a gallop and busted it good. Drunk as a skunk is what he was. I'll be surprised if he even felt it break."

I laughed. "That's hilarious! Oh, my Lord, wait until I tell the boys."

"Maybe that'll slow his mean streak," Ben said.

There was a pause, and we both looked at one another and said at the same time, "Doubt it."

After a good belly laugh, we loaded up his rifle, took the crates to the small wagon out back, and after I loaded my Winchester, covered them up and tied them down. Looking up at the sky, I saw a half moon, giving us some light for our ride. I wasn't sure if the werewolves in Lincoln would be out taking advantage of it as well, but I prayed to God they weren't.

"Billy?" Isaac said as we were about to leave. "When you get the chance, I have somethin' for you. From John."

"John…Tunstall?" I asked, clarifying.

"Yes, *that* John."

"Well, what is it?"

"It can wait. Get this done, and I'll show you later. It's not a quick affair."

I could tell there was no budging ol' Isaac on this, so I nodded, and Ben snapped the reins. We took the winding drive out to the main road and headed west. Winchester on my lap and eyes peeled for wolves, all was fine until we reached the Juan Patron Store. That's when I felt a tingle go up my spine, and I cocked my rifle.

Ben noticed the change in my demeanor immediately. "Problem?"

"Not sure…feels wrong. Pick up the pace. Not so that we draw attention to the townsfolk but so that we're not sitting ducks out here."

Ben urged our horse, who barely picked up speed at all, until she heard a howl that cut the night air clean through. Pulling on a bit of my soul energy, the world brightened to my eyes, and I scanned the area. Because of this, it didn't take long to spot who was watching us: two wolves running along beside us in the shadows.

I was about to give orders to Ben when they bolted out onto the road in front of us, causing the old mare to rear up, kick her front feet into the air, and charge toward them. Stunned as I was at the horse's reaction to two wolves in her way, I was even more shocked when the two wolves split, one going left and one to the right.

The furry beast closest to Ben jumped up to take a snap at him, and I pulled the trigger on the Winchester. The sound could've woke the dead and likely would cause ringing in Ben's ear for a week.

"Oh my God, did you get him?" Ben shouted.

My vision sharpened without my need to pull on the reservoir of soul-energy, and I wasn't dizzy. "Injured him, didn't kill him. Hurry up."

"Like ya have to tell me that!" He snapped the reins, and Mable picked up speed, a determination in her countenance.

If they were gonna come in close, I needed my pistols. I cocked my rifle and set it down at our feet since Ben's was on the long seat, the barrel behind me. Pulling on extra energy to flood my system for steadiness and strength, I stood up and pulled both six-shooters.

"They are runnin' along both sides, Billy! What do we do?" Ben yelled as jaws kept snapping up at him, luckily just missing.

"I know, just drive. Don't make any sudden movement that'd put you in the way of a bullet."

A wolf leapt up to get Ben, and I shot, hitting the creature in the head.

"No sudden movements? You're funny. You know we have a crazed horse, right?"

The full weight of the wolf's life force hit me, and I almost lost balance and fell.

"Shit."

Racing down the street, I got my bearings and decided I'd only fire at the wolves that got close. There were now three on my right and two on the left. One jumped into the bed of the wagon. I fired at him, and he dodged, my silver grazing the wolf behind him still on the ground, putting a hole through his ear.

They were fast. I had to be smarter or we were dead. With my next breath, I shot from each weapon. With my outstretched arm, I fired directly toward the beast while I waited a count and shot from my second gun, aiming to the side. As I hoped, the wolf focused on my primary arm and dodged that bullet, stepping into the path of my second, taking that bullet in the chest.

The wolf's eyes went from brown to glowing a copper color.

"That's new," I muttered and shot again, catching him in the leg, causing him to jump out.

I'd now used four of my twelve shots, so I had to make my last eight count. Sure, we had two rifles, but these guys were up close and personal.

A loud shot fired, vibrating behind my knees. I turned in time to see a wolf's head come clean off as his body fell lifeless onto the road. That's when I realized Ben had shot his rifle from the seat where it sat.

"He was about to take your ass!" he explained.

"Thanks!" I yelled over pounding hooves and the growling of three new wolves that had joined the party as we passed the Torreon. "It's not even a full moon! Jeez!" I shot, killing the next wolf who got close. This time I sat down before my head did a loopty-loop.

"Hang on!" Ben yelled as he directed the horse to make a sharp right just as we passed the McSween house.

Pulling her to a stop, I leapt down, grabbed my rifle, and turned to see not one furry bastard. I glanced at Ben, standing on the seat, rifle in position.

"Where'd they go?" he asked.

"Hell if I know. Come on, let's get this stuff loaded into—"

"Could you two be any louder? Both of you, comin' down the street like drunken hooligans!" came a female voice behind us.

Turning, we saw Mrs. Susan McSween holding an oil lantern. Her dark hair piled high, still wearing her traveling attire, gloves and all.

"Ma'am, you should get inside," I said.

She walked toward us, eyed the covered contents of the wagon bed, then her gaze met mine. "I certainly will not go inside, not until you tell me what in blazes you are doin' ridin' onto my property like Hell is on your heels!" She sat the lantern on the seat of the wagon. "And give me that before you shoot a passerby, for God's sake."

She grabbed my rifle, and for no reason I can fathom, I let her take it.

"Well, we sort of did have Hell on our heels, ma'am," Ben said. "There were these wolves and—"

I cut him off before he said too much. "Just two of nature's creatures, Mrs. McSween. They spooked the horse and us a bit, if we're to be truthful. Took a shot or two and they ran off. We apologize if we disturbed you. To be honest, we didn't know you'd returned from Missouri."

"Just got in a short bit ago," she said, walking past me to stand on my left, her eyes again flitting to the lump of things under the blankets in the wagon bed. "Found my husband gone to who knows where and a letter. I'm hopin' you can explain some of this to me."

Susan had been gone to see family since before John's murder, so there would be a lot to cover and many lies to tell. I saw a long night ahead of me and was prone to a grumble, until my stomach did so instead.

"Dear heavens, I could hear that from here. When did you eat last? Never mind, seein' as Alex took both servants with him, I'm sure my sister or I can fill your belly for your time and information. What are you unloadin' there and where does it need to go?" Her dark eyes bore into me as she raised an elegant eyebrow.

"I'll explain inside. First, we should get you and these inside, away from the Murphes," I said, using the word Charlie had made up.

Ben jumped down from the wagon and pulled the blanket back, saying, "It's just some—"

A wolf, smaller than most I'd seen, leapt out from under the blanket at Ben. I pulled my revolver and was about to fire when a loud blast went off and hit the animal in the head moments before his jaws would've sunk into Ben, who had frozen in fear.

Turning to see who'd taken the shot, I found Susan with my rifle raised up, perfectly poised, in firing position. Ben and I just stared at her for a moment.

"Silver?" she asked.

I nodded, for that's all I could seem to do.

"Good, then that's done. Let's move your...?"

"Ammunition, ma'am," I squeezed out, voice a bit higher than usual.

"Let's move your ammunition inside. And don't dawdle! I'm not savin' your ass from another one of them bastards tonight."

I watched Susan's tall frame walk into the house and questioned everything I knew about the woman. How much did she know about this word, why did she know, and what the hell was I going to do about it?

10

SUSAN MCSWEEN AND THE MAN FROM ENGLAND

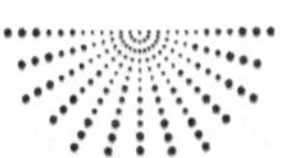

Ben and I shared a glance and then got to work. Carrying the second crate in, Ben looked at me and said, "A heads up about werewolves comin' for us next time, okay?"

I almost dropped my side of the crate. "What are you talkin' about?"

"Silver ammunition, wolves attackin' us, comments about the moon...I'm not an idiot, Billy. Besides, my dad and I know some of what John was really doin' here. Not all of it, but enough for me to know there's some supernatural mumbo-jumbo goin' on and you've not been honest with me."

That stopped me in my tracks. "Look, Ben, there are rules about..." Susan opened the door, holding it for us, so I finished with, "Ya know what, never mind."

Susan McSween was a tall woman with a walk that said she meant business. Without a word, she directed us to the front room of the west wing, which was the bedroom of Mr. and Mrs. McSween. Heading to the far wall, which was the front of the house, she pulled back the drapery there to reveal a large storage space with a bar that ran along near the top with shelving above. Hanging from the bar were summer clothes for both the McSweens, with his belongings to the left and hers to the right.

Susan examined the floor of the closet. "It would seem my husband took his trunk with him. That's likely for the best. It leaves room for you to fit that crate in here without difficulty. Slide it behind my dresses. That'll hide it best. Then bring the opened crate into the parlor." She opened the door that led to that room and stepped through.

Turning back to us as we maneuvered around the bed with the crate, she said, "Oh, and don't be startled, the gentleman in the parlor is a friend of Mr. Chisum's who assisted him with his trials in Las Vegas. I think you'll like him, he's a crusader like you, but he tends to attack his enemies with words, like an adult."

She walked out and shut the door.

I looked to Ben and whispered, "Was that an insult?"

Ben only partially hid his smile and quietly replied, "I think it was."

I grinned with a shake of my head, then we worked at placing the crate in the closet as instructed. To do so, I had to back up into the space. Once inside and surrounded by walls and garments, I whispered to Ben, "Why do I have a feelin' that Mrs. McSween knows more than she's sayin'?"

"'Cause she does," Ben said. "And it's probably a hell of a lot more than me, so you're gonna fill me in, or this is the last time my father or I help you, Billy. God as my witness, I want answers."

I thought back to Regulator training, to Garrett's emphatic rule of, "Tell no one without my permission." How many knew now? Obviously, I shouldn't tell him, but we couldn't lose the Ellis's assistance in this war, what with John's store not open for business anymore.

"I'm not kiddin', Billy," he prompted.

"I know you ain't," I snapped. "Damn it." I took a moment to adjust the dresses over the case and gather my thoughts. In doing so, I noticed a locked trunk in the back-right corner with three decorative initials in capital script. It said RLN, the L larger than the R and N.

With a shrug, I stepped back into the room and pulled the tin Garrett had given me from my pocket and flipped it open. "Hell, my hide is already poised for a good tanning, might as well make it worth it." I took out a toothpick, set it between my teeth, and closed the tin. "Come on, you'll get your answers, but first, let's meet this crusader of words and see why he's come to Lincoln."

"You don't trust anyone, do you?"

I slid the metal container into my pocket. "Not as a general rule, no."

"After you, then," Ben said, motioning for me to go first.

With a nod, I opened the door to the main front room. Carpeted like the rest of the house, it was lit with oil lamps as well as candles on the long table in the center of the room. A roaring fire in the fireplace on the back wall added further light and sitting beside it on the couch was an Anglo man easily pushing fifty. He had short, thick hair pushed back from his face, a full beard and mustache, and wore a British styled suit not unlike many I'd seen on Tunstall.

Sipping something from a porcelain cup, the man eyed Ben and I over the rim. Setting it down, the fine china clinked on the matching saucer. Next to it lay a metal tin that matched the one I'd just put in my pocket, the one Garrett gave to me and all the sworn-in Regulators.

"Mr. Bonney, I've heard a lot about you," the man said, his British accent stronger than Tunstall's. Standing, he put his hand out toward me. "Montague Richard Leverson, fellow Regulator here to help the cause."

I shook Mr. Leverson's hand and pulled one of the six table chairs over so I could sit opposite him while Ben sat at the other end of the couch.

"Is he sworn in?" Leverson asked, motioning to Ben.

"Of course," I lied without hesitation.

"Rightly so, good. Can't be too careful now, can we?" Leverson said as he sat back down.

"What brings you to Lincoln, Mr. Leverson?" I asked, leaning back in the chair to appear casual and unassuming.

"Many things. Off the record, I'm here because of Tunstall's death. My plan is to use my influence with those who have the power, in this country and mine, to obtain the dismissal of Governor Axtell and take his place."

"On the record?" I prompted.

"I'm in America seeking a location for an English colony."

"And you think Lincoln is that place?" Ben asked with a light chuckle.

Leverson shrugged. "Why not?"

"Uh, because they just killed an Englishman," Ben replied.

"Like I said, that's just my cover story. I plan to assist Alex with writing letters to get the government to investigate the Santa Fe Ring and their plot to murder John. I'm not of an age to fight the demons physically, but I can go at them another route."

"Well, good luck with that, Mr. Leverson. I plan to use my guns. In fact, we already have. The man who shot John is dead, as are two others who were involved, while a fourth is injured and in jail."

Leverson sat forward in his seat. "When did this happen?"

"Over the weekend. We're hopeful to take more of them out when we regroup in ten days."

"Regroup?" he asked.

I filled him in on Governor Axtel's actions and how that affected us.

Leverson stood and began to pace. "This isn't good. We need to find a way to combat this."

"We have. It's called huntin' them bastards down anyway," I said.

"You can't be serious, Billy!" Ben said.

"I've been an outlaw before, and I'm sure after this, I'll be one again. I'm not scared of the Santa Fe Ring. Let 'em come at me."

Leverson picked up his cup, which appeared to be tea, and sat. "Easy for you to say, but the rest of us don't heal like you, Mr. Bonney."

I stopped breathing and swallowed the words on my tongue. I didn't know this man and just because he had a matching tin to mine didn't mean I was gonna be putting him on my Christmas list, so I chose my next words carefully. "I don't know what you've been told,

Mr. Leverson, but the only thing special about me is my obnoxiously good aim with *either* hand."

"And his obnoxious personality," Susan added as she walked in, her presence seeming to shut Leverson up on the subject immediately. "Would you like a refill on your tea, Montague?"

"That would be lovely, thank you, Susan," he replied.

"Boys?" she asked.

"I'm not really a tea person," I said. "Do you have any coffee?"

"Of course. Ben?"

"Coffee, please, Mrs. McSween," he replied.

"Be right back. You boys behave," she said.

The bite to her words was either to warn me to not say something rude, or it was to warn Leverson not to say too much. With no idea which it was, I just smiled while Leverson picked up the fire poker and moved the logs around.

Ben, feeling the tension, stood up and said, "How about I come help you out in the kitchen, Mrs. McSween."

"That would be lovely, thank you, Ben."

He left the room following behind Susan's bustle and petticoats with a glare at me that said I had better be telling him things later. I rolled my eyes and nodded at him before he left, plastering a calm and blank expression on my face by the time Leverson turned around and sat in a chair this time around.

"I take it Ben doesn't know about your...abilities."

"My curse," I corrected him. Leaning in toward him, not hiding my irritation even a little bit, I kept my voice low and my eyes on his, and said, "Question is, why do you?"

Fear lit behind his eyes, and he swallowed it down as best he could before he spoke. "I was sworn in with full knowledge of the situation here on the ground before I left England."

"Includin' John's death?"

"Of course not. But I have John's letters to his father that mention he believed you were one of Scáthach's chosen warriors. I wasn't sure you were until you walked in here."

I leaned back in my chair, hand on my gun, fingers tapping a random beat on the handle. "And how is that? Is there some invisible mark on me that only you can see, Mr. Leverson?" I didn't like that a man I didn't know knew my secret. It was unsettling.

"The way you move."

"Excuse me?"

"I've only known one of your kind, and when you are full of soul-energy, which you would be, considering you just killed a bunch of demons on the way here, you move like them. It's not obvious to others, but it is to me. How many souls are in the well?"

"Who have you told?"

"No one."

I quickly stood and leaned over the man, with a hand braced on the chair arms on either side of him. "If I find out you've told anyone, I'll remove you from the equation here, Mr. Leverson. Do I make myself clear?"

Eyes wide, he nodded. I smelled fear on him, much like a wolf would, and I sat back down, not allowing how this realization upset me. "Good. So long as we understand one another."

He swallowed. "We do."

"Excellent. And if I've counted right, I have five or six in the well, as you call it."

Susan entered with Ben on her heels. They had coffee and plates of food.

I smiled a genuine, toothy grin at her and stood. "Coffee and food? Mrs. McSween, you are a goddess. Thank you so very much."

She eyed me with suspicion, but when Leverson also smiled at her, she seemed to decide we'd behaved and set the food and coffee on the table. "Well, come and eat. Then you two would be smart to spend the night here. With Alex and David gone, I'll bunk with my sister and her children in the east wing. Montague, you can use Alex's and my room while Billy and Ben can bunk in east bedroom as it has two beds."

I sat at the table. "Thank you, Mrs. McSween."

Ben parroted me and also sat down to eat.

"Well, we can't have you boys headin' out until after the moon sets, and that's not until almost two in the mornin'. You both will get some rest here and get back to the Ellis' before it rises again tomorrow around eleven in the mornin'.'"

Ben stared at her, a fork poised in his hand with food on it, frozen in the air.

"Mr. Ellis, eat your food before it gets cold."

"Yes ma'am," was all he said before focusing on his food.

To distract from his awkward behavior, I swallowed my food and said, "Thank you for lettin' us stay. Go help your sister. We'll clean up these dishes."

As if on cue, Susan's sister came into the room, evidently pregnant. I didn't know how far along she was, but it was enough that she was showing. "Don't you boys worry about those dishes. I've got you taken care of."

"Mrs. Shield, really, it's no bother," I said, and I meant it.

"It's good for my children to help out around here," she said. "The boys are teenagers, for goodness sakes. They can help."

This was true. George was seventeen, and David Curtis was fourteen. I saw them helping in the Tunstall Store back before everything went to hell in a handbasket.

I noticed a girl in the doorway behind Mrs. Shield and remembered Elizabeth Shield's youngest living child. "And how old are you, Mary?"

Mrs. Shield spun about. "Mary, what are you doin' up this late? I told you to get to bed."

Mary lifted her defiant chin just a touch and stepped from the shadows and into the parlor. "I'm ten, and I'm not tired. Besides, George is horrible at doin' dishes. He leaves all kinds of things stuck to the plates."

I fought a grin at her seriousness on the topic as my nose picked up a scent that was not from inside this house. I turned my attention to her and examined everything about her as I said, "That is a serious accusation, Miss Mary. Have you not shown him where he is lackin'?"

She sighed dramatically. "I have! He doesn't care. He's a boy."

I quickly noticed she was in shoes and that what I smelled was the grass and dirt on her feet. It was fresh. Unsure as to why, I stood and stepped past her mother to her. "Well, I'm a boy, and I do a fantastic job at cleanin' dishes. In fact, I used to wash them at a hotel as a kid. I'd be glad to show George how to for you, Miss Mary, if you'll go to bed like your mother asked."

Her eyes stared me down, and I read something in them that caused me to step in such a way that blocked Susan as well as her sister from seeing the child. "Shake hands on it?" she asked.

"Of course," I replied, and reached out to shake her hand.

I never saw the bit of paper, her sleight of hand better than most I'd met. However, I caught the tightness around her eyes, so when she loosened her grip, I paid attention. Feeling the piece of paper, I closed my fingers around it. "It's a done deal then. If I fail, I'll owe you one."

A sly smile slid over her face as she caught my second meaning and carefully took her hand back. "Deal. Goodnight then." She curtsied to us and left the room in a hurry.

I put my hands in my pockets casually and moseyed to my seat at the table. "Easy as pie."

"How you are so good with children, I will never understand," Mrs. Shield said.

"Because he still is one," Susan replied.

"Ouch," Ben muttered in jest.

"At heart, maybe, Mrs. McSween," I said, depositing the note in my pocket before pulling my hand out. Sitting, I said, "But I'm also good with the ladies, so…"

Susan rolled her eyes. "And with that, I'm goin' to make sure Mary went to bed. If you're so good with dishes, they're yours. Goodnight, all." She left, and I shooed her sister to follow along behind her.

"Great, now we have dish duty," Ben said.

"It's hardly nothin' compared to the free food and hospitality."

I noticed then that Leverson hadn't said anything. Looking toward him, I saw he was almost finished with his food, a strange smile on his face.

"Entertained, Mr. Leverson?"

"Oh, very."

I laughed and dug into my food. Finishing, I picked up my dishes. "Come on, Ben. I'll teach you how to do dishes, too."

Ben picked up his plates. "Har har. I do plenty of dishes at home, thank you very much." He headed for the smaller kitchen of the two in the U-shaped home, it being located at the tip of the west wing. Dishes in one hand, the oil lamp that'd lit the parlor in the other, he left.

Used to carrying more than one or two, I collected the dishes of our visiting Brit as well. "I'll take you to pay your respects to John in the mornin', Mr. Leverson. Sleep well."

Once dishes were washed and dried, we headed to the east bedroom to retire. Being the one room without windows, it was the safest by far. Sitting on the bed, I took off my boots.

Ben shut the door. "Okay. Spill it, Billy."

"Now?" I was exhausted and knew the next day would be busy. I just wanted some rest. "Tomorrow, I'll explain tomorrow. I promise. Let's just get some rest."

Ben sat on the other bed and took off his boots. "No, now."

I sighed. "Fine."

As I removed my cartridge belt, guns, and outer clothes, I told him as much as I dared. Mostly about me and my affliction and what Regulators really were.

"Well, shit. That's a lot to carry around, Billy," he said, getting into bed.

"The understatement of the year," I said, reaching into the pocket of my pants.

"What's that?"

I opened it. "A note from Roy."

"Well, what does it say?"

I read it, and the food still in my stomach flipped about, attempting to come back up. Swallowing it down, I just said, "Nothin'. Just warnin' me that the wolves are waitin' for us and we should stay in for the night." I reached over and shoved the note back into my pants pocket and got into bed.

Ben turned the oil lamp down, and I positioned the pillow under my neck the way I liked. Weaving the fingers of my hands together, I rested them on my stomach and closed my eyes.

"I want in on this, you know. I want to help."

"Jesus Christ," I muttered. "No. I told you to keep you safe, not put you in harm's way."

"But—"

"No."

"You're gonna need me, you'll see."

I hoped he was wrong. But with what Roy's note really said, I wasn't so sure. It hadn't warned of wolves at the door, but that Scáthach herself was in town looking for me.

* * *

Sun rose just after six in the morning and so did we. Once washed up and dressed, Ben and I joined the rest of the household for a big breakfast before taking Leverson to the empty plot east of the Tunstall Store. At the back of the property, we'd started a little cemetery, and that's where John was buried.

"Why here?" Leverson asked.

"Mr. McSween plans to build a church here on this property," I explained.

Leverson nodded in understanding.

"I'll leave you to say a few words."

* * *

Standing over a cross that was marked as John's grave now in 1949, I thought of the day I'd taken Leverson to pay his respects. However, it wasn't where I currently stood.

"You do know he's not buried here, right?" I asked the ranger who'd been the man with the keys going into The House, which was now a museum, as was the Tunstall Store. The store had just opened recently and had marked the graves of John and Alex directly behind the store in what used to be the corral area.

"We know, but that there's private property now and they didn't want trespassers stompin' all over their backyard," the ranger told me.

I nodded. "In fact, I think we're standin' where a bunch of bottles of beer were durin' that battle in July."

"And you'd know that how, stranger?"

"Oh, I uh, I met a man who was here at the time. He drew me a map of things."

He raised an eyebrow at me. "If you say so, Mr. Kidwell."

"Oh, please call me William."

"All right then, William. I must be goin' on back. Is there anythin' else I can help you with?"

"Just, where is the new sheriff's office?"

"Know someone there, too?" he prodded.

"Nope. But I plan to. Have a scheduled meetin' with Sheriff Sally Ortiz, and I'd rather get movin'. I'd hate to keep her waiting."

The ranger chuckled. "Yep, ya don't wanna do that."

He gave me directions and the name of where to grab some lunch. With a thank you and a monetary donation to the museum, I got back in my car and headed east on Highway 380. I drove through Capitan to the new sheriff's office located in the new county seat of Carrizozo. The sheriff had a much nicer building than in my days of living in New Mexico...of course, that wouldn't take much, considering.

Getting into my car, I headed down to the Ellis Store, just wanting to make sure it was still standing and all. I hated to admit it, but as much as I'd dreaded coming here because of the memories, it wasn't those that were bothering me as much as how my beloved town had died. Now to find out if my co-worker had, too.

11

COLONEL

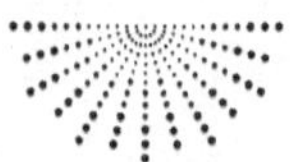

After leaving Leverson and Mrs. McSween to their day, Ben and I headed back to the Ellis Store where his father quickly sent Ben off to do chores and took me out back.

"John left you somethin'," Isaac said. "Follow me."

Into the stable we went, and I watched with curiosity as the older man reached up and pulled on a piece of wood, tilting it like one would a book on a shelf. I heard a click, and Isaac pressed a section of the wall, causing it to move inward.

"He's back here."

"He?" I asked, stepping through the new doorway.

"This was John's special stall. Being a Regulator, he wanted a spot to hide things." He shut the door and led me down a short hallway. "He told me the night of the sixteenth that if anythin' should happen to him, you were who he wanted to be shown Colonel."

"Who is..." My words failed me as I stepped into a small room to find a black stallion, around fifteen hands high, standing in a corner stall. This was only the left side of a small room, which held riding gear and other necessities. On the far side sat a four-foot long trunk nestled beside a desk with stool to one side and an armchair to the other, and in the corner, a cot.

"Let him hear and smell you. He's blind, so he needs to meet you differently."

"Blind?"

"He's special. John said he wouldn't take one-hundred and fifty for him today. Here, he left you this." Isaac handed me a wax-sealed envelope. "I'll leave you to get acquainted." Isaac showed me how to open the door from this side and left.

Standing there confused, I said, "Colonel, I'm Billy, and I have no idea what is goin' on."

Carefully, I ran my hand down his neck, and then I inspected him. He was a specimen of equine perfection, without a doubt. Likely a Morgan horse and jet black as coal.

"So why did John want me to have you?" I broke the seal with the JHT monogram pressed into it, pulled the tri-fold paper out to read.

Billy,

You are very likely discombobulated at the moment. I'm sorry for that. It seems I ran out of time to tell you the truth about who I believe you are and why I hired you. I say this because the only way you would receive this letter is in the case of my early passing. By now I would guess that Garrett has arrived to tell you the truth, so I won't bore you with all those details.

I will, however, tell you about this black beauty Isaac has shown you. I've named him Colonel, being that I got him for 27½ dollars at a sale of old condemned army stuff. I never saw a prettier horse or thrown my leg over a finer saddle horse in my life. He walks fast enough to keep my Long Tom horse in a slow jog trot, he can canter on a cabbage leaf, and gallop very finely.

I think he's likely a thoroughbred and not more than seven years old. Best road horse I ever came across, does an easy six miles to the hour if it's just you in the saddle, and he won't make a mistake unless you get careless. Unfortunately, he was run blind by the army, so I was unable to have his eyes repaired.

You have great abilities, Billy. Things you've not even begun to tap into. The way you channel energy is something that could have no bounds. I'm very sad I have been taken from this world so soon, if for no other reason than to see what you are going to be capable of. Well, that and I'd have loved to have seen how my younger sisters grow into the magnificent women they are bound to be. I trust Alex and Rob are seeing to their financial stability with all I put in place. If they do not, I ask you to make sure my sisters are okay. With me gone, all my sisters are in danger of being without a penny or dowry if something were to happen to my parents. It's up to you, Alex, and Rob to make sure they are okay.

I should get to the point. I tend to expound on things too much sometimes, or so my elder sister says. The point being, all my Regulator things are in the safe here in this room. For fear of it being seen, it is under the floorboards in the far corner near the painting on the wall of the New Mexico landscape. Remove it from the wall, and you'll see. Colonel has the combination. He's a magnificent horse, Billy. Take good care of him.

I hate tasking you with all these things. I should've been here to help you become a Regulator. When we learned about you, I was the closest to you (being as I was in California looking to get into the sheep business), and so I was given orders to come find you. I wrote to my family that I was told to head east for better land opportunities, but my father knows the truth.

You'll find more information inside the safe, of course, but most important of all is an envelope in there for my father and other members of my family, also sealed with my stamp, that explains my Regulator business. It has postage on it. I need you to mail it from somewhere Scáthach's pawns aren't prowling about. Only you can tell if they are a demon or not. If not now, in time. I beg you to find a safe spot and mail them.

As Garrett has likely told you, Alex doesn't know the truth about you or me, nor does Rob. Please keep it that way. Safer for you and them.

Regulator Brothers, Even After Death,

- John

My world had changed, yet I'd not moved an inch. I looked up into the large, prominent eyes of the beautiful horse before me.

"So, you hold the combination. How is that possible? And how am I to find someone to cure your eyes if John couldn't?"

Frustrated, I folded the letter and stuffed it into my pocket. With no other option, I stepped over to the painting on a thick box frame and took it down. Behind it was a lever.

"Well, that's easy enough."

I pulled the lever downward and it resisted. Yanking it harder, it slowly came down, and I felt the floor vibrate. Looking behind me, I noticed a line on the floor that hadn't been there before. Squatting, I carefully slid my fingers into the separation and lifted the trap door.

Settled snugly into a hole dug in the dirt under the wooden floor was a metal safe, door facing up at me with a combination lock.

I looked back over my shoulder at Colonel. "You have the combination to this, do ya? Don't suppose that Englishman taught you to speak the numbers, did he?"

Colonel whinnied lightly and shook his mane.

"Well now, I suppose I can forgive you this once." I carefully shut the trap door until it clicked, causing the lever on the wall to raise back up.

I hung the light painting on the lever and walked over to the black beauty. "You want to go for a ride? He bragged about you so hard I feel I need to see this miracle for myself."

Knowing the boys in San Pat weren't waiting on me, I didn't rush. I carefully fitted him with his riding gear, talking to him the whole time, sometimes singing.

Hand on his face, reins in my hand, I stood there perplexed, for the door I'd come in through was way too small for Colonel to fit through. "Well, they got you in here somehow."

As if understanding me, Colonel lifted his back leg and kicked lightly, his hoof hitting a metal plate at the back of his stall. Easily missed as it was close to the ground, it appeared to be a piece of junk used for repair.

A moment later, the smell of a blooming apple orchard filled my senses, and Colonel whinnied, his feet dancing on the floor. I'd opened my mouth to ask him what was so exciting when I saw something peculiar. The section of wall between the painting and where the stall began started to shimmer like heat rising off a hot flat surface in the afternoon summer sun. As the haze vanished, a pair of large barn doors appeared.

"Well I'll be damned. Tunstall had a witchy friend." Placing my hands on the doors, I pushed, and they swung open. "I suppose that's our cue."

I led him out and swung up into the saddle as the doors closed on their own and vanished to the naked eye. Knowing what to look for now, I noted a metal plate way up high and knew I'd need to be riding Colonel to reach it.

"Let's see what you can do," I said, then groaning at my wording. With a gentle hand on his neck, I rephrased. "I mean, let's find out what you can do, and I'll direct you. Sorry."

I felt a gentle pulse of energy pass between my hand and his neck with my heartfelt apology.

Colonel shook his beautiful mane and, though they weren't words specifically, I had the distinct feeling he'd told me it was all right. Scared yet fascinated, I slowly took my hand back, got ahold of the reins, and gave his sides a light tap with my heels.

John wasn't wrong. Colonel handled better than any horse I'd ever been on, and as someone who tends to steal them often, I'd ridden many. By the time we returned to the Ellis Store, it was twilight, and Colonel smelled something off, and before I understood why, he reared up, front legs kicking out defensively.

"Gave you his champion, did he?" came a woman's voice from somewhere in the dark.

I pulled my gun. "Who's there?"

A woman with dark hair past her waist stepped from the shadows, her nightgown flowing effortlessly in the light breeze, its material thin and revealing. I might've gotten ideas, but then I recognized her features.

"Scáthach," I said, her name acid on my tongue.

She snapped her fingers, and the wick inside the lantern in her hand lit, showing her features more clearly. "*A bheil sibh fhathast a 'bruidhinn a' chànain ar dachaigh?*"

The answer was yes, I did still speak Gaelic, but I wasn't stupid enough to let her know that. "It's adorable how you think I still understand that archaic language. My mother spoke it, as you already know since you have Mary's memory, but I've had no use for it."

"*Tuilleadh an truas. Bhon tha mi an dùil a mharbhadh thu an seo agus a-nis.*"

I didn't flinch to her promise to kill me here and now. I just stared her down, breathing easy. After a good ten seconds passed, I replied, "I heard you were in town. Did you want somethin'?"

She sashayed toward us, and Colonel backed away without my encouragement.

I laid my hand on his neck, patting nonchalantly, this time intentionally attempting to move the meaning of my words to him. "It's okay, Colonel, I'm aware."

Again, the vibration of heat transferred from my fingers into his body. He immediately stopped, stood tall and proud, and huffed out air through his nose, pounding his front hooves into the dirt while moving toward her by a foot or two. It stopped her advance immediately.

"Smart horse," I said, staring at her face, the only thing the lantern lit up fully. "State your peace and be gone. I have to rub him down for the night."

"I saw you ride by and followed you. I was not aware John had kept him. He's magnificent."

"Too bad he's blind."

"*Ro dhona nach eil sibh a 'tuigsinn faodaidh sibh leigheas.*"

This time I fought the desperate need to reply. If I could really heal Colonel's eyes, I wanted to know how. Instead, I sighed heavily. "You did not just see me and decide to come say hello. You've been waitin' for me."

She smiled, but for whatever reason, it reminded me of when my friend's sheepdog quietly showed his front teeth. It had the appearance of a grin, but it was a silent warning. "You are correct. I thought maybe you might want to meet now that you know the truth."

"That I'm cursed."

"It's not a curse, Henry Antrim."

"I don't go by that name anymore."

"I couldn't care less," she said flatly.

"Are you here to kill me?"

She laughed. "No. Not today. I wanted to introduce myself."

That seemed oddly wrong. "That's not all."

"Perceptive. As always." She walked around Colonel and me, her grace far surpassing any woman I'd ever met. "I smell the hint of a magic signature on him. It's one of a woman I thought to be dead. Your stallion has either been near a spell of hers or she touched him herself at some point...that intrigues me."

"When did she die?"

"Not long before I claimed Mary the first time around."

"That was only five years ago. This horse is older than that. It's possible she met Colonel in his army days. Besides, if a witch had been near him, don't you think she'd have healed him?"

This seemed to satisfy her in an odd way; the quizzical mask of confusion she'd worn since I rode up slid away, and she nodded. "You are quite right. She would have. She loved horses, and they loved her."

A look of nostalgia passed over Scáthach's face, and for a moment, her mind appeared to be in a different time and place. Coming back to the present, she gave me a weak smile and said, "Goodnight, Henry." Turning, she walked off, stopping near the stable. With a sigh, she uttered only two words, "Oh, Zahara." They were full of sorrow and longing with an undercoat of bitterness. After that, she disappeared into the night.

I must've sat there in the dark for five minutes, my mind playing the whole interaction over and over again until I felt the chill of night working through my attire.

Tapping the metal lever, we entered the stable, and as the doors became a wall again, I unsaddled Colonel and rubbed his muscles down as I sang to him. I ended the regiment with a blanket draped over his back before I eyed the small cot I'd questioned earlier.

"Oh, now I see. It's the only safe spot to rest."

For the first time in ages, I removed my gun and cartridge belt without worry. I slid off my trousers and draped my shirt on the chair before laying down for the deepest night of sleep I'd had in years.

* * *

Thunder boomed, waking me slightly as the walls shook. It wasn't until Colonel stomped about, whinnying loudly, that I was fully awake. Quickly, I was up and across the small room to him.

"Shh...it's okay, it's thunder. You're safe."

He was having none of it when thunder clapped so loud it made me jump. He was now scared enough that I worried about him destroying the stall. Because of this, I intentionally shoved energy through my hands into him, wishing he'd be calm and feel safe. Immediately he became quiet and nuzzled my arm. I breathed a sigh of relief.

"Must be hard not bein' able to see what the noise is, huh, big guy?"

After fumbling about for a bit, I found the matches and lit the oil lamp on the desk. Grabbing the brush by the stall, I began to work on Colonel's mane as more thunder crashed outside as rain hit the roof with a diligence that renewed one's healthy fear of Mother Nature.

"Shh...nothing to worry 'bout. I'm right here."

Looking at his big eyes as they tried to look around, my heart hurt. He was such a beautiful animal, easily the best horse I'd ever ridden, and if he'd been taken care of properly by the military, he'd not be blind.

Scáthach's words about me being able to heal him resounded in my mind as lightning and thunder played their troublesome song outside. I rushed to lay my hand on his neck in case he freaked out, but he appeared fine, and that's when I had an idea. If the soul energy could heal my wounds, and I could push some of that into Colonel, could I heal him? It was worth a shot.

Setting the brush down, I fetched an apple from the box and came to face to face with the stallion. "I'm gonna try something. Eat this and let's see if you'll let me touch your eyes."

I palmed the apple to his nose. Without hesitation, he took it from me, crunching it with a profound satisfaction. As he did, I reached up and placed a hand on one of his eyes. Closing my own, I focused energy into my palms like when I'd wanted to calm him, except this time I pushed harder and with intent to heal. A stinging sensation of extreme heat lit my palm on fire and gave Colonel a jolt.

"I'm tryin' to help you. Stay still," I said.

He did as I asked, and I pictured dark eyes of an amber brown, clear and healthy. With one last shove, the sky boomed again, and I pulled my hand away.

Colonel stepped back, blinking his eyes and shaking his mane. When he stopped, he turned his head, and the left eye looked at me for the first time.

I waved once and smiled. "Hey there. Can you see me?"

Colonel began to dance about in his stall, and I think if he'd been outside, he'd have kicked and leapt about with joy.

"Well, I'll be...that's what she meant. Let me see your right eye."

I followed the same process, and though it burned like hell, when I'd finished, Colonel's whiskey brown eyes could see. I was as excited as he was, if not more so, and whooped and hollered in joy, dancing around the room. "Oh, how I wish John was here to see this. He'd be so happy."

Remembering the safe, I went and opened the spot on the floor. Touching the stallion's neck, I said, "Colonel, John says you have the combination."

The horse's head moved up and down, and he pawed the ground with his hoof five times. Not waiting a lick, I ran to sit by the safe. "Five," I said and turned the combination lock three times past the five.

Colonel pounded the ground ten times, and I moved the dial to ten. Then he tapped for a while. I counted twenty-five and finished the sequence. Turning the handle, it clicked and opened.

"Well done, Colonel!" Inside were many things. I brought them all over to the desk and laid them out. "Well, here's the letter to his father, one to his sister, and one to an office in London." I picked up a book and unwrapped the leather strap that wound about it. Opening it, I found the missing ledger that Rob had talked about. Looking through it, I read notes regarding both businesses: the store and with the Regulators.

Not far in, I found a note that simply said, "Billy, if you find this and cannot hand it to my father personally, burn it."

"Well, that seems drastic."

After cataloging all the items, I put them all back, locking them safely away, and went back to bed. Tomorrow I would leave the Ellis Store and meet back up with the Regulators.

* * *

Thankfully the Ellis Store still stood. I didn't drive on back to it, for it was enough just to see her and the stable where I'd met Colonel still stood. Turning around, I headed west on Hwy 380 through Capitan to the new sheriff's office located in the new county seat of Carrizozo. It was a much nicer building than the sheriff had in my day...of course, anything with indoor plumbing and electricity is a nicer building to back then, but still...definitely in better shape.

Parking my car, I headed on into the two-story, rectangular adobe building and walked up to a long counter.

"Can I help you?"

I turned to see a woman in a skirt suit approaching. I pulled the American credentials given to those who worked for the MI-4 division of SIS and handed them to her. "Hi, my name is Agent William Kidwell. I have an appointment with Sheriff Sally Ortiz."

The woman looked at me, then my badge, and checked her books. "I see you listed here, Agent Kidwell. You're a bit early. Please have a seat."

I nodded and took back my identification from her before doing as she suggested. By the time I was called, I'd decided on a course of action to get Sally to tell me the truth. That was, until I was led through a large open room filled with a lot of desks where individuals worked and taken to an office with glass walls between those desks and me.

"Please wait here. The sheriff will be with you in a moment."

I tipped my hat to her. "Thank you, ma'am."

She smiled and left.

Too anxious to sit, I stared out at those watching me. I felt like I was a fish in a bowl and soon sat with my back to those in the bullpen.

"Thank you for waitin'. I'm not normally runnin' behind, but my two-year old son is sick, and I had to run something home to my wife for him."

I turned and stared at the man wearing a sheriff's uniform.

"Sheriff Sally Ortiz?" I asked as I stood, extending my hand.

He took my hand in his and shook it. "Yes, that'd be me." He paused, and then grinned. "Thought I was a woman because of the nickname, did ya?"

"No," I lied, letting go.

He laughed and sat behind his desk. Motioning to a chair that faced him, he said, "Sally is a nickname for Salvador. Have a seat, Agent Kidwell."

Feeling mighty stupid, I sat. "I apologize. I was only given your nickname, so I assumed...I am sincerely sorry."

Lacing his fingers in front of him, he shook his head slightly. "No need to apologize, Agent. I get it a lot. Now, how can I help you and why is the FBI interested in Lincoln County?"

12

THE MEDICINE MAN'S APPRENTICE

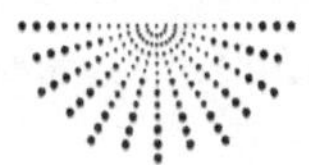

Waking up the next morning, I saddled Colonel and rode him on out and around to the regular stable. While transferring my belongings over from Centauro, the horse I'd arrived on, to Colonel, Dr. Reverend Ealy approached me. He was a pleasant man with a fiery hatred for the Murphes, though I think he disliked them as much for being Catholic as he did for everything else.

"Morning, Billy! What are you doing in town? You shouldn't be here. Governor Axtel—"

"I know, Reverend, but I needed to come in for a delivery and ended staying a night or two. I'm headin' outta here in a few minutes."

"How is Dick's shoulder?"

This stopped my feet. "Did he let you look at it?"

"He did. It was one simple round wound. He wouldn't tell me who shot him, but I gave him some salve and told him to keep it clean. It shouldn't be hurtin' him anymore at this point."

"Not that I know of," I lied. "Just salve, you say?"

"Oh, and that some colloidal silver. It's not a common item, but it's a great disinfectant. Truth be told, he asked for it by name, and I happened to have a small jar, so I sold it to him."

"Does that got real silver in it?"

"Yes, there are small pieces suspended in the liquid, easily absorbed into the body."

Speaking of pieces, the ones surrounding Dick's odd behavior began to fit together, and my stomach dropped to my knees. "Thank you, Reverend. I appreciate it. I best get goin'."

"Please do, and here—" He opened his bag and pulled out a bottle of clear liquid, tiny bits of silver floating about in it. "Here's a new bottle if he needs it. He paid me for two, so I owe this to him. You'll be seeing him today?"

I took the bottle reluctantly. "I will be now. In fact, I think I'll head over there immediately."

"Thanks so much, I appreciate it. I wasn't wantin' to ride out to his ranch, what with all the fightin' going on."

I tucked the disinfectant into my pocket. "I can understand. Have no fear, I'm happy to help."

Isaac walked by with a hearty hello for the Reverend and turned to me. "I see you're takin' Colonel with ya."

"Yes, sir. That's all right, isn't it?"

"He's your horse now, Billy."

"I mucked out his stall. Please keep an eye on it for me. I may need it from time to time. I also will leave Centauro with you. Use him as you see fit until either I can come get him or send one of the Coes to fetch him."

"Not a problem."

I thanked him, hoisted myself up into Colonel's saddle, and gave his sides a tap. We were off like lightning, even with the loads of silver ammunition in the bags. I was almost off the property when I ran into Ben.

"You left me some, right?" he asked.

"I did. A few boxes."

He nodded and was about to walk off when I said, "Are you sure you want to be involved in all of this? You're not a sworn Regulator, you don't need to—"

"Don't start soundin' like my dad, Billy. My friends and family are workin' with y'all, even if they don't know the whole truth. That puts me smack dab in the middle of it. Now, how do I get word to you?"

I hemmed and hawed on this, then pulled my tin of toothpicks out, figuring I'd replace it with one of those I'd packed up, and tossed it to him. "Take this. The symbol inside, find it here in Lincoln. The emblem won't be in an obvious spot. But it should be on or near a hidden compartment. My bet? It's not far from the Tunstall Store."

I explained how the one in San Pat looked and worked. "We call it the Regulator Network. Roy works with them. He delivers for us, sends messages and such. Use that to get in touch with me, or if you see him, he can do it. Learn more, and I'll be in touch with more information."

Ben nodded. "I'll let you know what I find out. Where will you be?"

"I'm heading to Brewer's ranch then to San Pat. Whatever you do, don't deliver to me at his ranch. Take all correspondence to the San Pat spot I told you about...I'll go there for messages."

"Easy enough. Be safe."

I nodded and snapped the reins. Where I was going was not safe for him, or possibly me either, for that matter, especially if my inclinations were correct. I hoped they weren't.

* * *

Riding up to Brewer's ranch at the Ruidoso, my mind went back to all the great times we'd had here, both with John and without. Dick had bought the old Horrell brothers' place and renovated it. Now it was a neat, twenty by forty-foot house with sixteen-inch-thick adobe walls and a new flat roof supported by vigas.

I dismounted and tethered Colonel to the gate as I walked up to the door, which was open. Hesitantly, I leaned in. "Dick?" He wasn't there, but it was evident why the door was open. It was stuffy inside due to all the days he'd been gone. It didn't help that the building had no windows. There were portholes, though, in the walls along the ceiling on all four sides of the home, for ventilation and shooting.

There was only one spot he'd be if not in the house and that would be his masterpiece of a barn. Dick had built the first real barn New Mexico had ever seen, complete with a steepled and pitched roof, which was unheard of around here. Flat roofs were the usual due to the snow being so light that it blew right off them. But not Dick's barn. He wanted it to look like the one he'd grown up with in Wisconsin.

Entering, I kept quiet and listened close for where he could be. Didn't take long to hear the sound of an ax hitting wood and knew he was out back, chopping firewood for his beehive fireplace. Door open all day, he'd want that tonight for sure.

I quickly glanced around the corner of the building to see Dick taking out some aggression of a serious nature on dead trees. Raising the ax, he came down hard, yelling out along the way, splitting the small log in half. As pieces dropped in opposite directions, he set the ax down and pulled off his sweat-soaked shirt, and with my enhanced vision, I could see the wound as clear as if I were inches from it.

The hole in his shoulder was red and inflamed, puffy even, and appeared as if it would be hot to the touch. It had to hurt like hell, yet here he was, chopping firewood. In fact, as he chopped the next piece, I saw the wound break open and ooze, making him curse.

He reached for a bag that wasn't far from his feet. In it was a small bottle identical to the one in my pocket. He appeared to be contemplating using the last of it, and I couldn't let him do that.

"I wouldn't use that any more if I were you," I said.

Dick jumped and quickly slid the bottle into the bag. "Shit! Scare the hell outta me, Billy. What are ya doin' here? Is there news already?"

"Not necessarily. Unless you count Ben Ellis and I bein' chased by werewolves night before last, Mrs. McSween killin' one without blinkin' an eye, and me hirin' Ben to help out our new Regulator Network guy who finally showed up." I leaned against the barn and crossed my arms over my chest. "If you call that news, then yeah, there's been a few things."

"Of course that's news," he said, eyeing his shirt and keeping his left shoulder turned away from me.

"Got a few more life essences inside me to go with Baker and Morton, meaning my eyesight is rather good. So stop trying to hide the wound. I've seen it."

"Keep your nose...or eyes, rather, out of my business," he snarked, picking up the axe.

"Did that happen the last night of trainin'? Did you take a bullet? Doesn't look like a bullet wound."

"It's nothin'. I'm puttin' stuff from the doctor on it. Just leave it be, Billy."

"Leave it be...right, leave it be. Cause I came all the way out here with another bottle of colloidal silver from the Reverend so I could leave it be."

Dick's blue eyes focused hard on mine. "Where is it? I'm almost out."

"Give it to you on one condition. Tell me, is that a puncture from a wolf's canine?"

He went still.

"If it is, then the silver is gonna make it hurt more and promote infection, not disinfect it."

"Just give it to me."

I stared him down and saw the answer in his eyes.

"No wonder you look and feel like hell. You're treatin' a werewolf bite with silver!"

Dick threw the ax farther than I'd have thought capable before turning on me. "What else is there to do?" he screamed. "If silver is the only thing that can kill 'em, then it's the only thing that can maybe keep me from losin' my soul and becomin' one of the things we hunt and kill."

"We need to talk to Garrett. See if there is a treatment for it. Maybe I can—"

"No! There's no tellin' anyone. You hear me? I won't have them put me down like a dog."

I smiled. "Well, technically..."

"Shut up, Billy! Now is not the time for your tension humor."

I wiped the smile off my face and stepped over to him. "You're right. But let's find someone who knows about this. Let's go talk to one a medicine man of The People. We won't say it's for you. How long until the next full moon?"

Dick sat down on the stump. "It's a week away. I've got a week to live, Billy. I just...I just want to be on my farm and enjoy my last days. Can you not just let me do that?"

What if he was right? What if what I'd seen in Baker's eyes had been my imagination? He should be able to spend his last week how he wished.

"I can do both. If anyone asks, you say I'm in San Pat with the Regulators. I'm gonna try to find answers."

"In six days' time you're just gonna find all the answers? Not even you can do that, Billy. You're a lot of things, and resourceful is one of them, but today is the twelfth of March. The full moon is the eighteenth."

"All right, so I have six days. I've escaped from jail in less time, so I think I can do this. Don't you give up though...and for God's sake, don't use the silver shit anymore. That's just makin' it worse."

"Or it's killin' the virus," he said.

I sighed. He could be right, what the hell did I know? "Fine, here." I reached into my pocket and handed him the next bottle. "Don't overuse it. Maybe cut back. How often have you been using it?"

"Four times a day."

"Cut it to two and see if it feels a bit better. You'll still be gettin' the silver in there, but maybe you won't feel or look so damn sick. Have you seen yourself in the mirror lately?"

Dick shoved the waves of hair out of his eyes. "I feel like hell."

"You look like it, too."

A small smile touched his lips. "Don't sugarcoat it for me or anythin'."

"I'd never dream of it."

He laughed lightly, eyes on the ground. Silence lingered for a few seconds between us, and I was about to go when he said, "It's okay if you can't, you know."

"Can't what?"

Looking up at me, he said, "Save the day."

"What's that supposed to mean?"

He stood, a stupid grin on his face. "You're always tryin' to ride in and save the day. I'm just sayin' that it's okay if you can't this time."

"I do not try to ride in and...look, I'm not out to save the day, ever. I will try to save you. I'll be back no later than early mornin' on the fifteenth. Pack a bag, prep your best horse, and be ready to go."

"Where to?"

"Far from here so you don't hurt anyone else that night. I'll take you out to that cave I was trapped in that one time, with the Indians outside. Remember that story?"

"Who can forget? You tell it all the time," he teased, walking toward the ax he'd thrown.

"Shut up, I do not."

He looked over his shoulder and squinched an eyebrow down in a way that said I was full of crap.

"Even if I do...that's not the point."

"What is, then?"

"The point is that it's far from here. A two-day ride for sure. I'll take you way out there so if you do change, you won't hurt anyone, and no one will kill you."

He picked up the axe. "Except you."

"I'm not going to kill you."

"You don't know that."

I turned and started to leave. "I'm not gonna have to. I'm goin' to figure out how to...what was it you said? Save the day? I'm gonna try to do that right now. Don't go do anythin' stupid, all right?"

The big man walked over, picked up a log, and set it on the chopping stump. "I already am. I'm lettin' you try this."

"You're funny. But seriously...I'm goin' to do all I can, okay?"

His face became serious again, and he nodded. "Okay."

With a nod, I left him to curse and take out his aggression on the firewood once more. I just prayed there wasn't as much aggression as before. That is the one thing Garrett was right about. Having a friend to share in your troubles did make a difference. Dick was there for me when I found out about my curse, and he'd not blinked an eye at it or treated me any different. I wasn't about to deny him the same courtesy.

Now shouldering some of Dick's worry on my shoulders, I mounted Colonel and headed off to see if I could get an audience with the medicine man of the Mescalero Apache over on their territory. If I approached this wrong, it would be my life on the line. I had to be careful.

* * *

Mescalero Apache were prevalent in New Mexico. It so happened that I knew a few of The Nit'ahéndé, the People Who Live Against the Mountains. They lived along the Rio Bonito and the Rio Hondo rivers, as well as in both the Capitan and Sacramento Mountains. Their chief, San Juan, and a few members of his Tribe had needed help once when I'd come across their path and lent my assistance. If I was lucky, they'd remember they owed me one.

Riding toward their territory, I had my rifle resting across my lap while I chatted with Colonel. "If you see a deer before me, do tell. Only way we're getting past the Chief's guards is with a gift."

It wasn't San Juan I need to speak with though; it was his medicine man, Dasan. He and I'd crossed paths before Tunstall hired me. Back when I rode with Jessie Evans' gang, which I'd hated every minute of, but it was money and protection. During that time is when I came across a member of The Nit'ahéndé and ended up saving Dasan's life. He told me he owed me a life boon. So now I would collect on that. The life he'd be saving wasn't mine, but that was fine by me. In fact, in my opinion, it was a life worth more than mine ever would be.

Thankfully, it didn't take long to hunt a deer, load him up, and deliver him to San Juan as a gift. I requested to speak to Dasan and was taken to where he sat by a fire, tending to a young boy's cut leg.

When his eyes landed on me, he didn't smile, but he didn't order me away either. Instead, he told them to leave me there and go.

I took a seat by the fire and waited.

Once finished with the boy, who ran off to play again, Dasan turned to me. "I did not think I would see you so soon, Williamson. I believe I told you to send word. You are not word. You are white eyes in the flesh on our land. The reason you come must be very important to take a risk such as this."

"It is, and private. Is there somewhere we can talk?"

"We are talking now."

"Don't be difficult with me, Dasan. You know what I mean. This is a private issue." I pulled out a bag from my inside jacket pocket. It contained half of the tobacco I had left. "Smoke and talk. Yes? If you can't help me, I'll leave."

He considered this, and then with a simple nod, he stood and motioned me to follow him. As we left, I noticed two members of the tribe come to tend to the fire we left behind. Where they'd come from I didn't know since it had appeared as if he and I'd been alone, making me feel like I was being watched, even now. I did my best to shake it off and followed him to a teepee on the outskirts of camp.

"Remove your boots," he instructed, as he took off his hand-sewn leather slippers.

I complied without question, hopping about to get them off before stepping inside. Many teepees are similar to tents the army uses, sleeping three or four people. This one was different, though, as it was the same size but only housed Dasan.

The floor was covered in animal fur, mainly deer and buffalo, which felt good on my feet after a day in boots. He instructed me to start a fire, and I selected a few pieces of wood from the pile to the left of the entrance and sat by the ring of stones at center. The base of the fire pit was filled with sand, and he placed some dry moss in the center of the circle.

Setting up a triangular build of wood over the moss, I did my best to use the flint rocks to get a spark to light the kindling. While I did this, I glanced around the cozy surroundings. The area directly across from the entrance lay Dasan's bedding. Near the wood pile, I saw a Dutch oven pot and a few other cooking items, and along the wall were books, many of them.

I looked over my shoulder to see the medicine man select a small wooden box that sat beside what appeared to be a woven mat attached to an x-crossed set of vertical wooden poles. This created a seat and backrest, which I found fascinating and inventive. Coming over to sit next to me, he opened the box and showed me its contents, a grin on his face.

"You could've just said you have matches, Dasan," I chided, happy to set the flint rocks down and light the moss with one of his matches, which took the flame and lit the thin wood pieces above it in an instant.

"Maybe I wanted to watch you try the old way first."

I laughed. "I am capable enough the old way, but this is much better, faster."

"And I feel time is of an issue for you," he said, setting the box down between us, which also held a pipe and the instruments for cleaning and packing it.

"Yes, or I'd not have come and bothered you."

Dasan took the pipe in one hand while putting out his other toward me. "I understand."

I handed him the tobacco. "I won that from a man in the southeast of the country, fresh from his tobacco plants."

Dasan only nodded in appreciation and began to pack the pipe as I tended to the fire, which warmed the round room quickly, smoke traveling upward and out the top perfectly. Once he finished, he selected a thin piece of wood from his box and set the tip of it in the fire. The flames discovered it immediately and fire overtook the end of it. Pulling it back out, Dasan used it to light the tobacco in his pipe.

After a few draws to light it, he blew out the smoke while sticking the thin wood into the sand to extinguish the fire on the tip. "This is good tobacco. You came well prepared, Williamson. Ask your question."

How was I supposed to explain this? What if he didn't believe in werewolves? I'd be right where I started, and Dick would be no closer to a cure, if there was one.

"Do you believe in magic?"

In the firelight, I saw the surprise on his face at my question before he replied. "I may be but an apprentice of our medicine man, but I believe in the magic of the earth, of what it provides, and of the spirits of our people." He handed me the pipe. "Why do you ask?"

"Because what I'm about to ask you next is gonna sound impossible." When he said nothing, I took a puff on the pipe and slowly let out the smoke. "Do you believe in the lycanthrope?"

Dasan stood and backed away from me. "You come to talk of dark spirit magic to me? In my home? On my land? Get out!"

"I wish I could just walk away. But I have a friend in need of help, a man I respect like you do your chief, and I cannot let him down. Please, Dasan, listen to me. If you cannot help, then I'll go. But hear me out."

Cautiously, he walked around the fire pit, sitting across from me this time, his back against a large trunk with a flat top, where he displayed photographs that he'd affixed to pieces of smoothed wood. "Tell me and then you must go."

I kept it vague and hoped he didn't press for more. He didn't seem to want to know anything he didn't need to, so that was on my side.

"There is nothing you can do. If what I've heard about this myth is true, your friend is infected, and he will change as of the next full moon and be dead to you. The best thing you can do is put a silver bullet in his brain."

"That's not gonna happen if I can help it. There has to be somethin' to pull this poison from his body. Leeches or colloidal silver or hell, I don't know, somethin'. There's magic in the world, Dasan. Because of that, I feel there's somethin' I'm missing that can help him."

He stared at me for a moment, then said, "I am not educated about such things, but I know of someone who is more...aware, shall we say. She used to be a medicine apprentice like me, but many began to call her a witch, and she left the tribe. She's not far though. I'll tell you where, but you'll need to have payment. She is not free, and unlike me, she doesn't owe you a life debt."

"Does she believe in this type of magic?"

"She does."

"Then I have payment for her enough."

He handed me a large skeleton key. "You'll need this."

Placing the key in my pocket, I said, "Okay. Where do I go?"

* * *

It would be easy to miss unless you were looking for it: an apple orchard along the side of a tall mountain rock. Dasan told me to find a door in the side of the wall of stone, not far from a creek that carried water from the reservation past the orchards that camouflaged the hillside.

Riding through, I plucked an apple from one of the trees and was about to take a bite when a voice, somewhere near but seemingly all around, spoke to me.

"Is that your apple?"

Remembering Dasan's words, I said, "It is if you'll let me eat it, my lady. I can pay for it and your guidance. Dasan sent me."

"Prove it," the voice said.

I pulled out the key Dasan had given me. "He gave me this."

Movement caught my eye to my right, and soon an Indian woman, very likely in her mid-to-late forties, stepped around a tree and up to my horse, apple in hand. Feeding it to him, her eyes of gold looked up at me, a stark contrast to her dark skin and hair that hung to her waist. She was a beautiful woman, and for a moment, I felt entranced by her and could see why some might call her a witch.

Shaking it off, I tore my eyes away from her to my stallion, happily munching his apple as she stroked his neck, her fingers swollen and knobby.

"He is a beautiful horse," she said.

"And he knows it," I told her.

"We all know our worth, do we not?" she said, her voice a silky purr.

I patted his neck. "He seems to like you."

"You are not human," she said so matter of fact like that I almost agreed with her.

"Well, that's changin' the subject, isn't it?" I said. When she said nothing, I added, "I am actually human. Why would you say I'm not?"

"My magic works on humans. If it doesn't work on you and you're human, there's some sort of magic in you."

I visibly relaxed in the saddle and said, "Yes."

"You intrigue me, magical human. What is your name?"

I paused for a split second to choose which name to give her. "Henry Antrim," I told her. "And you are...?"

She said nothing aloud, but inside my head, I heard the name Zahara as if whispered on the wind, and my stomach twisted. This was the woman Scáthach thought was dead, the one whose magic she smelled on Colonel.

"You're the witch who spelled the stable for Colonel, aren't you? That's why he likes you, he *knows* you!"

She stopped and stared. "You seem rather informed for a human who has just entered my magical grove, Mr. Antrim. Tell me what you are in need of."

"Knowledge on the lycanthrope."

Her eyes grew, and a smile of intrigue lit behind them. "I can help you. For I know much about the lycanthrope...and Scáthach's other children. But what magic have you come to share with me in return?"

"Share?"

"Yes. For you want information on this so badly that you are prepared to do whatever it takes to get it. That I can read plainly. The question is, what will you pay for it?"

"I will do whatever it takes and pay you all I can, dependin' on the information you share. If you hold back, so will I."

"I see, Mr. Antrim, you do like to play the game."

I smiled at her. "You can call me Henry, and yes, I do like a good game. But I'll warn you, Zahara, I tend to win."

"Mmmm..." She hummed as she nuzzled my stallion's neck. Laying her cheek on it, her eyes looked up at me. "But you see, Henry of the blue eyes and human magic, so do I."

Electric silence bounced between us, and suddenly I felt a desperate need for the information she knew. If I played it right, tonight I could learn more than just how to save Dick. I might learn how to save myself.

THE WITCH OF SCÁTHACH

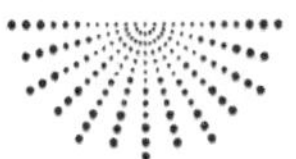

With no urging required, Colonel followed her like she was made of peppermints and apples. He either was in love with her or her magics held him in thrall. Laying low, I draped across his neck to avoid the apple tree boughs from smacking me in the face until we reached the wall of the mountain, not far from a painted-on door.

The wall here appeared to be covered in vines, yet as I dismounted and approached the curious sight, I noted that it was a wall of interwoven plants, black in pigment and covered in thorns. They writhed when she approached and coiled back without a second thought, revealing an opening and a path beyond it.

I'd seen enough traps in my time to become wary. "You are a child of Scáthach yourself, are you not?"

Zahara turned to me. "I am one of the few she blessed with the gift of magic, that is true. In fact, I am the first one on this continent she bestowed the gift upon. However, I am no longer her child. I earned my freedom and hold no allegiance to her."

I stared her down, debating what I was to do. Garrett said we were to kill all Scáthach's demon children. But I wasn't about to kill Dick, so did I need to kill Zahara?

"Oh, I see now," she said with a laugh and a smile. "You're one of her warriors. Are you here to kill me, Henry?"

"Should I?"

"It would be interesting to see you try," she said, raising her hands, causing the thorned vines to writhe about and a few to slither toward me.

"I didn't come here to fight you. I came for answers to help a friend."

She sniffed the air. "That smells of truth, warrior of Scáthach. Tell me, what help is it you seek?"

"His shoulder was punctured by a single werewolf tooth in battle when it fell upon him in death. We are approachin' the first full moon after the event. I have no idea if he'll change, but I want to stop him from losin' his soul." When she said nothing, I added, "He's a good and noble man. He doesn't deserve this."

"You speak of it as if it's a curse."

"It is!"

"It's a gift, warrior child. He will live for a thousand years, see things others only dream of. He will save lives and build a world where magic lives and breathes. It is a glorious chance to be extraordinary, and you want to rob him of that?"

"He has asked me to put a silver bullet in his head. I am not the one who wants to rob him of anythin'. He does not want to become a demon for Scáthach...a pawn in her game."

"All must sacrifice who they are until they earn it back. He will, in time, regain his mind and will."

This caught my attention, and my hand moved away from my gun. "What? Demons are not prone to lettin' go of their human host."

She held her snakelike vines in place for a moment, but then lowered her arms, the thorny plants going back to a harmless posi-tion. "Demons. You think they are demons? Who told you that? Wait, let me guess, you're one of those Regulators, aren't you?"

"Only recently inducted."

"Oh, they must be so excited to have a warrior of Scáthach on their team. Be very careful, Henry, for they will try to use you for their own gain."

"I thought that was to regulate the supernatural in this country and send them back to Ireland."

She laughed. "That depends on which generation of Regulator you ask. The new leader of the Regulators in England is a bloodthirsty man who desires nothing more than to eradicate all the supernatural from the Earth. His predecessor was a man with heart, who only wished to remove those who were tainted and hurt others. Some believe he was killed by the man who now heads the organization, but proving it will be most impossible."

"Why?"

"But *that* is not why you are here. You wish to know about the lycanthrope. How the taint of blood carries the gift of sharing mind and body with the elegant creature of the wolf. If your friend was punctured deep enough to bleed, he is infected, there is little to do about that. However, if you kill the one who bit him—"

"I already did," I said.

"Well, look at you, little warrior. Tell me, is that life force still in your soul chamber?"

"No, it was used to save my life from a bullet to the chest."

She tapped her finger to her lips and then, waving her arms up and out, she said, "*Sherlathada.*"

The vines began to move again, this time spreading to make an opening high and wide enough for us all, including Colonel, to walk through. Without a word, Zahara entered and disappeared into the mountain. With no other choice, I did the same. Once we were all the way in, the vines closed behind us, enveloping us in the black.

Unsure which way to go, I called out, "Zahara?"

"*Luminaire,*" she said somewhere in the distance, and suddenly the path, wide enough to drive a wagon through, was easy to see.

Bending down to get a better look, I realized that the small road was lined on both sides with small pieces of the stone used for bahvah-lamps, and they are what illuminated the way. But that wasn't all. Flowers and plants I'd never seen before began to come alive in every color of the rainbow, shining in the darkness. One would bloom and then the one next to it would as well, and then the next, traveling quickly until the cavern in which I stood became a garden of light.

"Holy Mary, mother of God..." I said.

"No, just me," I heard Zahara say, now far from me.

Cautiously, I led Colonel along the path, asking, "You sure you still like her?"

He whinnied and began to prance, pulling me faster down the trail. "Okay, if you say so."

It didn't take long to find Zahara. She stood in an enormous cavern lit by a large fire in the center, surrounded by pine trees.

"Are we inside the mountain?" I asked.

"Yes."

Tilting my head back, I gazed in wonder to the colors of the setting sun that illuminated the top of the cavern. "Are you sure?"

A laugh, lighter than the one she'd had before, bubbled out of her. "Yes. That's just magic. Come further into the light, warrior of Scáthach. Eat, drink, be nourished, and let's talk of magic, yours, mine, and your friend's."

She stepped to the fire and ladled out something into a stone bowl, and I couldn't help but stare. She looked different, younger and more vibrant. The gray streaks in her hair were gold, like her eyes, and she now wore a dress made of draped, deep red fabric.

"That's a change," I said.

"Here you see my spirit self...how I am on the inside." She turned to face me, and she looked surprised. "Why, young warrior of Scáthach, is that your true spirit? I have to admit, even I am impressed."

I looked down at myself to see a man clad in leather and chainmail armor. My arms and legs were stronger looking than I was used to, and as she approached me, I noted I was taller as well. "This is different."

"The true spirit is something no one can hide from me in here...and if you had come to do harm, it would show. Instead, it is your heart I see. I will help you as best I can. Come, sit by the fire, and

I will tell you of the lore that now surrounds your friend who you hold in such high esteem that you would die for him."

"I never said I would—"

"You don't have to say things here for me to know them. Come, sit, eat with me and drink some wine. I will teach you what you need to know to disconnect your friend from Scáthach's will."

* * *

It was the morning on the fourteenth when she led me out of the Forest of True Spirit, her name for it, not mine. Stepping out into the real world, the air felt harsh on my flesh, and I again looked like myself, as did she.

"Now that we are in the world where your soul chamber is yours to wield, I do ask for payment."

"And I keep my word. Hold out your hands."

I had forgotten while inside the magical forest, but her hands appeared older than she did, twisted and knobby with arthritis that I'd seen on women in their late years of life. I took her hands in mine and smiled at her. Holding eye contact, I focused the energy of those in my soul chamber and sent that power into her hands, sacrificing two chances of saving myself from death. This was my payment to her for what I'd learned.

I had the option to split one life between her hands, but she'd given me more than I could have asked for. The swelling and twisted look of the joints went down completely, and she wiggled her fingers like a piano player excited to touch the keys.

Tears filled her eyes, and she leaned forward to kiss my cheek. "You gave more than promised. Did you think I would not notice? Your friend is a lucky man."

"I don't know how long that will last," I told her.

"I guess we'll see soon enough."

This reminded me of a thought I'd had as I'd fallen asleep the night previous. "Tell me, could my power to heal help my friend's wound?"

She shook her head. "No. And do not try it. Your magic kills the wolf, but not the infection. If you try, you'll kill him. His only chance is if you do as we discussed. Checks and balances, remember?"

"I do."

She patted my hand. "Good luck, Henry. I wish you all the best. If you are ever in need of me again, you know where I'll be."

"How do I find this place again?"

"Once you've been inside the Forest of True Spirit, it will always show itself to you. No one else can see this place though, not without a talisman of mine."

"The key Dasan gave me," I said with understanding.

She nodded. "Yes."

I smiled and tipped my hat to her. "If you need me, you send me a letter. Find Ben Ellis in Lincoln. He will deliver it."

"Good to know. Travel safe, young warrior."

I put my hat back on and mounted Colonel, who whinnied at her.

"Oh, I could never forget you, handsome." Zahara kissed Colonel's nose and palmed an apple to him out of nowhere.

He munched and swished his tail, making noises at her that made me roll my eyes. "We'll be back, ya big lug. Come on, we gotta go. We only have a day to find what we need."

"The man I mentioned should be able to help you. Just give my name."

I nodded. "Thank you."

Getting Colonel to leave her was difficult, but soon he trotted out of her orchard, and we headed to get all our supplies. Dick and I were in for a rough couple of nights in the desert, but if I did this right, he wouldn't owe Scáthach a moment of his life. If I failed, his soul would vanish, and he could end up killing me.

It was a risk I was willing to take.

* * *

By the time I returned to Brewer's ranch, it was late in the morning of the fifteenth, and I found him lying in bed in such a miserable state that he didn't even move when I came into the room.

On the floor lay a packed bag, and next to his bed lay an empty bottle of the colloidal silver.

"Jesus, Dick! How did you use the whole thing in a matter of three days?"

He muttered something, and I couldn't hear him as well as before, which was a result of sacrificing two of the souls in my chamber, I was certain. I stepped closer, and he repeated himself.

"Did you just say you drank it?" I asked, more astonished that he could get it down than shocked that he tried.

Dick hummed what appeared to be a positive confirmation as his reply, and I sat on the end of his bed. "And how do you feel about that decision, Mr. Brewer?"

"Muck-oo," was what I heard, but I knew what he meant to say.

Laughing, I said, "Bet you feel like utter shit, partner. I'm shocked you didn't vomit it up."

"Ah-must," he muttered.

"Almost? Not surprisin' since you just poisoned yourself. Look, it's almost ten in the mornin', and we need to get movin'. Can you stand?"

"Mather lot," was what came out of his mouth.

I sighed. "But you're going to, even if I have to pull you out of there. You have until I've packed up the wagon."

With that, I went into his kitchen, grabbed his Dutch oven, filled it with whatever food he had, grabbing his packed bag, and opened the door. He groaned when light spilled in.

"Werewolf, not vampire, stop with the theatrics!" I said before shutting the door.

I sang as I loaded the items into the covered wagon I'd borrowed from someone dumb enough to leave it unattended. I'd return it when we were done, and I'd already sent the horses back. Colonel had followed beside us the whole way, and the moment I unhitched them, he whinnied, they replied, and off they went, back the way we came.

With Dick moaning inside with the regret of those who drink too much alcohol, I hooked up Colonel and Mattie to pull the wagon. Then I tossed four two-string hay bales into the very back, leaving an opening at center in case Dick needed to crawl in and pass out for the ride. I collected two more bales to set in once he laid down to hide him and all the other items I'd brought with me from town.

Heading back into the ranch, I noticed a crow perched above the door, the black of his feathers gleaming in the sun. I tilted my head to look at him, and he mirrored my movement as the wind gently blew his feathers, exposing a base color of white instead of gray. This told me my first assumption was incorrect.

"Well hello there, Chihuahua Raven," I said. "I've not seen one of you in a while."

He flapped his wings at me, and I couldn't help but smile. My mother had loved birds and taught me the difference between the types of crows and ravens, and how to tell them apart. This one was a beauty. Now that I looked more carefully I saw he, or she, was bigger than a crow but not as large as a regular raven, with a black and slightly curved beak the size of a crow's bill, hence my earlier mistake.

"Hello there, scavenger of the desert, are you guardin' the door or can I go get him?"

The raven tapped his feet like a clog-dancer while making a *quark-quark* sound, which isn't as throaty as a regular raven, yet not as harsh as the caw of the crow.

With a chuckle, I ducked through the doorway and went down the steps into the ranch, where I found Dick hadn't moved an inch. "Great. You're still not up. Good thing I have two souls in the well to give me extra strength." I pulled the covers down, happy to find him in pants, and squatted down to ease the big man's arm over my shoulder. Holding it in place with one hand, I put my other one around his waist.

"On the count of three, help me out, okay?"

"Weave me ah-wone," he said.

"I'd laugh if I wasn't damn sure that'd solidify your decision to not help me at all. Now...one, two, three!"

I pulled him up, and with a little bit of assistance from him, I got him on his feet. "We just need to get you to the wagon and you can lie down."

"Okay," he said.

"Come on, out the door we go. Man, you're heavy. How is such a fit man so heavy? And hot. You're burning up."

We went up the steps and through the door. As the sunshine hit his face, he doubled over, taking me down, too. Pivoting around, I kept Dick from face-planting into the dirt.

I squatted in front of him, a hand on each shoulder to hold him up. "You okay? What is it?"

"Mooo," he said, and I had no idea what that was supposed to mean, until he vomited the colloidal silver all over my boots.

I stared down as his stomach contents emptied yet again. "Excellent. Just excellent."

Dick sat down on the ground. "I told you to move."

"Oh, is that what you said? Because I heard you moo like a cow and then you threw up all over my boots."

He looked up at me. "I feel better now though."

"Muck-oo!" I said and stomped off to the creek that ran in front of his home to clean myself off. I wasn't there more than thirty seconds when he came walking toward me with a bucket and a towel. "I don't need that."

"I do. I think I've been in that bed for two days straight."

"Oh, by all means, do wash," I said, and stepping out and over to him, taking the bucket.

"How's the temperature today?"

I grinned, filling the bucket. "It's rather warm for this time of year, actually."

He nodded, and I set the bucket down, walking away. Not moments later, I heard him dump the water over himself and scream like a little girl.

I turned about to see his backside, buck-naked by the creek, his hair soaked.

I grinned, hooking my thumbs on my belt. "How's the water?"

"You're so dead," he said, his voice low and mad.

I burst out laughing as the raven from earlier flew overhead, its cry almost sounding like it chuckled at us as well. "Now we're even!"

He flipped me off, making me laugh harder. "Hurry up there. We don't have all day for you to frolic in the creek." I smiled and headed for the wagon as he cursed me out.

I'd just finished putting in the last two bales of hay along the back of the wagon bed when he came walking up, towel wrapped around his waist.

"You can wear that, but I'm not to blame if your, what did Tunstall call them, twig and berries, get chaffed."

Now Brewer smiled. "Yeah, that's what he said that time. We all must've laughed for half an hour." After a short pause of reflective silence, he added, "I've got a change of clothes set out inside. I'll be right out."

He was fast about it, and we were on our way. The sun was warm, but he'd thrown on a spring jacket over his regular attire.

"Cold?" I asked.

"Shut up."

But then we both started to laugh, and my hopes for my plan squeezed my heart. I had to make this work, for both our sakes.

14

BEING FOLLOWED

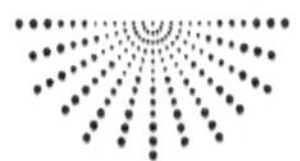

We'd traveled about a third of the way to our destination as the sun began to set. There was nothing for miles, but I pulled the wagon off the road and around the side of the mountain that had a good number of shrubs at its base. By putting the back end of the wagon toward the mountain, it would make for only one real entrance and a quicker hook up and getaway if needed.

Dick detached the horses and began to give them a good rub down while I made a fire and emptied two cans of soup into the Dutch oven pot. While that heated, I pulled a bale of hay out and fed the horses. Once they were settled, he and I sat down, using the wheels of the wagon as back rests, the fire at our feet between us. Tearing into the smoked jerky I'd brought, I ladled soup into bowls.

"Why are you doin' this?" Dick asked once food was done and we were sitting by the fire.

"I'd want someone to do it for me, I suppose. You're a good man, Dick, and a great friend. You and George gave me work when I first got to town and helped me get in with Tunstall. I've never been able to thank you for that."

Dick huffed a laugh. "Yeah, we got you involved in more than you bargained for."

"Oh, I was already cursed by that woman before I ever met up with you all."

"I meant the war, Billy. John's death. All of this."

"I know, but it was my choice to stay, just like it was yours. I coulda left back when it started to get tight. But John trusted me to be one of his main gunmen. That's a big thing to me. He gave me a family and friends, a sense of belongin' and unity. That's not somethin' an orphan takes lightly, Dick. We just don't."

He was silent, and I sat there listening to the insects and the other wildlife making noises around us as I thought about my mother. Would she be proud of me or would she be disappointed of where I'd ended up? God only knew.

"I still miss her," I said aloud without really meaning to. Feeling my face redden with embarrassment, I stood up. "I'm going to go prep the inside of the wagon for some rest. Should we sleep in shifts, or do we think we're solid out here?"

"Shifts isn't a bad idea," he said to me. "You go first. The moon is up, and I'm wide awake."

I nodded and climbed up onto the driving bench of the wagon. I was about to step into the covered area when he spoke to me again.

"I miss mine, too, you know. There's nothin' wrong with missin' your mom, Billy. Dead or alive."

I nodded. "Thanks. Night."

"Night."

I crawled into the wagon bed and set out my bed roll in the open space. Laying down, I let my head wander to the information Zahara had given me and wondered if I'd be able to pull it off. Next to me was a crate of chains, steel nails, and different sized cuffs that I hoped would at least give me the chance to try. We'd know in forty-eight hours. It felt like a lifetime away and yet just around the corner.

I shuddered at the thought of failing and pushed it from my mind. I needed sleep to keep my optimism up. I closed my eyes and let myself drift off. Dick didn't wake me until a few hours before sunrise, so while he slept, I got the horses fed and hitched. By the time I made food and coffee, he was awake. Stepping down from the wagon, the cry of a desert raven filled the air.

Looking up, I saw him perched on top of the wagon cover. "You again?"

"Just cause they all look alike doesn't mean it's the same crow you saw somewhere else," Dick said, taking the coffee I handed him.

"That's a raven, Dick. Learn your birds."

He rolled his eyes at me and drank.

"Only four hours down. That can't be good," I said.

"I'm havin' issues with sleep. After I eat somethin', I'll get a second mug of coffee down me, and I should be all right. We need to get movin'."

Once we ate and filled Dick with coffee, we hit the road where he finally asked the question I knew was coming eventually. "You never told me who you found or what they said about my...condition."

No, I had not. I was hoping to avoid that talk for a bit longer, but if I tried to evade now, it'd be obvious. "It's a long story."

"I think we've got the time."

I sighed. "That we do. Well, it starts with a medicine man and ends with a witch."

* * *

During World War I, Regulators became absorbed by England's Secret Intelligence Service and renamed MI-4. After the war, that division signed a deal with the FBI so our agents could work in America more easily and assist with the Red Scare, which was not just about communism in America. Scáthach was busy causing trouble and we'd been called in to help. But that's a story for another time.

By doing this, I was able to carry FBI credentials while in America. This was helpful on multiple fronts. It opened doors, but mostly it stopped us from ruffling feathers, so to speak. Local police and sheriffs in the United States don't care too much for Federal muckity-mucks coming in and messing with their investigations, but they despise law enforcement from other countries even more. Hell, they barely even recognize SIS as law officers or give us any rights in America. Meaning the FBI papers Sheriff Ortiz had on me weren't a total lie, just partially.

Trying to stay relaxed in his office, I said, "Look, I'm not here to get in your way of anythin'. I'm just goin' to be in the area investigatin' a few things and was told to stop here first."

"Yes, I spoke to your boss."

I raised an eyebrow. "You checked my references?"

"Of course I did, and he told me about your assignment. Do you have a picture of your missing agent?"

"I do." I pulled out the picture of Agent Fletcher Calhoun and handed it to him. "Last we heard from him, he was in Lincoln County. He coulda just been passin' through or he might've been lookin' into somethin' here. I have to poke around a bit and see. Does he look familiar to you at all?"

"He does. The name didn't ring a bell for me since he introduced himself as a PI from New York. Went by the name, what was it, oh, Fletcher O'Conner."

"That's one of his aliases, so I'm not surprised. He might've been tryin' to keep his federal ties out of it all. We get a lot of heat from local law enforcement, as you can guess."

The sheriff nodded. "He said he was in town lookin' for a man by the name of Blue-Jaw somethin'."

"Yeah, Seymour 'Blue-Jaw' Magoon. Did he explain why?"

"Somethin' to do with some mob guys back in New York if I remember correctly."

"Yep. Ya see, after a short stint in the can, Blue-Jaw took off and disappeared. We heard rumor he'd headed back out west, and Calhoun found evidence of him comin' to New Mexico not that long ago, so he came out here to see if he could locate Blue-Jaw."

"What for?"

"Just makin' sure he isn't dead and tryin' to keep him safe. Word on the street out east is that there's a hit out on him."

This, of course, was complete and utter bullshit. Not the hit, that was legit. But the reason the MI-4 team was looking at him had nothing to do with that. It was because Blue-Jaw had gotten himself wrapped up with some werewolves working in the illegal gambling business and folks were dying or disappearing, and President Truman had asked us for help.

"Well, I got a great artist here. If you got a picture of Blue-Jaw, we can have drawings done of him and Agent Calhoun really quick and I can use them to ask around."

"That'd be great." I pulled out Magoon's mug shot and handed it to the sheriff. "I'll come on by tomorrow and get those back, if that'd be all right?"

"Sure thing."

I paused a moment, then decided to ask for some help. "Problem is, I was plannin' to stay at The Wortley Hotel if I was goin' to be here overnight but—"

"That burned down in the thirties. No one's had the inclination to fix it up," the sheriff told me, looking at the two pictures in his hands.

"That's too bad. I'm hungry and in need of lodging for the night. Any suggestions?"

"Got a few good places here where the grub's worth more than they charge and a little bed and breakfast I send family to. I'll give Lois a call and see if she can take ya in."

"That's mighty kind of ya. I'd appreciate it."

"Not a problem." He picked up the phone and dialed up the B&B. From what was said, it seemed I had a place to stay for the night. He was almost off the phone when he said, "Lois, did that private detective stay with you back in April?"

This got my attention, and I stared holes through the man until he said, "Mmm hmm...all righty then. Agent William Kidwell is comin' on over there then. Put him up for me on the city's account if you would. Tell him whatever he needs to know about that PI. Okay? I'll send him your way in a little while. Yes ma'am, you too. Bye." He hung up the phone and jotted something down on a piece of paper. Standing, he handed it to me. "This is the address. Know your way around well enough to find that?"

I looked down at the address. "Sure do." Standing, I put my hand out to him. "Appreciate all your help, Sheriff."

He shook my hand firmly. "Not a problem. I'll walk ya out and introduce you to our artist."

"Sounds right as rain, sir."

Sheriff Ortiz led me back to the artist. He explained to the young man how I needed my pictures back the next day and then walked with me out to the lobby. to the lobby.

Looking at his watch, Sheriff Ortiz said, "Ya know what? It's lunchtime and a beautiful day out. Come on, I'll take ya on over for some lunch at the diner."

"You don't have to do that," I said.

"We'll take my car."

"Really, ya don't—"

"I do. You need to know about Las Cruces. Lois said your friend was headed there when he left her place."

"I've been to Las Cruces before, Sheriff. I think I know—"

"No, you don't. Take my word for it." He pulled out his keys. "Come on. I'll tell ya more when we're away from here. It's best you understand what you'll be walkin' into...ya need to know about Sheriff Alfonso Luchini Apodaca."

We got in Ortiz's car and headed on out, and it was evident by the way he was driving that we were going out of our way to make sure we weren't followed. I commented on this, and all he said was, "I want to live to see tomorrow, Don't you?"

I hadn't understood his desperate need to explain this sheriff to me until now. However, now that I did, I wasn't so sure my trip to New Mexico was going to be as simple as I'd thought. Especially if he was worried about being followed. This was not what it seemed.

* * *

Quark-quark, sang the desert scavenger.

"Is it just me or is that raven followin' us?" I asked, chewing on my last bite of dinner.

We'd made good time that day and had camped about an hour past where I thought we'd stop for the night. Again, we were up against a mountain, but it was nice enough out that we'd set our bed rolls by the fire.

"No idea," Dick replied, leaning back against a rock, a sheen of sweat covering his face and arms. He'd eaten for two and seemed green in the gut.

"You okay?" I pried.

"I hurt everywhere."

"Stomach?"

"Only place that's fine. I mean, I'm a bit hungry still, but if I'd eaten until full, you'd not have gotten any."

Eyebrow raised, I handed him the last piece of bread and remnants of my bowl of stew. "How you fitting that all in? I mean, I know you're a big guy, but this is a lot, even for you."

He took the bread and bowl. "You sure?"

I waved him on. "Where does it hurt?"

He used the bread to mop up the last bits of my stew and ate it before answering me. "Everywhere else. Like growing pains...not that you had those..."

I laughed. "I thought I was the funny one. That was good, Brewer. That was good."

He grinned and finished off my dinner.

Personally, I was surprised the big man could still stay jovial considering all that had and was about to happen. Looking up at the moon, almost full, I worried about many things. None of which was if I'd be hungry later, and that was a first.

Finishing with a resounding belch, Dick eased himself to lay down onto his sleeping mat. "That was fantastic. No idea where you learned to cook, Billy, but you missed your callin'."

"I do love food," I said, unsure how else to respond.

The throaty noise of the raven I'd asked Brewer about earlier filled the air again. This time, it sounded like a warning call.

Standing, I pulled my gun. "Who's there?"

Silence replied with the sound of wind rippling the covering on the wagon. I reached my hearing out farther, like the witch had taught me. Now I heard it, the breathing of an animal. It could be wolf, coyote, mountain lion, or a cattle-herding dog, for that matter.

I toed Brewer's boot with my own. "We have company."

Brewer didn't move an inch. "It's a coyote. Not as close as ya think. Lay down and sleep. He's just lookin' for a calf."

"How can you know that? Besides, I'm about the size of a calf, thank you very much, but probably not as tasty."

A wide smile filled Brewer's handsome face. "Don't sell yourself short."

I sighed at the bad pun.

Brewer opened one eye, still smiling like an idiot. "Short, get it?"

"Shut up, Dick." I sat, gun still in hand.

He laughed heartily. Once it faded away, he said, seriously this time, "I know because I can smell him. I can hear his movements like you can. But I can tell how far away he is and in what direction."

"How can you do that?"

"I'm not in pain before a full moon for no reason, Billy. I'm startin' to change."

"We're going to stop that."

"I don't think that's possible now." Sitting up with much effort, Dick looked at me, the remaining firelight casting angular shadows on his face. "You have to make me a promise."

"Um, okay...why?"

"Because if nothin' else, Billy Bonney, you're a man of your word. And I need that right now. It's either your sworn promise or I'll slice my wrists and bleed out by mornin'."

"What the hell are you talking about? Why would you do something stupid like that?"

"Because I don't want to lose my soul, become some demon!" he shouted, his frustration finally showing.

"Oh, do alert all to our location, please," I complained.

"Between the small fire, dinner, and how much I'm sweatin' right now, trust me, every animal knows we are here."

I sighed. He was right. "Fine, what is the promise?"

"That you'll kill me if I change into a demon."

"Dick, that's—"

"It's goin' to happen. I'm going to change into a wolf. If my soul goes, you kill me. Ya got that?" His blue eyes appeared almost silver in the dark as he leaned toward me, the intensity of his stare a palpable thing.

"Even if you can earn it back in time?"

"Even if. I don't want her to own me for a second. Okay?" When I didn't answer, he pressed. "Okay?!"

"Yeah, I got it. You have my word."

He put his hand out, and we shook on it. Laying back down, he said, "And yeah, that damn raven has been followin' us since we left the ranch."

"Dammit."

15

GAAX

It didn't take long for Dick to fall asleep. I, on the other hand, tossed and turned, the instructions the witch gave me swimming 'round in my head. Eventually I slipped into slumber. Not long after, or so it felt, the loud *quark-quark* of our party-crashing raven woke me. I ignored it and rolled over. Again, it cried out, and again, I refused to move, my head sucked into a beautiful dream of a sensuous Mexican woman dancing with me in a large room with ceilings so high it couldn't be a real building.

QUARK-QUARK! QUARK-QUARK!

The raven jumped onto my head and beat its wings, yanking me from the dream completely. Cursing, I swung at him and missed as he dove at something in the dark.

Pulling on my enhanced sight, I could see the coyote, big for his breed, pacing the side of our camp that wasn't up against the mountain.

I slowly reached for my gun, whispering, "Dick? Are you awake?"

The big man didn't do much more than snort and roll over, and the coyote leapt at him. I reached for my gun, but I was going to be too late.

QUARK-QUARK!

Out of the darkness, the raven flew at the beast, attacking its face with claws and beak. The coyote screamed in pain, swiping at the bird and knocking it to the ground. But before he could move another inch, I shot the beast in the head, learning suddenly that he was not a coyote.

The rush of soul power hit me, and I tottered backward, holding onto the wagon to stay upright. Head spinning, I watched as Brewer's immense frame shot to a standing position in seconds, rifle spinning up from his side, rising into firing position out of nowhere. He pulled the trigger, blowing the wolf's head off before he'd even had a chance to fall over and change back to his human form.

My ears rang for a moment as we both stood there, breathing hard. I listened for the second member of his hunting party but heard nothing. Not sure I trusted that, I slid my gun into my pocket and kept my hand close, saying to Brewer, "Well, Dick, that was overkill if I ever saw it."

Dick turned, eyes glowing silver in the dark, aiming the rifle at me.

"Whoa...whatcha doing, big man?" When he didn't reply, I said, "Dick! Put the damn gun down!"

Instead, he slowly advanced on me, and I backed up along the wagon until I reached the end. Hands up, I said, "Richard Brewer, can you even hear me?"

The poor raven, somewhere in the dark, made a horrible noise, and it distracted Brewer enough that his eyes ticked to his left. Immediately, I grabbed the barrel of his 1873 Winchester, still a bit hot from the previous firing. Using my accelerated speed and strength, I yanked it toward me and shoved the barrel away from me, lining up the shoulder curve right where I wanted it. With one hard push, I rammed the butt of the gun into Brewer's head. He let go of the rifle and dropped to the ground, where he promptly rolled over and snored.

I, too, fell to the ground, landing hard on my ass. "Sleep shooting? Are you fuckin' kiddin' me? I hate you sometimes, Brewer. I really do."

A growl, low and steady, sounded close, and I spun around as I pulled Brewer's rifle into firing position to see a wolf twice the size of the other staring me down. I didn't hesitate, because he wouldn't either, and I fired. It hit him in the chest, but he kept running. I cocked the gun and fired again. The silver bullet hit the wolf in the face, and he dropped, sliding toward me on the ground, nose stopping two inches from my boot.

The eyes found mine, and again, I saw the human behind the wolf. I opened my mouth to ask him a question, but he died, and his soul hit me like six horses pulling a carriage ran me over. Once I was more aware, I crawled to my bed roll and located my honeycomb calcite. *"Luminaire,"* I said, and it lit from within, pooling light all around me, making it possible for me to find the raven in the dark, even with a swimming head. He wasn't far from the first dead wolf, now a headless boy, no more than sixteen. My heart squeezed, and I turned away.

Sitting by the raven, I said, "Let's see how badly injured you are."

He quarked at me, trying to peck at my hand.

"Hey, I'm not gonna hurt you. I'm goin' to try and, well, heal you. I've only ever done this once, but I think I can replicate it. Least I can do for you savin' my ass."

As if understanding me, he stopped fighting and went silent. Carefully, I lifted him as the sun began to lighten the sky.

"Sun's coming up. A new day means a new chance to make a difference. That's what my mom would say. I used to think that was hogwash until recently. Now let's take a look atcha."

Moving the light around him, I saw his right eye was destroyed, as well as his right wing, broken for sure. As was a foot.

"You're a mess, little one. Let's see what I can do."

I set the light down and rested the black bird on his back in my cupped palms. First, I sent energy into his foot, then his wing. As they healed, he tried to flutter.

"Shhh...I got one more thing. This'll take the longest. But, being as you're so small, it might not be so bad."

Laying a hand on his head, careful not to press hard, I pictured the eye of a raven and all it saw from above. I imagined myself high in the air with him, seeing all he saw as I pushed healing energy into him, just as the sun came up over the horizon.

Suddenly the air around me changed, as if my energy expounded, sending a swirling of gray mist around us that felt static-like, flashing like lightning bugs were zooming about inside it. Still connected to healing the raven's right eye, I felt a tug on my own. The force pulled my face toward the bird, as if connecting us like a rubber band.

Opening my mouth to cry out in pain, I removed my fingers from his eye, and my vision changed. I saw myself from the bird's point of view. I was enormous and obviously in pain. Afraid of my power and yet determined to save this bird's eye and life, I tried to give one more push of healing energy.

The sun slid over the horizon, bathing us both in golden light. The clarity of vision I had through the bird's eyes became perfectly clear, letting me know his sight was repaired. I pulled my energy back, and the connection between us snapped. My sight returned, and I opened both of my eyes in time to watch the raven jump from my hands, good as new.

Happiness filled me and then, the next second, the raven was gone, and before me sat a naked Indian boy, no more than twelve or thirteen. He wore nothing but a leather necklace strung with what looked like bird bones. He inspected me, head tilting like a bird, as the flashing gray swirled around us for a moment longer before fading away like fog with the morning light. Heavy silence filled the air as the boy and I stared at one another for a moment until he placed a hand on his chest and uttered one word.

"Gaax," he said, the word coming out sounding like, "Gawkh."

It took a moment to understand he was giving me his name. I touched my chest and gave the name I always uttered to strangers. "Henry."

He looked over his shoulder at Brewer, sleeping sound in the dirt where he'd fallen.

"That's Richard," I said. "He is not on my Christmas list at the moment. What are you?"

Gaax looked back at me, an eyebrow raised.

"Damn, you may not speak English. Sadly, I don't speak any language of The People. I do know Spanish."

The boy smiled. "I know language of the white man. One cannot survive these days without that knowledge. I stare at you because you survived the magical place of shift. What are you?"

"What am I? What are you?"

The boy smiled. "Zahara said you were different, that you and your companion were special. But she didn't explain how."

Now it all made sense. The sense of being followed from her place. The raven following us from Brewer's to here. She'd sent a spy.

"You're a witch too then? Sent to what, watch us and report to her?" I said, standing, blazing anger roaring up from the depths of my gut.

The boy stood as well, calm and controlled, standing just under five feet tall. "No. I was sent to keep you safe. I am a shiftshaper. My people call them skinwalkers. I take the shape of the raven, as it is a sacred bird to my people. My job was watcher and protector of my tribe. But my family are long dead, so I work with Zahara." The boy, dark eyes old beyond his years, motioned toward me, insinuating it was my turn.

Holding my anger at bay, I said, "I'm a cursed warrior of Scáthach."

Eyes wide, a smile spread across his face. "Why, I've not seen one of you in many moons. That must mean she is here, causing trouble again."

"You could say that. How long?"

"Since before you were born, that is for sure. You're a new warrior then."

"Why would you say that?"

Gaax walked over to what was left of our fire and sat on Dick's sleeping mat. "Zahara wouldn't have sent me to a seasoned warrior, for he'd not have need of my help. And to be truthful, she'd not have sent me at all if she didn't care what happens to you."

"I see," was all I could say.

"Do you have any food? I'm starving."

"Yeah, I think we have enough breakfast to add you in, if Dick isn't still eatin' for two." I stepped over and sat on my bed roll. "I'll restart this fire if you'll find me some wood."

"Of course," he said, standing.

"Would you like clothes?"

"Why?"

"Oh, I don't know, so your privates don't get caught on sharp plants or get sunburned."

He sighed. "I hate clothes about as much as I hate being tied to the land. I would not have transformed back into this form if I'd not needed to heal."

"I thought I'd healed you."

"By sunrise you'd not completed, so my body automatically began the shift while we were connected. No one has ever been in the gray space with me before and gone unharmed. You are a powerful man, warrior-Henry, even if you do not know it yet."

With that, he walked off to find wood while I contemplated my situation and began to prepare breakfast. When he returned with the wood, he begrudgingly asked for some clothes. I found him a pair of my smallest pants and a belt to cinch them. Once on, he rolled up the bottoms before plopping down on Brewer's bedroll.

Once the fire was ready, I cooked up some bacon, hoping the smell would wake the big lug snoring in dirt like he'd drunk the night away. Thankfully, it did.

With a groan, Dick sat up and looked around. "What the hell am I doing over here, and why does my head hurt? And uh...who is this?"

Gaax waved. "Good morning."

"This is Gaax. He saved our lives last night, you almost shot me, and I knocked you out with the butt of your rifle."

"You what? Why? What smells?"

"If it smells good, it's bacon; if it smells bad, it's one of the two dead wolves, now humans," I said, placing two crispy pieces of bacon on a tin plate with some oatmeal flat-cakes I'd mixed up the night before, and handed it to Gaax.

"You knocked me out and left me over here? Really, now?"

"Do you want to keep bitchin' or have breakfast?"

Dick stopped, eased himself up onto his long yet sturdy legs, and headed toward the campfire like a hungover drunkard. Sitting down next to Gaax, he just stared at him. "Why are you all alone out here...and why are you wearin' Billy's pants?"

"Funny story... We'll eat, and I'll fill you in."

"Why do I have a feelin' that you say funny, but you don't mean it?" Dick said.

I narrowed my eyes at him. "Because, you sleep-walkin' fool, I did not find your gun in my face funny. Now eat and I'll explain."

Once I had caught our resident soon-to-be werewolf up to date, he apologized profusely; as if he got paid each time he said he was sorry. Finally, I had no choice but to forgive the big galoot and just ask he not sleep with a gun for a bit.

After breakfast was done, we packed the wagon for the last leg of the journey up to the caves. I wanted us to be there before sundown.

Looking at our new travel companion, I said, "Are ya comin' with us?"

"I am unable to shift until sunset, or I'll be too tired to fly, so you're stuck with me."

Dick and I shared a look.

"We might want to tell him where we're goin' and why, then," Dick said.

"I already know. Zahara told me that much."

"Well, great," I said, not really meaning it. "Let's all hop up into the wagon and get goin'." Climbing up into the wagon, our teenage guardian found room in the back, right behind the bench, between us so he could see the road.

With a chuckle, I said, "A cursed son of a bitch, a soon-to-be were-wolf, and a skinwalker walk into a bar. What could possibly go wrong?"

"We're going to a bar?" Gaax asked.

"No, just a turn of phrase," I said, snapping the reins on Colonel and Mattie. As they began to pull us back onto the road, I added, "Besides, aren't you a bit young to be goin' to a saloon?"

"I am well over sixty years old. I can go wherever I wish."

"What?" Dick sputtered, almost choking on his sip of water from the canteen.

"We don't age as long as we shift…I've only ever stopped shifting once, when sorrow drove me away from my homeland sixteen years ago. That is when I flew far away from the white man disease that annihilated my people."

"Smallpox," Dick said.

He nodded. "How did you know?"

"Your people aren't the only ones to have died from the disease," I said. "Hell, Dick here was sick with it for a while."

"And you survived?" Gaax asked, obviously stunned.

"So it would seem," Dick replied.

"You must be a hearty and healthy man."

"Well, he did have the help of his mom," I teased.

"Oh, shut it," Dick said.

"The love of a mother is to be cherished. I'm glad she was able to help you survive such a horrible disease."

This sobered my humor. "Yes, yes, they are to be cherished."

"We were plagued with three large outbreaks of this disease, and it killed a fourth of my people, taking all of my family. My father, before he died, ordered me to fly far from the plague, so I did. Unfortunately, I was injured and had to shift back and was found by a member of the Navajo tribe on their trudge to Fort Sumner. I did my best to help them there. I hated seeing our kind treated like cattle. I stayed with them for three years, aging physically to thirteen."

"So that's how you ended up in Lincoln," I said.

"Yes, and I'd have stayed with the family who'd taken me in, but they, too, died, and so I shifted and flew away from that horrible place. When I did, I realized how much I'd missed the sky, and I've not been on land for more than a day here or there since."

Brewer turned to face Gaax, his focus steady on the boy. "You *chose* to be the raven from the beginning then. This isn't a curse set upon you or an infection?"

"No. My family, a part of the Tsimshian Tribe, have always been shifters."

"Where is the Tsimshian Tribe from?" Brewer asked, doing his best to repeat how Gaax had said the tribe name.

Gaax laughed. "That was a good try, Mr. Richard, but it's Tsimshi-an," he said, pronouncing it, t'SHim-SHen. "To answer your question, my family once resided in what is now British Columbia. We lived off the sea and flourished...until the white man came."

He was silent, and neither Dick nor I felt we could do or say much to make him feel better for that, both of us being what killed his family, in a way.

Dick turned back around to face the front and handed me the canteen and I waved it off.

Gaax yawned. "But then I found Zahara's orchard, and I've been with her ever since."

"There is room to lie down back there if you want to take a nap," I said.

The boy hummed in agreement and made himself comfortable on the hay in the bed of the wagon. In no time at all, he fell asleep, and we all headed for an area of the desert that I prayed would be far enough away from people that if Dick lost his soul and I couldn't bring myself to shoot him, that he didn't kill anyone, including me or Gaax.

This was getting more and more complicated by the minute. To hide my growing fear, I sang songs to pass the time. However, Dick was looking worse and worse as we drove. After we'd stopped at a river to fill our canteens, eat, and wash up, Dick swapped out places with Gaax and curled up in the wagon, moaning in pain every now and again.

"The river didn't lower his fever enough. He is still in great discomfort," Gaax said as he climbed onto the wagon seat with me.

I pulled out the pocket watch John had given me. "It's five hours until sunset, so I'm not surprised. If we're lucky, we'll be at our desti-nation in the next two hours."

"Why do the hours to sunset matter?" Gaax asked.

I clicked at the horses as I lightly snapped the reins, urging them forward. "Because tonight the full moon will rise about fifteen minutes after the sun sets, and that is when my friend will change for the first time."

"And you will use what Zahara taught you to try and save his soul," Gaax offered.

"Yes."

"It has never been done before," Gaax explained to me.

"I know, but I like to be the one who breaks the rules, and dammit, I plan to break this one tonight or..." I let my thought fade away and began to whistle a tune instead. But Gaax wasn't one to accept less than all the information.

"Or what?" he prodded.

I stopped whistling but continued to stare ahead as we headed down the empty, rarely traveled road. Finally, I said, "Or die trying."

And I meant it.

16

FULL MOON

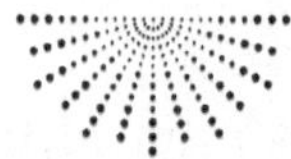

Sweat poured down Brewer's face as I attached the tenth set of chains around his body. "It won't be enough."

"You don't even know if you'll change," I pointed out as I tugged on the chains I'd wrapped around, and slightly under, a boulder. "Do you feel homicidal?"

"At you, maybe."

I stepped back from him and attempted to determine how honest that was.

He laughed. "No, I don't feel homicidal. I just feel...off. Like when I had smallpox. Like I want to scratch my skin off."

"That's disturbing enough."

"Hey, I could want to peel your skin off and eat it, so there's that difference."

"Point taken," I said, and did the one thing he wasn't aware of in the so-called plan: I pulled both guns and sat down.

"What are you doin'?"

"I'm gonna knit a sweater, Dick. What's it *look* like I'm gonna do?"

"The plan was for you to leave."

"No, that was your plan. My plan has always been to see you through all of it."

176

Dick opened his mouth to tell me off, but pain ripped through him so harshly that I could follow the trajectory from beginning to end. Eyes shut, head thrown back, he bellowed out a guttural sound that, if it were something visceral, would've ripped through flesh and bone, piercing my heart. As it was, mine currently felt as if it beat in my throat, making it hard to breathe. Recognizing my fear, I swallowed it down and waited for him to stop.

Moments later he slumped forward. I rushed to him and again picked up the cloth, soaked it in water, and wrung it out. When I lay it across the back of his neck, he sighed.

"Water," he whispered.

"Sure thing, champ. Hang on." I went to the canteen and poured a mug of water. Bringing it over, I held it to his mouth and helped him drink. He downed the entire thing, and I stepped back. "More?"

He shook his head slightly, still staring down. Drops of sweat fell to the rocky ground from the tips of his drenched waves of hair. I set the mug on a flat rock near the canteen and was about to sit back down when he spoke. Unable to understand him, I moved closer. "What was that?"

"Kill me."

I normally would've had a witty comeback for anyone who said that to me, but not Dick. Instead, I just stood there, flabbergasted. "What? No!"

"Please kill me."

"Yes, now that you said please, I'll get right on that," I said, my voice heavy with sarcasm. "Maybe you didn't hear me. I said no. No way in hell, to be specific, and that's where I'm probably headed but no, no, and no."

"Why?" he shouted, his head snapping up, wild eyes staring at me. "I know you know how! Just put the barrel of that silver bullet filled gun to my head and pull the trigger."

"No. That's the end of this discussion."

"Please, William, God, please?" he begged, his voice breaking, tears streaming down his face, now red from exertion. "Please. If I was ever your friend, put a bullet in my brain."

I approached him again, and squatting down in front of him, I lay my hand on his shoulder. "Brother, I'd as soon take my own life as take yours, and we all know I'm not ready to go. I gots me some demons, both figuratively and literally, to deal with first. It's not my time or yours."

After a moment, he nodded. "Just remember, you gave me your word. When I change, if it's not me anymore, if I lose my soul, you don't hesitate. You put a bullet in me. You hear me?"

In no way was I going to kill him. Not unless I had no choice. "I promised then, and I promise now." God help me, I was such a liar.

Not hearing my reservation in that statement, he nodded again. "Good. Good to know."

Silence hung heavy, and I sat down.

"Why are you doin' this?" Dick asked finally. "I'm about to become a demon, a monster you as a warrior of Scáthach are bound to kill on sight. That's the balance."

I picked up a small rock and rolled it about in my hand as I spoke. "Who says these men are demons? Fuckin' Garrett? Does he know for sure? When Charlie shot Baker, you remember he wasn't dead yet."

"I know."

"Well, his eyes looked at me in fear and knowledge as I lifted my gun on him. I think his human mind was present in that form." I threw a rock, still feeling the anguish from pulling the trigger that day. "Damn it, Dick. I think it's a curse, not a possession. I'm not killin' demons so much as men cursed...I'm killin' men like me."

"Not like you. I'm not about to be like you. I'm about to become a monster from storybooks and you...you just get to live forever!"

"You think that's a gift?" I screamed as I stood. "It's not! I already watched my mother die. The idea that anyone else I care about leavin' me terrifies my soul. You may have chosen to run away from your family, but mine were taken!"

"I didn't run from my family."

"From a broken heart then. Whatever. You ran from a nice home where you were loved. You weren't abandoned by everyone you thought loved you!"

"No, just by the one person who mattered most, the one I thought I'd spend my life with."

His voice was so steady and quiet I knew I'd stepped on something that mattered. Even so, I pressed. "Has it ever occurred to you that had to happen so you'd be here, with us? That you have a greater purpose than marryin' a woman who wasn't smart enough to keep you?"

"She was all I ever wanted," he said, voice cracking. "Matilda and I were a pair from our early teen years. She was supposed to be with me through it all, and she married my cousin."

Now I knew he was feeling like death because he was opening up to me about things he'd told no one before. Deciding it was best to keep his mind on anything except the possible change, I quietly said, "Did she say why?"

"She felt pressured into our marriage. Like everyone had decided on it but her." He shook his head. "My cousin was a bit older than me, like Matilda, and had more money. Plus, they shared a love of books and the city. The idea of bein' a farmer's wife wasn't who she was, or so she said the night she ended it.

"Thing is, I'd talked about nothin' else but my own farm for years. She knew where my heart lay, yet she kept me thinkin' we were meant." He fought to swallow and then added, "She also felt I was too much of a lone wolf, her words." To this, he burst out laughing. "If she only knew, right?"

"Dick, you may not—"

"Stop!" he yelled at me, his blue eyes lightening up to glow. "Stop lying to me like she did!"

I looked at my watch; it was ten after six. The sun would set fully any moment, and the full moon would rise fourteen minutes later. Those fourteen minutes were to be his most painful, and deep down, I knew it.

"Yes, you're right. I'm lying, but not to you, to me. I'm lying to myself because the idea of having to shoot you is not something I can bear."

Dick breathed in, wheezing like my mom had when her lungs hurt.

Exhaling, he made the same sound. "You shoot me if I hurt you or anyone else. You hear me?"

"Yes," I muttered.

"You hear me?!" he screamed in agony.

Tears came to my eyes, but I held them back as I saw hair begin to grow on his neck and chest. I'd not cried since my momma died, and I wasn't going to start again now.

"Yes! But damn it, Dick, you stay you!" Though fear coursed through me, the idea the Zahara had given me rang through my mind. I had one shot, and I was going to take it.

I grabbed the mug of water and dumped it out. Pulling the knife from my pocket, I drew it rapidly across my wrist and let the blood pour into it until the wound healed. I then poured some into my empty mug and added water. The scent hit Dick just as the sun went down, and his eyes hit the full fever glow, a blue with silver behind it, like the moon shone from behind his eyes.

Another wave of pain hit, the full moon now rising. Dick dropped to his knees, chest out, arms splayed to the sides as he threw his head back in excruciating pain. He yelled out Matilda's name, and my heart broke for him.

As this wave of pain let up, he sat back on his heels and tears slid down his face, arms limp at his sides but fists clenched. If I was going to try, now was my only window.

With the courage of ten men, I approached the changing werewolf with both mugs, unsure when Dick would cease to be, and said, "Do you trust me?"

Panting from pain, he nodded, and I set both mugs down. Without waiting for him to ask for something to drink, I grabbed the mug I'd added water to and brought it to his lips. Without second-guessing the contents, he allowed me to pour the bloody water down his throat. After I'd gotten enough down him, he tasted it and knocked the mug away.

"What are you doing?" he growled.

"I'm tryin' to save you," I said, coating my palms with the remaining blood and placing them on either side of his long face. "The only way I was told how." Concentrating on the energy stored inside me, I pushed some of that into Dick, and said, "So given to me, I give to you freely, out of love for you, my brother, my family, my friend. This gift is yours."

For the first time ever, the transference of energy hurt like the dickens. I shouted out, fighting to keep my palms on his face.

Dick's eyes once again grew large and began to glow as he placed his great paws on my hands, and this time they really were paws. Before my eyes, I watched bones break and shift as fur sprouted under my hands and his face elongated, coming toward me with teeth the size of a shark's.

Finally, the energy stopped its transference, and I backed away quickly. Reaching the two pistols I'd set on the rock on the other side of the cave near the exit, I picked them both up. Turning to face my friend, his body began to change. Bones broke, shifted. Muscles detached, moved, adhered to the new form.

Once he had completely changed, Dick stood there on all fours, breathing hard, and he was massive. Obviously large human bone structure equated to the same in wolf form. However, due to muscle restructure, the chains I had attached to his wrists and ankles had snapped, and he stepped out of them, leaving only the ones around his neck and his center attached.

Head low and eyes on me, he growled and lunged, the neck chain holding him back while the center one slipped down near his rear. He snapped large jaws in anger, and with a wiggle of his behind, the next to last chain slid off.

"Aw shit," I muttered to myself and began to back away, toward the cave opening.

The wolf growled and pulled again, putting immense stress on the thickest chain of them all, the one around the boulder.

"That's my exit cue!" I said, then turned and ran down the shaft and into the bright moonlight.

Following the plan to a tee, I holstered one gun and tucked the second into my belt before I began to climb up the mountain. There was no way a wolf could scale up the same wall, so once I reached the first plateau, I stopped to wait.

A roar from within the cavern sounded and made me shudder. Moments later, Dick ran out into the moonlight, raised his nose to the sky, and damn it if he wasn't beautiful. He stopped dead in his tracks to howl at the moon, I got a good look at him. His fur was a dark gray-tipped silver with what appeared to be flames of a lighter silver shooting up his face, starting at his nose, which scented me out right away.

He turned to me and huffed. Shaking his head, he tried to remove the iron, but it just caused the tail of chain to swing round and smack him in the ass.

I laughed and I shouldn't have. He turned toward my direction and growled, blue eyes so bright they glowed in the dark. Tracking the sound, he found me. Lowing his head slightly, he bared his teeth for a moment before he ran at the wall. Leaping up toward me, he tried to get to the cliff I rested on and almost made it, scaring the piss out of me. He tried two more times before he stopped, howled, and without warning, ran off.

The quark-quark of the raven sounded as Gaax flew over me.

"Follow him!" I shouted.

Gaax answered and disappeared.

I sat back and sighed but stayed alert another half hour. But nothing happened. I was about to kick back for some rest when I heard a noise from above. Pulling my gun, I backed up near the edge and looked up to find a pair of blue eyes staring down at me.

"Dag-nabbit, Dick. How the hell did you...? Aw, never mind. Are you gonna come down here and try to kill me or what?"

Gaax sounded a warning cry as he flew over me.

"You're a little late, bird boy," I muttered. "I see him."

The wolf let out a bark that for the love of the Almighty Creator sounded like the word "help." Next thing I knew, the chain to his neck shackle dropped over the edge.

"You want that off, I take it?"

The wolf shook his head before laying on his belly, using his paws to try and remove the shackle.

"Okay, but I'm staying down here." I holstered my gun and grabbed the chain good and tight. "Pull!"

Without waiting to be asked twice, Dick pulled by backing up. Problem was, with the leverage of being above me, he was stronger by far. Before I knew it, my feet were pressed against the wall for more resistance, and then I was walking right up it.

I thought of letting go and falling, but there was no promise I'd land on that ledge and stop. I lifted up a prayer and went to meet my friend or my death. It all depended on if my earlier theory was correct, and I wasn't right that often. I expected the worst as I flew up the side of the mountain, my heart racing as I prepared to pull my gun as the top approached.

I placed the center of my boot on the edge of the cliff, and as soon as the momentum vaulted me upright, I let go of the chain, stood my ground, legs apart, and pulled both six-shooters.

Dick flew backward. Landing, he shook off the fall and stood on all fours, staring me down before slowly coming toward me. Was it a ruse, or was Dick still in there? I had to know.

I cocked both pistols. "That's far enough." But he kept coming, and I held my ground. "If you are trying to force me to kill you, think about Matilda. How do we tell her you died?"

This stopped him completely. He laid down on his belly and crawled toward me.

"Well I'll be...it is you in there." I holstered my weapon and knelt, setting my second weapon on the ground. The wolf lay his long nose at my knee and whimpered as he tried to pull the shackle off. "I'll get that, Mr. No-Thumbs."

Pulling the key from my pant pocket, I slowly reached to the metal ring and unlocked it. Opening the hinge, I tossed it aside. Without warning, the gratitude of the wolf part of Dick's brain won, and against the human side's better judgment, he sat up and licked my face in appreciation.

"Oh man, you did not just do that!"

The wolf looked as disgusted as I felt, and I had to laugh. "You should see your face! Oh man!"

His eyes narrowed at me, and I halted my laughter. Without knowing how much control Dick had over instinct, I thought it best to behave.

"No, really, you should see your face. The pattern on your face is like flames." Fascination won out over caution, and I reached one hand toward his face. Surprisingly, he didn't move. "The pattern is so striking and unusual, I wish you could..."

I stopped as I lay my hand on the pattern to find it matched exactly. I put my other hand in place and muttered the words from earlier, "So given to me, I give to you freely, out of love for you, my brother, my family, my friend. This gift is yours."

The energy inside me slid into the wolf and back again, taking my breath away.

"What was that?"

"I don't know," I replied and then realized no one had spoken, unless... "Uh, Dick, did you just ask me a question?"

"Can you get your hands off my face? You mean that kinda question?"

I let go of his face, and he now looked back at me in a weird way. Silence held steady as we stared at each other. He barked, and it was just barking. I understood nothing, so I reached out and touched his body. "Bark again but mean something by it."

He huffed and barked. "I meant something just then, thank you very much. This is ridiculous."

"It is not ridiculous."

"You can understand me?"

"Hot damn! I can! But only when I'm touching you."

"Have you been able to, with any of the other wolves?"

"No, but I tend to shoot them if they're this close."

"Good point."

"I have no idea what happened. Maybe it has something to do with my blood or the energy I used as you changed. My plan was to stop the process, not alter it."

"Well, looks like your plan failed." With that, he stepped away from me and walked to the edge of the cliff as Gaax called to us and swooped down to sit on my shoulder.

"He's himself. That part worked," I told Gaax.

The raven's head bobbed up and down, his feet tapping out a happy dance before he flew off.

I have no idea how long Dick stood there, but I sat quietly by. He lifted his nose to the sky at one point and howled into the night, a cry of sorrow if I'd ever heard one. I said nothing. He was right; I'd failed him. I'd not stopped the change, and though he had his wits about him, would he when Scáthach called? That alone dug at my core like an icepick, and if it hurt me that badly, I didn't dare think of how he felt.

I eventually let him lead me the long way back down to the cave we'd started out in. He stayed outside while I lay my bedroll out inside where it was warmer. Unable to sleep at first, I tossed and turned, eventually falling asleep.

I woke to find the sun already over the horizon, filling the front of the cave with light. I looked to see where the wolf was to get a shocking view.

"Well damn, Dick, aren't you cold?"

Dick Brewer, all six-foot-three of him, lay naked on his bedroll that I'd laid out next to mine. Thankfully, he was curled up on his side with his back to me.

I tossed my blanket over him and headed out to go take a piss. When I returned, he was still out cold. I stole his blanket from his pack in the corner and lay back down to catch a few extra hours of rest seeing as it was another full moon tonight.

He was still out when I woke for the second time, so I headed out to hunt. Only once I walked back in with Gaax on my shoulder and some dead rabbits in my hands did he sit up.

"What time is it?" he asked, voice deep and gravely.

"Wow, you sound like you're hung over," I said. "It's around three."

"In the afternoon?" he asked, obviously shocked.

I put the rabbits down. "Well, you probably didn't pass out until the moon went down shortly after sunrise, so I'm not surprised."

He rubbed his face. "Any chance you made coffee?"

I chuckled. "Sure, hours ago, while you got your oh-so-naked beauty sleep. That was not what I expected to wake up to. Talk about a moon..."

Dick looked down and realized the truth of the matter. "Where are the clothes I had on when I changed?"

I sat and Gaax flew over to the bowl of water I'd set out for him earlier. "It's no big deal, Dick. We all been traveling together for a while, bathing in rivers and stuff. It ain't like I've not seen all the Regulators naked at one point or another. Just wasn't expecting you to be all curled up next to me. Didn't know ya felt that way..."

"I don't..." he sputtered. "I'm not...you thought that I...?"

"Hey, it's fine by me if you swing that way, I don't, but I'd love ya anyway, big man."

He stood in frustration, thankfully holding the blanket in front of him. "I would not make advances on someone in that manner, even if I was like Murphy!"

I couldn't hold it in any longer and burst out laughing.

Realizing my joke, his brow furrowed, and a light growl escaped him before saying, "Oh, fuck you!" To emphasize his annoyance, he threw the blanket over my head. "I'm gonna take a piss. You want to live through the night, you better make some damn coffee!"

Guessing he'd walked out, I began to laugh so hard my eyes watered. Pulling the blanket from my face, I looked at Gaax. "So worth it."

"*Quark-quark,*" he replied, as usual, but it sounded like laughter to me, and that made me roll in a fit of my own.

17

GEORGE COE'S RIDE FROM HELL

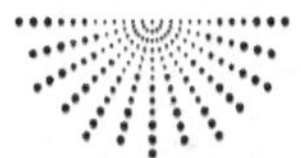

That night's transformation wasn't much easier, but it was faster, and since he wasn't wrapped in chains, he wasn't in a rage afterward. Instead, we worked on discovering his abilities in his new form, specifically how far away he could hear and smell me or food. We hunted and played hide and seek, Gaax joining in on the fun, and that is when everything changed.

Walking around a brush area, trying to find where Dick had hidden, I heard Gaax call out in warning far above me. When I didn't react, my vision shifted, pain radiating through my skull. Losing my footing, I stumbled to kneel in the dirt and rock, blinking my eyes. Closing one and then the other. With my left eye, my sight was normal, yet with my right eye, I saw a different view. I could see exactly what Gaax did, from high above, and that is when I saw two wolves, Dick and a visitor we'd not planned on.

Due to the pattern on his face, it was easy to identify which of the two was Dick. Plus, he was larger than the new arrival. Dick was evident by the pattern on his head, but there was a second, smaller furry friend on the mountain with us.

Trying to figure out where I was in the bird's eye view, I reached up, removed my hat, and waved it. Seeing where I was, I could tell that our party-crasher was closer to me than Dick was. Placing my hat back on my head, I closed my right eye to focus on what was in front of me. Slowly, I pulled my gun with the silver bullets and moved toward the creature quietly, sniffing the air. I opened my right eye and watched the second wolf and I approach one another.

Then, out of nowhere, I saw Dick moving in toward the creature as well. He must've gotten the scent and headed our way. Unsure if he knew where I was, I paused and watched from above in awe of how Dick almost slithered toward the creature, who didn't notice his approach.

Focused solely on me, the smaller wolf didn't notice the threat until it was too late and Dick was air bound, leaping at the creature. Fear at the scuffle gripped me, and before I realized it, I was running toward them.

Arriving, I found Dick holding the living creature in his jaws. The smaller wolf was making sounds like I'd only heard a New Mexican shepherd make, like he was talking. Dick grunted in reply, and I desperately wanted to reach out and touch him to see if I could understand the conversation, but Dick's body language told me to stay put.

Soon enough, he let go of the creature, and it bolted away. I followed it as long as Gaax did and then, suddenly, as quickly as the pain and aerial vision had begun, it stopped. I sat and blinked a few times to regain my bearings as Gaax came and sat on my shoulder.

Turning my head to him, I said, "What was that?"

He pecked my forehead.

"Ow! What the hell was that for?"

Quark-quark-quark!

I sighed. "I don't understand..." I stopped and touched him with my hand. "What was that again?"

This time, as he quarked at me, I understood him saying, "It appears we are connected. I wanted you to see the danger and suddenly you did. The minute the threat was gone, the connection stopped."

"Can you see from my eye when you do this?"

He bobbed his head up and down.

"I can't hear Colonel and I healed his eyes."

"He's not a magical being, nor has something magical connected the two of you," Gaax explained. When I didn't reply, he continued. "I think it is because our right eyes were still connected when in the gray space, so they became permanently linked."

"Permanently?" I said

Gaax's head bobbed but he said, "Most likely."

Dick padded over, and I touched his side with my hand. "Why'd you let it go? Was it a wolf of hers?"

"Yes. He came to collect me."

"And?"

"I sent him with a message." He paused, and I waited. "I told him that if she wants me, she can come and get me herself."

I whistled long and low. "She's gonna be mad as a March hare."

The three of us just sat there for a moment.

"Well, we still have a few hours of moonlight, so let's finish training, specifically this new vision thing."

"Vision thing?" Dick asked.

I explained, then said, "I can't go falling over every time it happens. Let's see how we can use it to our advantage."

We played with this newfound ability and used it, along with Dick's nose, to hunt rabbits until we had enough for me to make us all some dinner. However, though it disgusted the human side of him, Dick realized in this form he preferred his meat raw. I tossed him the biggest rabbit and set to skinning and roasting the others. Gaax, on the other hand, shifted until sunrise so he could eat with me in human form.

Learning from his mistakes, Dick slid under a blanket as the sun rose, since the moon would set twelve minutes later. Wanting to see how the reverse happened, I stayed awake to watch his body shift back into a man. This seemed smoother, less painful, and the minute it finished, he fell asleep.

Thankfully, the next night would be a waning gibbous moon, and he'd only have to transform if he couldn't fight it. Rumor was, even though new, if he stayed focused on something else, he'd be able to stay in human form. For his sake, I hoped that was true.

* * *

By the twenty-third, Dick and I had returned to his ranch since he was able to fight the call of the moon and stay in human form when the moon wasn't full. Gaax didn't come with us however, instead he flew to fill Zahara in on what had happened. The next day, we saddled up and headed to meet with the Regulators in San Patricio as previously planned.

Half a mile out, Dick brought his horse to a halt. "I'm not so sure this is a good idea."

I turned Colonel around and brought him up next to Mattie. "What are you talkin' about?"

He rolled his eyes at me. "Really, Billy? I don't know, what could I possibly be worried about, hmm...I wonder."

"That sarcasm is super thick, even for you."

"Well, if you didn't ask stupid questions..."

"Dick, they won't be able to tell you're a werewolf just by lookin' at ya. Hell, I'm supposed to be the only one who can do that, and I can't yet. So, your secret is safe. Just breathe, okay? Now, you start actin' weird or get that silver glowing-eye-shit goin' on, *then* they'll begin to ask questions. So just relax...and don't piss off any of the dogs."

Dick rubbed his face with a groan. "If my eyes start to glow..."

"I'll double-tap your arm if you're near me. Stomp twice, somethin'. I promise to help."

He thought about it for a moment. "All right then. Let's go."

"Thank you," I muttered, and we headed off.

Arriving in town, we found MacNab had returned, but now Doc was gone. Went to spend time with his family and tend to his farm. But the rest met up behind the church to figure out our next plan of action. This is when we learned about George Coe's run-in with the sheriff.

"He might be primed and ready to join us now," Henry Brown said. "We could use him."

"He and Frank told me in no uncertain terms they wanted nothin' to do with this," I replied.

Fred lit a smoke. "Word from Uncle Ike is he'll be at Newcomb's tomorrow. I say we check in on that again. See if he's changed his mind."

"Then that's what we'll do," MacNab said.

Dick looked at him, raising one eyebrow.

"I mean, don't ya think we should, Dick?"

"Yes, but not all of us. We need to cover more ground. Charlie, Billy, Big Jim, Henry, Middleton, and I will go see what's goin' on with George. The rest of ya stay here and look for recruits. MacNab, you're in charge until I return. Look to the Hispanic community. They sided with Tunstall more than the Anglos, so they'll likely side with us now."

"Sure thing," MacNab said. "What about Doc?"

"We won't be far from his farm. We'll snag him on our way back," Dick said.

"Good. We need all the men we can get," MacNab said. "You think George will join us?"

"If he does, he'll be a solid addition to the fight," Charlie told him.

"Boy, would he ever!" I added.

"And if George comes on board, my bet is Frank will, too," Charlie added.

Frank Coe, born Benjamin Franklin Coe, was George Coe's cousin and friend. The two of them had been living and farming this county for a good spell and made a good life for themselves. They kept their noses clean, which is why I was surprised that Sheriff Brady had anything on George at all.

"Charlie's right," I told them. "I can tell you this—I've been huntin' with both them boys and there's no one better for a long shot with a rifle than the Coe cousins. They're good men and can keep a level head in a fight. They'd be assets for sure."

* * *

Next morning those of us bound for Newcomb Ranch headed off early, arriving at his place around lunchtime. For a man in his late forties, John Newcomb was an agile man with spirit in his step as he answered the door.

"George isn't here yet, but come on in, boys! It's good to have some company."

Newcomb and his wife, Andrea, prepared a hearty lunch for us, and just as we all were sitting to partake, a knock came at the door.

John motioned for his wife to stay seated, stepped up to answer, and in walked a slender man with dark hair, light eyes, a prominent nose, and lips hidden by a full mustache and beard. His kind face was rosy from the wind, and he gave John a smile, but the jovial look that had lived behind his eyes ever since I met him appeared to be missing.

"Well, look what the cat dragged in," Charlie said, getting up and going over to George, embracing him. "How the hell are ya?"

"Aren't you all a sight for sore eyes!" George said, hugging him hard.

"Well come on and sit, eat some grub, and tell us what happened," Charlie said.

"What a fine welcome to raise my spirits," George said, taking off his riding gloves and sticking them in the pockets of his coat.

I smelled blood at the same moment Dick did, and both of us turned heads to stare at his hands. George noticed and held them out for everyone. Encircling both wrists were rope burns that'd torn at the flesh bad enough that the rings of red still wept, blood staining his cuffs.

Andrea stood. "I'll get you some salve for those."

"Mrs. Newcomb, you don't need to—"

"I can't hear you," she said, turning her back to him and heading off.

I fought a grin. "Ya better take a woman's help when she offers it, George, or she'll make ya wish you had."

Everyone at the table laughed.

"Ain't that the truth," George said.

Andrea returned and motioned George over to her. He made a face that made us laugh as he went over. Once she'd cleaned his wounds and wrapped them, he sat down to a plate of food and began to tell us what happened.

"I was workin' in the field when around three o'clock, I looked up to see my house surrounded by a company of soldiers. A sergeant ran up to me with a request that I come to the house. Of course, I went immediately, findin' Sheriff Brady and a company of negro soldiers with him."

"What'd they want?" I asked.

"Well, Brady approached me and said, 'I suppose you know who I am, Coe.' Thing is, sure, I'd seen him and knew who he was, but I'd never met the man. Before I could say squat about it though, he goes, 'I'm the sheriff and a deputy United States Marshal. You may now consider yourself under arrest.'"

Charlie sat his glass of water down so hard some sloshed onto the table. "What the hell for?"

"That's what I wanted to know. Astonished, I said, 'Now, Mr. Sheriff, what have I done?'"

"He had a good reason, right?" I offered.

"Hell, no! Bastard just says that no matter what I've done, I was going to Lincoln that night. And that's when I saw Doc."

"Wait, Scurlock was with the sheriff?" Middleton blurted out.

"Not by his own choice," George said. "I asked him what he was doin' as a part of this party, and he told me, 'Well, I guess I'm goin' into Lincoln with you tonight.' Brady then asked me if I had a horse to ride, and I told him that I didn't, so what does he say? Bastard goes, 'Well, I'm sorry for you, but you're goin' to Lincoln with me, horse or no horse.'"

"How did he expect you to get there? Walk?" Charlie asked.

"That was my fear! I mean, the outlook appeared serious, and I remonstrated, tellin' him I was all alone with no one to watch the property. I thought he'd give me a chance since I'm no criminal or anythin'. But he was indifferent to my plight and said that my neighbors could take care of my place for me since I was goin' to Lincoln. Thankfully, we saw my cousin, Ab Saunders, as we rode by his place, and I shouted out at him to look after my stuff until I got back."

Jim French finally spoke up, going, "Wait, he still hadn't said why he was takin' you in?"

"Nope. He did ask if I had a gun, and I had to hand over my newly purchased rifle. She *was* a beauty! Well-oiled scabbard and well taken care of." George wiped his mouth and tossed his napkin down. "The bastard took it, handed it to a soldier, and I was an idiot who exclaimed somethin' about bein' careful with it. He then says to me that it made no difference about my gun either."

George rose up from the table and fetched his rifle from where he'd set it. Bringing it back to the table, he said, "Scabbard is gone. Some wretch stole that for sure. The rest looks like this now." Holding it up, we all could see that it was scarred and crisscrossed with saddle marks. More than one of us let out a low whistle at its state.

Shaking his head in frustrated sorrow, he put it back and returned to the table. "And that's not even the worst of it. He ordered me to get up behind Scurlock on his little Spanish bronc. Poor thing was havin' a hard-enough time with Doc, but now had to also try and carry my one-hundred-and-sixty pounds as well?"

"Wait, where'd he sit ya?" I asked.

Newcomb piped up on this. "Behind Doc on the *bare* low back of the horse."

Horror of this memory registered on George's face, the way it does to any man when they remember excruciating pain. "That'd be correct."

We all winced and groaned with our friend. It was a thirty-five-mile ride to Lincoln from George's farm, and being cowboys ourselves, we understood better than most the misery of riding behind another man on a lean, little pony without the comfort of a saddle blanket.

"Sadly, it does not stop there. It was rainin' and dark by the time we reached the big hill about two miles from your place, Dick, and the officers decided to take no chance of Doc and I makin' a break for freedom in the dark of the night. Brady called a halt and said to the sergeant to tie up the prisoners."

I set my fork down, for I could no longer eat a thing, my stomach turning about from what George had gone through.

"They used horse hobbles to tie Doc's and my feet under the horse's belly. Then they had me wrap my arms around Doc's waist, binding my hands together with bed-cord. We rode that way in the drizzle, which caused the cords on my wrists to tighten, for three more hours. It was the ride from hell, boys. And I'll admit, I forgot my pride somewhere between bleedin' wrists and an achin' rear end. I turned to a sergeant and asked him to tell Brady I'm bein' tortured, the cords had to come off my wrists."

"What did he say?" Charlie asked, his voice an acidic growl.

"What do you think he said? That he was obeyin' orders and that he couldn't ask."

"Sons of bitches!" I blurted out, standing up to pace about.

"I even sent word to Lieutenant Smith, for I know him personally, and it must've never gotten to him or he didn't care, for I stayed tied up until—"

"Until they reached here," Newcomb said.

"By then, I won't lie, I was cryin' aloud in pain. Seein' this, Brady finally softened and asked John to give me a bed, supper, and breakfast and charge it to the county."

Newcomb stood now, too, and selected two more logs for the fire. "I got in Brady's face and gave him a verbal lashin' about how I'd never seen George so badly in need of a little consideration and help...and that I'd not charge anyone anythin' for lookin' after a friend and neighbor. The nerve of that man..." He tossed the logs into the fireplace, sparks shootin' out like an extension of his anger.

"You're a good man, John," George said. "You made sure the rest of the way I had a horse and a saddle. Thank you. I promised you I'd return him and that's why I'm here today."

"As if helpin' find Tunstall and bringin' him back to town for a proper burial wasn't enough to upset *The House*, you did this, too?" Big Jim said, breaking his silence. "You must not fear the law of this county much."

"He's not the law; he just wears a badge," Newcomb grumbled as he sat back down.

"Truer words were ne'er spoken," I said.

"Well, if there's ever anything we can do for you, John, all you have to do is ask," Dick said.

Newcomb replied by just giving Brewer a nod.

"So, what was the charge, George?" I asked.

"Well, when we got in front of the Justice of Peace, it was stated that Doc and me were harborin' murderers. They placed us under a bond of a thousand dollars each, and we were told to appear at the fall term of court."

"A thousand dollars! Are they crazy? Where was you gonna get that?" Middleton exclaimed.

"And that's not countin' the bail money. I went down to Isaac Ellis' store with the bailiff and poor Isaac, I unloaded all my anger at him. Poor man, he just stood there and let me spit bitter venom about revenge. I told him if he'd let me have a Winchester and a hundred cartridges that he won't need to go post bail for me, I'll just sell out and kill 'em all. It would cost me my life, but I'd have done it, boys."

"I don't blame ya, George!" I said.

"What did Uncle Ike say?" Charlie asked, usin' our nickname for Isaac Ellis.

"You know Isaac...he was the voice of reason for me. He was all, 'my boy, I know just how you feel, but you mustn't do it. I can't let you throw your life away or get into a shootin' scrape either. I'll pay your bail and you go on back to your ranch. This'll all wear off in a few days.'

"I tell you, I was blind with rage. If I'd not loved and respected Uncle Ike for so many years, his words wouldn't have carried any weight, but they did. Finally, he made me agree not to go kill them bastards right then and there."

"Can't say I'd have had the same restraint, George," I said. "No way in hell."

"I told him he'd been a father to me for years and that I'd take his advice. But he was dead wrong on one score. There won't be any wearing-off with me. This affair has been rubbed into my very bones, and it's there to stay."

All the Regulators at the table made noises of agreement.

"Either way, he accompanied me to the Justice's office to pay bail and get my gun. When I asked for it, well, you saw what they gave me back. If Uncle Ike hadn't held me back, there wouldn't have been no sheriff on duty today. So, boys, I'm with you now no matter what comes. The first hard day's work I do, I am goin' to get that bunch at Lincoln."

It was silent for a moment, and I sat on a stool by the fire. Quietly, I said, "They've killed Tunstall, the first man to treat me as one myself, and they've darn near killed George, one of my best friends." I pulled my ivory-handled pistol and laid it on my lap. "George, I'll bet you my pistol against five cents that I'll get even with that outfit before you do."

George laughed. "All right, Billy, I'll just call your hand on that."

Dick took that moment to make the pitch. "George, we want you to join us. You're the best rifle shot in the county!"

"I can't go with you now. I've got to walk back home and do somethin' with my stuff first."

"Walk?" I said. "No need for that. Tunstall has a lot of horses at Brewer's, which ain't far from here. We'll go fetch you a mount for your journey home. When you're ready to join us, you send word."

"Thank you, Billy. I will."

Brewer and I fetched George a horse from Tunstall's herd and headed back to Newcomb's with that mare in tow. Not wanting to be away from his farm any longer than he already had, George thanked us and headed off alone. But not before warning us of how they were looking for large groups traveling on horseback and to be careful.

Hearing this, Dick and I decided to cut our numbers, sending Middleton, Henry, Charlie, and Big Jim back to San Patricio to warn the rest. Dick and I though, we decided we should go check on another member of our team, and off we went to check on Doc Scurlock. We were hoping he'd be able to come back out and join us, but we'd have to wait and see.

18

HOPE YOUR WELL ISN'T DRY

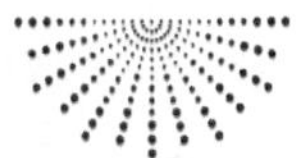

Dick and I arrived at Doc's ranch late in the day and we were downright pleased to see he wasn't in as bad of shape as George. His dogs, on the other hand, were sure riled up at our arrival, though. Or rather, at Dick's arrival.

"Quiet down, ya mangy mutts!" Doc shouted. "What's wrong with them?"

Dick cringed.

"Ya stupid mongrels, it's just Billy and Dick, you know them!"

Dick crouched down and stared at them a second before dropping his head to look at the ground. Surprisingly enough, they calmed down.

"No idea why that worked, but you always did have a way with animals, Dick," Doc said. "Come with me. I got a few more chores left."

Dick stood, and though they were quiet, the dogs kept their distance as we all headed into the stable. I wanted to say something encouraging to Brewer, but I didn't know what to say to make him feel better, or more human, so I patted his shoulder when Doc was turned about. Dick nodded at me, and I had to hope my sentiments were understood.

"I'm glad you two are here," Doc said, grabbing a bale of hay and tossing it into a stall. "I've set all affairs here in order 'cause we've got work to do. Tomorrow we should start headin' to San Pat. Stop a few times along the way. See if we can't pick ourselves up some more Regulators from men I know and trust."

"If you trust 'em, so do we," Dick said.

"Good to know." Doc looked at the sky and added, "Sun's settin'; we should get in."

I pulled out my moon cheat sheet from my vest pocket. "Moon rise isn't until about half past one in the mornin', so let's tend to all your horses here before we head in. Moon don't set until eleven tomorrow mornin', so we'd be smart to get a late start." This way Brewer would also be in the right state of mind and not a walking stick of dynamite.

Doc wiped his hand on his trousers. "Sounds good. Best we not leave the farm until those soulless bastards can't shift. Good thinking."

Dick flinched, but Doc missed it.

"I'll tend to my last horse here and then we can head on in for some dinner," Doc continued. George stopped by on his way home and told us you all was comin'. Antonia's parents are here spendin' time with their grandbaby, so she offered to make us up a nice dinner. She also prepared some sleepin' quarters for you both. Come on, if we don't have time to be cleaned up right and proper for supper, she'll have my ass."

I laughed. "God bless your wife!"

"I say that every day," Doc said with a grin, exposing the two missing front teeth he lost in a shoot-out in Mexico over a game of cards. "Please feel free to tend to your horses and get them settled for the night while I see to my pregnant mare here at the end of the row. That way we should be on time for supper."

Once everything was squared away in the stable, we headed in to clean up and enjoy a nice hot meal with the Herreras; Doc's wife, who was pregnant again; and their seven-month-old daughter, María Elena. We stayed up for a drink or two with Doc's father-in-law, Fernando, before heading to bed, seeing as we weren't getting up as early as usual tomorrow. Dick, however, excused himself after the first drink, heading to bed around the time the moon rose.

"He all right?" Doc asked as he handed me a new beer.

"Just on edge a bit. Been feelin' under the weather on and off ever since gettin' the smallpox back in December."

Doc sat in his rocking chair and drank. "If you say so. He just seems...different."

My heart began to beat harder, and I took a slow breath in and out to settle my nerves. "He's fine. Just gettin' used to this lifestyle. You know Dick, he's a lone wolf...used to it just being him and his animals on the farm and comin' into town when he was in the mood to see folks. Now we're up his ass day and night. Can't fault the man for wantin' some time to himself."

I tilted the bottle up to hide my face from the firelight, so if any of my lies were visible, he'd not see them. Not that I was full out lying to Doc, but that wasn't the difference Doc was noticing, and I had to hope my half-truths pacified him well enough.

They seemed to, and as his father-in-law returned from taking a leak, Doc asked me to tell one of his favorite stories from my past. Happy to change the subject, I obliged, and we all headed to bed a little drunk, sore from laughing, and thoughts of Dick's odd behavior forgotten...or so I hoped.

* * *

Nine in the morning came earlier than I'd have thought, what with staying up late, but by ten we were outside starting to prep the horses for the trip when Doc's dogs began going haywire. Without hesitation, Dick and I pulled our guns loaded with silver and stepped over to the door of the stable.

"They seem to dislike somethin' more than you two yesterday," Doc teased, having no idea what he was saying.

Dick and I shared a worried glance.

"Stay here, Doc," I said. "Dick?"

He holstered his gun. "I'll go high."

I nodded, and he ran for the back exit of the stable. Once I noticed he'd gone out, I listened and heard him when he landed on the roof. Taking that as my cue, I stepped out and sniffed the air. I caught the approaching wolf's scent in seconds. He wasn't even trying to hide it, which I thought odd. I smelled a second werewolf as well. Brewer had somehow removed his clothes quick enough to shift. He now sat hunched on the roof, ready to strike if needed.

I looked up and caught his eye. He motioned with his nose out to the right and I nodded. We both smelled him coming from upwind, like an amateur. In moments, he was visible, running full tilt in our direction. However, he wore something I'd never seen: a white bandana. I held up a hand to signal Brewer to stay put and heard him growl. He'd stay put for now, but I knew he was itching for a fight after a night of restless sleep. And Doc as witness or no, I was pretty sure Dick would jump into the fray no matter what.

Reaching the ten-foot mark, the werewolf stopped and bowed at me. In doing so, I noticed that at the back of the bandana was a small tube. Carefully, I approached the animal and, while keeping my gun trained on him, reached for it. It clicked open as if by the magic of my touch and exposed a scroll.

I pulled it out and closed the wooden tube. The wolf backed away, head down, and waited.

Unrolling the scroll, I read and cursed quietly before saying, "Tell her I'll be there."

The wolf stood, bowed his head in understanding, turned, and ran off.

Looking up to the roof, I saw the quizzical look on Dick's face. He was not going to be happy.

* * *

Ya sure about this?" Doc asked as we reached the turn off for Lincoln on the twenty-eighth.

"No," I lied. "But Brewer will be with me, so I've got backup." Another lie. I wasn't letting him anywhere near her.

"There is no backup equal to her," Doc whispered.

"That's what I told him, too, but he doesn't seem to think she's called him to kill him," Dick said. "Funny thing is, I agree with that...but plans can change when someone makes you upset."

"You say that like I'm gonna go in there and purposefully make her mad," I told him.

Dick raised an eyebrow. "What you plan to do and what you do are not always one and the same thing, Billy Bonney."

I rolled my eyes. "Scáthach has no interest in killin' me just yet, or she'd have done it by now. We'll see you tonight, Doc. Now get movin'! If one of us don't show up in San Pat soon, MacNab is gonna send the cavalry to look for us."

Doc sighed. "All right, but you better be right about this."

"If I'm not, you can dance on my grave. Now go!"

Doc spun his pony about and headed toward San Pat while Dick and I headed into the lion's den. Not only were we wanted outlaws, but Scáthach was in town. That would make *The House* either feel more powerful or laid back. It was either the worst or the best time to come into town...and honestly, I had no idea which it was.

Tapping Colonel's sides, I said, "Well, here goes nothin'."

Dick cursed under his breath and followed me into town where we ran straight into Deputy George Peppin and a few of his fellas.

"Well, if it isn't William H. Bonney and Richard M. Brewer..." Peppin said.

"We really don't have time for this," I said. "I was expected somewhere ten minutes ago."

A deputy I didn't recognize stepped forward. "And we got warrants for your arrest!"

"Didn't I just say we didn't have time for them right now?" I asked Dick.

With a grin, the big man pulled his gun with lead in it. "I don't think they heard you."

"I don't either." I pulled my lead-filled gun as well, and we both began to fire at Peppin and his deputies' feet.

The useless whelp that he was, Peppin ran for cover, and so did the rest of his men. Not waiting for them to make decisions, Dick and I rode through town like a bat outta hell and onward to a bar in Capitan where I was told to meet Scáthach.

I pulled Colonel up to a halt near the turn off to the Salazar property and looked down at Mattie's front right hoof as Brewer came to a stop. "Go see Eugene and tend to Mattie's shoe. She threw one back there."

"I thought you said I was your backup."

"To be honest, I don't want her near you. I don't want her knowin' your soul is free or why. Not yet. Please go take care of Mattie, and I'll come back for you."

"And if you don't?"

"Then you can dance with Doc on my grave," I said, and without waiting for his reply, I shouted as I hit Colonel's sides with my heels, and we were off to see the devil.

* * *

When Sheriff Ortiz informed the waitress at the Capitan diner that this was a working lunch, she sat us in a back corner away from everyone. We sat at a booth, and she gave us the specials before heading off.

"I recommend the burgers...you can't go wrong with 'em," he told me.

"I'll take your word for it."

She returned with a Coke for each of us. Ortiz ordered two of the classic cheeseburgers, and she left us alone.

"It's best you know what you're walkin' into in Las Cruces."

"So you said before," I commented.

"Word on the street is that Apodaca has the politicians of Santa Fe in his pocket, and they have him wrapped around their little fingers. The leash is long, but it's there. If they yank, he follows, ya hear me?"

"Loud and clear," I said, thinking about how the Santa Fe Ring and the Lincoln County sheriff were just like that during the Lincoln County War. "I've dealt with crooked law before."

He nodded. "And how did you do?"

"We lost."

"Exactly. The Santa Fe Ring still exists, Agent Kidwell, and the minute you pop on their radar, they'll be watchin' you...especially since you're the law. They're gonna want to know if you're on the right side, the wrong side, or if you're willin' to walk the line between 'em."

He drank his soda and just looked at me, waiting for an answer. If I was honest, I was willing to walk the line a bit...but I couldn't say that.

"I'm on the right side of the law, Sheriff Ortiz."

"Please, call me Sally."

That felt weird, but I nodded anyway. "Sure thing, likewise. I mean, do call me William...or Billy...I answer to either."

"Billy fits your face better." He paused as food was delivered, and I watched as the waitress delivered to us the best lookin' burger and fries I'd seen in ages.

"This looks amazin'," I said, my stomach growling.

"Dig in. While we eat, I'll fill you in on a bit of the gamblin' history out there. When we finish eatin', I'll take ya out to speak to my friend in Capitan, he's from Lincoln. You'll wanna see him before you head out there, too."

I took a bite of the food and hummed in pleasure. Swallowing, I dragged a fry through my ketchup. "And why does this man know so much about what's going on in Las Cruces?"

Sally chewed his food with a grin. Finally, he said, "You wouldn't believe me if I told ya."

"Try me."

"He is one of the last survivors of the Lincoln County War, and he knows a lot about the Santa Fe Ring."

I almost choked on my fry but washed it down and passed it off as shock instead of fear. If this person really was around back then and they recognized me, things were going to get sticky awfully fast...and in Capitan no less. Why was I not surprised?

* * *

Riding into Capitan, I found the saloon Scáthach told me to meet her at and discovered not one horse tied up outside.

Dismounting Colonel, I said, "That can't be a good sign."

Colonel turned his head toward me.

"No witnesses," I explained.

He whinnied and pawed the ground twice.

"I'll be careful. But if she comes out the front before me, you get outta here fast. Go find Dick and bring him back here, you understand?"

He pounded the ground once.

"Good."

With a deep breath, I crossed myself like the Catholic I'd been and walked into the dark saloon. The only people there was an older gent behind the bar, likely the owner, and a woman with dark hair piled high, sitting on a stool at the bar. She wore a dress of dark blue, complete with bustle, and appeared to be sipping whiskey.

Sure, I'd seen her before this. But it'd been dark, she'd worn her hair down, and I'd been more focused on Colonel than her. But now I had a moment, and I stared in disbelief at how exactly she looked like Mary Richards, my teacher from Silver City. But was she really Mary or not? That was the question.

"You're late," she said.

"Ran into a few of your idiots who held us up," I said, hands on my guns as I walked over to and around her, my eyes telling me one thing and my head telling me another. "You're not the real Mary."

"Not in spirit, no. She was herself though, when you first met her, if that helps. But right now, she's...on vacation." The creature laughed, sounding just like the woman I'd cared for, and I gripped my guns tighter as goosebumps traveled up my arms. "Go ahead, shoot me, and you can watch the real Mary die." When I didn't fire, she added, "I thought not. Shall we have a drink?"

"I'm good."

"Ah yes, I've heard you're no fun anymore." She downed the rest of her drink and waved over the bartender. "I'll have another whiskey, straight up, and my friend here will have a water."

The man raised an eyebrow but got to pouring the two items.

Scáthach pulled out a cigarette. Lighting it, she waved the match out, her hazel eyes watching me. "Oh, do take your hands off those. You're not goin' to shoot me, and I'm probably not goin' to kill you. Just sit and relax."

"I can sit, but I won't be relaxed," I muttered as I considered the situation, deciding to do as she said. For as much as I hated to admit it, I wasn't going to shoot her. Hell, I was pretty sure I couldn't even get myself to give her a paper cut. Thus, I took a seat at the bar and waited.

Once we had our drinks, she took a sip and looked at me the way she had when I was a child in her classroom. "You're dyin' to ask, so ask."

"Why me?"

"Because you needed direction. You were a mess."

"Of course I was! My mother had died, my stepfather was useless, and my brother was removed to another family. I had nothin' and no one...and I trusted her!"

"I saw the bond you two had, and for that, I gave you a gift. A rare one at that. I only create an immortal once a century."

"A gift? You call it a gift? It's a curse, and you know it."

She smiled, and it both warmed my heart to see again yet chilled my soul, if I still had one.

"Fine, curse, whatever. Either way, it's a form of checks and balances. My monsters are very powerful, and I own their soul unless you release them."

"You mean, kill them?"

"Is it really killing if their soul isn't there?" she asked with a lazy shrug.

"Then why make someone like me at all?"

"If I didn't create a few avengin' warriors, my monsters would take over the world, and that cannot happen either. It's up to men like you to challenge me, to save me from utter boredom."

"Wait, we're here to entertain you? This is all a big game to you? What are your monsters then, expendable?"

She laughed, and this time it sounded nothing like the Mary I'd known. "Yes, it is, and yes, they are. See, you learn quickly! I always knew you were the smart one."

I thought of Brewer, not far from where we sat, and all he'd gone through over the past month and without using those smarts she'd just praised, knocked the drink out of her hand. It hit the floor with a crash, glass traveling about the floor. The bartender didn't move, nor did she, until the tinkling of the last bit stopped moving.

Once it had, faster than lightning, her hand was on the back of my neck, the pressure created as she squeezed was like nothing I'd ever known. She lifted me off the stool and up onto the tips of my toes. "I sincerely hope your well isn't dry," she said, and broke my neck, dropping me to the ground.

19

FRANCISCO GÓMEZ

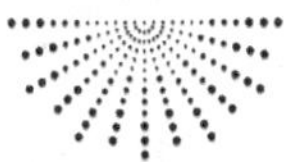

Sheriff Salvatore "Sally" Ortiz and I pulled up to a house of a man I desperately did not want to see me. I'd aged all of a few years since he'd seen me last. Besides, he thought I'd been dead since 1881. In short, this was not going to go well.

Sally turned his car off. "Now, he's old, so you might have to speak up a bit for him to hear you, and sometimes he rambles...but what do you expect, he's in his early nineties."

"And he's from Lincoln, you say?"

"Yeah, family stayed outta the war, but he knew Billy the Kid, the McSweens, and the rest of them. Come on, he's a character." Sally opened his door. "I'll warn you though, he doesn't speak a lick of English...but he understands it pretty well."

I stepped out of the car and shut the door. "I speak fluent Spanish. Have since I was in my teens. I'll be okay."

Sally shut his door. "All right then."

We both headed up to the house, and I had visions of shooting a man in his nineties, knocking out the sheriff, and hauling ass out of town. All of which would be a bad idea, but if this man recognized me, it would jeopardize more than just this mission.

Sally knocked, and an older woman came to the door. She was

209

likely in her early sixties and spry for her age. Her smile lit up her face, and her blue eyes reminded me of someone I couldn't place.

"Sally, what are you doin'? Shouldn't you be keepin' the county safe and all?"

He grinned. "Bess, I didn't know you'd be here. You visitin' with the group? Did Carrie come with you?"

Bess's eyes flitted to me for a moment but returned to the sheriff. "No, she's not here today. Too much goin' on with that brood of hers." Bess looked toward me to explain. "My sister has seven kids not countin' spouses and grandchildren, so you can imagine."

"That I can, ma'am," I said, taking my hat off.

"Me, however, I couldn't pass up on comin' by to see Francisco. You know how much I love his stories."

"That I do. And that's why we are here. To speak to him. Oh, I'm sorry, I've not introduced you. Bess, this is Agent William Kidwell of the FBI. He's my guest at the moment, here lookin' for a fellow agent of his that went missin' a month or so back. He's gonna have to head down to Las Cruces to deal with law there, and I thought—"

"Blimey, that's not where I'd want to be goin', but if I was a handsome young man like you, I think I'd fare better than a woman at my age."

"Oh, don't you start with that age talk, Bessie," Sally started to tell her.

"¿Quien esta en la puerta?" A man shouted a bit too loud for how far he was from us, asking who was at the door.

"And there he is, the wanted man," she whispered to us. Raising her voice, she shouted, "It's Sheriff Ortiz and the FBI here to see you, Francisco. What did you do this time?" Her tone was playful, and the old man who came around the corner using a cane for balance chuckled lightly, his head down.

"¿A mi edad, qué podría haber hecho?" he said.

"I'm sure you could still get in trouble at your age, you silly old man," Bessie said, laying a hand on the man's shoulder as he came to stand next to her.

Raising his head to look out the screen door, his smile at Sally turned to frozen terror when he saw me, and I knew this visit was a grave mistake.

* * *

Everything was dark for a moment. No sound, no smell, no nothing. I didn't even breathe. Then I felt the vertebrae heal, and everything returned. With some difficulty, I stood, found my balance, and glared at her. She sipped a new glass of whiskey, looking as perfectly put-together as before I'd died.

"Sit," was all she said, and I complied. "Now, where were we? Oh yes, my monsters are expendable, and I see this all as a great game. It is true. You see, Henry, I need a challenge. I'm bored, so I wormed my way into the hearts of a few men, and I've started a war. I find it all very excitin'."

She drank again, and I fought everything in me that wanted to pull my silver six-shooter and blow a hole in her head. Instead, I pretended I was Dick. What would Brewer do? He'd let her talk herself into a corner. Hoping for that, I sat there, just breathing.

"What? You don't even want to know which men?"

"Murphy? Catron? Dolan? Dudley?" I offered.

"Dolan? Please, he's an angry, drunk Irishman with a serious temper and God complex...he is a fun pawn to set on his course, but no. Murphy? Maybe. Carton? Kinney? Definitely. Rynerson? Very much so."

"The Santa Fe Ring...that's your construct," I said, realization hitting me.

"Do give the young man a free beer! He is correct!" She laughed, head thrown back, and for a moment, I saw the demon under the skin of the woman I'd loved like a mother. "You don't think men thought up that on their own, do you? I can look like and be whoever I want. I can wriggle into men's dreams and make them believe they've come up with the most marvelous plan..."

She drank again and glanced at me. "Oh, Henry, your rage is so heavy upon you that it's almost a tangible thing. Shoot me if you wish, but you'll kill this body, and I'll find another host. Just think of all I could do if they were a willing one. Mary, well, let's just say she's been difficult."

"Serves you right. Where does her family think she is?"

"Visiting family. Oh, I've not been in here all these years. Only long enough to curse you, as you put it, train you, and then once you ran from Silver City, I moved on as well. I only returned to borrow her for this event. I just wanted to see your face. Besides, the devil you know makes this so much more...fun." A cackle escaped her before she drank more.

"Why not take the face of my mother?"

"I can only be physically present with a breathing human being, but I can exist outside of one and cause harm. However, not with my own two hands, and I do like to get my hands dirty." She downed the rest of her whiskey. "But you can't kill me, Henry. So...what will you do? Wait! don't tell me, I love not knowin'!" She stood and leaned into my face. "We are gonna have such fun, you and I."

She exited out the back of the bar, and I sat there stunned. Can't kill her? I highly doubted that was true. Everything could die, even me, so there had to be something I could do to hurt her. But first, I needed her out of Mary's body. To do that, I need to see a witch. Exiting the bar, I jumped onto Colonel's back and hurried to meet up with Dick at the Salazar place, only to find him dozing under a tree.

"Glad to see you're so concerned about my life," I said. "Is Mattie good to go? We have a long ride ahead of us."

Dick yawned. "Glad to see she didn't kill you...and San Pat isn't that far of a ride."

"She killed me once, but we'll talk about that later. We need to send a note to the boys in San Pat that we'll see them in a few days. We need to go see a witch first...it's time you met Zahara."

* * *

Bessie steadied the old man when he wavered. "Francisco, are you all right?"

He swallowed and nodded, backing away from the door with his wide eyes still on me. Quietly, he muttered words the rest couldn't hear, but I did. "El diablo ha venido por mi."

"I can assure you, Mr....?" I said.

"Gómez," Bessie told me.

I felt my stomach drop to my toes. This man did know me, and I knew him. He'd only been in his early twenties when we'd been acquainted. He'd helped George Peppin build the McSween house. I'd even gone on a hunt for some outlaws with him once.

Everything now depended on how I handled this and what he did with it.

"I can assure you, Mr. Gómez, I'm not here to hurt you or your family." I pulled my badge and credentials, showing them to Bessie and Francisco. "I'm just here for some help findin' a friend and fellow agent."

Francisco stopped backing up, but his gaze bore into me, and I saw he truly had all his faculties. "¿Está aquí para matarme?"

Bessie guffawed. "Francisco, why would the FBI be here to kill you? Now stop that." She looked at me. "I'm so sorry, Agent Kidwell. He's not usually like this." She opened the door. "Sally, do come in. Let me get him settled back down and see if he is of a state of mind to talk to you both."

"Of course," Sally said, and entered the house.

I followed him and quietly shut the door behind me.

"They'll be in the kitchen at the table if they are playing cribbage," Sally explained.

I only nodded and followed along. When we entered the kitchen, Bessie was giving Francisco a glass of water.

"Creo que necesito algo mas fuerte," he said.

Another woman walked out from a back room and said, "No, you don't need somethin' stronger to drink, Francisco. It's just the FBI, and you've done nothin' wrong." She looked to me. "He's not done anythin' wrong, right?"

I laughed. "I'm not here for anythin' he's done, though, I do have some questions for him if he's able."

This wasn't a lie. The last time I'd seen Francisco, he'd been in his early twenties lyin' on the stand to discredit Susan McSween. In truth, I just wanted to know why he'd done that. But more importantly, I needed to hear what he knew about the hold the Santa Fe Ring had on the sheriff of Doña Ana County.

"Quiero hablar con el solo," he said.

Sally appeared perplexed. "You're not goin' to say anythin' I don't already know, Francisco. You're not puttin' me in any danger."

"Quiero hablar con el solo," he said again.

"Well then, let's leave 'em alone," Bessie said, setting a glass of water on the table for me. "If you need anythin' else, please let us know. We'll just be in the livin' room listenin' to The Guiding Light...it's about be on the radio. I'm sure it'll drive Sally crazy." She winked at me and turned her attention to Francisco. "You behave."

He waved her off, and I sat down. Unsure if I should just be honest or if I should lie, I drank some water and let him take the lead.

"Billy," was all he said, and I knew.

"Not here I'm not. It's important you say nothin' to them."

"I heard rumor," he said, struggling for the English. "You survive. You immortal. Evil. The devil owns you."

"She's not the devil, per se. But yes, until I earn my soul back, I hunt her and the monsters she makes. I did that in 1878, and I'm here to do it again. Will you help me?"

He paused, and I could tell he wasn't sure what was best.

"If not for me, for Susan. You lied for the Murphes, Francisco. You let Dudley walk away clean. I don't know why you did that, and that's between you and God. But I need the truth of what you know."

He looked out the window above the kitchen sink. "I probate judge for Lincoln. Four years. Did you know?"

"I did not."

Tears filled the old man's eyes, but he wouldn't look at me. "Took dinero, I did. Lied. Every day I try. Earn absolución. But here you are..." His eyes found mine, and the tears fell.

My heart broke for him, and I reached out and took his hand. "I'm not here to avenge Susan for your lies. I'm not goin' to harm you. I need your help. Can you to fill me in on the Santa Fe Ring's hold on Las Cruces before that radio show is over?"

He nodded.

"And you can do so in Spanish, remember?" I tapped my chest with my free hand. "Lo hablo con fluidez."

A hint of a smile touched his face, and he laid his other hand on top of mine. "Yes. I remember."

"And most importantly...I ridded this land of the wolves that took men's souls before, but if they are back, I must know."

Francisco's hand trembled. "The wolf inside has returned."

I laid my second hand on top of his until it steadied. "Tell me everything you know."

* * *

The sounds of evening filled the orchard with the song of Mother Nature as Colonel trotted in happy anticipation of apples and peppermints. He must've conveyed as much to Mattie, for she, too, appeared eager.

"She spoils you. No wonder you like it here," I said.

Colonel whinnied, shaking his mane, and I couldn't help but laugh as he picked up the pace, no longer in need of being led through the magical group of trees to that spot on the side of the mountain. Approaching the secret entrance, the vines peeled back gracefully, opening without me needing to shout for her.

"It appears someone already knows we're here," I said.

"You sure I'm welcome to enter?" Dick asked.

"If you weren't, she'd have shown up out here instead of opening the pathway for us. This is her orchard; she knows who comes in and out of here the minute they step in."

"Uh huh..."

"Trust me," I said.

Dick only raised an eyebrow. "Nothin' good happens when you say that."

"Not true."

"Want me to give examples?"

"No...just be quiet and follow me."

Entering the enchanted garden of light, the vines quickly closed us in behind Mattie, causing her to swish her tail in agitation.

"Are those bahvah-lamp stones linin' the path?"

"She *is* a witch," I explained.

Unable to keep Colonel from moving swiftly through the forest of light, I whooped with enjoyment as we galloped along the path to the opening of her inner realm. There she stood, arms crossed, and a skeptical look on her face.

"I didn't think you'd bring him so soon."

"I needed to see you, and I thought you two should meet since you—"

"Saved his soul," she said. "Richard Brewer, I presume."

When Dick didn't reply, I turned to see him in wolf form sitting there next to Mattie, his clothes tattered on the ground next to him. His blue eyes narrowed with agitation at something.

"Uh, why did you shift?" I muttered to him, and he huffed in recognizable indignation.

"The same reason you appear different when you step into the clearing," she replied before walking away toward the fire.

I took a step and felt the weight of the leather and chainmail. "Damn it." I began to peel the armor off, saying, "You said this was the inner me...a warrior."

"Yes, and Richard has a wolf within him. Hence, he will be in wolf form when he's in here."

"I see Gaax got the news to you that I saved his soul."

"If you'd not, he'd have died upon entrance."

Dick huffed air out his nose, and if looks could kill, I'd be dead.

"I didn't know that, and you're fine, so stop lookin' at me that way."

With one more huff, Dick stood, sniffed the air, and padded on over to Zahara, who was holding something out toward him. Colonel, thinking this was an invite, also trotted over, Mattie right behind him.

Zahara laid a plate with something on it between herself and Brewer. He sniffed it, and then lay to eat it as Colonel nuzzled her hair. She laughed. "All right, all right, here you go...you and your lady." She stood and directed them to some hay and gave them each an apple before coming back to the fire.

By now, I'd put the armor aside and headed toward the fire in time for Dick to finish eating whatever it was she'd given him and lay down in a happy stupor.

"I need your help," I told her.

"That's what I like about you, Henry. You always get to the point. Well, that and you bring me such interesting visitors." She reached out and pet Dick's face, scratching his ears as he closed his eyes in happiness. She looked up at me. "Tell me about her."

"Her who?"

"Scáthach. You reek of her."

"She has a scent?"

"Evil always has a smell to me. Especially old evil like hers. I'll make you tea. It'll cleanse you so you can be free of the taint she leaves in her wake. Then we can speak of your needs. Meanwhile, talk to me about this pattern on Richard's fur."

I knew not to argue with her, so I set my impatience on the back burner. We had tea as I spoke of how I'd saved Dick's soul.

"My idea worked. By binding his soul to you instead of her he stayed himself."

"Wait, what? That was your plan? Cause, he's not bound to me. He has control of his own choices. I just sorta claimed him, I guess."

"Then his soul is under your protection and care then. Fascinating. You, Mr. Brewer, are one of a kind. I hope you realize what he's done for you. Only someone who truly loved you could have pulled this off."

Hearing this, both Brewer and I backed away from one another as I sputtered something about not being in love with the son of a bitch.

Zahara laughed heartily. "Not that kind of love, you idiot. The love that ties true friends to one another. That, in my opinion, is more precious than the 'in love' variety. It also lasts longer...can stand the test of time and trials of fire." She put her hand out to Brewer again, and he came to lay beside her, his head on her lap. "You are a beautiful wolf. I look forward to seeing your human form."

I finished my tea and set the empty cup by the fire. "Am I clean enough yet?"

She leaned down toward Brewer. "I should make him bathe just to be mean, but I have a feeling you two do not have long to spend with me this time around." Dick chuffed, and she gazed up at me. "Tell me what happened."

20

ZAHARA

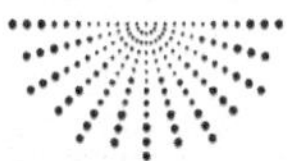

"**S**o...knowing all that, how do I get Scáthach out of Mary's body?" I asked.

Zahara laughed. "Most men want to know how to get a woman out of her clothes...you want her out of the whole body?"

I grinned. "I thought I was the funny one."

She laughed from the gut, and in the echo of it, I heard the chorus of thousands of years of her people. I couldn't help but feel a sense of kinship with her at that moment, and it made me wonder at the level of her power.

"Yes," I continued. "There has to be a way to force her out. I can't hurt her while she is in Mary's body. I just can't."

Zahara nodded. "I understand. But this will take some work. I don't just know this, Henry."

I sighed. "I figured that might be the case. How long?"

"I don't know. But I will begin to work on it. She says she is an unwilling guest, that her host is uncooperative. That'll be the key. That was a bragging error. We'll use it to our advantage. Plus, you know the real name of the woman, and she knows you, so it will help. I promise."

"Good because I'm pretty sure I can't fight her."

"Not the way you think, but you can."

A silence slid comfortably into place as she ladled stew into two bowls, handing me one. "Eat. You look starved, and you'll not train well if you're not fed."

"Train?" I asked as Dick's head came up off her lap to stare as well.

"Yes. Since you are here, and she's stepped up her game, we should train. How are you *without* a gun?"

I laughed. "In case you don't remember my true stature in the real world, I'm a small guy. That's the whole reason I learned to use a gun in the first place. I've never been strong enough to fight a man and win without one."

She stood. "It's not about strength where my family comes from. It's about skill. My father was an Apache warrior who wasn't graced with a son. Because of this, he secretly trained my sister and me. As did my mother's brother, a Dog Soldier of the Cheyenne clan in Colorado. Now I will teach you."

"A dog soldier? What is that?"

A wickedly playful smile touched her face. "A Dog Warrior is a man who his enemies knew was prepared to die trying to kill them. He is skilled in combat, with his own life on the line if he does not complete his task. You are in this same predicament often.

"For you, though, it is a much more dire situation, as it's your eternal soul you fight to save, not just your body. What would you do if attacked by a pack of wolves twice your size? That gun of yours only holds six chances to save your soul; I say we up the odds." She let that hang there a moment before saying, "Shall we begin?"

I stood. "Teach me."

* * *

Not much was said between Sheriff Sally and I on our way back to the precinct. But as we got closer, he finally spoke.

"Did Francisco tell you why he was so afraid of you? The man was a judge; I cannot fathom why he would fear the FBI."

"He felt I was there to punish him for somethin' he did wrong many years ago. I told him that was not the case, that those lies on the stand as a young man were between him and God."

"Francisco would never lie on the stand!" Sally blustered.

"His words, not mine. He was young, caught up in a war, broke, and was tryin' to keep he and his family safe. And it's good he did. Between the information you gave me and what he knew, I'm not goin' to be headin' into Las Cruces blind. Thank you."

Sally's jaw was too set still to say anything, so he nodded.

Once we returned to the court house, he dropped me at my car and told me how to find the B&B that Fletcher had stayed at. I thanked him again and was on my way. I hoped Lois could give me more information on Fletch and let me use her phone. I was going to need help on this, and as much as my partner was going to hate coming back here, I had to call him in.

Man, was he gonna be pissed.

* * *

I ached everywhere the next day. But she healed my muscles, and we began again, with Dick watching and learning. It wasn't just hand-to-hand, but knives as well. I spent the day learning ways to fight as she proceeded to kick my ass repeatedly. Later that day, we went out into the orchard so Dick and I could practice the moves on one another.

It was close to sunset by the time we took a break.

"Have you ever been to Agua Negra?" Zahara asked.

We both nodded.

"Only in passin' really, though," I told her. "Why?"

She handed me two canteens. "Fill these with the black water there."

"What for?" I asked, sitting on a stump to truly rest my aching bones a moment.

"It can help Richard not feel the pull of the moon so much." She looked to him. "You can work up a tolerance to it, so don't overuse it. Also, you must be careful collecting it."

Dick drank from our canteen. Handing it to me, he said, "Why?"

"Not you. It won't work if you gather it. It must be a warrior of Scáthach. But there's a twist. Now that your gift is triggered."

"Curse," I corrected her and drank.

"Fine. Now that your *curse* is triggered, you cannot let the water touch your skin. It can paralyze you."

"What?" I sputtered, almost choking on the water I drank.

"And your body will not recognize that as an invader, and it will not know to heal you."

"So, no touchy the water. Got it. How do I get it into the...never mind, I'll figure it out."

"Maybe you shouldn't bother," Dick said. "I don't need it that bad."

Quark-quark came the familiar cry of Gaax seconds before he swooped in and landed on Zahara's shoulder. Tied around his leg was a small slip of paper.

"What do we have here? May I?" she asked. Gaax held up a leg, and she untied the tiny document. Unrolling it, she handed it to me. "It's for you."

I stepped toward her. "Me? From who?"

"The Regulators."

Quickly, I took the note and read the words Doc had sent us. I looked to Dick. "We've been called to meet with McSween at Uncle John's tomorrow mornin'."

Dick grabbed his shirt from a nearby tree. "I know a shortcut from here."

"Good," she said. "Then you can leave at dawn. The sun is setting, so traveling now is not wise. We'll eat and rest, so you can both leave at sunrise. Come, let's head on in."

Dick stopped in mid-dressing and took the shirt off again with a sigh. "Can I not be in human form this time?"

"I'm sorry, but that's not how Forest of True Spirit works. Besides, if you weren't a wolf, there's a chance you'd have been a lion...count your blessings."

Dick and I shared a glance, but neither of us asked her what she meant, and after collecting our weapons, we headed inside.

* * *

We awoke with the sun and ate. As we did, I asked a question that'd plagued my mind since the night before. "Why do I feel like an old man after yesterday's beatings while you appear even younger now than when I arrived?"

"These two days brought back good memories of my family and renewed my love for them in a way I've not felt since I was a young girl." She laid an open palm on my cheek. "You are far from trained. But you will fare better now. Put what you have learned into practice, warrior child, and return soon. There is still much I need to show you." Then, she spoke the rest inside my mind. "Come alone next time. What I have to teach is for you and you alone."

I nodded. "I understand."

She kissed my other cheek, then walked over to Colonel. With dramatically spread arms, she wrapped around his neck, burying her face in his mane. "I'm going to miss you most of all."

"Wow, really, Zahara?" I said in jest as Dick laughed in wolf form.

She pulled back to look Colonel in the eye. "Don't you pay his crankiness no mind. He's just jealous. It's good for him." She looked over a shoulder at me for a moment before returning attention to the black stallion. Kissing his nose, she ran a gentle hand along his jaw and then leaned to whisper into his ear. Whatever she said won her an enthusiastic whinny and a front hoof pound in the dirt.

I shouldered my bag and headed over. "I hate to take ya from her, pal, but we gotta go." I tied my bag onto the side of his saddle and swung up into its seat. "I'll be back for more training when I get a chance."

"You mean, you'll be back to get your ass beat by a woman as soon as your pride heals," she said with enough sass that I knew she was just trying to get my goat.

"You aren't wrong," I replied with a hearty laugh as I led Colonel in an arch to turn him toward the exit.

"Come on, Dick, time to be a man again."

With happy panting, he ran up, licked Zahara's face when she bent down to say goodbye, and then headed off into the garden of light.

"He really hates being a wolf," I said.

"I know, but he'll learn to love what it gives him."

"When?"

"In time."

I snorted a laugh. "Well, we know we both got a lot of that now, Don't we?"

"In theory," she replied.

"Hey, everything works in theory," I said with a silly grin on my face. "Come on, Mattie."

The bay mare accepted hugs and an apple from Zahara before following us out through the garden and into the dawn. Richard stood there, now in human form, buckling his pants. Grabbing his shirt and coat, he slid them on and smiled at Mattie as she trotted to him. It'd taken her a bit to get used to his new smell, but she now had no problem with him.

"There's my girl. Let's show these two a shorter way to Uncle John's than they know." He hoisted himself into the saddle and got a good hold on the reins.

"You think you know a faster route?" I asked. "Well then, lead away!"

* * *

Dismounting from Colonel at South Spring Ranch, the black beauty pranced about with Mattie at his excitement to get a rest. As farmhands took him and Mattie for some water, food, and a healthy rubdown, Dick and I wandered toward the house. Not even to the gate yet, we heard the pounding of hooves behind us.

Turning about, we saw a group of men on horseback trotting toward the ranch. Dick and I shared a glance of worry, so I cupped my mouth with my hands and let out a loud whooping call, only to have it answered in kind, telling me it was none other than my pal Charlie Bowdre and the rest of the Regulators.

"Looks like they got a few more recruits," Dick said.

"Looks like." I turned to him. "You okay?"

"Don't I look okay?"

"No. You look like a pig when its intestines are tight."

"Oh, the imagery," Dick muttered.

"Well, ya do. Now listen here...you did fine last time, and you'll do so again."

"More people. More to notice I move different or that dogs are strange around me or—"

"Stop," I begged, holding the 'o' out longer than usual. "I've got your back. Remember the deal? If I notice somethin' is off, I'll double-tap your arm or stomp twice or somthin', okay? Besides, it feels good to be back to normal life, don't it?"

He huffed a short laugh. "It does." With that, he dropped the topic and walked toward the arriving Regulators with his usual swagger, which I'd not seen since February.

I looked back at Uncle John's one-story home to examine it for weaknesses like Zahara had taught us. Smoke coiled out of both chimneys, which were equidistant from either end of the long building. This made me eager to get out of the damp chill of the morning and inside the warm, dry home where Miss Sallie had likely prepared coffee and cakes for us all.

Anxious to head in, I turned my attention to my arriving compadres. Dismounting from their horses were Charlie, as suspected, Doc, MacNab, Middleton, Fred, Henry, Big Jim French, and a new addition, Joe Smith. I noted also that Chavez y Chavez and a few other Mexicans I knew were bringing up the rear.

Charlie dismounted, his auburn hair catching the sun as he took off his hat to resituate it on his head. "Glad to see you got our message. Was wonderin' if you'd beat us here." He clasped hands with Dick. "Good to see you're both all right. Doc here told me you had a meetin' with...you know."

"That went as well as could be expected," I said.

"She killed him only once," Dick said with a laugh to make those who didn't know about my curse to think he was just kidding around.

"Only once, musta been your birthday," Charlie teased, grabbing me for a hug that turned into an arm around my neck. He dragged me down, grumbling something that sounded like, "You're an idiot...next time we all go with ya." Taking my hat with a whoop of fun to hide his growling message, he let me up. Tossing my sugarloaf sombrero to MacNab he said, "We thought maybe that woman had gotten the better of ya."

I walked toward MacNab for my hat. "Nope, just had to run an errand after the meetin'."

MacNab tossed my hat to Middleton. "You missed out on some good huntin'."

I eyed Middleton and my hat. "I will scale you like the tree you are. Give me my damn hat!"

"Oh, is this yours?"

Standing my ground, I crossed my arms and raised my eyebrows at him. "I got at least two in the chamber. Give me the hat."

"Sure thing," Middleton said, his gruff voice sounding strange with the words as he extended my hat toward me.

I reached for it, and he tossed the hat to Fred Waite, who was to my left. "If you know what's good for you, Fred—" I started to say.

"Boys, stop the lolly-gagging and get in the house," Susan McSween yelled out at us. "Alex is waitin' on you."

"Yes, ma'am," Dick said, opening the gate of the three-foot-high picket fence. "Fred?" He motioned giving me the hat.

Fred grinned and walked up to me, handing me the hat. I reached for it, and he pulled it away. Switching hands, Fred placed it on his right shoulder, hitched it up, and leaned toward me, causing the hat to roll across his shoulders, down his arm, and into his left hand. He set the sombrero on my noggin' and headed for the house.

"Points for style, Waite," MacNab said with a laugh as he went through the gate. He punched Dick on the shoulder to say hello, but the big man didn't move an inch. "Ow! You been throwin' bales of hay since we last saw ya? Damn!" He shook the pain from his hand and kept moving.

If Dick had been a boulder before, he was a mountain of strength now. He looked at me with worry, and I shook my head with a laugh to let him know he was being hypersensitive. In retaliation for me laughing, he hit the top of my hat, indenting my sugarloaf sombrero again.

"Damn it, Dick, I just fixed that."

"I like it that way," a young lady's voice said from the doorway. "That high top looked too formal for the likes of you, Billy."

I looked up to see Sallie standing there in a pretty blue dress with a white lace pattern at the top. "Why, Miss Chisum, don't you look lovely, and what for? A bunch of filthy cowboys comin' in to dirty up your home?"

She grinned. "You all will be takin' your boots off as you enter, and you'll let Miss Mary Ann give you all a damp cloth to wipe your clothes off with."

I took my hat off to her as I stepped behind the adobe wall that blocked the main door. "Really? Better with the dent?"

"Without question."

I hummed in acknowledgment as I followed the rest of the men into the house. Here by the door, each of the cowboys was working to take their boots off, hopping this way and that. Trying not to laugh at the sight of all the big bunch of cowboys jumping around, I leaned my backside against the wall and pulled my boots off with ease. "The beauty of having small feet and boots that are always a bit too big."

Setting them in the corner, I took a cloth from Miss Mary Ann and wiped the dirt and horse hair from my britches. Tossing it in a pail near the door, I noticed the man who'd been safeguarding McSween, Deputy Sheriff Barrier, enter the little foyer. With a polite nod toward me, he grabbed his shoes and was out the door before I could ask where he was going. I threw a questioning look at Sallie, but she just shrugged her shoulders.

I peered out the door at him and it was apparent he was leaving. This wasn't a good sign.

Looking in toward the rest of the house I wondered if McSween knew his protection had just left the building. Either way, that small detail was going to change things for us in a big way. With a last nod at Sally, I went off to find out what that change would be.

21

SOME BAD NEWS, AND SOME MORE BAD NEWS

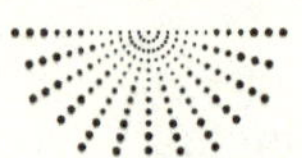

I headed into the parlor of John Chisum's home, which was only one of eight rooms, all of which surrounded a patio at center. My eyes landed on Alexander McSween first. He sat in a rocking chair near the fireplace with Susan standing beside to his right, her hand on his shoulder. He patted it, and she smiled down on him, her other hand smoothing out a section of his bright red hair, which was thinning a bit, but we were never dumb enough to mention that.

Without knowing if Susan had mentioned to her husband that Ben and I visited the house about three weeks ago, I walked up to her and gave her a peck on the cheek. "Good to see you're back in town, ma'am."

MacNab took her hand and kissed the top of it. "Good to see you are safely here, Mrs. McSween."

She, as well as the Regulators sworn by oath, knew the real meaning of this. We were happy she had made it safely to the Chisum ranch after suggesting she and Leverson come here to be away from Lincoln town.

"Thank you, Billy, Frank. It's good to be back. Missouri was relaxin', but it's always nice to be home."

"I wish you were returnin' to more pleasant news," Dick said.

"Yes, I'm so very sorry to hear about John. He was a dear friend to us all. Alex here sent me a letter while I was away to let me know about that and the arrest warrant."

"We're not gonna let him be arrested, ma'am," Dick said.

She laid a hand on Brewer's arm. "I know he is safe with you keepin' an eye on him, Richard."

Coffee and cakes were served as more pleasantries were exchanged, then McSween cleared his throat and began. "I'm glad you all got my message. Thank you for comin'. Now, as to *why* you are here..."

"I'm guessin' it's for the same reason Barrier left or because he did," I offered.

"Deputy Barrier left?" Fred asked.

"Out the door like his backside was on fire," I said.

Squelched laughter could be heard all around the room and McSween said, "He has left to be with his family."

"What?" Dick said, and he wasn't the only rumblings in the room, just the loudest. "But he's your assigned protection until spring term of court."

McSween smoothed his long mustache, which ran all the way to his jaw line. "He's been with me non-stop for three months. He was anxious to return home to his family."

"Umm...did I miss somethin'?" I said. "Do you not need protection anymore?"

Susan spoke up. "Captain Smith from Fort Stanton was here yesterday and gave his word as an officer and a gentleman that Sheriff Brady would make no attempt to serve the warrant he had for Alex's arrest."

Leverson stepped out from the kitchen with a fresh cup of tea and addressed us all as he came to sit on the couch beside Alex's rocking chair. "I believe his words were, 'You may make a football of my head if a hair of his head is injured or if the least insult be given him by word or sign for the highest to the lowest, madam.'"

"Is he gonna tell Sheriff Brady that?" Middleton asked.

"No need," Leverson replied. "Brady was standing right next to the military captain when he said it."

This caused the room to burst into chatter with earnest concern that Brady was here at all, let along just yesterday.

"What was he doin' here, and with a military escort?" Middleton demanded to know.

"It seems he was unable to convince any civilians to travel with him down to the Pecos Valley to summon folks for grand and petit jury duty. He apologized for showing up with soldiers," Leverson explained.

"Oh, well, isn't that just swell of him," I said sarcastically. "Because that makes it all okay."

"That's why Barrier has left," Alex said. "Now that I've been promised military protection, he headed home. I would've preferred he stayed, but I can understand bein' away from your wife and missin' her, so I can't fault him much." He reached up and took Susan's hand from his shoulder and kissed it, letting his eyes stay on her just a moment before turning back to us.

"However," Susan said, "Leverson and I still believe that as soon as Alex arrives in Lincoln, that Brady is goin' to try to arrest him."

"Yes," McSween said. "That's why I called you all here, to say you shouldn't let him get away with it. If I'm arrested, they'll lynch me for sure."

"What do you wish we should do, Governor?" Middleton asked, using a name we'd started to call McSween since he'd taken charge of the fight. Not just for justice concerning Tunstall on a legal front, but as the bank roll for the Regulators as well.

"Seein' as I'm to believe I'm fully under the protection of the military, I want you boys to head out, as if you're no longer actin' as my protection either. But I want some of you in Lincoln on Sunday when I come through town with Brady and Smith on my way to Fort Stanton. If Brady goes against his word to follow Smith's orders, you stop him."

"Are we to kill him, Governor?" Jim asked.

McSween shook his head. "I'd love nothing more than to tell you to kill Brady and earn a mighty reward, but I'll give no such command."

It was evident by his tone and facial expression that if we saved him from Brady, there would be a reward. And though Alex abhorred violence, he appeared to be giving us a pass on if we killed Brady in the process. There was no way I'd been the only person to catch the other meaning of his words, but no one said anything about it.

Instead, Chavez y Chavez stepped forward and addressed our two other main concerns. "I'm low on ammunition, sir, and in the purse, if you get my meanin'."

"I do," McSween said. "That's why I want those of you who head to Lincoln to go into the store and take anythin' you wish prior to meetin' me there. For those who wait for further orders in San Pat, I have a bit of coin for you after we are done here."

Once we discussed the logistics of his surrender at Fort Stanton, there wasn't much more to cover, so McSween dismissed us. We spent the day at the ranch relaxing, socializing, and getting a good meal in. However, before it got too late, I mentioned the fandango I'd heard about that was going on over in Berrendo, a small hamlet east of South Springs, and suggested we attend.

"A fandango?" Sallie asked with light laughter. "What is that?"

"You know," I said, doing a few dance moves. "It's a dance. But this one is done in triple time by couples with castanets." I snapped my fingers in place of the wooden instrument and took a silly pose that made her laugh.

"Oh, Billy, you've a weak spot for dance parties."

"And for the pretty Latina women who go to them," Charlie said quietly.

I hit his arm. "That is not the only reason I like to go, and you know it."

"But it is one of them," Sallie said, her smile accusing me in a playful manner.

"Maybe, but I'll not admit to such things in such company."

Sallie set empty coffee mugs on a tray Mary Ann held as she

walked by. "Oh, so you think we ladies don't know you boys attend dances to flirt with the skirts?"

"Miss Sallie!" Mary Ann said, her tone mildly astonished.

"Oh, please, Mary Ann, that wasn't nothin'," Sallie said before looking to me. "So, do you?"

"I'm goin' to plead the fifth right about now," I said. "But you should come with us and see for yourself."

"Thank you, Billy. That's sweet of you. But this time I must stay here and tend to our guests."

"And tend them well you will, I'm sure," I said, placing a peck on her cheek. "We will be gettin' out of your way then." I gave her a slight bow and headed for my shoes.

She followed me toward the door and looked down at the pile of boots, most of which were the same make and brand, and said, "How do you all tell which ones are whose? They all look the same."

"Well, Dick's are too big for anyone other than maybe Middleton, so they usually set theirs far apart from each other," I said, shoving my foot into one of mine as we watched Fred put a boot on and take it off again, picking up another. "Or we try on and try again," I explained, giving her a big smile before picking up my second one.

"And you know those are yours because they are smaller than most?"

I couldn't help but laugh. "No, because I etched my initials inside 'em," I told her, showing her the inside of my other boot.

"Well, look at you, usin' your smarts," she said.

I couldn't help but beam at her as I put my second boot on. With a wink, I said, "It can happen from time to time, but don't get used to it now."

She laughed, and Dick walked up, grabbing his big ol' boots, and said, "We best get goin' before sunset."

"Yes, yes we should," I agreed, and stepped out the door, turning back to Sallie. "As always, it was good to see you again, Miss Chisum," I said with a slight bow, my hat on my chest.

"It's good to see you too, Mr. Bonney," she replied with a small curtsey.

I put on my hat, dent in the top and all, and walked out, unsure when I'd see her again. The boys all followed me to the stable to fetch our horses and we headed off to Berrendo, a fun night of dancing and music ahead of us.

* * *

I'd finally gotten the *señorita* I'd had my eye on for the first half hour onto the dance floor when I spotted someone in the crowd I'd not expected. It was the young man from the Regulator Network, the one Isaac Ellis called Roy. As always, he blended in so well that most didn't even pay him any attention. He wore a long coat that covered his attire, and he moved like a cat as he wove through the crowd. Catching my eye, he motioned toward the door.

Once I could take my leave for more than a moment, I followed after him, taking Charlie, Dick, and MacNab with me. Once Roy put some distance between the dance and himself, he stopped and waited for us to catch up.

I took note of his tall boots as we approached and cataloged my thought for later. Instead, I asked the obvious question. "What are you doing here?"

"Miss Sallie said you were here, so I raced over to bring you some information and on the way noticed about fifty of the Murphy/Dolan gang headin' this way."

I looked to Dick. "That's more than us by just a small bit."

"Just a small bit," Charlie said, understanding my humor, for there was no way the twenty of us could stand against fifty and do all that well.

"Then we best be gettin' outta town," Dick said. "I'd hate to bring a fight to this here party and have innocent people get hurt. MacNab and I'll head back in and let the boys know."

Before anything else could be said, they were gone, leaving me with Roy and Charlie.

I didn't wait two seconds before asking the next question. "Why were you comin' to find us at Chisum's and does it have anythin' to do with your unusual attire?"

"His attire?" Charlie asked. "It's a coat, in March. I think that's pretty normal."

"It's not the coat; it's his boots. Those are military. Am I right?"

One side of Roy's mouth slid up into a side grin. "Nice catch." He opened his coat a bit to show he was indeed dressed as a soldier. "I infiltrated Captain Smith's soldiers, the ones that joined Brady's posse, and I overheard talk between Brady and one of his deputies."

"Why do I have a feeling this is not good news," Charlie said.

"Because it's not," Roy replied. "Brady and his men are not goin' to give Smith the chance to protect McSween. If they have to, they plan to kill Smith and frame McSween for it. Brady has his soul set on servin' that arrest warrant come hell or high water."

"Did you tell McSween that?"

"I did. He said to tell you and the Regulators that he's going to find a reason to stay the night in San Patricio on Sunday and not come into Lincoln until Monday. This'll give him the chance to separate Smith and Brady by tellin' them to go on ahead and just meet Smith at Fort Stanton. That should save his life."

"Smart thinkin'," I said. "But what about Monday?"

Roy shrugged. "I don't know just yet. But I would bet that Brady will find a way to cut him off from makin' it to Fort Stanton if he doesn't get the chance he wants on Sunday."

I looked at Charlie. "We can't let that happen. McSween has to make it home or to the fort."

Charlie nodded. "Do we tell Dick?"

I thought on it and remembered my research. The last slip of the moon would be up all day on Monday, making Dick unpredictable. "No. He's been lookin' forward to gettin' some work done on his farm for a couple days, and we can handle gettin' McSween through town."

"Anythin' goes wrong, he's gonna be mad as hell."

"Yeah, well, it's a risk I'm willin' to take."

"It's your funeral," Charlie said, unaware of how right he might actually be.

"Speakin' of, here comes Dick and the rest," I said, then turned to Roy. "Can you sneak back into the formation without a problem? In case we need more information by the time we hit Lincoln?"

He nodded. "Of course. What about San Pat?"

"We'll send some of us there," Charlie said.

"We got everyone," Dick said, causing Charlie and I to look in his direction.

"Good, we'll just tell—" I turned to make sure Roy was set, and he was nowhere to be seen. "Never mind."

Charlie looked at me. "That kinda creeps me out."

"You and me both," I admitted.

The Regulators mounted up and headed outta town. Not a half a mile out, we heard gunshots.

I turned Colonel around to face the gunfire behind us. "Someone is bound to tell 'em we headed this way."

Dick agreed. "We either make a stand or we run for it."

"I say we make a stand," Charlie said. "I ain't no runner, that's for sure. And especially not from the likes of Dolan and his crew."

The group agreed to stay, seeing as we were now far enough from the small town to keep the innocent out of harm's way. Quickly, I assessed the area, and we began to come up with a plan, placing ourselves in different positions to ambush the Murphes when they came by. But they never did. We waited an hour and nothing happened.

"They probably joined the party instead of tryin' to find all of us out here in the dark," Fred offered up.

"Very likely," I replied.

Dick came over and pulled me aside. "It's late, and the moon, no matter how small, is goin' to rise around four in the mornin'. I didn't change the past few nights, so I can feel it comin' on. I need to go home for a night."

"That's a good idea. I'll head to Lincoln and make sure McSween gets where he is supposed to be. I could even swing through Agua Negra on the way."

"You don't have to—"

"Don't try to change my mind. I'm gonna go."

Dick sighed. "Fine. I'll meet y'all tomorrow night so we're there for McSween on Sunday."

"McSween ain't arrivin' until Monday now. Roy told us while you were gatherin' everyone."

Dick looked at me, left eyebrow raised, right eye squinted. "You don't really think I believe that's all the news he gave you, right?"

"Brady plans to arrest him no matter what. We're gonna make sure that doesn't happen."

"And how are you going to do that?" he asked before his breath was taken away by the wolf fever. "You know what? I don't want to know. Just try not to kill the bastard, okay?"

"I'm not makin' any promises, Dick."

"I can't hear you," he said, finding the strength to stand up. "Send word to me on Monday mornin' if ya need anythin' from me."

"All right, now go!"

Without another word, he hoisted himself onto Mattie and rode off as I explained to the rest of the boys how he was feelin' mighty sick again and that I needed to head up to Agua Negra for some medicine.

"After that, we shouldn't split up," MacNab said.

"I agree," Fred said. "We'll all ride with you to Agua Negra, and then we'll take the straight shot down to Lincoln from there since we have until Monday now."

The gang agreed and we began to ride north, hoping we reached Agua Negra by daybreak.

2 2

AGUA NEGRA

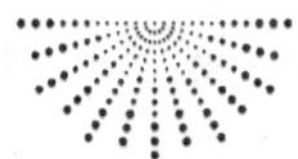

The B&B was north of the sheriff's office on Highway 54, and Lois was kneeling in the dirt planting something by her front porch as I pulled in. Standing up, she stood just over five feet tall; a sturdy woman with curves and a strong build.

Turning off the car, I placed the keys in my jacket pocket. Stepping out, I inhaled deeply of the late March air, warm enough that I could see why she was working in the yard. Well, that and I knew she was keeping an eye out for me. Sally woulda called her, telling her I was en route.

"Sally tell you I was on my way?" I asked as I shut the door, curious if I was right.

She took off a gardening glove. "Sure did, but he didn't mention you had such a nice car. If you're lookin' to blend in around here, you're not gonna." She put out her clean hand. "Lois Gutierrez, glad to meet ya, Agent Kidwell."

I shook her hand. "Please, call me Will, or Billy, I answer to either."

She gave me a firm nod. "Well then, Billy, come on in, and I'll show you to your room."

Letting go of her hand, I went to the trunk of my car. Opening it, I

237

said, "It's been a long day. I think I'll grab an hour down after I make a call. Any chance I could use your phone?"

She removed her second glove and tossed it onto the ground with the other. "Sure thing."

I pulled my suitcase out and shut the trunk of my car, leaving my magical toys in their lockbox inside. "I appreciate it."

She led me into the two-story home and up the stairs to the right of the foyer. "I've got three rooms up here and a bathroom. Don't got any other tenants right now, so you've got your pick."

I quickly took the front room that overlooked the driveway and set my suitcase by the door. "I greatly appreciate this, takin' me in on such short notice and all."

"Tis no big deal, seein' as I'm empty. Oh, and since you missed my breakfast, I'll whip us up somethin' for dinner so we can talk about your friend. Bathroom is here next to your room, and how does six o'clock sound for dinner?"

"That would be great, Lois. Thank you."

"Of course," she said, and began to head down the stairs. Stopping, she said, "Funny thing, your pal chose the same room. You rest a bit. I'll see you in two hours. There's a phone there by the bed. If you're callin' long distance, be sure to pay that before you leave."

"Of course, ma'am."

Without another word, she went on down the stairs, and I stepped over to the mirror above the dresser. Pulling the dresser out, I found what I was hoping for: a word written in chalk on the thin wood casing. All it said was ROSE.

Confused on what that could mean, I moved the dresser back and sat on the bed, staring at the phone, knowing it was time to ruin someone's day. He'd be getting up around now anyway.

"Best get it over with."

With a deep breath in and a slow exhale, I picked up the receiver to call my reluctant reinforcement and dialed the emergency number. The operator put me through, and soon his handler answered.

"Hello?"

"Hey, James. Is he there?"

There was a pause, then, "Who's calling?"

"Really? You're goin' to ask me—"

"Please hold."

I rolled my eyes. "Why does he always make things difficult? Oh yeah, because he's him."

I heard a connection go through and then a phone receiver being fumbled before a deep, groggy voice said, "This better be good, Billy."

"Sorry to wake you," I said.

"No, you're not."

I laughed. "You're right. I'm not."

There was a pause, and he finally said, "What do you need, now that I'm marginally awake?"

"I need you in New Mexico."

"Aw hell, Billy, seriously? New fuckin' Mexico? I told you I never wanted to—"

"I know, I know, but trust me, I have a good reason...I'll explain when you get here."

I heard him grunt and knew he was sitting up now. "This must be pretty big if you're makin' me come back there."

"It is, pal. It really is."

"Is this work?"

"Yeah. So...MI-4 will pay you back or I will. Just buy a train ticket and get here."

"Damn straight someone will pay me back. Where am I headin' into?"

"Albuquerque is best."

"Santa Fe has better food."

I laughed. "We'll be headin' to Santa Fe after you arrive. But I have to head to Las Cruces first, so Albuquerque is best. Besides, they have a great train station. Send word through the agency when you'll arrive, and I'll be there to pick you up."

"I'm supposed to be on leave, you know," he said.

"I know."

"They can't possibly be happy I'm comin' in."

"I didn't ask. Better to get reprimanded after the fact than be told no. I need you here, no one else. They're gonna have to suck it up."

He whistled low. "They're gonna be mad as hell."

"I couldn't care less."

"I know. But you're gonna owe me for this. We had a deal."

I rolled my eyes. "I was hopin' you'd forgotten about that."

"No, sir."

"Look, I wouldn't call if it wasn't necessary. And yes, I know the deal we made."

He grunted a noncommittal sound. "I'll be there by the end of the week."

"By the thirtieth," I countered. "Later in the day if you can."

"Shit," he sighed out. "That means I need to leave like, now. You best have answers for me when I get there."

"I will."

"Fine. The thirtieth. See you then. Bye, Billy."

"Bye, and thanks so—" The line went dead. "I hate it when he does that."

I hung up the phone and looked out the window at the dying light. Clouds were gathering, and I thought we might end up getting some rain tonight or tomorrow. Neither of which bothered me. Driving around in the rain was nothing like riding a horse all day in it.

I laid down to rest my eyes for a bit before dinner, and my mind went back to a long trek in the rain on horseback. It was bad. In fact, the whole trip to Agua Negra was horrible.

* * *

Not long after the sun rose, clouds started rolling in. Seeing this, I pulled the group together and sent them into town to find a spot for a hot breakfast. Sharing a bit of my speed with Colonel, we headed for the "black water." When I arrived at the body of water that gave the town its name, I took the two special canteens from Zahara to the edge of the lake. Remembering what she'd told me about what would happen if I touched the water, I held the strap of each canteen and dropped them into the water.

Using my boot to help them fill all the way, I lifted them out, being careful to use a towel to dry them off and screw the tops back on. Thunder boomed above, and I slid both canteens into a bag lined with beeswax. Mounting back up onto Colonel, I felt dizzy and checked to make sure there were no black spots on me from the water. At first, I didn't see any, but then the shade of gray showed on my hands, and I realized some of the water must've passed through the towel.

"Damn it," I said, and pitched forward, my face landing on Colonel's mane. I felt my body quickly begin to go into paralysis. Stiff like I'd done ranch work for twelve hours without stopping, I fought to reach the knife in my boot.

The tips of my fingers found the hilt, but I was becoming so stiff I wasn't sure I'd be able to grab it. With one last push, I grasped the handle and yanked the blade out. Without hesitation, I stabbed myself in the leg, creating a blood-gushing wound. Praying that the healing powers of my gift to renew my body would also attack the poison, I pulled the knife out. With the last of my mobility, I kicked Colonel's sides, and he headed off.

Using our mental connection, I told him where to go once we were on the road, where the wound began to heal. At first, I thought the soul magic wouldn't attack the poison, but as Colonel trotted into town, I felt my legs come back to me, then my arms and torso. By the time we found the rest of the boys, I was still a good ten percent stiff and fought not to fall off Colonel as he stopped behind an inn.

Landing on my ass, I cursed and grabbed the stirrup to hoist myself back up. Colonel was greatly amused, as was the boy who tended the horses out back of the inn.

"It's been a rough twenty-four hours," I said, and as if on cue, it started to downpour. "Great. Just great." I groaned and limped my way to the front of the inn.

Thunder rolled across the sky, and I opened the door, surprised to see the place only filled up with the Regulators. I walked over to

Charlie and asked what was going on as I marched out my limbs to get rid of the stiffness.

"We walked in, and the few that were here scampered out. What in tarnation are you doin'?"

"I'm stiff. Been a long ride. We best not stay long. Did you order me some grub?"

"Sure did. Barkeep is busy fillin' the order now. Seems they are a hand short in the kitchen."

This gave me an idea. "I'll be back." I headed into the kitchen area like I'd worked there my whole life and offered to lend a helping hand.

"*Voy tan rápido como puedo,*" the man said, telling me he was going as fast as he could.

With a smile, I placed a hand on his shoulder and spoke to him in Spanish, letting him know I'd grown up helping out in kitchens and asking him to show me where things were.

With my help, food was on the table faster than it would've been. The owner knew after our chat that we didn't want any trouble, so he hung a sign out front that they were closed until lunch and locked the door.

"*Gracias, señor,*" I said.

With an accepting nod, he disappeared into the back.

I turned my attention to the Regulators. "We need to find a way to get McSween through town without gettin' arrested."

"Or killed," Charlie added.

"And how do we do that?" Big Jim asked.

"We put some fear into that man and his deputies," someone said.

Then one of José's Hispanic recruits, whose name I wasn't sure of, spoke up. "We just need to be there. Show Brady we're there to keep him honest."

"'Cause that worked so well for Tunstall," Joe Smith said.

Faster than I could blink, Middleton had ahold of Smith's shirt and was lifting him up out of his chair. "You weren't there. You have no idea how that all went down. I suggest you leave your rude insinuations to yourself."

It was quiet for a second while no one breathed.

Quietly, I said, "John, set him down. He didn't mean nothin' by it, did you, Joe?"

Eyes bugging out of his head, Joe said, "I didn't...I meant y'all were overpowered, that's all."

"Put him down; it's all right," I said again.

This time Middleton seemed to hear me and dropped Joe into his seat before sitting back down to finish eating his breakfast.

Charlie breathed a sigh of relief. "All right then, let's talk strategy on what to do if there are a ton of men."

"Why can we not just threaten him?" a new man to the group, John Scroggins, asked.

José Chavez y Chavez spoke up as he filled his coffee from a carafe left on the table. "He's not the type of man who will respond to threats, *mi amigo*. Just like Dolan, Brady will only respect force. We need to take Lincoln back."

Charlie hummed in agreement and swallowed some food down with a gulp of coffee. "I'm with José on this. I say we get supplies at the store and watch and wait. McSween will have to pass us to get to *The House*, where Brady will likely be sitting in wait. We'll join McSween there and surround him, and we'll be his escort to Fort Stanton."

"We'll never all get into town without bein' noticed," Fred pointed out.

"We will if we go in small groups," I said, since Charlie had put another bite of food in his mouth. "We send some of us to San Pat, some will position themselves at the Ellis Store, and the rest of us will be at Tunstall's, and those in town go in shifts."

Without Dick there to lead, MacNab stepped up to make decisions. "We'll need no more than nine in the center of town, but less would be good. Three is too small, though."

"Nine Anglos," I said. "None of you Mexican boys will go."

José bristled. "Why don't you want the Mexicans? You know the other Americans aren't any braver than I am."

"Don't be annoyed, José. It has nothin' to do with who's brave or a good shot. Brady is married to a Mexican woman, and everyone is always sympathetic to their own kind...and we can't be havin' changed minds partway through this. Besides, I'd hate to put your families in that predicament. If a fight breaks out and Brady dies, leavin' his wife a widow, you need to have clean hands. *Comprendé?*"

José thought, then nodded. "You're right. It would put my family in a tough place."

"Let's do this," I said. "Charlie, me, MacNab, Middleton, Henry, and Fred will go to the Tunstall Store. The rest of you will split, four men to Ellis and the rest to San Patricio to meet with McSween."

"Ya know, I gotta ask," Frank MacNab asked. "Why do you use everyone's first names but mine and John's?"

"Huh? Oh! 'Cause I already know a man named Frank and way too many men named John. This is simpler."

MacNab frowned. "That's the dumbest—"

"It's my reason. If you like, I can call you Frances," I offered, a grin sliding across my face.

"MacNab is fine."

I slapped him on the shoulder. "Glad to hear it. Now, if we six—"

"I said we should have nine," MacNab said, interrupting me again.

"There will be. Don't forget, we've got Reverend Ealy, Robert Widenmann, and Sam Corbett in town. By droppin' the number tryin' to sneak into the center of town to six, our chance of being noticed drops considerably."

MacNab agreed, and we all finished our food. I left a nice tip for the owner by the register, and we all slipped out the back, saddled up, and headed out. The San Pat group of Mexicans went one way; the Ellis group of Anglos went another, leaving the five I'd appointed with myself left to ride alone to Lincoln in the rain.

"They'll be to San Pat by mid-day," Charlie pointed out.

"That's why I sent a letter for Roy with José."

"Roy?" Henry asked at the same time Fred did.

"It's what Isaac and Ben call that blond Regulator Network guy. No idea what his real name is. Anyway, it'll let Reverend Ealy know we're comin'. Let's go the long way 'round. That way, chances are we won't be seen as we'll arrive after dark. Easier to slip into town that way. Besides, if we stay off the heavily traveled roads, the mud shouldn't be as bad."

"Shouldn't is the key word in that sentence," Charlie said, pulling his hat down to protect his face against the blowing rain.

Thunder boomed, and I smiled. "Great day for a ride, gentleman. Let's try to enjoy it!"

"He's your best pal," Henry said with a chuckle.

"I never said he was normal," Charlie replied.

I started to laugh and gave Colonel a light kick to the ribs, and we headed for Lincoln.

* * *

Standing out on the front porch, I smoked a cigarette and stared in awe as the sun, which had set a while back, still escaped from below the horizon.

Lois stepped out onto the porch without saying a thing and stood next to me. In the porch light, she looked younger than her years, which I'd placed around forty. Her eyes, green as the grass, appeared to be able to watch me and the horizon at the same time.

Feeling a bit uneasy at the silence, I said, "Ya know, the sun doesn't do that everywhere."

"What? Set?"

I chuckled. "No, come up from the ground like that. I've only seen that out here. It appears to light up the sky longer here. No idea how or why, but I've missed that."

"I'll have to take your word for it, as I've pretty much just been here in New Mexico my whole life. How long has it been since you were here?"

"Early 1940s," I said, lying. The last time I'd enjoyed watching the land lit from below woulda been February 1898. But I wasn't going to tell her that.

"When you were what? A teenager?" she teased.

"I'm older than I look. Good genes."

"Uh-huh. Well, do those good genes have an appetite to go with 'em?"

"Sure do!"

"Well then, come in and get washed up. Dinner will be ready in a few minutes." Without another word, she walked back into the house.

I finished my cigarette and did as she told me. By the time we were halfway through our meal, she began to talk about Fletcher.

"Nice man, he was. Kept to himself mostly but seemed to enjoy going out and being social. I take it Sally already told you he left here for Las Cruces."

"Yes, ma'am."

"Well, he wasn't even considering that area until he'd spent some time over at Bobby's Bar and Grill."

"Oh?" I asked before eating another bite of the best mashed potatoes I'd had in a decade.

"He met someone there that tipped him in that direction. He didn't say who, but I know it was a woman. Not surprisin'."

"Why do ya say that?"

"Fletcher was like you. Handsome and easy goin'. He had quite a few visitors when he was here, men and women, with information for him. It was amazin' to see how easily he could get them to tell him their life story."

"That was Fletch all right. With that thick black hair and dark blue eyes, he was never hurtin' for a date, and he had a way about him that put folks at ease. We used to say that if Fletcher couldn't get a confession outta someone, no one could. Hell, there were folks who admitted to things without even realizin' they did!"

"I can believe it," she said, putting more butter on a roll. "He has that kinda gift where he brightens up a room. I sincerely hope no one has put that light out."

The mood switched quickly, her somber note hitting me hard. "Me either, Lois. Me either."

The rest of dinner she filled me in on his full stay, the day-to-day, and when I got back upstairs, I jotted all I could remember into my notebook before an idea hit me.

I headed out to the stairs and started down them as she came down the hall.

"Yes, Agent Kidwell?"

I smiled. "Any chance that bar you mentioned would be open tonight?"

"Sure, but it's a Monday night, so they won't be open past midnight."

"Great. I think I'll go check it out."

"They're havin' some sorta cook-off tomorrow afternoon if you'd rather go then. Everyone will be there."

The sliver of a moon had already set but would be up tomorrow during the day. My safest bet was tonight. "I think maybe I'll do both. Don't you wait up for me now, ya hear?"

"Me? No sir, I'll be in bed by nine."

"Sleep well then. I'll see you for breakfast."

"Eight o'clock sharp, Billy."

"Yes, ma'am," I said, and headed upstairs to get my dancing boots on. If I was lucky, I'd run into this woman that Lois mentioned. Maybe she could tell me why Fletcher had gone to Las Cruces. And maybe her name was Rose.

ALL FOOLS DAY

Whether it was the rain/sleet/snow mix that fell all day or the path taken, we never saw a soul on our journey to Lincoln. Plus, by staying on the grass and stone areas, we weren't as covered in mud as we could've been if we'd traveled the main roads. However, we were soaked to the skin and quite miserable.

Around an hour after sunset, the six of us rode into town, keeping it slow and steady so as to not draw attention. Reaching the Tunstall Store, MacNab dismounted and approached the gate, which opened easily, meaning Reverend Ealy got our message.

We all breathed a sigh of relief. Having six men show up without warning on a night like tonight, what with the tensions in town being the way they were, would've been disruptive, to say the least. Reverend Ealy lived with not just his wife, but his two children and a teacher by the name of Susan Gates.

MacNab led his horse through the gate, and we all rode in behind him into the corral. With no stables here, we were stuck grabbing our bags and leaving our horses outside in the rain. I sent an apology through touch to Colonel. Seeing as we might have to leave quickly, it was best if we didn't take them to McSween's stable or remove their saddles. I promised him a longer visit with Zahara, and that seemed to appease him.

We all headed for the back door, what'd been the entrance to Tunstall's living quarters. I knocked once, and the door opened. The Reverend stood there, lantern in hand, his eyes flitting over each of us holding our bed rolls and bags.

"Get in, get in, but head straight into the store and take off your wet clothes and boots, or my wife will have words with ya."

"Understandable, Reverend," I replied.

We all filed in and took an immediate sharp right through the open door that led into the back area of the Tunstall Store. We all removed our boots and would've continued with our soaked clothes, but we heard a noise close to the main entrance. There we noted the shape of a woman building a fire in the stove that heated the front of the store.

Shutting the door to the stove, the light dimmed, but I recognized Mary Ealy's voice the moment she spoke. "We heard you come into the corral, so I started this for you."

"Much obliged, ma'am," I said, placing my dirty boots against the wall under the back window.

"I see you picked up the store a bit," Charlie said. "Last I knew, this place had been ransacked."

Mary set the poker down and came toward us. "A shipment John made before he died finally came in. The doctor assisted Rob and Sam with restockin' the shelves while Miss Gates and I cleaned the place up."

She always referred to her husband as "the doctor," and I never really understood why she didn't call him Taylor or Reverend. But that was her way I supposed.

"Rob wants to open the store back up for business to help pay for all the work y'all been doin'. Problem is, with all that is goin' on with the legal paperwork, well, he can't open it up until after the spring term of court," she said.

"He can only do that if McSween is acquitted of charges or found not guilty," Fred pointed out.

"He will be," MacNab said. "They've got nothin' on him, and they know it. It's Murphy and Dolan's last effort to get some money to save their store. Mark my words, if McSween wins, they'll have to close down."

"God willin'," Mary said. "I'll leave you boys to dry off and get warm. There's more wood and matches there by the fireplace. I reckon you'll want to start that as well. I have some coffee on the stove in our room. I'll bring you some shortly. Have you eaten?"

"Not since this afternoon, ma'am," Middleton replied.

She eyed the large man with a small smile. "Well, we'll see what we can do to remedy that. Please, get warm and rest a bit. Y'all been ridin' in the rain all day, and that is hard enough without addin' on all the other stress."

Without waiting on a reply, she walked through the door that separated their apartment from the store and shut it behind her. None of us dallied in removing our wet clothes and putting on the driest thing we could find. While we did, I told the Reverend of McSween's orders.

Once we were all decent, he opened the door to his apartments. "Mary, could you bring me the other lantern?"

I stepped into the doorway to see his wife at the small stove. She didn't move a muscle. Instead, she replied, "Suzie has it. Miss Gates? The doctor requires the lantern."

"Of course," came the voice of the school teacher from the second room. A moment later, Miss Gates softly swept into the room, still in her dress from the day, her hair piled high on her head, and slippers on her feet. She crossed the room and handed the lantern to the Reverend who gave it to me. Noticing us, she said, "Good evenin', gentlemen."

Each of us replied in kind in our own unique way, yet as Suzie opened her mouth to reply, she stopped, distracted by the feel of someone tugging on her skirts. Standing there was the Reverend's eldest daughter, Anna, her hair down and nightgown on.

"What are you doin' out of bed, sweetheart? Come now, let's get you back."

"But it's so dark," Anna complained.

"We'll light a candle," Miss Gates told her as thunder boomed outside, causing the adobe walls to shake and the girl, no more than three-feet-high, to grasp Miss Gates's leg. Bending down, Suzie picked up the three-year old and propped the girl on her hip. "Better yet, we'll light two. How's that sound?"

Anna nodded. "But why's it so loud?"

"Oh, that's nothing but our Heavenly Father and his angels bowling in Heaven, love," Mary Ealy said, a metal candle holder in her hand, complete with a tall, lit taper snuggly fit into the center. "Ya see, you have nothin' to fear." She handed the candle to Miss Gates, who set Anna back down so she could take it. "Now go on back to bed, and Suzie will finish readin' to you, all right?"

Anna nodded again, even though she didn't appear sold on the explanation about God and the angels bowling in Heaven. I wondered if I'd ever believed my mother when she'd told me the same story. I was in the middle of thinking about this when a knock came at the rear door to the Ealy apartments.

I looked to the Reverend. "Are you expectin' anyone else?"

"No. Just y'all," he told us.

Mary placed her hand on the teacher's back. "Come, time to head to bed and hear Suzie read us a story," she said, leading them toward the second room, closer to the front of the building.

"But who's at the door?" Anna asked.

"None of our business. That's for the men to take care of. Come now, into the room with you." Mary shared a look with Miss Gates before she shut the door between them and the rest of us, including her.

"Mary, go with her," the Reverend said.

"It's my home, too. I'm stayin' right here," she replied, walking back to the stove.

"Strong-willed women..." the Reverend started to say.

"I like 'em that way," I told him, trying to relieve the tension. It was totally true, but it still didn't work the way I'd wanted, so I added. "I'll get the door. Safest choice for all of us."

Doing so, I found Roy standing there, still in his military attire. "Twice in two days, this is getting—" I stopped, noting the look on his face and the blood on the front of his jacket. "Are you okay?"

"It's not my blood," he clarified, yet not answering my question fully.

"Good to know, but are you okay?"

He laughed lightly. "No, not really. But I will be. I have news, and I need a place to clean up. Can I come in?"

"Who is it?" Middleton said, looming over me from behind.

"How is that a safe spot to be, John?" I asked.

He ignored me, his eyes landing on Roy. "You again."

Eyebrows raised, he nodded. "Yes, me again."

"You don't tend to bring good news," Middleton said.

Roy pressed his lips together for a moment before saying, "I don't bring it now either, but better you know than not."

"He has a point," I said. "Reverend?"

"You trust him?" he asked me.

"With my life," I replied.

"Then come in, young man. It's not safe outside. And you look a mess."

Roy turned to me for the okay, and I gave it. We quickly ushered him into the store where he set his bag down and immediately began to remove his wet attire while filling us in. "Just before you all rode into town, Brady, Smith, and his troops did, too."

"Without McSween?" I verified.

"Yes. McSween used the rain as an excuse to stop traveling. He, his wife, Leverson, and Chisum all stopped off in San Patricio. Alex told Captain Smith that he would come to Fort Stanton in the afternoon to surrender. Smith began to argue, but of course, Brady supported the idea. So, the two of them and the rest of the regiment pressed on to Fort Stanton."

"Brady went to the fort?" Henry asked.

"No, he went home. But before he did, he handed his messenger some notes to deliver."

"Any idea who they are for?" I asked.

"Yes. George Hindman, Billy Mathews, George Peppin, and Jack Long."

"That sounds like the beginnings of a plan," I said, sitting on a short stool. Selecting kindling, I began to put little sticks of wood into the fireplace. "Is there a way we can find out what they said?"

"I already know."

This stopped all the shuffling in the room.

"How do you know?" MacNab asked.

"I killed him and delivered them myself, after readin' them first, of course," Roy said, motioning to his bloody jacket as proof.

The still room was now so silent that I wasn't sure anyone was breathing. Lightning flashed outside the window behind Roy, and I lit the kindling.

"What did you do?" I quietly asked.

Roy unbuttoned the top portion of his undergarments, exposing his chest before pulling his arms out. "Regulator Network men and women are quiet and fast. We carry a myriad of weapons. For example, I have a small six-shooter that fits in a pocket. The idea is to look harmless so no one gives us a second thought. We also carry knives we are trained to use." He mimicked slicing his throat.

I blew on the kindling, watching as the flames began to take hold, considering this new information.

Fred set a small wash basin full of warm water and washcloth on the windowsill. "Here. So you can clean up."

Roy appeared relieved even though he shivered in the cold of the room. "Thank you." He wrung out the cloth and began to wipe down any exposed skin. "I've just never had to help a Regulator to this extent before. We're trained, sure, but puttin' into practice is different. Thus, I'm a little shook up."

"Understandable," I said, trying not to gawk at this new Network information while I selected a few logs and set them into the fireplace.

He gave me a sad smile when I turned about. "You didn't know, did you? That's why you sent Ben to find me."

"No, I had no idea you were trained assassins," I confessed.

"Don't worry. Ben is still useful. But he can't be sent away for trainin' at this point and still be useful for the war."

"I'd not want him sent to be trained. Ever."

"Noted," Roy replied, wringing out the cloth and setting it aside before grabbing his bag.

The Reverend handed Roy a warmed towel to dry off with. "What did you learn from the letters?"

Roy used the towel to dry off before pulling out a dry change of clothes that told me his bag was like ours, spelled to keep the contents dry. It also had something embroidered on the side, and as I attempted to see what it said, he began to dress while answering Middleton's question. "The letters to each deputy told them to meet him at the Murphy/Dolan Store at eight o'clock and to come armed because they are going to arrest McSween as he comes into town."

Middleton looked to me. "Now what?"

"We go through with the plan," Charlie told him. "Right, Billy?"

"We should take positions to make arrestin' him impossible," I said, looking to MacNab.

With a nod, MacNab sat on the chair by the fire. "If we put enough Regulators around him, we'll outnumber Brady and his deputies, and it would mean we'd probably be able to get McSween to Fort Stanton alive."

"That could work," Roy said, toweling his blond hair.

"Or they could just shoot us all," Middleton said.

"Brady wouldn't allow that," Reverend Ealy said.

"What he allows and what Scáthach compels her minions to do are two different things," Roy said, putting his boots back on.

"He's right," I replied, fanning the flames of the fire, relishing in the heat on my skin. "He may not be one of her monsters, but she can get into their heads."

"How do you know that?" Roy asked, putting things into his bag.

"She got braggy and told me," I replied, and focused my eyes on Roy's bag, the initials becoming clear. They were familiar somehow, but I couldn't remember where I'd seen them. I shoved that thought into the back of my mind and focused on Reverend Ealy, who'd stepped up.

"Well then, you all best get warm and make plans. Let's get some coffee for you boys, especially you...?" He let the sentence hang, hoping Roy would give his name.

"I was never here," he said, pulling something small from his bag. "You can't tell a soul how you know the information I gave you, and you can't tell anyone you saw me. Understood?"

Everyone looked at one another, confused.

"Regulator swear," he said, putting his hand out—a flat, round piece of honeycomb calcite in the palm of his hand. Seeing as it was what we used for bahvah-lamps, we all understood this stone held magic, thus making this an official and binding promise.

The seriousness of this made the air feel heavy, yet no one hesitated to place a hand on Roy's or another Regulator's and swear to keep Roy's secret.

"Thank you," he said, putting the calcite into the pocket of his pants. Grabbing his raincoat, he put it on. "I must go. If I learn more, I'll make sure you know."

Unsure what to say, we all shook his hand, and he disappeared into the night. Mary brought us coffee, and we worked on our strategy to protect McSween. Little did we know our plan would be useless.

* * *

The next morning, I woke after sunrise, the rain/sleet mix having ceased not long after Roy had vanished into the night. However, that didn't stop the day from holding a damp chill. Even though sunlight lit up the room where we all slept, it was cold.

The only one awake so far, I put more wood into the stove causing the two others near me to roll over and grunt at the disturbance.

I glanced toward the back of the store to see Fred kneeling in front of the fireplace in his long underwear, adding logs to the fire. I was about to head toward him when the clip-clop of horse hooves outside got my attention. Staying low, I peeked out one of the front windows to see Sheriff Brady riding by toward the west end of town.

Fred quietly walked up behind me. "It's half past seven. We better wake everyone up."

With groans and curses, the men woke and took turns peeing out the back window before getting dressed and collecting the supplies we'd come to town for. Once we'd finished, I lightly knocked on the door that separated the store from Ealy's main room. It opened to reveal the Reverend and his wife already dressed and ready for their day.

"Mornin', Billy. Coffee?" Mary asked.

"Thank you, that would be great."

As she prepared coffee and breakfast, the rest of us took the supplies we'd gathered the night before and loaded up our horses with them. By the time we'd finished, food was ready. We'd just sat down to eat when a knock came at the back door, and this time, I recognized the pattern.

Standing up, I set my coffee mug down. "Roy's here."

"Is he ever *not* at the back door?" Ealy asked in jest and opened it. "Morning, R—"

But standing there were three men. Roy, Sam Corbett, and Rob Widenmann.

"Good mornin', Dr. Ealy," Roy said before looking to me. "Billy, we have a problem and only minutes to make a decision."

* * *

And we're sure they're coming this way?" Middleton asked.

"I heard them discussing it over breakfast at The Wortley," Roy said. "They plan to kill McSween as he enters town and make it look like self-defense, just like with John."

"Then this is our only chance to stop it," Rob Widenmann said.

"Hindman is mine," MacNab growled.

Middleton huffed out a laugh. "You are claimin' the crippled man. You don't think much of your skills then I take it."

"Oh, it has nothin' to do with my confidence with my gun. I am not lackin' in that department," MacNab said with a wink and a grab of his belt buckle.

Fred laughed at the double-entendre, but when Middleton glared at him, he shut up.

I tapped MacNab with my elbow. "Some past grievance to share, pretty boy?"

"Nope. Just got a score to settle from when we be livin' in Texas."

"Good enough for me," Henry Brown said.

Movement to the right caught my attention. Glancing over, I saw Sam Corbett hand Rob a tin bowl. Punch, Tunstall's bulldog, began to do circles in excitement, and I understood. Widenmann was going to feed Punch to keep the pup from giving us away when the time came.

Checking my guns, I glanced out the window and saw George Peppin walking by, real close to the store, followed by Jack Long to his right and a few steps behind. Both wore long coats and carried rifles. "Shit! They're early! Go, go, go!"

No one hesitated but me. They ran out the back door into the corral, and I went to the window. There were five of them, as Roy had said. After Long was Hindman. Not only was he in the middle of the group, but he was walking down the center of the road. Brady was after him, jogging a bit to catch up, with Billy Mathews bringing up the rear.

Taking no more time to watch, I ran out the door behind the last of the group, leaving Sam, Suzie, and the Ealys inside. Exiting, I noticed Punch's attention was focused on Rob, who held the dog's food near the storage shed to my left and that all the boys to my right had taken places at the corral door.

Blood pumping fast, I barely felt the cold wet of the morning, even standing in the mud by the corral door taking aim. Brady had already passed the door, but without a building to our left, we had a wide range of view. Once I was in place, MacNab whispered, "Now!"

Six shots went off, shattering the morning stillness. A single shot hit George Hindman, who lurched forward a few steps before collapsing in the road. Brady took multiple hits. One to the head, as well as a few to his back and left side, causing him to fall into a sitting position. With my abilities, I heard him say, "Oh dear," before he fell over, likely dead.

Jack Long took a hit but still ran for safety near the Torreon. George Peppin and Billy Mathews ran for Lola Sisnero's house for shelter. We fired on them but missed, one of us accidentally hitting John Wilson in the buttocks while he worked in his garden. With a yelp, he threw his hoe in the air and hobbled out of the line of fire.

"Damn it, poor Wilson. Hope he's okay," Big Jim said.

"Is that my carbine Brady has in his hand?" I said, recognizing my rifle. "It is! Son of a bitch..."

"Water!" Hindman called out from the road. "Help, someone!"

That someone appeared just out of our line of sight and began to drag him toward Ike Stockton's Saloon.

"What was that about your confidence?" Middleton chided MacNab.

"Fuck you, John," MacNab said, taking careful aim and firing again.

This shot hit Hindman in the head, and he was done, causing the person helping him to run for his life back into the saloon.

Widenmann ran over to us. "We need that arrest warrant Brady's carrying!"

"He's right," MacNab said. "If we can get that, we take away their power for the time bein' with concern to McSween. Who'll run out to get it?"

"I will," Big Jim French said.

"The hell you will!" I told him. "I'm the wisest choice here. I'll go."

But Jim was stubborn. "You think I can't pull my weight?"

"It's not that, I just think—"

I didn't get to finish, for Jim opened the gate and was running diagonally to the left toward Brady's body.

"Damn it all to hell! Cover us!" I said.

Dropping the rifle I'd been using, I ran after Big Jim. Pulling on some soul-energy for speed, I passed him just before he reached Brady. Gunfire erupted from Peppin and Mathews at Lola's house, and I moved to shield Big Jim. However, he wasn't called "big" for no reason, and a bullet missed me and hit him in the side.

Cursing with pain, Jim stumbled sideways as Long, who was hiding at the Torreon, began to shoot at us as well.

Caught in crossfire, I shouted at Jim, "Get outta here. You don't heal like I do! I'll get the warrant!"

He began to argue when a bullet clipped my hip and healed, followed by another, which passed through my left thigh. Damn thing took my breath away, dropping me to my knees. My hand flew to the second wound as blood gushed out of it, not healing like it should.

I was in trouble.

2 4

KILLING FEVER

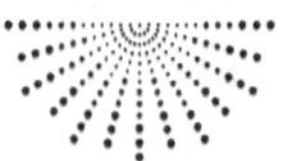

Blood poured out between my fingers. "Son of a bitch! I'm not healing, Jim!"

Seeing the situation, Big Jim got an arm around me, helped me up, and we rushed back to the Tunstall Store as fast as we could go. Bullets zipped past us as we ran, and I prayed we didn't get hit again.

Jim and I got back to the corral where MacNab immediately shut the gate behind us.

"We've both been hit," I told him.

Jim winced but only said, "Billy is hurt badly."

"Can't you—" MacNab began.

"The well must be dry," I explained, watching the rest of the Regulators mount their horses.

"Can you ride?"

"No way in hell. I need the doc."

MacNab looked to the boys and me.

"Go!" I shouted at him. "I'll be fine. You too, Jim. Saddle up and ride outta here!"

They both began to argue when I let go of Jim and used the

building to hold me up as I worked my way to the back door, leaving a blood trail along the wall.

Not needing to be told twice, Jim and MacNab hurried to their horses and hoisted into the saddles.

Riding up to me at the back corner of the building, Jim said, "Billy, I—"

They didn't have time, so I smacked his horse on the ass and said, "Ride!"

The five Regulators burst from the corral on horseback, riding out into the street, firing their guns and hollering for all they were worth.

I moved to the back door and fell into the Ealys' quarters. "Reverend!"

Sam Corbett reached me first. "Billy! What the—"

"Shot in the leg, where's the doc?"

"Right here," Ealy said, rushing over to us.

Motioning to the blood soaking my pants, I said, "I'm thinking we might need to bandage this up."

"Not right now we can't," Ealy said, helping Sam drag me farther inside. "Look, with the Regulators riding out, Peppin and the rest won't hesitate to rush back here."

Sam shut the door and dropped the bar to lock it. "He's right, Billy, but I got an idea!" Stepping into the store, he grabbed the small handsaw and ran back into the living quarters. Bypassing Ealy and me, Sam dropped to his knees next to the Ealys' bed in the corner. Ducking under, he used his shoulders to lift the frame and began to saw into the wooden floor.

"Mrs. Ealy, you got a blanket?"

"What the tarnation are you doing?" Ealy said as he wrapped a long strip of fabric around my leg a few times.

"I think I know what he's doin'," Mary Ealy said, opening a trunk and pulling out a quilt. Walking over to Sam, she added, "Will this do?"

"Sure will! Billy, come here!"

"I see what he's about," I told the Reverend. "Help me over to him."

Ealy tied the material off to slow the bleeding down, put his arm around me, and helped me to where Sam knelt on the floor, the hole now big enough for a man to fall through.

"Give me your guns and get in," Sam said as he lay the blanket under the wooden floor on the dirt below.

"I'm not giving you—"

"I need to reload them," Sam explained.

"Oh." I handed my guns over.

As the Reverend held the bed up, I eased myself down into the hole. I laid down on the blanket with a groan as Sam filled both six-shooters with silver-shot. Once situated, Sam handed me the guns, one revolver in each hand.

I looked up at Reverend Ealy. "All of ya get outta this room so you can claim to knowin' nothin' if I'm found. With a nod, Ealy lowered the bed as his wife fetched the children and Suzie. I watched as they all filed into the store just as Sam began to put the wood back over me.

"And what do I do if they find me?" I whispered to Sam.

"Shoot 'em," he said, as he eased the edge of the area rug to just cover the cut line. I could still see out through the cracks, though, and saw Sam salute me as he left to join the Ealys.

It wasn't quiet long. Soon a desperate pounding came at the back door, and my heart rose to my throat. I did not want to be the reason this family got hurt or arrested. They didn't deserve that.

"Reverend Ealy, open up!" Deputy George Peppin shouted through the closed and locked door.

"I'm in the store, hold on!" he yelled out, moving with a steady pace to the door. Opening it, Peppin barged into Ealy's apartment, along with Long and a few others of the Dolan faction.

"Tear this place apart...one of them bastards is still here. Find him!"

The men of *The House* swarmed into the store like locusts and tore the place apart. I could hear Sam being roughed up a bit, and I cocked both guns. If they didn't stop, I was going to come out and kill them all.

Soon, Suzie came into the room with the children, followed by Ealy and his wife.

"I don't know what you're lookin' for, no one is here."

"The blood trail leads into here," Peppin said.

"Yes. I tied off his wound, and as far as I know, hurt too bad to ride, he ran on foot the other direction while the Regulators drew your attention the other way as they rode out of town."

I grinned. Ealy was one smart man.

I watched as Matthews stepped into view, and my blood heated. If he so much as touched this family, I'd kill him here and now.

A man I didn't know came into the room. He smelled of wolf, and the wound in my leg throbbed with fervor. It desired to be healed and the urge to burst out shooting became overwhelming, like I was some horny fifteen-year-old boy again with no control of how my body reacted to the sight of a beautiful woman.

To give in and explode prematurely out of my hiding spot would put the Ealys in harm's way, so I fought it. I stopped breathing and with the smell not tugging at my needs, the fever building in me to kill him eased away. He needed to leave the room soon though.

George Peppin entered and forced his way into the other rooms of the Ealys' apartments, pawing through the belongings of Suzie and the young girls in the front room as Suzie objected loudly to him getting his dirty hands on her things. Stepping back out into the main room, not more than ten feet from me, Miss Suzie Gates was on his tail, face red with anger.

"Anythin'?" Peppin asked the werewolf man I didn't recognize.

"No one is here, Sheriff," he replied.

Suzie scoffed. "Sheriff? Brady's body still lays in the street, not even cold yet, and you've already decided you're just the man to replace him? I think not."

Peppin whirled around, his face in hers, but bit back the words he wanted to say. Instead, he muttered to Ealy, "I suggest you keep her in line, Reverend."

Ealy raised an eyebrow at Peppin. "She's a grown woman, and I'm not her father. She can say as she pleases. You, however, have barged in and destroyed my home, and you will not disrespect the women in it as well. Now get out."

Peppin hesitated for a moment as Suzie stared him, hands on hips, not flinching an inch. With his eyes still on hers, he said, "Let's go, men. He isn't here."

The others noisily left, their muddy boots pounding out the door back into the wet and cold as I slowly let myself breathe, out of my mouth only, hoping to not get a whiff of the werewolf among them again.

Thankfully, they were all out soon enough, and with the door shut and locked again, Mary drew the curtains, and Sam helped me out of my hiding spot.

"I can't thank you enough," I told them, sliding both guns into their respective holsters.

Ealy grunted, obviously unhappy. I wasn't sure if that irritation was more for me, for what had occurred here today, or Peppin. I decided it was likely all three and limped away from him.

"Where do you think you're going?" Suzie said. "They are swarming out there, and you're bleeding again. Doc?"

"What? Oh, yes, yes. Billy, come into the store and let me tend to that properly now. Sam, fetch me something to sterilize the wound with."

I noticed Sam's nose was bleeding and my blood boiled again. "Sam, are you okay?"

"This ain't nothin'. Don't you worry 'bout it," he told me and headed into the store to find what Ealy asked for.

We followed him into the store, the front windows covered so no one on the street could see in, and the Reverend motioned me toward the back window so he'd have good light. "Pull your pants down so I can see the wound better."

I undid the bandage he'd tied around my wound, undid my belt, and let my drawers and long undergarments drop to my knees. Doing my best to cover my manhood with my long shirt that'd been tucked in, I sat on the stool in a way where the light hit my wounded leg.

Unfazed by either my nakedness or the blood, the doctor examined the wound. "You're lucky, the bullet exited the other side."

"Funny, I don't feel lucky about now," I said, the wound hurting me like it was on fire as Ealy pushed on it.

Sam ran up. "This is all I could find," he said, handing something to Ealy.

"You're about to feel even less lucky," Ealy told me, "so bite down on somethin'."

I pulled my leather belt from the straps of my pants and put it between my teeth as Ealy had tied a piece of material to the carved loop at the end of a slim, well-sanded, four-inch rod of wood. "Soak this," he told Sam.

When he did, I smelled the kerosene. Yet, before I could panic further, the Reverend took action. Quick as lighting, he slipped the newly alcohol-covered wooden item into the hole the bullet had made, entering the thigh on one side and exiting out the other, pulling the material through it.

Screaming with my teeth clenched on the belt, my eyes watered as I fought to stay conscious.

"This silk handkerchief is all I had handy," Ealy said as he cut the material off the wooden needle. Tying the two ends together, he added, "That should help stop the bleeding too."

I nodded, the pain too much to reply in words, as I pulled up my pants.

"Best you stay put for a bit," Ealy told me.

"Come rest in here for a while," Mary said from the door between the store and living quarters. "Suzie made you a spot to lie down."

Removing the belt from my teeth, I squeezed out, "Thank you," before weaving my belt back through the loops of my pants. Once the buckle was set, I limped into the apartment and found that Suzie had cleaned off and brought out a single mattress into the back room from the front.

Covering it with a fresh blanket, Suzie motioned toward it. "Lay down and rest."

I eased myself onto the straw mattress and thanked her. As she walked away though, I added, "The way you stood up to Peppin, that was applause worthy."

She grinned. "Thank you, Mr. Bonney. But Peppin is a pervert and deserved it. Pawing through my things like you'd be hidin' in my dresser drawers." With an exasperated huff and eye roll, she walked away to gather the older child and took her to sit on her mom and dad's bed.

I fell asleep listening to Suzie reading a book to the little girl, waking up about an hour or so later. When I woke, I found a note next to my head. I recognized the handwriting: Roy.

Opening it, I read that the Regulators were at Brewer's waiting on me and that if I was going to ride with them, I needed to hurry along soon.

With a groan, I stood, shoved the note in my pocket, and made my way to the door.

"You are in no shape to ride," Ealy said.

"Tell me somethin' I don't know," I replied. "But I have to get movin' on if I'm gonna rejoin the men. Besides, if I wait too long, Peppin and his crew are goin' to surround the town waitin' on me and I'd rather not get pinned in. Besides, it puts you all in danger."

Ealy handed me my coat. "Keep the wound clean, and it should heal in a few weeks."

I shuddered at that idea and slipped on the long jacket. "It doesn't hurt too bad, to be honest," I lied. "But here's to hopin' it takes less time than that to be back to normal."

Truth was, I was praying I'd run into a werewolf or two so I could heal as soon as possible, for my leg hurt like the dickens. Grabbing my hat from a corner, I opened the back door and whistled for Colonel. The black beauty trotted up and bumped me with his nose.

I put my hat on my head. "I'm okay, big fella."

With pain ripping through me like fire, I hoisted myself into the saddle. Reins in one hand, gun in the other, I thanked the Ealys again, and with a prayer on my lips, I bolted out of the corral about two hours after everything had gone down.

Riding out into the street, I saw Amelia Bolton and some other children and hoped they'd not been out on the street when we'd ambushed Brady. I smiled at her, and though it hurt like hell, I kicked Colonel's sides and we were off.

We'd only gone a short distance when bullets started to fly toward me. Leaning down over Colonel's neck, I fired my gun behind me three times and kept going. Just before the bend in the road, the man who'd smelled like a werewolf from earlier ran toward me, close enough for me to see his white teeth grinning at me as he pulled his weapon.

Our eyes met, I saw his pupils glow golden, and before I could even think about it, instinct kicked in, and I shot him in the forehead and rode out of town.

Power slammed into me, and I felt the wound try to heal. It stung more than it should, and I remembered the silk tied into the wound. As quick as I could while riding, I reached for my small knife, then undid my pants. Reaching down into my drawers, I cut the silk and pulled it out of the wound with a grunt. It healed, and I did up my pants.

Putting the knife away, I rode Colonel up onto the knoll just east of the Ellis store. The hill was just high up enough to see the whole town and for them to see me. With my wound now healed, I leapt down from Colonel onto steady legs. With a smile on my face, I removed my hat and made a big sweeping bow to the town.

With a laugh, I easily pulled myself back into the saddle, waved my hat again at the town, and rode on out of it, headed for Brewer's. However, when I arrived, what I saw there was not what I'd been expecting.

Wolves, at least ten of them, had Brewer's barn surrounded with my friends inside. They were firing off a shot here and there, but it was evident they were saving ammunition. One glance told me they were also cut off from their horses, where their rifles and extra silver bullets would be.

None of them had seen me, and luckily, I was downwind, so the wolves hadn't smelled me either. Easing Colonel and I behind some of the trees nearby, I replaced the silver bullets I'd fired leaving town, and without thinking about it too much, I locked the cylinder back into place and leaned down to speak in Colonel's ear.

"We need to go in full tilt, and I got no energy to share. Can you do it?"

Seeming to understand, he pranced quietly in place.

"Good, we need to clear a path to their horses. Let's go!"

We needed a bit more space to build up speed, so I rode Colonel away from the ranch a bit. Once far enough away, I turned him about, took a settling breath, and said, "Full out, Colonel."

He nodded in his way and I hit his sides with my heels. He took off like the devil himself was on our ass. Coming around the bend into sight, I dropped my body to the side of the horse like I'd seen the Apache warriors do. I barreled toward the group who blocked my friends from their horses. Riding at a right angle, they couldn't see anything but a big black horse running toward them, until it was too late.

I knew I had to do it quickly and get out of there before their souls hit me and I got too dizzy to stay on the horse. Falling off Colonel with wolves about and my head spinning would be suicide. But I needed souls in the chamber, and my men needed their horses.

Taking aim, I hit the biggest wolf first, then another and another, until I was empty. I pulled myself up seconds before the souls hit me. I lay with my face in Colonel's mane, the world spinning, watching some of the Regulators run for their rifles as I reached the barn.

Counting the souls as they hit me, I said, "One, two, four...what comes after five?"

"Damn it, he's worthless," Charlie said, taking the rifle off my saddle. "It's up to us. Fire!"

My rifle and those behind me went off, and as they did, I saw three more men run to their horses. They mounted, grabbed up their silver-loaded weapons, and chased down the other wolves. They scattered and soon all was quiet, save for the voice of Dick Brewer.

"You have a lot to answer for, asshole."

He was already swearing, which meant, in short, it was gonna be a long day.

* * *

To say Brewer was "merely upset" with our actions that morning would be like saying an avalanche was nothing more than a snowball. The man couldn't even get a full sentence out without cursing one of us out.

"What the hell were you thinkin'?" Brewer's voice boomed.

My head was no longer spinning, but taking that many souls at once had me feeling hung over. "Do you need to yell?"

"Yes! Yes, I need to yell! It's either that or beat the shit out of you...out of you *all!*" Brewer shouted as he looked from one man to another, finally zeroing in on me. "Do you have any idea what you've done? You've kicked the hornet's nest, Billy. Any kind of sympathy we had on our side for *The House* killin' John will go out the door. And with what Axtel did, we needed that advantage."

"If we'd had any other choice," MacNab started to say.

"You did!" Dick said. Walking over to the Scotsman he added, "You are not the leader of this group and the sooner your big head can fathom that, the better. There were many ways to handle this and you chose the worst way possible."

MacNab opened his mouth but something in Brewer's eyes stopped him.

"What's even better is you then lead all of them bastards to my home. My fucking home. I should beat the hell out of you for that alone." Dick turned back to me. "And you, lettin' the well go dry you almost got yourself and the others killed. You can't let that happen again. Ever. Do you hear me?"

I heard fear in his voice now and understood part of his reaction stemmed from knowing I almost died. Because of that, I didn't reply in kind. Instead, I said, "You're right. I'll keep a better eye on that."

"Damn straight you will." He walked away and hit a wall of the barn, putting a hole in it. Thinking fast on his feet to explain that, he added, "Damn termites."

Everything was silent as we all waited for him to say something else. But instead, he left the barn and headed to his home without so much as another look at us.

We took that as a sign and headed off to San Pat for the night hoping that by the next day he'd calmed down a bit. Thankfully, he had. Not by a lot, but enough to understand we'd been trying to save McSween from being killed like John had.

"Look, I'm not happy with what y'all did," he said to start off with. "I understand it wasn't a planned thing, that you made call, a *bad* call, but you really had no other option. Problem is, you killed the sheriff, so we gotta get outta here."

"Where to, Captain?" Middleton asked.

"We need more men. Let's go see if the Coes are ready to join us."

With all in agreement, we hit George Coe's place first.

Entering his home, I yelled out, "Come across, George, and pay me that five cents you bet me. I've won it!"

George came out from his room. "So I heard." Reaching in his pocket, he pulled out a five-cent piece and handed it to me. "Here you go."

"Thank you, good sir," I said, stuffing it in my pocket. "Now pack up your stuff and come with us."

"Where ya headed?"

Dick walked in. "Spring term of court is comin' up, which means Judge Bristol is on his way to town. We were thinkin' that we might run into him on his journey, see if we could have a chat. But on the way, we was thinkin' of payin' a visit to George Davis."

"Isn't he the outlaw who's been stealin' our horses?"

"One and the same," Dick said. "Heard rumor he's gonna be on the Tularosa side of Rinconada for a rendezvous."

"Thought we might blot him off the map," I said.

Dick sighed. "Not if we can encourage him to move on to another part of town."

"Or that," I said, pointing at Brewer.

"Well, I'm in," George said. "Frank?"

George's cousin nodded. "Same."

"What about Ab?" I asked.

Ab Saunders came into the main room. A slight young man with a pleasant face and demeanor. "I'm stayin' out this time 'round. Besides, we gotta leave someone here to tend to the farm, don't we?"

"Smart thinkin'," Dick said. Turning to the Coes, he said, "Get a war bag packed, both of ya, and let's get movin'."

The Coes nodded and headed off to prep for our new mission.

BRAVE AS A LION

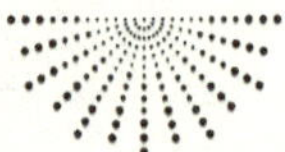

We started out on our new mission, and because we were passing by the old Dowlin Mill on the way, we stopped to pick up supplies at his store and eat something. That's when he informed us that there was a one-hundred-dollar reward for each head of the Regulators, dead or alive. George was a hair startled to hear this, but I was a bit offended.

"Only a hundred? That's just shameful," I said.

"You rather it be higher so more would try and kill you?" Frank asked.

I thought on that. "Well, when you put it that way…"

Dick laughed. "Billy likes to speak and act before he thinks."

"Better than not actin' at all if you ask me," I retorted.

"I concur," Charlie agreed.

I grinned but could feel Brewer was still mad about Brady, so I shut my mouth, and we mounted back up.

We rode through to Rinconada on Wednesday the third, where we camped for the night, eating good on a steer we butchered earlier that evening. I thought we would lose our kill to the Apaches who were nearby watching us, but they didn't speak to us. Either we got lucky or they had a Supernatural Tracker with them. Word was, one of those could smell a werewolf a mile away and they likely smelled Brewer and thought we had one tailing us, so they stayed far away.

"Billy cooked, so y'all boys can clean it up and fetch more wood for the fire," Brewer told them. "If ya aren't doin' that, help the Coes with settlin' the horses in for the night."

The group quickly began to do as he asked, leaving me alone with Dick. This was obviously his objective, since the minute we were alone, he spoke to me without a snide tone under it for the first time in days.

"Did you get the black water?"

"Oh, now you want to know."

Dick glared at me. "Did you or didn't you?"

"Yeah, I did." I went and grabbed the sack from my saddle and handed it to him.

He looked inside. "Two? Wow, I guess you did do somethin' worth a damn while I was gone. Here, keep one just in case."

"Sure," I said, taking the sack back from him. When he said nothing, my anger became sarcastic rage. "Thanks, Billy, I know you put your life on the line to get that for me. Oh, you're welcome, Dick. It was no problem at all. Not like I got paralyzed doin' it and was lucky enough to figure out how to stop the poison before I was useless. But sure...you go on and just keep being a prick about Monday mornin'."

Mad as hell, I threw the sack toward my things and headed back to the fire, being sure to hit him with my shoulder as I went past. This knocked him off balance, which surprised him and me, but I said nothing and went back to stoking the fire.

It was quiet, the only sound the crickets and other animals coming out for their nightly prowl, as I pulled out a cigarette and lit it. Tossing the match into the flames, I decided to use my elevated sight to help find more wood and walked off.

"Billy, wait," Dick said.

I stopped but didn't turn toward him.

"I'm sorry," Dick said, his voice quiet as a mouse behind me.

Too mad to reply, I just stood there smoking my cigarette, wishing my feet would take me out to hunt for wood, but they seemed rooted to the spot.

"Thank you for this," Dick added. "I'm sure it'll help me stay human during the day when the moon's up."

"You're welcome," I said, my jaw clenched.

"Billy, I'm allowed to be mad that you killed Brady."

I turned on him. "Did I say you couldn't be mad? I did not! But you weren't there! We had to make a decision, and I'm sorry if you don't like it, but it's done, and we saved two men's lives and took out a pivotal component in Scáthach's army."

Brewer sighed. "I know. It's just...it makes us look bad. Public opinion matters, and I'd bet we just lost a lot of credibility due to your stunt. Not to mention Jim's side is hurtin' him bad. I'm sendin' him back to Fort Stanton to be seen."

"Soul well was empty, and I was worse off. I had no choice but to let him leave injured. It's been eatin' me up inside." I inhaled on my cigarette in the silence that followed.

"Ya can't save everyone."

Blowing out the smoke, I laughed as I turned around to face him. "First you say I shoulda not left him injured, and now I can't save everyone? Which is it, Dick? 'Cause I'd like to know."

Brewer sighed, and his head dropped backward. Looking up at the stars, he said, "You're right, I'm sorry. It's just...it's the new moon and I'm all messed up. I know you did what ya had to. That you coulda died savin' McSween...that you almost died gettin' me the black water. I'm grateful. I really am."

After a moment, I said, "Don't thank me yet. Wait and see if it helps."

He laughed lightly. "Good point...but thanks anyways."

"Men are comin' back, I can hear 'em," I said. "Are we good?"

He lowered his head to look at me. "Yeah. We're good. I'm gonna go put this with my things." He got a few feet away from me and added, "Ya know killin' Brady is gonna come back to bite you in the ass, right?"

I inhaled on the cigarette, slowly exhaling the smoke with a sigh, and said with utmost sincerity, "Yeah. Yeah, I know."

With a nod, Dick left as the men returned with wood, and I headed to check on Colonel.

* * *

Sitting around the large bonfire drinking coffee spiked with a touch of whiskey, the fifteen of us also began to pass the bottle around for a little extra swig here and there. The men swapped stories, bragging about how they were going to wipe out the little bunch on the other side of the mountains. Then they talked about riding into Lincoln and settling in short order all the difficulties that were troubling the people there.

They sounded like a brave band of heroes to hear them tell it, and I couldn't help but laugh. Most of these men were an inexperienced bunch of greenhorns, and as I looked around the campsite, the proof of this was staring me in the face; guns lay all over the campsite, carelessly left here and there near trees and out of arms' reach. I sat near Dick and whispered this under my breath.

"What do you want to do?" he whispered so quietly that no one but me could hear him.

I told him my plan.

He grinned and gave a nod.

As they told story after story, I found a chance to slip five or six lead cartridges out of my belt and toss them into the fire. I sat and waited as they continued to chat, wondering what they would do. After about a minute, I found out.

The cartridges started to explode in the fire, going off one by one. Lo and behold, all the men, except Dick and I, made a mad dash for the tall timber faster than anything I'd ever seen, taking nothing with them. Dick stepped aside to let me take the fall for this prank, which was fine by me. I stood by the fire, arms folded, and unconcerned.

Slowly they returned to the fire like whipped curs, and I said,

"You're a damn fine bunch of soldiers, aren't ya? Runnin' like a bunch of coyotes and forgettin' to take your guns."

"Damn you, Billy!" someone shouted.

"I just want to break you in a little before we met the enemy, and, boys, I'm sure proud of your nerve." I smiled and laughed. "You should've seen your faces!"

For a moment, they seemed to stand there, embarrassed and upset. But they soon swallowed their medicine and laughed along with me.

* * *

Leaving my car parked a short distance from the entrance, I walked past a man smoking a cigarette and into Bobby's Bar and Grill to find it was more bar than grill. The primary seating was at the bar, with a few tables scattered about that didn't seat more than two each. Most folks stood, beer in hand, talking with their friends as I made my way through the crowd to the back. Here I noted that the building took a sharp turn to the right, and the short part of the L-shaped building held a pool table. Currently, it was in use, coins lined up on the side for those waiting their turn to play the winner.

The green of the pool table was a bit worse for wear, as were the bar's walls, floor, and stools, but no one seemed to mind. I ordered a whiskey on the rocks and knowing how Fletcher loved to play pool, I requested my change be in coins. Laying down enough to hold my spot in line, I sat down at the back of the bar to keep an eye on both rooms. If Fletcher had met someone who gave him info, it would've been at this pool table or the bar.

Drinking my whiskey, thinking about my upcoming trip, my mind drifted back to April third, the last night the Regulators were all together. It was a fun evening of drinking whiskey by the fire as George Coe told us a story about Brewer and his trip to where I'd soon be heading, Las Cruces.

* * *

W ere you in on this prank, Dick?" Charlie asked.

Brewer just grinned.

"Of course he was," George said. "If he hadn't been, he'd have had his gun out and shooting. Have you all not heard of Richard M. Brewer's resolve?"

"George, don't start," Dick said, looking embarrassed, which was a new thing to see.

"Oh, do start, George," I said. "What are you talkin' about?"

"That's right, this was before you got to Lincoln, Billy. I must say this here is my favorite Brewer story ever."

"Must you, George?" Dick pleaded.

"Oh, I *must* tell how you stuck it to The Boys and the Caseys in the same month. Come now, this is a fun story!"

Dick sighed. "I'm goin' to bed then." He stood, his tall frame lit by the fire, and added, "Don't believe all he tells you."

Brewer headed to his bedroll, the one farthest from the fire, saying he could keep an eye on us all better from there, but I knew it was because he just ran hotter than the rest of us now.

As he bunked down, everyone else fetched their guns and kept them handy as they sat back down by the fire for the story.

George took a sip of whiskey and began. "As many of you know, Tunstall was travelin' this summer to purchase items for the store. On his way home, he contracted smallpox and was laid up in Las Vegas. Well, Dick bein' foreman an' all, that left him in charge when The Boys stole John's horses. So, what does Dick do? He gets Charlie and Doc, and they chase 'em down."

Charlie picked up the tale. "We ride through the Tularosa valley, skirtin' 'round the White Sands area, and head on to Shedd's ranch."

"Why there?" I asked, pretending I had no idea what was out there.

"Everyone, well not everyone if *you* don't know," Doc said, "but *most* everyone knows that's the clearin' house for stolen stock. It's located on the eastern slope of the San Agustin pass."

"So, we get there," Charlie says, "and I'll be damned if the animals weren't right there in plain sight! Obviously, Dick goes to talk to the seven Boys that are there at the time. Has a long parley with them and finally they tell him, 'Well, we'll give you back your horses and keep the balance to pay our expenses in the matter.'"

"And what does Dick say?" Doc said, laughing. "He said somethin' that could only come out of his mouth, 'If you can't give me the Englishman's, you can keep them all and go to hell.'"

"Brave as a lion, that man!" George said with pride and a chuckle.

"Agreed!" Doc replied. "Of course, he doesn't stop there. He then goes on to Las Cruces and tries to round up men to assist him to go back and take The Boys on. Thing is, everyone in that town is either friends of The Boys or members. After three days he had nothin'. Even the sheriff there was crooked, and he tells Dick that there's nothin' he can do since the actual theft didn't happen in his jurisdiction."

"Of course he did!" I said with a laugh. "If that was the case, what did y'all do?"

"We went back to Lincoln to tell McSween. Thankfully, he'd heard that The Boys were down at Seven Rivers. He went to Sheriff Brady and demanded that he appoint Brewer a deputy sheriff, raise a posse, and go after 'em. He even offered to supply the arms and provisions from the store."

I took the bottle passed to me. "Let me guess, Brady still said no."

"At first," Doc said, "but eventually he agreed. So, on the twelfth of October, fifteen men thundered down the valley toward the Pecos and Seven Rivers."

"Oh, remember how when we hit Peñasco, Brady wanted to turn back?" Charlie said. "Guess what does Dick does! He says he's pushin' on and asks what men will follow him."

"Hell, Dick woulda gone on alone if no one had agreed to go," Doc said.

"Truth!" Charlie shouted, pointing at Doc. "But all of 'em wanted to follow Dick. So we rode all night, and in the gray dawn, we surrounded the place. It was one of those houses built over a hole so that when you're inside, half of the room is underground while half is above ground.

"We yelled out that they were surrounded and should surrender.

They started firin' at us, and we returned it. A lot of shots were fired that day. Hell, three shots were within four or five inches of Dick but missed."

Doc hummed in agreement. "Later on, Jessie admitted that he had taken those three shots and had no idea how he missed, seein' as he had good square shots at him, and he'd saved those for him alone."

"How'd you get them to surrender?" I asked.

"Dick told them that he meant to take them dead or alive, and comin' from him, they knew he meant it," Charlie said.

George took the whiskey bottle from me. "Plus, Brady promised them they wouldn't be lynched if they surrendered, so they came out with their hands up."

"But that's not where the tale ends," Charlie said. "Tunstall made it back from Las Vegas around this time and was on his way to the Hondo Valley to deliver somethin' to Chisum when he ran into Dick and The Boys. He came to a halt and says," Charlie stopped, stood, and put on a British accent. "Why, I thought you boys went out to round up some wild stock.'"

Doc stood. "The posse-men and Brewer laughed, as did The Boys, and Tunstall musta looked uncertain of what was goin' on, so one of 'em speaks back at him in the same accent." Facing Charlie, Doc sneered like one of The Boys mighta and finished in a bad English accent, "By Jove! He don't know if Dick has got us or if we've got him."

Everyone laughed.

Continuing to play out the scene, Doc goes, "Do you got any whiskey, Englishman?"

"Merely a dram," Charlie said, sounding just like Tunstall to my ear. "If you knew me, you would know that I don't need any to keep my blood warm, but if you met me at Lincoln, I'd soak you if you wished."

"We'll be in the jug by then, but you can come soak us there," Doc replied.

"Who was this?" I asked.

Charlie turned to me. "Tom Hill."

"Did he ever soak 'em?" I replied.

"He did, once, I do believe," Charlie said, sitting back down. "I think he was tryin' to learn where his dapple-gray mules were. He loved those two."

"He had to know that they'd not actually be charged or held once in Brady's custody," I said.

"Oh, Brewer was under no illusions about what would happen when The Boys got to Lincoln," Doc said. "He told Tunstall, 'They'll get out of jail sure as fate. They have more friends in the country than enemies, and you mark me, those chaps will get let out. Brady will let 'em go for sure.'"

"That's not what I sound like, Doc!" Brewer yelled out at us.

Everyone began to laugh.

"You sure about that?" I shouted back.

"You all can bugger off!"

"Too much time with Tunstall! Pickin' up them British words," Charlie teased.

George stood. "But that wasn't the end of Tunstall's issues or Dick's. No sooner was Brewer back than McSween told him about how the widow Casey had left town for Texas with the cattle she'd sold to Tunstall at auction *plus* some others from his herd."

"McSween was beside himself and he asked Dick what was to be done," Charlie said. "And Dick goes—"

"I must rack out on the road again and bring 'em back, to be sure I ain't goin' to see John run over," came Dick's deep voice from behind me.

"Thought you was goin' to bed," I joked.

"Well, I hate for y'all to get it wrong."

"Okay then, what did you do?" I asked.

"I gathered a posse of fifteen men, most of which were Mexicans, and I went out after 'em."

I laughed. "Of course you did! But did you find 'em?"

"Sure did. Came across them about fifteen or twenty miles across the Texas line. I demanded a portion of the cattle, explainin' I knew they were the property of Tunstall and McSween. After some heated discussion, they let me take 'em. I plucked four hundred head out of the herd and began to take them back to Lincoln."

"I heard you went back the next day and threw guns down on the two Casey boys," George said. "Brought them to Lincoln without a warrant, forcin' them to come along."

"I did. Figured that the Caseys might try to pull this again and the only way that wouldn't happen would be if they were put out by the whole affair. That's why I snatched the boys up and took 'em with the cattle back to Lincoln and had them charged for theft."

"But you hit a snag, didn't ya, big fella?" Doc said. "Ya see, Billy, their mother was a day behind, chasin' after her boys, and she just so happened to run into John Chisum and told him what Dick had done."

Dick rolled his eyes and crossed his arms over his chest. "He just had to get involved."

"In fact," Doc continued, "Uncle John escorted her to Lincoln and used his influence with you to drop the charges, didn't he?"

"Well, damn it, Doc. It wasn't like I was plannin' to go through with it. I just wanted to teach them boys a lesson about stealin' other people's property."

"That you did, big man...that you did," Doc said.

I stood and slapped Brewer on the shoulder. "So...what you're sayin' is Dick's got the courage of a lion but the big lovin' heart of house cat."

Dick immediately spun me, wrapping his arm around my neck from behind, and used his other hand to mess up my hair before pulling me to the ground. "What was that you were sayin'?"

I laughed so hard, tears filled my eyes. "All right, all right! I give! Heart and soul of a fierce lion are you!"

Dick let go. "That's more like it."

I sat back on my bed roll and looked up at him. "I'll say this, I bet them kids never stole livestock again! You may have a big heart, but you can be scary when you have to be. I wish I'd been there to see you arrest 'em. It woulda been a hoot!"

* * *

The loud crack of fifteen racked pool balls breaking pulled me from my memories. Glancing over, I was a bit shocked to note that the person who'd broke them so forcefully was a woman. She was about my height with dark hair pulled back into a French braid and skin the lovely color of someone from parents of different races. She was a slip of a girl, likely in her mid to late thirties, and while I watched, she called a pocket and hit a solid in. I stood and wandered over as she did that again, and only missing by a smidgen on her third.

"All yours, Sam," she said, her voice holding a slight Irish lilt to it.

"Damn it, Rose, ya left me with nothin'," her opponent complained.

"Not if you know what you're doin'," she replied.

I chuckled, which got Sam's attention.

"Somethin' funny, pretty boy?"

I didn't reply, as I didn't think he was talking to me. But when his buddy gave me a shove from behind, I clued in.

"I'm talkin' to you, blondie."

I raised an eyebrow at him. "My hair is light golden brown, thank you, and yes, somethin' is funny."

"Oh?" Sam retorted.

"She's not wrong. You have a few shots, but you'd have to really know the game and how to use the bumpers to your advantage to do 'em."

"Care to show me how, hotshot?"

"No way in hell. Those are my coins sittin' there, so I'm next. I want to see if she can whoop my ass."

"Oh, you think I'm gonna lose, do ya?" Sam asked.

"Look at the table," I said. When he didn't seem to get what I was sayin, I followed my comment up with, "Yes. Now play and prove me wrong."

There was a moment where it appeared they were considering kicking my ass instead, but he finally just chalked the end of his cue and took his shot, missing by more than he should have.

Rose stepped up and gave me a flirty look before calling a pocket, sinking her next ball, then another, and then the eight-ball.

I downed the rest of my drink and set the glass down. "I rest my case."

Sam shoved his pool cue at his friend and took a step toward me like he was going to challenge me to a fight. "How about I show you my case."

Purposefully, I put my hands in my pockets in such a way as to reveal the badge I'd clipped to my belt. "I really wouldn't."

Sam's buddy, the same man I'd seen smoking out front when I arrived, grabbed his arm. "Horse feathers, he's a cop."

"No...but you're close. Still wanna show me your case?"

"Come on, Sam, let's go," his buddy said.

Reluctantly, Sam backed up and walked off. His pal gently set the pool cue on the table, and with a nod at me, they left.

"Well, you sure do know how to enter a game with flair," Rose said. "Rack 'em."

"You won the last game, that's your honor, ma'am."

"And I say, rack 'em."

I snagged the triangular rack. "All right, I'll do as the lady says." Placing the balls into it, I added, "William Kidwell, but you can call me Billy or Will if you'd like."

"Rose McMasters, nice to meet ya. So, if you're not a cop, what are ya?"

I could tell the whole room was listening, so I quickly weighed the options and decided it'd be best to be up front. "Fed," I told her as I carefully lifted the rack from the balls and put it away.

"Now that's interesting," she said, tossing the chalk to me.

Catching it, I picked up the pool cue and began to apply chalk to the tip. "Why's that?"

"No reason," she said, and it sounded like a lie.

Grabbing the cue ball on my way around the table, I purposefully stood close enough to feel her body heat. Looking into her light green eyes, I said, "I doubt you say anything without a reason, Miss Rose."

Her body temp rose as her cheeks flushed just a bit. I grinned and headed to the end of the table, setting the cue ball in position.

Leaning down, I took aim. "If I win, you tell me the reason. Deal?"

A nervous laugh skittered out of her, but when I lifted my eyes up to find hers, she said, "Okay, and if I win, you tell me why you're here."

A big grin filled my face. "You're on." Without looking away from her, I hit the cue ball, and it smashed into the balls at the other end, sending two solids into pockets. "Looks like you're stripes."

THE BATTLE AT BLAZER'S MILL

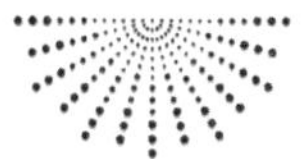

Just before noon on April fourth, we arrived at Blazer's Mill, located on a hillside halfway between Lincoln and Tularosa. Dr. Joseph H. Blazer, a retired dentist, owned the mill and had turned the land it was on into a little village of its own. Other than the sawmill, there was a roadhouse where you could get food, rest your horses, and stay the night if need be. If the county's Indian Agent, Fred Godfroy, a Murphy/Dolan supporter, hadn't lived on this property, it would've been a perfect spot to take a rest, but I was leery.

"We sure it's safe to stop here?" I asked.

"Why wouldn't it be?" George Coe asked.

"Well, in case y'all have forgotten, Fred Godfroy is a big supporter of *The House*, and he lives here with his family," I said, pointing at the older and smaller building of the pair of two-story buildings on the property. "In fact, his wife runs the roadhouse, cookin' and such."

"So?" Dick said. "There's fifteen of us and one of him. I think we're okay."

"They have a telegraph machine here, Dick," I reminded him. "And soldiers aren't far from this location either. We might be smart to keep on movin'."

Frank Coe heard us and rode up next to me. "We've known Doc

Blazer for years, Billy. We're fine. Besides, Fred Godfroy might be a tool of *The House*, but his wife is lovely and an amazin' cook…and I'm starvin'!"

The others laughed and agreed, so I was overruled.

Dick dismounted and ran into the two-story adobe roadhouse to make sure they could accommodate all of us for lunch. The Blazers had originally lived in this home but had recently built a three-story home to its right, which was where they lived now.

While the boys waited on Brewer, I rode Colonel to inspect the area on the other side of the road. Looking down the hill at the creek, I counted eight small, adobe homes on the property. These likely housed those who worked at the mill, blacksmith shop, and the post office with the store located on the back of the two-story roadhouse.

I was watching the paddle wheel of the sawmill gently turn through the water of the stream when Dick exited.

"She can accommodate us, so I put in an order for us," he said. With a nod toward the plank corral, he added, "We'll let the doc's son take care of the horses for us while we eat. Almer is a good kid."

We rode across the bridge and handed the horses off to Almer and two other teenage boys, Si Maxwell and Willie Pitts. While they took care of our ponies, we hung out front by the creek until Doctor Blazer himself came out to tell us the meal was ready.

Blazer was a tall man with broad shoulders and a wide chest, both of which made him appear taller and more upright. In the bright sunshine, his thick, well-groomed beard was a shade darker than his short hair, the latter of which had this tendency to naturally stand up on end before sweeping back from a high forehead.

Dressed for a day of working outside, Blazer leaned against the wide adobe archway at the south entrance as we approached, saying, "No guns inside, house rules and you know it."

"That we do, Joe," Dick said before turning to all of us. "Boys, leave your guns." The men grumbled but removed their belts and weapons as Dick continued, "A couple of us might as well stand guard while the others eat, though, if we got the enemy nearby and us goin' in without our weapons."

George Coe spoke up, knocking dirt from his boots, "I'll be one of the two, Dick."

Middleton smoothed his handlebar mustache and said, "I'm not as hungry as the rest of ya are at the moment. I can eat after y'all are done."

George then chimed in with, "Just make sure whoever finishes first comes out to take our places. I love me some of Mrs. Godfroy's cooking!"

Dick grinned as he removed his gun belt lined with cartridges. "You got it."

I was never comfortable without my gun on me, but currently my hunger was stronger than my desire to keep my weapons on me. I took my belt off, set it aside along with my Winchester, and followed the rest of the team through the south entrance. Hanging a right into the dining room, I looked out the window, for I had a bad feeling about this I couldn't shake. If I were making bets right then and bet on us, I had a feeling I'd lose, and I hate losing.

* * *

I set a drink down in front of Rose at the bar. Sitting on the stool beside her, I grinned. "Here you go."

"You won the game. Shouldn't I be the one buyin' you a drink?" she said.

"You only lost one more game than I did," I said, trying to make her feel better.

After I won the first game, she'd challenged me to best out of three, which had become best of five, finally relenting after I sank the eight ball first on our fifth game, my third win.

"Too true," she said, and drank some of the beer I'd sat before her.

"Ya know what? I'll still answer your question, but you have to honestly answer mine after that. Deal?"

With a coy look, she drank again before saying, "All right."

I set my whiskey down. "I'm here lookin' for a friend of mine who has gone missin'. Name is Fletcher, and I know he came through here not long ago. He stayed with Ms. Lois Gutierrez, and she told me this place had a pool table. Now, I know Fletcher like a brother, and he loves to play pool, so I came out this way to see if anyone might have seen him."

"And you figured since I was sharkin' the boys that Fletch woulda played me for a challenge, like you did."

I winked at her. "You're on the money, darlin'. So, did you? Is that the reason you said it was interestin' that I was here?"

"Why would you say that?" she said, looking a tad uncomfortable, yet covering it with a playful look in her eyes.

"For starters, 'cause ya called him Fletch, not Fletcher like I did, and I know he tells folks to call him that. Secondly, he's Irish, like you, so you'd have zeroed in on him in a heartbeat the minute you heard him talk."

Her face flushed a bit, and she drank. Setting the bottle down, she slowly wove her fingers together and rested her hands on the bar in front of her. "I'm only half Irish."

I grinned. "Still...he'd have heard it."

She casually looked around the bar to see who was near us, which was no one since it was close to closing time. With a sigh, she said, "Yeah, I met Fletcher. We got to know each other a little bit, and he told me who he was."

"Did he tell ya why he was here?"

"You mean his hunt for that New York mobster? Yeah, he told me. But that was only after I mentioned Mr. Magoon as the other New Yorker who'd been around recently. It's not like we get a lot of New Yorkers here in Carrizozo, New Mexico. You're the third in two months—that's more than likely been here in three years."

"You have a point. Are you the one that pointed him to Las Cruces then?"

"Yes. Seymour said he was headin' that way to make it rich in gamblin'. I told him he should stick to pool sharkin', but he just laughed, sayin' I didn't know where the real money was."

"Did he, by any chance, say who he was goin' to be meeting up in Las Cruces?"

"Seymour did mention a guy, but all I remembered was the name Sandman, so that's what I gave Fletch."

"We're closin' up in a few minutes," the bartender said.

I pulled out some money for a tip and placed it on the bar. "Come on, I'll walk ya to your car. It's late."

"I can promise you, Agent Kidwell, I know how to handle myself."

"I'm sure you do, but I'm still walkin' ya to your car."

With an eye roll, she got down off the stool. "Fine. Night, Pete!"

"Night, Rose!"

With a wave at the bartender, I opened the door for her, and we stepped out into the chill of a March evening in New Mexico.

Pulling her coat tight around her, Rose said, "I'm over this way."

"As am I, that's handy."

She laughed as we approached our cars, not far from one another, but quickly her laugh became a groan. "Oh no."

"What?" I asked, suddenly alert, my free hand reaching for my gun.

"Is that sporty car yours?"

"Yeah, why?"

"It appears Sam and his pal had to have the last word after all."

Fear gripped me, and I quickly looked over at my baby and saw what she'd seen before me. "Damn it!" I ran over to the car and squatted by one of the four flat tires. "He slashed 'em. Son of a bitch! Oh, he's gonna be a sorry man come tomorrow."

"Well, not much you can do now. I'll give ya a ride back to Lois's, and we'll get you towed in the mornin'. I'll go let Pete know."

Before I could stop her, she turned and ran back into the bar. I used that moment to examine the wards I'd put on the car. He hadn't, so everything else was fine. "Next time I get a protection ward, it's gonna include the tires, damn it," I grumbled.

"Pete says you'll be safe to leave your car here overnight. No one will tow it. Said he'd leave a note for the openin' bartender, too. Come on, I'll give ya a lift."

With a sigh of resignation, I agreed and got into her car. I was supposed to leave for Las Cruces in the morning...looked like I was gonna be late. I hated being late.

* * *

We can't be staying here too long," I told Dick. "We'll be late and miss that stagecoach."

"We'll be fine, Billy," he replied, still eating his food.

Frank Coe finished eating first. "I'm with Billy on this. We can't be dawdlin' here. I'll head on out and switch places with George, so we can get movin' sooner."

With that, he headed out, only for both of the boys standing guard to come rushing into the dining room.

"We got a situation, Cap'n," Middleton said, causing the whole gang to go silent.

Before Dick could reply, George said, "Buckshot Roberts just rode up to the post office."

Some of the gang who'd finished eating already stood and wandered over to our table while Dick yanked up his satchel and pulled out some papers from the front pocket.

"I have a warrant for him right here," Dick said, laying the paper in the center of the table.

"I know, I know," George said. "But Frank and I know him, he's got himself a ranch on the Ruidoso not too far from us. Mind you, we used to know him just as Bill Williams, but, well..."

"For God's sake, spit it out, George," I said with a laugh.

"Frank's gone to talk to him, I couldn't stop him. Said he was gonna try and convince him to turn himself in."

"What if he don't?" MacNab proposed, now standing between Charlie and me.

Dick looked from them to the rest of us and said, "Boys, he's a bad hombre, well-armed, and I ain't gonna ask anyone to go and get him, but who will volunteer? Anybody?"

Charlie was the first to pipe up. "You bet, I'll go for one."

"I'll go, too," Henry Brown chimed in, wiping his mustache of food remnants.

"You know you can count me in," Middleton said.

I wasn't surprised at any of their offers. It was the next voice I'd not expected.

"I'll be another to go, Dick," George said, likely volunteering to make sure nothing bad happened to his cousin.

Me knowing how pissed off Charlie still was from last week and our run-in with Roberts, I said, "I'd hate to miss this little frolic, so I guess I'll go, too."

"Good!" Brewer said.

More food was set down, and George looked at it longingly. "Think we can give Frank a bit of time to talk to him though?"

"Is that your head or your stomach talkin', George?" I teased.

"The least we can do is give Frank a chance for us to bring him in quietly...and let me eat."

Dick laughed. "Sit, eat, we'll give him some time."

Middleton and George sat down and eagerly dug into the food on the table. But Dick didn't plan to just wait and hope for the best.

"Billy, can you get an ear in on that?"

"Yeah, I can do that. Be right back."

I headed out into the hall that ran through the middle of the bottom level of the home. To my left was the door we'd come in from, to my far right was another door. I hustled to that and went through it and into the store. With a finger to my lips, I looked to the man working behind the counter. He was smart and said nothing.

Ear to the door that led out onto the porch where Frank sat with Roberts, I listened, recognizing Frank's voice easily.

"I had no idea you were sellin' your ranch."

"It's time for me to be movin' on," Roberts replied.

Frank sighed, and I knew he was about to broach the subject.

"Thing is, the Regulators have a warrant for your arrest."

"The hell you have," Roberts blurted out.

"Yes, and I'm glad you rode up because now we won't have the trouble of huntin' for you. You better come in the house and see Brewer and surrender."

"Me, surrender?" Roberts asked with a laugh.

"Why, of course. There ain't any way out of it now," Frank

told him.

"Well, we'll see about that."

"There are fifteen total in the gang, Bill," Frank said, "and if you don't surrender peaceable, it means simply they'll kill you. You wouldn't have a chance on Earth."

"As long as I've got a load in old Betsy here," Roberts said, my ears picking up the sound of him patting something, likely a rifle, "there ain't nobody goin' to arrest me, least of all this gang."

"Now, don't be foolish, Bill," Frank argued. "There ain't no sense in resistin' and gettin' yourself killed."

"I'd be killed if I surrendered."

"What makes ya think that?" Frank asked him, genuinely interested.

"Didn't I try to kill Billy Bonney and Charlie Bowdre last week? If those two fellows got their hands on me now, they'd kill me for sure."

"No, they wouldn't. You surrender and nobody will hurt you."

Not likely, but Frank sounded like he believed it.

"Yes," said Roberts. "That's what they told Morton and Baker. I know this gang."

I didn't wait around any longer, I'd heard enough. Roberts wasn't going to turn himself in, no way in hell. I went back into the dining room and brought everyone up to date. Roberts might've been slightly crippled from all his years in the service dealing with Indians, unable to lift a gun higher than his waist, but he was a good shot nonetheless.

Dick had this look on his face that told me he was feeling a bit bloodthirsty, and I knew his mind was made up—he wanted to take Roberts, regardless of the consequences.

I pulled him aside. "Moon's up. Did you drink any of the black water?"

"No. We don't know exactly what it does, and now ain't the time to test that out. Why?"

I sighed. "'Cause ya got that look in your eye."

"I'll be fine," he said, then stepped around me to the group. "Those of you who volunteered, go get suited back up. We're takin' this one today."

Charlie stood, a glint in his eye, too. "Said my name, did he, Billy? Well, let's see who comes out on top, shall we?" He tossed his napkin down on the table and headed out of the dining room.

I followed the boys out of the dining room and into the hall, with George right behind me, still chewing his last bit of food.

Heading toward the back porch, Dick said, "If he kills that little bunch, the rest of us will take a hand."

I looked to George. "Not so sure Dick's got a lot of confidence in us."

Stepping out the door, I took up my belt from Charlie who was handing it to me.

"Lead or silver?" George asked me quietly.

Middleton's heavyset and swarthy self pushed between us to his belongings. "He's human; lead is fine. Let's not waste the silver."

"What he said," I commented to George as Middleton loomed over me.

"You got it," George said and began to load his pistol and Winchester, as did the rest of us.

Coming close to me, Charlie said, "Is Brewer all right? He seems a bit...edgy. More vengeful than usual, if that's even a word to use for the gentle giant. Man's got blood in his eye."

Oh, if only I could tell him the truth. I wanted so badly to say, "Well, he's only been a werewolf for over two weeks, and the moon is out right now so he's got a bit of bloodlust going on, so go get a silver stake, I'll knock him out with it, and we'll just let Roberts go." Thing is, I couldn't. I'd made Dick a promise, and I would keep it. Plus, I knew Buckshot had a hand in Tunstall's murder, so there was no way we could let him leave.

We all finished loading up and headed around the east side of the house to sneak up on Roberts on the plank walkway out back. We all reached the corner, and Charlie gave me a look before he went around the bend, saying, "Roberts, hands up! You're under arrest!"

"Not much, Mary Ann..." Roberts said as an insult to Charlie.

The rest of us came around the corner and two shots fired simultaneously, Charlie's pistol and Roberts' rifle.

Pulling on my abilities, I began to see things slower than they were happening. Unable to stop it in time, I watched as Roberts's shot hit Charlie in the gut, glancing off the buckle of his cartridge belt. From there, the bullet hit George's gun, traveled up the barrel, hit his hand, sending the gun flying off the plank walkway.

Charlie went down, but not George. Instead, he ran at Roberts in a rage as I rushed to Charlie. Middleton shot at Roberts and missed. Standing, Roberts fired three times from the hip as he backed up around the front of the store. The first bullet missed George somehow while the second grazed my arm. The third caught Middleton in the chest, and he went down as Roberts went around the northwest corner of the building.

Henry and I were the only ones left standing with a gun seeing as Frank never had a weapon to begin with. I ordered Henry to check on Middleton, ran past the Coes, and then around the front of the store. Peering around the northwest corner, I saw Roberts step backward up onto the plank porch outside Dr. Blazer's office. I tried to see if he was hit, but couldn't tell, so I fired. Unfortunately, he'd just stepped into the recess of the door to the office, and my bullet missed.

Roberts must've opened the door and backed into the room, for all that stuck out toward me was the barrel of his Winchester. He fired, but it was empty. The door slammed shut, and I heard the lock turn. With a curse my momma would've slapped me for, I turned and ran back to the store entrance where I found Middleton coughing up blood and George Coe sitting with his cousin, nursing a hand that was bleeding rather profusely.

Dick came running around the northeast side of the building with Frank MacNab, Fred Waite, and Big Jim French.

"Where are the rest?" I asked, meaning Steve Stephens, John Scroggins, and Ignacio Gonzales.

"Went around the other side," Waite said, walking over to Frank Coe and handing him his guns and belt.

"What happened?" Frank MacNab demanded to know.

At the same time, Dick asked, "Where is he?"

MacNab wasn't in charge, so I answered Dick first, "He's locked himself in Blazer's office." Looking over at Charlie, who was curled up in pain on the ground, I gave the short version of what had occurred and explained that even though Charlie wasn't bleeding externally, he likely was on the inside from the hit he took that severed his cartridge belt.

"Are you okay?" Fred Waite asked George, looking down at his bleeding hand.

"Bastard took my trigger finger and busted up my hand really bad, Fred. I'm out."

Dick went over and knelt by Middleton, who coughed up more blood. Brewer looked up at us and said, "He's really bad. I'll get that bastard now at any cost. I'm gonna go talk to Blazer." With that, Dick stood and went into the store, running into Blazer's foreman, David Easton.

"I have a warrant for the man hiding in Blazer's office. I need you to go in there and bring him out."

Easton refused, begging Brewer and the rest of us to leave.

Having none of that, Brewer entered the house to go find Doctor Blazer, and I sat by Middleton. We all could hear Brewer's loud, bass voice demanding that the doctor bring Roberts out or he'd burn the house down. Seeing as Dick stormed out even madder than before, we all assumed Blazer told him no. The doc was neutral to the core, and if you were in his house, you were safe from either side of this war.

"I've got an idea. Let's move," Dick said.

MacNab stepped in Dick's way. "Pardon me for sayin' so, but shouldn't we be gettin' our injured to a doctor instead?"

Dick's eyes filled with silver fever-light, and I spun him about.

Tapping Dick's arm twice, I said, "MacNab has a point, we can go after Roberts, have a few of the others work at gettin' us outta here if it doesn't all go well."

Dick shut his eyes for a moment and took a deep breath. Letting it out, he opened them back up again, the light now gone, and said, "Fine, MacNab, you see if you can get a wagon from Blazer for our wounded. Big Jim will help you load. Frank, Fred, and Billy? Come with me."

Frank looked at George, who nodded and told him to go. We all followed Dick back around as he explained our plan of attack. Frank grabbed his Winchester once we reached the south entrance, and we all split up. Frank and Dick ran over the creek bridge and down the hill. His long legs carrying him, Dick ran to the mill itself and positioned himself behind a log pile at the end of the second building.

Frank kept running, through an open area, to the next building where he used the southeast corner for cover as he raised his rifle and took aim at the Blazers' house. They both might've been fifty feet below the house on an angle, be they had a direct line of sight to the window to Blazer's office from where they stood.

There was a small wagon just around the southwest corner, on the west side, just before you got to the plank porch in front of Blazer's office. Fred and I crouched around that, ready to take the shot if he stepped out. When he didn't, Dick fired his weapon from the woodpile, straight into the window of the office. Smoke rose from his weapon as he slunk down behind the logs.

When all stayed silent for a minute, I was wondering if Dick had hit the son of a bitch. Curious as to what was going on, I peeked out just as a gun went off. With the power of the supernatural in my system, I saw the bullet go past me, and my head swiveled to the left, following it down to where Dick had also raised up to see what was going on.

"No!" I shouted, but it happened anyway.

The bullet from Roberts hit Brewer in the head, causing him to drop face first onto the wood pile. Panic froze my voice, but not my feet. Without thinking twice, I ran for Brewer. Frank and Fred laid down cover fire for me and I prayed that everyone else was so focused on taking cover that they'd not notice my supernatural speed. I jumped the creek and ran behind the mill building before rushing to where Dick was at, not knowing what I'd find.

If Roberts had fired a silver bullet, Dick was dead for certain, for that bullet hit Brewer in the head. I saw it. Hell, we all saw it. Worse yet, if he wasn't dead, Dick was going to have to do the one thing he never wanted: tell the Regulators the truth.

RUNNING OUT OF TIME

Frank Coe was the closest to Brewer at the time of the shot, but thankfully, he was too busy covering me to reach Dick's side first. The big man had slid down from where he'd landed on the logs, now laying on his back lengthwise along the log pile to his right.

Dropping to my knees to the left of Brewer's head to block Frank's view of it, I saw blood around a hole that seemed to sink into his left eyebrow. However, as I watched, the bullet worked itself out and rolled down the side of his face to the ground.

Shocked, I picked it up. "Thank God. Dick, can you hear me?"

"Kid! Get away from there!" Frank yelled as he moved closer.

Gunfire erupted from the office window, and everyone, including Frank, put his focus there.

Dick groaned. "That son of a bitch."

"Don't you move," I whispered. "They all saw that bullet hit your head. If you sit up all fine and dandy, they'll know. Which I'm cool with, but are you?"

Dick lay perfectly still, which gave me his answer.

Noting movement our way, I held up a hand toward all parties.

"Don't come closer. It blew a section of his head clean off. He'd not want you to see this."

"Damn it!" Frank said. Turning his attention on the now silent window where Roberts was, he fired a few times while yelling out in emotional anguish.

I used that moment to pull my bandana off and wrap it around Dick's head, as if hiding the wound. "You're gonna have to pretend to be dead. Are you sure you just don't want to tell—"

"No! They can't know!" he whispered, heartbreak plastered all over his face. "Billy, they—"

"Okay. Shush!"

The gunfire ceased.

"Kid! Come on, we have to go! MacNab is loadin' up Charlie and the rest. If we're to save Middleton, we need to get him to Fort Stanton."

"We can't leave Dick here like this!" I shouted out.

"Dick would understand," Frank said.

"The hell I would," Dick muttered so quietly I almost didn't hear him.

"Go fetch your horse, mine too," I said. "I'll be right there." I quickly closed Dick's eyes and placed my white handkerchief over his left eye and eyebrow area, the blood soaking into it.

Frank came over and laid a hand on my shoulder. "He really was the best of us."

"I tied the part of his head back on," I explained.

"Roberts got him right on the forehead? Man, at least it was quick. Come on, say your goodbyes, kid, we've gotta go." Frank stopped a moment by Dick's head, crossed himself even though he wasn't a religious man, and ran toward the corral.

I bowed over Dick like I was praying for his soul. "You need to make a run for it, or you're gonna have to play dead."

"Shit. What if they bury me? What then?"

I'd not thought of that. "Uhh...I'll come back once it's safe and pull you out if that happens."

"I could run out of air by the time you get back here."

"I'll be back before that. I promise. But if you run now, you'll be runnin' forever, and they'll be on your ass. And not just Dolan's freak show, the Regulators, too."

I looked at the scene. There wasn't enough blood to sell the story. With a curse, I pulled my knife and cut my wrist and prayed enough blood hit the ground to be believable before my wound healed.

"What are you—"

"Shh!" I said, watching blood pool under his head from my arm. Once it closed, there wasn't a lot of blood on the ground and bandana, but it was going to have to do. Pulling Dick's extra bandana, I tied it around his head to secure the first one, then sat his head back down into the pool of blood I'd created.

"Billy, we got soldiers comin'!" Frank Coe shouted down at me.

"Damn it all to hell," I muttered. "I gotta go."

"Billy..." Dick said.

"I'll come back for you."

"And if I get found out before that?"

"Then you fuckin' run for it and kill a few of them sons of bitches while you're at it. You hear me? No judgment here."

"I can't let them learn—" Dick started to say.

"If it's your life or theirs, you are more important, you hear me?"

"Says who?"

"I do, damn it, so that's the end of it. Play dead, Dick." I watched him reluctantly close his eyes and slack the muscles of his face. "Good boy. Now stay, I'll be back."

"You wish I should sit and fetch, too?"

I grinned. He was joking, which was a good sign that he might listen to me and not end up dead for real. "Only if you're a good boy." I stood and saw MacNab driving the government wagon Blazer appeared to be lending us. I bent to pick up Dick's hat. "I'll hold onto this for ya."

"You best have a plan," he muttered, eyes open again and fixed tight on me.

I stared back and stayed low so no one could see my lips move. "Nope. But I will by the time I'm back."

"Don't you be late."

"You know how I feel about that. See you soon. Good luck." Standing, I turned and ran away from one of the best men I'd ever known, leaving him to possibly be buried alive or worse, die for real. Yeah, I was a great friend. Just great.

* * *

I hated being late so much so that without realizing it, I'd pressed down on the gas pedal of my car more than I should've on Highway 70. It was quarter after eleven o'clock at night on the twenty-ninth, and I'd just crossed over into Doña Ana County on my way to see the sheriff of Las Cruces.

I'd wanted to be here twelve hours previous, but getting the right tires for my car had proved to be a pain in the ass. God bless Rose or I'd still be in that town. Thankfully, her uncle ran a garage and was able to get the tires I needed from Roswell and on my car by the time they closed at seven. By then, Miss Lois had demanded I eat before I leave. I used this chance to call my partner again and was told when he'd arrive in Albuquerque.

Because of all this delay, I'd not pulled out of town until half past nine o'clock at night. With Las Cruces being a two-hour drive from Carrizozo, I was running out of time to make the deadline to check in at the hotel.

Before I could calm down enough to lay off the gas, police lights lit up behind me, along with a siren I barely heard over my blaring radio.

"Son of a bitch!" I said, checking my speed. "Aw, hell." It was at one hundred miles an hour. I was in a lot of trouble.

Pulling over, I turned the radio off, rolled my window down, and though I knew they'd prefer I turned the car off, I wasn't about to do that. No way in hell. The moon might not be up, but that didn't mean Scáthach's men behaved themselves in human form.

One cop approached my side as well as another at the passenger side of the car. The one on my side leaned down and looked at me.

His name tag said, "FLORES." "Evening, sir. Turn off the vehicle and hand over your license, registration, and proof of insurance."

"Of course," I said as the other officer tapped on the closed window of my passenger side. "I'm going to open my glove compartment and get it for you and open the window for your partner. Okay?"

Flores nodded, and I did as I said, noticing the name on the second officer's chest read, "LUCERO." The minute I did, he spoke to me.

"Turn your car off, sir."

"No can do."

Without hesitation, Lucero pulled his gun on me.

"Are you kiddin' me?" I said.

Lucero did not look amused. "Turn off the car!"

"No, I will not," I said calmly as I handed my items to Flores. "The starter is havin' some trouble, and I do not want to get stuck out here or have y'all drive me into town. And put that damn gun away before you do somethin' stupid, Lucero."

"Excuse me?" Lucero and Flores said at the same time.

Ignoring them, I said, "I'm goin' to reach into my coat pocket for my Federal ID. All right?"

"Your what?" Lucero said.

I rolled my eyes and took a chance at a bullet by reaching into my jacket pocket instead of answering his stupid question.

This prompted Flores to pull his gun on me as well. "Slowly!"

I did as he ordered and carefully pulled out my credentials. "Federal ID, as in, I'm FBI." I handed the bi-fold to Flores.

Keeping his gun on me, Flores said, "Open it so I can see."

"Seriously?" I sighed in disgust and flipped it open to show the ID and badge. "Happy?"

Reading it, Flores put his gun away and took it from me. "I have to verify this."

"Well, no kiddin'. I'll wait, but if you could make it quick, I'd really appreciate it."

"Stay on him," Flores said, and went back to the police car.

After a moment of nothing but the sound of my engine purring, Lucero said, "Do you know how fast you were going, sir?"

"It's Agent, and I don't know, I'm guessin' really fast?" I replied, my sarcasm thick.

"You think you're funny, but you're not," Lucero said. "You were going ninety-nine miles an hour accordin' to our brand-new radar detectin' machine."

"How did you all get one of those all the way out here?" I asked, mildly impressed.

"Our sheriff has friends in Santa Fe," Lucero bragged.

"Would that be Sheriff Apodaca?"

The officer seemed surprised. "Yes. How'd you know that?"

"I research the cities I'm goin' to be stayin' in and alert them when I'm in town."

"I see," was all he said. Awkward silence again slid into place and lingered just long enough for me to start whistling, "Turkey in The Straw," prompting him to interrupt me.

"Fed, huh?" Lucero said. "If so, what you doin' out here?"

"Heading to Las Cruces," I said, being vague and annoying on purpose because I could be, and because he still had his damn gun on me like I was some criminal. Not that it would kill me, but it could damage my coat or my car and then I'd be mad.

"For what?" he prodded.

"Stuff," I replied curtly.

Now he knew I was being rude just for the sake of it, and his face contorted, showing his irritation. "That's not an answer."

"It's classified," I finally said. "Way above your pay-grade."

"Oh, is that so? Well, let me tell you, wannabe fed-boy, I can—"

"Cool it, Vincent," Flores said to his partner as he approached my car door. "Sorry to detain you, Agent Kidwell. No way we coulda known seein' as your car isn't government issued."

Actually, it was, just not his government, but I wasn't going to clarify. "That's all right. Just doin' your job, I know the drill."

Flores handed me back all my items. "Why the hurry, if you don't mind me askin'?"

"Says it's classified," Lucero said, his bitter sarcasm not hidden in the least.

Deciding to mess with him, I said, "No, I told you the reason I was going to be in town was classified. I'm in a hurry because after midnight, the check-in desk will be closed, and I'm not a fan of sleepin' in my car, Officer Lucero," I said, pronouncing his last name wrong on purpose.

"It's Lu-sare-oh," he corrected me.

"Where are you stayin'?" Flores asked.

"The Campbell Hotel," I replied.

Flores nodded. "Are you just passin' through?"

I set the items on the passenger seat. "Yep, just stayin' the one night in Las Cruces and then I'll be on my way to Albuquerque later tomorrow if all goes as planned."

Flores nodded. "All right then. Sorry to keep you. Maybe next time try to go a bit slower through here, all right? This beauty of a machine can handle the speed, but you're only human, and accidents can happen on this windin' road."

I grinned at his "only human" comment and placed my credentials back inside my jacket pocket. "I'll keep that in mind."

"Thank you. In fact, we'll radio dispatch and have them call the Campbell and alert them that you're on your way, so you can take it at the speed limit."

"I appreciate it," I told him, and I did.

"Of course, please keep in mind though that while you're in the city, we ask that you not overstep your bounds. Just because you're FBI doesn't put you outside the law, you hear me?"

I raised an eyebrow at his snarky tone. "Uh, yeah. I hear you. Can I go now?"

"Yes, but—"

"Great, thanks so much!"

Then, without waiting for another word from them, I put the car into drive, drove off, and because I'd been a smartass, kept it at the speed limit...just in case.

* * *

On our journey to Fort Stanton, the assistant surgeon of the fort came riding by with two guards. Seems he'd received a telegraph from Blazer's Mill asking for medical assistance. Yet, before he could continue on, we had him look at our wounded.

Using the end of the wagon like an operating table, we had Middleton lay out to be looked at. Soon his blood covered a good portion of the wagon as well as the doctor himself.

Dr. Appel was doing all he could to save Middleton from the bullet to his chest, but I knew we were going to lose him, and I was torn. I should try and help save John, but every moment I waited for an opportunity to get past Appel, Dick was likely in a coffin, losing air. I had to make a decision and soon. If it came down to one life or the other, I would have to choose. I desperately didn't want that job.

I glanced at the pocket watch Tunstall had given me. It was getting late. How much time did Dick have left? Supernatural or cursed, he could still die without air. Would he save his own life and risk others seeing him rise from the ground? No. Dick would die first. He'd take his secrets to the other side. That's the kind of man he was. Which pissed me off.

"You all right? You're fidgetin' like a two-year old in church," Frank said, coming to stand next to me.

I looked at him and blew out the breath I hadn't even realized I'd been holding. "I healed Colonel's eyes, did you know that? I think I can heal people, too...if I could get to Middleton..."

John screamed, cutting me off.

Dr. Appel cursed. "Hold still or the bullet near your heart could move and puncture it."

"You can't help Middleton, Billy. You'll risk too much. You can't expose your gifts in front of Appel or the new Regulators who don't know everythin'."

"Curse, not gift," I corrected him.

Frank rolled his eyes at me. "Depends on your view, Billy."

"I couldn't save Dick," I said, and I felt the emotion of that statement tighten my chest. I was talking of the night Brewer first changed, but Frank didn't need to know that.

Frank placed a hand on my shoulder. "Kid, you can't carry that weight, too."

I walked away, the energy of the lives I carried were bouncing about inside of me like jumping beans, and I needed to be moving. "Then why does it feel like—"

"I'm losin' him!" Appel said.

Without a second thought, I said to Frank, "Follow my lead."

I rushed to the wagon, then, as Appel turned away to get another instrument, I bumped him, causing him to drop the item he'd fetched from his bag.

"Kid, you can't help!" Frank said, stepping in between the doctor and me, blocking Appel's view with his wide chest and tall form. He placed a hand on me like he would pull me back when in truth he was holding me steadily in place.

"They can't take another one of us today," I said as I laid my hand over John's heart. "What's mine is yours," I whispered and willed only half of the energy I'd use to heal one of Colonel's eyes into him since I couldn't fully heal him in present company. However, I could help just enough to give John a fighting chance.

I felt it flow out of me and into John just before the furious doctor stepped around to take my other arm and "assisted" Frank in pulling me away.

"Interfere with me again, and I'll kill you!" Appel yelled, pointing his gun at me with his free hand. "Now move away from here!"

With a nod, Frank pulled me to my horse and handed me a handkerchief from his pocket, quietly saying, "Clean your hands off, Billy."

I could see he was mad, so I did as he asked with my mouth shut. Once they were clean, I handed it back to him.

He yanked it from my hands and smacked me with it, whispering in a gruff voice, "Do you want to be discovered? We can't get justice for Tunstall without you. Damn it all to hell!" He walked away from me but was back in a minute or two, being sure to whisper at a level he knew only I would hear. "Were you able to—?"

"I don't know. I tried something new, I only used half a push of energy. I'm hopin' it's enough to save him if the doc keeps workin'."

"That's all I can do," Appel said. "Get him to a hospital."

George stepped forward. "Doctor, I want you to look at my hand and see what's the matter with it."

Appel examined George's hand, who did his best not to cringe in pain each time the assistant surgeon touched it. "George, you've got a very bad hand. The bones are all shot to pieces." Pulling his kit toward him, Appel did a small procedure on the bones as we all stood and watched. Once he was done, he said, "You need to go to a hospital too or you could lose that hand. I can try to get you into the one at Fort Stanton. I may not be able to do it, but I'll try."

"Now, Doc," George said, his voice strained but steady, "don't you worry about that because I'm not goin' to that hospital."

Appel handed George a roll of gauze. "Then I'll tell you what to do and you must do it quickly. Get a bottle of carbolic acid, then dilute it, and keep the hand saturated with it."

"Where can I get that?" George asked.

"Fort Stanton is about the only place I know of," Appel told him. "But I can send it to you in Lincoln."

Evidently becoming distraught, George said, "No, that's worse yet."

Seeing that the doctor was at his wit's end, I stepped up. "Send it to Isaac Ellis's place in Lincoln. I'll get it for George."

Appel nodded. "I'll have it there tomorrow evenin', I promise."

Quickly, he loaded up his things, mounted his horse, and rode off with his two companions toward Blazer's Mill. Once they were out of sight, I pulled George to the side.

"I can heal what he did for the bones in your hand. I have enough energy in me to do that. I can't regrow your finger, but I can solidify what he did so you hurt less."

"Billy, ya can't go wastin' your energy on me."

"It's going to be thirty-six hours without medical aid. That's a lot of time your hand doesn't have. Do you really want to take a chance that you need to go to Fort Stanton?"

He hemmed and hawed while I fetched the gauze and came back with Frank behind me.

"Frank, lay your right hand out." When he did, I instructed George to lay his on top of it. Once he'd done this, I lay mine on top of his and urged energy through my hand, down into his. George moaned in pain as bones moved a bit and clicked into place, mending as best as they could without me using too much of my power.

"That's all I can do," I told them. "Frank, help me wrap his hand so the blood doesn't start flowing again and we hold the work Doc and I did as steady as possible."

Once George was set, we gathered to discuss our next move.

"Whoever doesn't have an open warrant on them, take Middleton to Fort Stanton," MacNab said. "Billy, you and Scroggins head to Lincoln to get the acid when it arrives. We'll be in San Patricio."

"Sure thing," I said, saddling up on Colonel. "Let's get moving."

A bit confused at the quick decision and my readiness to leave, Scroggins agreed without thinking it out and got on his horse. Quickly, we rode off in the direction of Lincoln, but as soon as we were too far away for riding back to make any sense, I pulled us to a halt.

"Okay, I need you to ride off to Lincoln and let Uncle Ike know what's coming and why. I'm gonna try and go get Brewer's horse. He loved Mattie. I need to get her so no one else gets their hands on her, like Dolan. Plus, he had a nice saddle Tunstall gave him. Another thing we wouldn't want his murderer to have."

"Well, what do I do with the acid if it gets there before you do?" Scroggins argued.

"Then you ride that shit out to George immediately. They'll understand why I went back."

"I don't think you should go, Billy. It's not smart. Those officers could still be—"

"I left Tunstall layin' out in the desert all night. I'm not leavin' Brewer to have who knows what done to him or let those sons of bitches have his possessions. I'll be there. If not, you tell George I'll be right behind ya. Okay?"

"But I—"

"Go! Now!" I said, reaching for my gun.

"Okay, okay...I'm going..."

With that, Scroggins rode off toward Lincoln.

I turned Colonel on a dime, and we hauled ass back to Blazer's Mill, hoping I was in time to save Dick from dying for real.

* * *

Tremendously exhausted, I parked my car, and turned off the engine. Rubbing my eyes, I reached for my hat in the passenger seat and paused. My skin tingled all over and I knew: the call they made wasn't just to the hotel. They'd contacted someone else and either that person was my welcoming party or they'd sent him. I could feel his presence, but it wasn't strong.

Looking up at the sky, I smiled, remembering that the moon had set at seven-thirty-five tonight and wouldn't rise again until about seven tomorrow morning. That was why the feeling was low level. He couldn't shift.

"Aw, poor baby," I said with zero sympathy and a heavy dose of sarcasm.

It didn't mean he couldn't be a danger, it just meant I only had to deal with a man, or men, and not the kind covered in fur with a plethora of sharp teeth and stinky breath. Well, they still could have bad breath, but I liked to give them the benefit of the doubt.

Pulling my weapons out of the glove compartment, I slide them into their holsters, including the one in my boot. Pulling my pant leg down, I grabbed my hat, and exited the car.

Whistling the song, "Turkey in the Straw," I placed my black hat on my head, shut the door, and lazily strolled to the trunk. I used that time to reach out with my senses and quickly pinpointed the location of the child of Scáthach who was sent to watch me. He'd staked himself out at the main entrance of the hotel, just standing there smoking a cigarette.

It didn't appear he had a friend, but there could be more inside.

Keeping that in mind, I unlocked the trunk, snagging my weapons bag, and slung it over my left shoulder. Grabbed hold of my suitcase and shut the trunk. Moving my suitcase to my left hand, I freed up my right to draw my weapon, and I made my way to the door, whistling the whole way.

I flipped the latch to free up my pistol and hooked my thumb on my jeans to justify my hand being close to my weapon. "Good evenin'," I said to the man with dark hair and matching, well-trimmed beard. "Nice night, isn't it? Let me guess, they don't let ya smoke in this here hotel, huh?"

His hooded eyes slowly moved toward me. "No idea. I just like smokin' outside. The desk is closed, stranger. So if you're lookin' to check in—"

I glanced through the glass on the doors to see no attendant. In fact, I saw no one at all, telling me they were merely curious and had only sent him. "Oh, they know I'm comin' in late. Cops even called to let them know they held me up."

Now I had his full attention. He stepped a hair closer to me and inhaled deeply through his nose, likely trying to see if I was a werewolf. The golden flecks of his eyes glowed as he used his heightened senses but I pretended not to notice that aspect.

"Can I help you?" I said, stepping back from him slightly.

He shook his head and stepped back. "No, sir. You have a nice night. Looks like the desk man has come back for ya."

I glanced inside and saw he was correct. I touched the brim of my hat. "Why, thank you. You have a nice night, sir." I turned my back to him and entered the hotel.

He grunted in what appeared to be confusion and I smiled. He likely smelled the magic on me, could tell I wasn't fully human, but had no idea what I was. Not surprising. These parts hadn't seen a Spirit Warrior since I left in 1880.

This meant that their top tracking dog, because they'd have sent their best, was confused but had enough information to go back with. He'd report his observations, and that information would either keep me safe or put a bullseye on me.

I was betting on the latter, because this is me we're talking about after all. That meant I was stepping from the frying pan into the fryer. The question now was, had the burner been set to low or high?

Either way, trouble wouldn't likely arrive until tomorrow after the moon rose. In order to handle that appropriately, I needed to go get a full night's rest, so I checked in. As I headed up the stairs, I got this foreboding feeling that the burner was likely set to high, or inching toward it with each moment I was in town. That meant they were up to something they shouldn't be, and I was going to have the honor of fixing that.

The next part of the adventure was about to begin and to be honest, I was itching to get to it.

THE END
To Be Continued in *The Torment of Richard Brewer*

ACKNOWLEDGEMENTS

First and foremost, I'd like to thank my support system: my parents, my best friends, my writing group, my wonderful editor, and those who live in Lincoln, NM. If it wasn't for the people in Lincoln, taking me in and helping me learn about Billy, this book never would have happened.

I'd like to lift a glass to all the people of Lincoln for sharing their knowledge, hospitality, and affection for Billy the Kid with me. Specifically, we should toast to, Drew & Elise Gomber, Marilyn Burchett, Jens Klingshirn, Bev & Bill Strauser, Tiffanie Owen, Beau Lucas, Annmarie LaMay, Kenneth Walter, John Schultz, Victoria Kubica, Marilyn & Murray Arrowsmith, Marla & Brandon Caughron, Sumi Ayame, Mitchell Harper, Nina & Brett McInnes, Rick Garcia, Tim & Ashley Roberts, and last but never least...Katherine, Troy, Willa, & Prue Nelson—your family is my heart.

I'd also like to thank Frederick Nolan. Most of my preferred research came from his books. If he'd not done so much leg work years ago, I'd not have had such a rich group of books to pull history from. So, a huge thank you to him and the other writers on my list of books listed at the back of this novel.

ABOUT THE AUTHOR

Tamsin Silver is a Fantasy author currently based out of Albuquerque, NM. Her Urban Fantasy works include the **Windfire** saga, **Mark of the Necromancer**, novellas based on her **Skye of the Damned** web series (*which can be seen free online*), and the **Moon Over Manhattan** series (*Falstaff Books, fall/winter 2020*).

She is also a writer for Faith Hunter's **Rogue Mage Anthologies** with *Lore Seekers Press*, the **We Are Not This** anthology for *Falstaff Books*, and the **Storming Area 51** anthology with *Bayonet Books*.

Tamsin graduated from Winthrop University in SC with a BA in Theatre and Secondary Education, along with a minor in Creative Writing and Shakespeare. She's taught middle school and high school drama in the Carolinas and run two successful theatre companies (one in NYC), where she holds awards in directing for both.

You can learn more about Tamsin by visiting www.tamsinsilver.com and www.skyeofthedamned.com.

AFTERWORD

Names, characters, and incidents depicted in this story are products of both actual history and the author's imagination. Though most of the history in this story is based on fact, the author would ask the reader to remember that this is historical fantasy, so if something is different on the page than in the history books, it is likely done in the service of the fantastical story.

The author did her best to keep the historical facts as exact as possible. However, seeing as there are varying recollections of the events that took place during the Lincoln County War of 1878, often she had to choose which she felt worked best for the story, and move on.

FRIENDS OF FALSTAFF

Thank You to All our Falstaff Books Patrons, who get extra digital content each month! To be featured here and see what other great rewards we offer, go to www.patreon.com/falstaffbooks.

PATRONS

Dino Hicks
John Hooks
John Kilgallon
Larissa Lichty
Travis & Casey Schilling
Staci-Leigh Santore
Sheryl R. Hayes
Scott Norris
Samuel Montgomery-Blinn
Junkle